The author was born in Stockport in 1947 and after leaving school was employed in widely differing capacities including being a police constable and sailing around the world in the Merchant Navy.

In the 1980s he started his own businesses, and in 2001 he became a volunteer, then professional yachtmaster, taking disabled people on sailing trips until 2008.

Since then he has been able to pursue his love of writing, living at home in Bournemouth with his wife.

MARIA'S PAPERS

This book is dedicated to my Great, Great Aunt Maria and my dearly missed, loving father Frank without whom I would not have had the Chance.

Stephen F Clegg

MARIA'S PAPERS

A CIP catalogue record for this title is available from the British Library.

ISBN 978 1 84963 130 3

www.austinmacauley.com

First Published (2012)
Austin & Macauley Publishers Ltd.
25 Canada Square
Canary Wharf
London
E14 5LB

For their endless patience, love and support I would like to thank my wife Jay, my daughter Nicola and my son Iain.
For their tireless and time consuming research into our family history I am absolutely indebted to my cousins John Clegg and Alan Finegan.
For their past and present kindnesses and understanding I would like to thank Annie and Alan Haworth and their daughter Joyce Booker of Whitewall Farm.
Finally, for encouraging me to get this story published and for his years of faith in it, I'd like to thank my good American friend and film producer Steve Robitaille.

Preface

24th July 2002. Whitewall Farm, Wordale Moor, Lancashire

"*Berserk?* What do you mean something's just gone berserk?"

"I mean exactly what I say; something just went absolutely mental in the room next to the finds room."

"For pity's sake," said Crowthorne, "you're supposed to be a scientist, explain yourself properly."

The forensic archaeologist looked across the farmyard and said, "Look, how the hell am I supposed to know. All I can tell you is that some, some, bloody huge sounding animal, a dog I think, just had a major conniption fit in what we thought was an empty room and it's scared the shit out of us…" he faltered as he saw the girl and said, "Sorry…"

"No problem," said Naomi. She shot a quick glance at the occupants of the police car and realised that she was the only one who might be able to explain what was happening. She closed her eyes and desperately hoped that she was wrong.

The archaeologist cut across her thoughts and said, "I'm not usually so crass but whatever made that noise put the fear of God up me."

Crowthorne looked across the deserted yard and said, "And have you checked to see if anything's in there?"

"Absolutely bloody not!" said the archaeologist, "I wouldn't go anywhere near that room. You should have heard it, it sounded totally deranged."

Crowthorne frowned, put his hand up to his mouth and stared at the door in question; for once in his life he didn't know what to do. He hated dogs and the thought of dealing with one, let alone a deranged one, filled him with concern. He took in a deep breath and turned back to face the others.

"All right," he said, "here's what we'll…"

"*Sir!*" The police driver pointed through the windscreen.

On the opposite side of the yard the door had opened and Francesca Drake one of the female team members had staggered out. She lunged forwards, stumbling and falling in an effort to get away from the room.

Without thinking Crowthorne jumped out of the car and ran towards her.

He got half way across the yard when a howl that would have stopped a charging bear erupted from the room in front of him. He didn't just hear it; he felt it. It plunged sickeningly icy fingers into his chest and squeezed his heart. Terror spread through him like a cold primeval wave and stopped him dead in his tracks.

He stood in petrified silence and listened as the sound of the horrendous howl receded across the top of the moors.

"Please help me..." begged Francesca.

Crowthorne heard her pleading but couldn't move, his legs felt like jelly. He remained motionless and stared intently at the door behind her.

"Please, Inspector..."

The second call for help shook Crowthorne into action; he ran forwards, grabbed the distraught woman and yanked her to her feet.

"Come on," he said pulling her towards the police car, "let's get you out of here." He looked up and saw the driver staring at him.

"Cooper get over here!" he shouted.

The driver didn't move.

Intent on dragging the stricken woman, Crowthorne didn't notice at first, but when he looked he was stunned to see that the driver hadn't moved.

"Cooper, get your arse over here now!" he shouted.

With an enormous bang, a door slammed behind him.

Francesca turned, looked back across the farmyard and said, "Oh God, no..."

Crowthorne could feel his heart hammering; he stared steadfastly at Cooper as he approached the police car but just knew that something bad was going to happen.

Suddenly, Cooper's eyes widened with fear and he involuntarily shifted backwards in his seat.

Chapter 1

August 1867. Wordale Moor

Silas Cartwright looked around at the moorland from the driving seat of his cab, he loved living in Hundersfield one of the subdivisions of Rochdale, it was such a mixture of growth and opportunity in the towns, and yet it was still ringed with breathtaking beauty once you took to the countryside.

He easily recalled the days of his youth when a lot of the area had been just farmland, but the mills and mines had taken a hold and the population had grown enormously. Rochdale was growing too with new civic buildings, parks and amenities complete with the endless rows of terraced houses, often with up to four families living together in separate rooms. He had read that in nearby Spotland alone the number of people living in the area had grown from about eighteen thousand in 1841 to over thirty thousand and he reckoned with no little amusement that if his old Pa had been alive he'd never have believed it.

All of this provided no end of employment for his horse and cab and as far as he could see, there would always be a need for his trade even with the railways spreading ever further across the country. The noisy, smokey cursed things might have been able to go from town to town quicksticks, but they couldn't go door to door like him and old Henry.

He reined the horse in to a walk as they breasted Wordale Moor and the familiar gateposts came into view. Remembering that her name was pronounced "Mariah" and not "Mareeya" he courteously tapped on the roof of the cab with his whip and called, "Drive's in view Miss Maria; would you like me to turn in or to stop?"

"Stop please Silas, it's a beautiful day, I'll walk."

The cabby stopped at the end of the drive and the elegant figure of Maria Chance stepped onto the roadside.

"You will wait?" she asked politely.

"Of course ma'am, I'll be here when you return."

Maria smiled and set off down the long drive.

Silas watched as she walked away from him; she wasn't exactly beautiful but some hard to define quality simply captivated him each time he saw her.

Maria looked from side to side at the panoramic view of the moors. She considered that it had been no wonder that her forebears had loved this place, it was stunning. From whichever direction she looked, she was confronted by rolling grassy farmland as striking as anywhere the country could offer. Cows and sheep grazed lazily in the warmth of the sun and the ubiquitary sound of insects filled the air; she inhaled the atmosphere and let it lift her.

As she made her way down the long drive she recounted the number of years that she'd been at the business. '*Heaven forbid,*' she thought to herself, '*seventeen long years!*'

When her father had charged her with her task she'd had no notion that it would take up so much time. '*Seventeen years!*' the words spun around her head, '*Good Lord the countless letters, solicitors, agents, and trips out to here…*'

The estate buildings came into view as she walked down the last part of the drive. They comprised two long grey sandstone constructions facing each other across an unmade courtyard, both only two storeys high and utterly devoid of any hint of classicism. On the right-hand side was the main house and servant's quarters, attached to which was a stable and barn; opposite was an equipment store, dairy and other ancillary rooms, whilst at the far end was a large byre.

As she crossed the courtyard her demeanour changed; she tilted her head slightly upwards, squared her shoulders and strode purposefully towards the main door. In doing so she caught sight of the hated inscription that was as surely carved into the stone lintel as it was indelibly carved into her memory.

In the form of a triangle she saw the three initials. At the top an 'L', below that the initials 'J' and 'M' separated by a colon, and the base of the triangle was the date 1748. The 'L' was that of Lincoln; the 'J' and 'M' were James and Montague respectively. *James Montague Lincoln - 1748.* She bristled with indignation every time she saw it.

She'd never met James Montague Lincoln: he'd died in 1788; thirty-two years before she'd been born and she'd had to conduct her business with his grandson Edward, a man of advanced years and at least an octogenarian himself. His years on God's good earth however had done nothing for his temperament, as she'd always found him to be a boorish and insufferable old man.

She was ready; she lifted her parasol and rapped loudly on the front door. The door opened and she was confronted by a presentable and attractive-looking woman who exuded warmth and self-assurance from the moment of her first smile.

"Good day," she said with the slightest bow of her head, "How may I help you?"

This threw Maria who quickly gathered her wits and recalled her reason for the visit.

"Good day to you too madam; my name is Maria Chance and I am here to see Mr. Lincoln on business. Would you please tell him that I am here yet again as promised, and that I have absolutely no intention of leaving until we have discoursed further on the subject of this estate."

"Mr. Lincoln you say?"

"Correct!" Maria confirmed.

The woman paused briefly as she assessed her visitor and then decided that some conversations were better held indoors. "Then you'd better come in; I have something to tell you."

'*Come in?*' Maria was astonished! In seventeen years of visiting the estate this was only the second time that she had been invited in. The last time had been her first visit in the autumn of 1850.

The woman led her into a small but tastefully decorated parlour. The small Tudor-style windows made the atmosphere rather stuffy and restricted the amount of natural daylight coming in. Numerous unlit candles in a variety of candle-holders were sitting atop various pieces of solid oak furniture in the darkest corners of the room and she surmised that the atmosphere would have been even stuffier with all of them alight.

She walked across to an offered chair and sat down.

"Now," said her host, "Please let me introduce myself; I am Margaret Johnson the daughter of Edward Lincoln."

"Daughter? But, I thought…"

"You thought that he was a bachelor without issue?" said Margaret taking the initiative.

Maria nodded.

"Well you were wrong."

Maria was taken aback by the bluntness of her host and said, "Forgive me madam it is not my intention to pry, but I have been coming to Whitewall these past seventeen years and have never seen you here before."

She watched as Margaret walked across to the window. The daylight illuminated the cut of her ankle length brown tweed skirt and her side-laced leather shoes.

Margaret turned and said, "That is not surprising because I didn't live here."

"But…"

"But nothing madam, you are a stranger to me and the details of the relationship between my father and me are of nobody's business but my own; suffice to say that I am indeed his daughter and was the subsequent heir to this estate."

Maria's feathers ruffled.

"The heir to this estate?" she said trying to remain calm after the curt riposte.

"Precisely my reason for asking you in. My father died fourteen months ago, taken by consumption in the end."

Maria needed time to compose herself. So much had changed with that one sentence. She appreciated that Edward Lincoln had been an elderly man but she had never entertained the possibility that he may die before they'd concluded their business together. She responded by being direct; the only way that she knew how.

"Since some considerable time has passed since the departure of your father from this earth, may I enquire if you were his sole heir?"

Margaret said, "I was."

"And do you think that sufficient time has now passed for you to attend to your late father's affairs?"

Margaret frowned and said, "To what exactly, do you refer?"

"To the Whitewall Estate."

Margaret raised her eyebrows, walked across to a vacant chair and sat down. She looked at Maria and guardedly said, "What about the Whitewall Estate?"

Maria turned to face her host and tried to assess her disposition; she seemed to be readily given to passion but this was not a time for meek submissiveness. She said, "I apologise if this comes to you as a shock, but your late father and his father before him conspired to cheat my family out of our rightful ownership of Whitewall and if he bequeathed it to you, he had no right to do so. It was not his to give!"

Chapter 2

7th May 2002. Walmsfield Borough Council Offices - 2 months
before the incident at Whitewall Farm

"Ooh, you bastard thing!" Sandra Miles aimed a hefty kick at the rickety stepladder and looked down at her broken fingernail.

"Bugger!" she said exasperatedly. She stared up at the old leather handle sticking out on the top shelf and cursed that every time she was asked for a dossier from the 'Inactive Files' room it always seemed to be the most difficult one to retrieve. She looked hawkishly at the stepladder and then manhandled it a little closer to her quarry; she climbed up slowly, grabbed the protruding handle and extracted the container from the tightly packed, dusty bundles. She saw the faded lettering 'Whitewall Farm' on a mostly detached gummed label and then climbed carefully back down.

Back in her office, she placed it on her desk and looked at it carefully. The Whitewall dossier was everybody's favourite; it looked like an old small brown travel case with crossed straps around it that were sealed with a hefty looking padlock. Nobody had a clue how old it was, or how long it had been in the Council's care, but now it had been requested by Naomi Draper from Historic Research and it was up to her to open it.

She carefully looked to see if a key was somehow attached, but there was none; she tried flicking open the case locks to see if she could lift a corner of the lid, but they too were locked. This meant another trip to the basement to see if a key had become detached from the case *and* manhandling again, the heavy wooden stepladder.

Half an hour later the only thing that she had to show for her effort was her broken fingernail and a good deal more dust up her nose.

She returned to her office, looked dejectedly at the case for a few minutes longer, then reached for her phone and dialled the Head of Planning.

"Carlton, Sandra here. I've had to retrieve that old Whitewall file from the basement and it's locked. Do we have any keys for it?"

"Now you're asking," said the puzzled Head, "I haven't seen that file for years, so if they aren't evident, Heaven knows where they could be. You'd better bring it up to my office and we'll see what we can do."

A few minutes later there was a tap at Carlton Wilkes' door and Sandra walked in with the case. She leaned over, carefully placed it in the space that he'd made on his desk, and sat down. The two of them looked at it for a few seconds as though it was a favourite meal about to be devoured.

"Well," said Carlton, "I'd forgotten this beauty and I don't think I've ever had to open anything like it before."

"Neither have I, and I thought you'd be interested."

"Quite right, my life has too little mystery in it nowadays, so something like this is a real bonus! Now let's see…"

He reached into his briefcase, extracted an impressive looking Swiss army knife and prized open the main blade. For several minutes he cut, hacked and poked, but to no avail. The straps were thick leather similar to horse trappings; their ages had toughened them up and try as he may, no function the knife had to offer could cut through them without potentially taking them way beyond office closing hours.

"Sorry Sandra," he finally said, "This is pointless. I'll take the case home tonight and set about it with a full set of tools. Come to my office in the morning I'll have it open for you".

Dejectedly Sandra bid her boss 'good night' and left the file in his care.

It was a lovely spring evening when Carlton wandered down to his shed with the Whitewall file. Despite being a widower he still prided himself on being able to prepare a good meal and having eaten, and partaken of a small beer he now had the immensely pleasurable task of opening the intriguing case.

He unlocked the shed door and stepped inside. The day long sunshine had warmed up the interior and the woodwork smelled pleasantly of creosote. This was his domain, even when his wife had been alive this had been his domain, it contained all of his tools, his old chair and workbench and all of those unidentifiable objects retrieved from long gone pieces of equipment. It really needed a good clear out, but that was never on the cards.

He placed the container on his workbench selected a small hacksaw and carefully sawed through the top leather strap; he then turned his attention to the side straps and sawed through them until he had full access to the lid. Next were the case locks; he recalled for a few moments the ease with which television detectives picked locks armed only with a small knife and a hairpin, but unlike them, and despite having a wide variety of tools at his disposal, he'd had to concede defeat within fifteen minutes. One or two hefty blows from his ballpein hammer and a blunt chisel, and the job was done; with a contented smile he put down his 'picklocks', lifted the lid and peered in.

Lying in the bottom and looking diminutive compared to the size of the container, were two items; a brown leather document holder tied around the middle with a faded red silk ribbon and an old envelope. He reached in, carefully picked up the envelope and saw a handwritten inscription on the front.

MOST IMPORTANT!

The accompanying documents and the contents of this envelope are to be read only by the incumbent Mayor and District Clerk.

By order of
Surnh Horrocks, Hundersfield District Clerk 1869.

This was both a surprise and a disappointment; the curious instruction made him want to investigate further but the letter was sealed with wax and he knew that if he opened it, it would be patently obvious to any subsequent examiners. He set it down and took out the folder. For a nano-second he considered looking in that too, but it was never going to happen; he was an honest, principled ex-military man and the use of sophism to defend his actions wasn't his style. With a resigned sigh he returned the items to the case, closed it and took it back indoors.

At 9:10am the next day Sandra sat resignedly in Carlton's office and being of a similar disposition to her boss, understood perfectly well why he hadn't opened the folder.

"I have an appointment with Giles Eaton at half past nine," said Carlton, "I think he's as intrigued about this situation as we are. You can't normally get to see him without at least two weeks' notice, but as soon as I told him what was written on the envelope he re-scheduled his early appointments."

Sandra's lack of vitriolic response about the Town Clerk, one of her least favourite characters, caused him to take a closer look at what she was doing. She appeared to be distracted as she studied the rear of the envelope from the Whitewall file.

"Have you noticed this?" Sandra leaned across the desk and pointed to what looked more like a stain than anything else.

Carlton took the envelope from her and looked carefully at where she had indicated.

"It's writing," he said.

"Yes, I know that, but what does it say?"

Carlton looked a little closer and said, "Part of it appears to be scribbled out but I can just about make out the rest."

"And?"

"It says 'Cestui que Vie'."

"What?"

"Cestui que Vie; or more correctly given the scribbled out part, 'Something or other,'- Cestui que Vie"

"What on earth is that?" said Sandra.

"I've no idea; I've never come across it before." Carlton glanced up at the gold plated carriage clock on his bookcase, a leaving gift from his old unit and said, "Time to go and see the Town Clerk, I'll ask him; he had an Oxbridge education so he may know. I'll pop in and see you when I get back."

Following Carlton's departure Sandra returned to her small office and sat down. On one side of her desk was a photo of her daughter Helen in the mortar-board hat and gown that she'd worn on her graduation day; she picked it up, kissed it and put it back down. It helped her get through the day sanely.

She quietly pondered the events of the past twenty-four hours and though there weren't many times that she enjoyed being at work anymore, she found herself hoping that there would be more intrigue for her to savour in the days to come.

She looked up at the clock on her wall; 10:10am. Seven hours and twenty minutes to home time; it ticked loudly as the seconds passed by. Tick, tock, tick, tock...

What Sandra didn't know was that the other clock had started ticking too, the one that had started the moment she'd retrieved the Whitewall file. But that one was on a three week countdown, and when it stopped she'd be brutally murdered.

Chapter 3

The Town Clerk's Office, Walmsfield Borough Council Offices

"Sit down er..."

"Carlton Wilkes... Head of Planning..." said Carlton with a soupcon of sarcasm as he sank into one of the Town Clerk's uncomfortable office armchairs.

Giles Eaton coughed awkwardly as he realised that he should at least have made the effort to find out the name of the departmental head visiting him.

"Yes of course; Carlton. Now what's all the mystery? You have me quite distracted up here."

Carlton opened the case and placed the contents on the Town Clerk's desk.

Giles picked up the envelope, studied both sides of it with furrowed eyebrows for awhile, put it down, and then examined the leather document folder without actually opening it.

"Hmm, intriguing," he said gently placing the folder down on his desk, "What do you think, should we open them now or do what's instructed and wait until the Mayor gets in?"

Carlton knew that the Town Clerk had no intention of opening either item but was making small talk in an effort to be pleasant. He said, "It's not my choice to make Mr. Eaton."

"No, no, of course not, forgive me, I wasn't thinking straight. Tell you what, I'll put a call in to him and I'll let you know what this is all about in due course."

The silence that ensued made Carlton realise that it was time to leave; he stood up and walked across to the door.

"Oh Mr. Eaton," he turned and said, "before I leave, did you notice the faded writing on the rear of the envelope?"

"Yes," said Giles off-handedly.

"Did you understand what it said?"

"What? Oh no, all a bit mumbo-jumbo to me; 'que' is Spanish for 'what' isn't it? 'Vie' is French for 'life'... you know, 'ce'st la vie' etcetera, and I don't know what the other bit is, so it's 'something or other - what life' as far as I can make out."

"O.K. thank you." Carlton closed the office door and frowned. Eaton had lied to him; there'd been no puzzled look when he'd read the wordage, he'd simply read it.

The early excitement of the day gave way to routine and by late afternoon Carlton was lost in one of his more pressing projects when the telephone rang on his desk; he picked it up and placed it to his ear.

"Carlton, Giles Eaton here. About the Whitewall documents, what exactly did someone want with them, and do you know who instigated the enquiry?"

"Sandra Miles is handling it and I didn't ask her who had requested the file."

There was a pause and he could hear muffled speech; clearly the Mayor was in with the Town Clerk.

"O.K. thank you, that will be all."

"Mr. Eaton is everything all right?" said Carlton quizzically, "We haven't compromised any procedures or anything have we?"

"What? No don't concern yourself old chap, Mr. Ramsbottom and I have got it all under control and we're going to handle things from here."

Carlton sat back in his chair and stroked his chin. The words *under control* puzzled him. The intrigue level stepped up another notch as he tried to consider what could possibly motivate the Town Clerk *and* the Mayor to handle an apparently routine enquiry?

He got up from his desk, went down to Sandra's office, courteously tapped on the door and let himself in. As he sat down he noticed that she had a puzzled expression on her face too.

"How odd," said Sandra, "Mr. Eaton just rang to ask the name of the person wanting the Whitewall file and when I told him that we'd got it from Naomi in Historic Research he told me that he'd be dealing with her direct from now on."

Carlton frowned and said, "He told me the same. Something odd's going on."

"I agree," said Sandra, "Giles Eaton doesn't get involved in routine office work. In fact thinking about it, I have no idea what the greasy slime ball *does* get involved in; so why he's got his

26

fake-suntanned snout in this trough is beyond me."

She paused as she saw Carlton give her a chiding look and then said, "So what do you think was in the file?"

Carlton shook his head and said, "I haven't the slightest idea, but there's more to this than meets the eye that's for sure."

The two of them sat in silence until Carlton finally drew in breath and stood up.

"Naomi Draper in Historic Research you said?"

"Yes."

"Right, first thing tomorrow I'm going down there."

"Are you sure that's a good idea? The Town Fart did tell us that he and the Mayor, God help us, would be dealing with things from now on."

Carlton gave Sandra another disapproving look and said, "That may be so, but he didn't impose any restrictions on me, so if I as Head of Planning have a few questions of my own, I see no reason why I'm not entitled to ask."

"It sounds as though you've made your mind up."

"I have," said Carlton heading for the door, "I'll be in touch."

Sandra watched as he walked out of her office. She knew that he was forty-ish; he was tall, strong and handsome with square shoulders and a full head of dark hair just starting to show traces of white around his temples. His military bearing and no-nonsense attitude was evident in everything he did and he appeared to be utterly unafraid of anything or anybody. Most of her office colleagues considered him to be a bit of a stuffed shirt but she disagreed; she could visualise him in combat situations, and on more than one or two occasions he had been the central character in some of her more intimate flights of fancy...

Upstairs in Giles' office the Mayor Tom Ramsbottom, was staring out of the window into the distance; he had a churning inside his stomach telling him that his ulcer was unhappy. Having taken in nothing of the vista, he lumbered across to one of the narrow green leather office armchairs and dropped his bulky frame into it. At first he thought that the springs had failed because he kept sinking farther and farther down, until with a sound a little too reminiscent of breaking wind, the cushions finally arrested his descent.

He was in no mood for niceties and didn't care whether Giles thought that he'd made the sound personally or not.

The Whitewall documents and the letter from Surnh Horrocks lay open on the desk and he eyed them irritably.

"How could this possibly be?" he said in his brusque manner, "How could this have gone on for all these years and us not know about it?

How could that bloody case sit on a shelf in our basement for a hundred and thirty years and us not know what's in it? It's bloody ludicrous!"

"But…" Giles tried to speak.

"And why the hell didn't anybody think to open it and look inside? The letter was addressed to us for Christ's sake!"

Giles remained silent.

"And what about all the other Town Clerks and Mayors, what were *they*, sodding Ostriches?"

"Maybe they were just as unaware of the contents as we were until today," said Giles mildly.

"Oh that's all right then, that makes me feel much better! Now what shall we do, jam our heads up our arses like all the other Town Clerks and Mayors and keep them there until it all goes away?"

Giles glanced across to the case, it looked small and unassuming and completely out of keeping with the explosive contents.

"And to think that we've been blithely going about our business completely unaware that we are sitting on documents that could bankrupt the shit out of us! Hah!" said Tom, "It's so bloody preposterous it's laughable!" He stopped speaking and shook his head.

Giles said, "We can't ignore it now, other people have seen it, and the contents."

Tom let out an exasperated snort, leaned forwards and held his head in his hands. A few seconds later he said, "This is intolerable Giles, if this old Horrocks guy is right, the consequences for this Council would be utterly unthinkable."

Giles was troubled, too, but knew that of the two of them, he would have to be the one that remained steady. He needed to buy time.

"I appreciate that Tom, but so far we are the only ones actually aware of what the contents say."

"That's as maybe; it could still become public knowledge, and this is just the sort of stuff the media would have a field day with."

Giles leaned forward in his larger and more sumptuous chair and said, "Look, let's just do nothing for now. I'll go and see the Draper woman in Historic Research tomorrow, establish where the enquiry originated and take it from there. Until then I suggest that we keep this strictly between ourselves."

Tom looked thoughtfully at Giles for a few seconds and then slowly nodded his head.

"And Tom," said Giles in his most patronising manner, "not even wives. Do you understand?"

To the straight-talking Mayor of Walmsfield Borough Council this was one of the more annoying habits he had to put up with from the Town Clerk; it immediately rubbed him up the wrong way.

"Perfectly!" he said in his most indignant manner, "You might think I'm nothing more than a thick farmer but even *I* can grasp how serious this could get, so I don't need wet nursing by the likes of you!"

"Sorry Tom, I didn't mean to offend," said Giles as obsequiously as he could muster, "but the thing is, it may just be an innocent enquiry and amount to nothing so it's best not to over-react right now."

Tom disliked Giles intensely but had to agree.

"I suppose so, but I'm warning you, I have a very bad feeling about this. In my entire working life I've never heard of anybody being put into such an outrageous and disastrous predicament as this, so I don't want you screwing it up now!"

Giles nodded and remained silent.

"*And*," said Tom, "if you think for one minute that things are getting out of hand I want to know about it immediately; do you understand?"

Giles said, "Yes, of course."

Tom placed both hands on the high arms of the office chair and pulled upwards; he was aware that he'd put weight on recently but getting out of the ludicrously soft and narrow armchair was a work of art for anybody with a few pounds on, let alone a person of his 'manly' stature. The struggle up aggravated his ulcer and gave him a nasty twinge.

"For Christ's sake Giles, who did you buy these ridiculous chairs for, Lowry's bloody stick people?"

Giles watched in silence as the Mayor wrestled his way out of the chair and then walked over to his office door.

Before leaving Tom turned and pointed to the contents of the Whitewall file.

"Be sure to put that lot under lock and key!"

"Of course I will. Trust me," said Giles, "you take yourself off home now and try not to worry about a thing. I'll be in touch as and when."

Tom closed the door behind him and trundled slowly down the corridor towards the lift. The words *'Trust me'* were ringing in his ears. *'Trust me'* indeed!'

He shook his head and quietly said, "I wouldn't trust you Eaton if you were the last man on God's bloody earth."

Giles listened to Tom muttering as he retreated down the corridor and knew that most of his ire would be vented on him.

He glanced across to the little case on his desk, reached over and pulled off the partially attached label. Now it was anonymous, now it was nothing more than a harmless bit of old luggage that could so easily be disposed of.

He stared at the innocuous looking container, tapped his fingers on his desk and quietly pondered his options.

Chapter 4

August 1867. The Whitewall Estate

"How dare you say such a thing?" said Margaret, "That was my father and I will not sit here and have his name blackened by you! Your explanation had better be a good one or I shall have you thrown off the Estate!"

Maria tried to maintain a semblance of calm; she'd been exceptionally blunt and could hardly guess how upset and angry her host must have been feeling.

"Well?" said Margaret.

This was the opportunity that Maria had been waiting for. She could hardly believe in her luck, for seventeen years she'd been trying to explain; to reason, to even just have a fair hearing from the impossibly intolerant and rude figure that had been this lady's father, and now she was being given the opportunity. She needed time to compose herself and in doing so, remembered that Silas was waiting at the top of the drive.

"Before I proceed madam, I have a horse and cab waiting at the end of the drive and I fear that he may well be wondering where I am if our discourse becomes protracted."

Margaret was considerate in her response and said, "Don't concern yourself Miss, or should I say Mrs. Chance?"

"Miss Chance."

"Very well, Miss Chance, I will send a man to dismiss your cab and once we have concluded our conversation I will see to it that you are taken to wherever you require."

Maria thanked Margaret and ordered her mind as instructions were imparted to her maidservant regarding Silas.

Presently Margaret returned to where she'd been sitting and said, "Now Miss Chance, please proceed."

Maria removed her black fingerless silk gloves, laid them in her lap and made herself comfortable in her chair.

"Very well; in March 1747, my great grandfather John Chance *leased* this Estate to your great grandfather James Montague

Lincoln for ninety nine years and one day. The terms of that lease came to an end twenty years ago and the Lincoln family have been illegally residing here ever since."

"What?"

"Leased, I reiterate," said Maria bringing the full import of her words to bear, "but your family, despite being in possession of documents attesting to the absolute and incontrovertible validity of my claim, have steadfastly maintained an historic deception that it was in fact not leased to them at all, but sold to them all those years ago!"

Margaret leapt to her feet and put her right hand in the air.

"Stop, stop!" she said indignantly, "This is too much now! What kind of nonsense is this? Are you really expecting me to believe that my forebears have carried out a huge deception? Have lived what, a lie of monumental magnitude? Please credit me with more sense than to be expecting me to believe a fantasy like this!"

Maria remained silent.

Following a few seconds of barely controllable exasperation Margaret sat back down, faced Maria and said, "Let me be perfectly clear on this issue Miss Chance, are you seriously trying to tell me that you believe your family to be the rightful owners of this estate?"

"I am not *seriously* trying to tell you anything Mrs Johnson;" said Maria defiantly, "I simply *am* telling you. I am the rightful owner of this estate!"

Margaret was dumbfounded. She didn't know how to respond; she looked at the slight figure of the woman opposite and marvelled at her sheer audacity. To have appeared at her front door and to have made such a claim, she either had to be verging on the criminally insane or indeed believing herself to be in possession of some compelling truth. But what a truth! If she was right, it would be unthinkable. She needed to know more.

"You truly have me at a loss Miss Chance, and I would be lying if I did not say that my immediate impulse is to dismiss you at once, but in deference to the simple truth that you have journeyed here, with this, this..." She bit back what she wanted to say and tried to remain dignified, "this tale of yours, I will endeavour to listen to your account with an open mind."

"Very well," said Maria, "then I shall acquaint you with the antecedents and let you be the judge. But I should tell you before I proceed, that *you irrefutably are* in possession of the documents proving my claim, and if you opt to continue the deception, you will find me an equally diligent and persistent thorn in your side, as did your father before you."

Margaret took in a quiet, deep breath. Maria Chance was the most forthright and determined person she had ever encountered; her size and appearance utterly belied her strength of character. She appeared to be no more than five feet in height, had a good figure, a feminine, but resolute looking face and was dressed in an expensive but ageing black dress. Her hair was dark with a parting on the left-hand side of her forehead and she had the most exceptional eyes. They were the brightest pale blue and were so alert that each time she looked in a different direction they appeared to coruscate.

Maria adjusted her position in her chair and re-started her narrative.

"As I said, in 1747 a lease was arranged between our two families, both of which were happy with the terms; its sheer length ensured that the tenancy could, providing that those terms were not compromised, be passed from father to son for at least two or three generations. As a measure of goodwill the original lease, signed by both parties and the deeds to the Estate were placed in the safekeeping of a firm of independent solicitors named Josiah Hubert and Sons in Hyde, Cheshire.

For fifteen years the terms of the tenancy were satisfactorily upheld, and then in the winter of 1762 my great grandfather John Chance died quite suddenly following the onset of a chest ailment. The very speed of his demise meant that he departed this world without leaving a will, with the consequence that a good many years passed before his financial dealings fully came to light. This difficult situation was further exacerbated because my grandfather Joseph was but fourteen years old when he inherited, and he was not aware of the original terms of the lease."

She paused long enough to give her host time to ask questions, but Margaret remained calm and in no apparent need to do so.

She continued, "It was several years before my grandfather became aware that payments had been made by the Lincoln family for the Whitewall Estate; and in order to clarify the details of these dealings he visited your great grandfather in 1768. There he was informed that the arrangement between his father John, and your forebear James had been a mortgage for the purchase of the estate, and not a tenancy agreement at all!"

She heard Margaret draw breath but make no attempt to halt the narrative.

"My grandfather Joseph had no reason to doubt such a man of substance as your great grandfather and he left the Lincolns that day satisfied that their business together was concluded; and I should say that at the time of his visit, he was living a comfortable life, because he was the joint heir to a considerable fortune and three other estates.

Seventy-one full years passed by without a single member of the Chance family ever knowing that they were the rightful owners of the estate, until in 1839 and through a caprice of fate, my father Thomas, finally learned the truth about the Whitewall ownership *and* the years of deception by the Lincoln family."

She heard Margaret expel a long slow breath and stopped speaking.

"Forgive my interruption Miss Chance, but this account is almost too much for me to take in at one time."

Maria appreciated that had the shoe been on the other foot, she, too, would have been equally aghast.

"Then I shall stop until you have had time to compose yourself."

"No, that will not be necessary," said Margaret calmly, "please do continue."

Maria sympathised with her host's position, tried to be as considerate as possible and said, "I cannot possibly understand the full extent of what must be going through your mind, but please let me assure you that this is no tale of fiction, and it is a hard fact that you have it entirely within your power to prove my claim."

"And I am not naturally of a disposition to automatically disbelieve you, indeed I cannot see a motivation for you to concoct such a story if it were to no avail, but please tell me, how did your father come to learn of the alleged deception?"

This was the one question that Maria didn't have an answer to.

"Frankly," she said, "I don't know. I do know, however, that he became aware that Hubert & Sons solicitors in Hyde held the legal documents that could have substantiated his claim; indeed he visited their establishment on numerous occasions and demanded to see them but by all accounts they steadfastly refused, informing him that they no longer belonged to his family and that he therefore had no right to view them.

But, following his last visit to their offices my father discovered that the solicitors were in receipt of an annual stipend from your family which made it hardly surprising that they adopted this stance.

Margaret frowned and said, "An annual stipend?"

"Yes, one that has been paid since the original deception in 1768."

"Wait! Are you inferring that it is still being paid Miss Chance? Because if you are…"

"It is." said Maria unemotionally.

Margaret was utterly dismayed by the contentious riposte and immediately took offence.

"I assure you that it is *not* being paid madam, and furthermore I take exception to the implication of such a comment!"

Maria was as forthright as Margaret was indignant.

"Well I apologise if this comes to you as a surprise madam, but I equally strongly assure you that it is! And according to my very reliable source, a payment was received just last week!"

Margaret could not have been more shocked, she jumped to her feet and said, "All right, that's enough! I refuse to sit here in my own parlour and be accused of dishonesty. I think you should leave."

Maria remained seated and said, "I apologise if I have offended you. You have been a most gracious host and I truly appreciate being given the opportunity to acquaint you with these facts; but that is all I am doing. It is not my intention to insult you so badly that you would ask me to leave, where would be the sense in that? I speak only truths here Mrs. Johnson, truths and nothing more."

Margaret stared at Maria for a little longer and then sat back down.

"Very well," she said, "but I too am speaking the truth when I tell you that I know nothing of any payment to this firm of solicitors though you may rest assured that I will most certainly investigate your claim."

Maria nodded and said, "Perhaps my time in pursuing this business has blunted my politesse and made me too forthright so I apologise for that also. I appreciate that this must be distressing for you and it certainly is not my intention to cause you any unnecessary disquiet."

Margaret looked closely at Maria. Some indistinguishable quality shone out; she couldn't easily place her finger upon it but Maria looked as innocent and uncomplicated as a childhood doll and she found it increasingly difficult to doubt her veracity.

"And how long have you been at this business?" she asked more calmly.

"Seventeen very trying years; I first approached your father in 1850 at the request of mine."

"And you imparted these same facts to him?"

"There was no need. He blustered, and denied all knowledge of any wrongdoing, but I am convinced that he knew the truth. We had repeatedly requested viewings of the estate documents but he unwaveringly refused. This to us was proof that he had something to hide."

Margaret slowly mulled over the imparted information; it should have been easy to dismiss, but disturbingly it felt as though she was being re-acquainted with a long kept, awful Lincoln family secret.

A question popped into her head. "If your family was so well placed, what made your father so determined to learn the truth? Surely it would have made life easier for you both if you had simply accepted the status quo?"

Maria looked down and said, "Circumstances." She paused briefly and then decided upon honest frankness. She looked up and said, "Following one of my father's disastrous business investments our family fortune collapsed; we lost everything including our home. Thereafter it became of paramount importance to try to reclaim what we believed to be rightfully ours, and in the knowledge that your father had become a man of considerable wealth owning at least two other estates whilst still illegally residing in the one owned by us, it seemed only fair to seek justice."

She paused for a second and then dropped her head.

"Just before my father died in 1850 he asked me to take over his quest to return Whitewall to the family, and I agreed.

I think about him every day; I feel that my diligence in this pursuit keeps us close together and I will not give it up until I have succeeded where he could not. That was my vow to him."

Margaret looked at Maria and all doubt vanished. She knew that it may have been a ridiculous supposition, but she simply believed her.

"And that," said Maria unaware of Margaret's thoughts, "is the reason for my visit today."

Margaret tried to comprehend the gravity of what she'd heard; she got up and walked over to the window deep in thought. Within a short while she returned to her seat and turned to face Maria.

"All right," she said, "I have listened to your story and I tend to believe you. Three things however, trouble me. Foremost is the apparent disservice done to your family by mine which I shall of course look into; next is your mention that my father owned at least two other estates in 1839, and finally…"

Without any hint of warning she suddenly remembered someone; someone that made the colour drain from her face. Her eyes widened and she put her hands up to her mouth. She tried to block out the memory but it was too late.

Maria saw the sudden change in her host and spun around expecting to see something fearful in the doorway behind her, but nothing was there. She looked back at Margaret and said, "Mrs. Johnson, what's wrong?"

Margaret remained motionless and silent.

"Mrs. Johnson, *please*?"

Margaret looked up and said, "I'm sorry."

Maria was stupefied; apart from her account, she had no idea what had happened.

"Please, is this my doing? I did not want…"

"No," whispered Margaret, "on the contrary, it was a recollection, something I never…" Once again she stopped speaking and sat with a troubled expression upon her face, but following a few more seconds of silence she managed to gather herself together.

"I'm sorry," she said more resolutely, "it is a family matter that troubles me and is something that I alone will have to deal with."

"Would you care to …?"

"No. Thank you for your kind consideration. Maybe one day I'll explain, but now is not the time."

Maria smiled and then sat in silence trying to comprehend what had just happened.

Finally Margaret regained her composure and said, "Now, getting back to your narrative. You must trust me when I tell you that I will fully investigate your claims and be honest with you in my conclusions but you have to make allowances for me. I have never seen you before today and though it is not my pre-disposition to think that you would come here with such a tale if indeed it were not true, I need to satisfy myself about its validity. Therefore I want to see some evidence of your endeavours, that is the letters, documents and other various journals relating to your claim, so that I may see them first hand and establish that they are indeed real and not a fiction."

Maria was shocked at what could have been taken as a slight on her integrity, but she realised that her host was being eminently fair and sensible.

Oblivious of Maria's dented feelings Margaret said, "If you satisfy me that your claim is valid I shall make it my first order of business to visit Messrs. Hubert and Sons in Hyde. I shall acquaint myself with the details of the stipend and examine the documents in their possession. Thereafter we shall meet again and discuss the results of my investigation." She looked at Maria and waited until she was sure that she'd understood her terms.

Maria accepted with a nod of her head.

"Good," concluded Margaret, "Now I would ask that we speak no further on matters concerning this estate."

Maria nodded again and closed her eyes. She was elated; it seemed almost impossible, but for the first time ever she dared to believe that it could be just a matter of months before her family was finally proven to be the rightful owners of Whitewall.

One hour later as the trap carrying Maria slowly wended its way down Wordale Moor, Margaret sat alone in her parlour and tried to rationalise her earlier feelings of distress. Her heart was beating quickly and she was deeply troubled. She told herself over and over again that she was being ridiculous, but from the top of her head to the tip of her toes, she was utterly and unambiguously afraid.

She knew of only two people who could benefit from perpetuating such a monstrous deception as the one Maria had spoken about; her estranged husband Abraham and her stepson Caleb.

She closed her eyes and took in a deep breath; she looked down at her hands and saw that they were trembling. It had been blessed years since she'd had anything to do with either of them and the very thought of those hideous, misogynistic characters coming back into her life had her gripped with abject fear and anxiety.

Chapter 5

May 2002. Walmsfield Borough Council Offices

At precisely 8:50am Naomi Draper stepped off her beloved orange and black 50cc motor scooter, removed her helmet and protective clothing and stowed them neatly away in the back box; she then fitted the security lock through the rear wheel, carefully locked it and made her way into the building. Five minutes later she entered the ladies rest room, checked her appearance and then headed for her small office on the lower ground floor.

She loved being in charge of the Historic Research Department, each day was a new adventure but as far as she was concerned the adventures started at 9:00am precisely and ended at 5:30pm. She didn't mind being a slave to routine, it structured her life; she always knew where she would be at any given time, her friends and family knew that any deviation from it would not exactly upset her, but...

'*My God, Giles Eaton*!' The thought flashed through her brain as she caught sight of the somewhat charismatic, but older figure of the Town Clerk through the glass partition of her office. She quickly checked her wristwatch, confirmed that it was indeed 08:59am and walked confidently into her office.

"Mr. Eaton, good morning," she said flashing a smile at the Town Clerk, "This is a surprise; to what do I owe the honour?"

Giles turned and smiled back. He was wearing a mid-grey suit with a thin black stripe, a white shirt and delicately patterned, pale blue silk tie offset with a dark blue crystal tiepin. The whiteness of his teeth accentuated the orange hue of his skin causing Naomi to be convinced that he was no stranger to more than just a few bottles of tanning lotion.

"Ah yes, Mrs. Draper good morning to you," he replied without moving from his seat, "Do you mind if I call you Naomi?"

"No, not at all." Naomi caught her breath as she became immersed in the invisible fog of his overly applied aftershave. "What brings you to my small office?"

"Yes, well er, nothing serious; just a simple question in fact. You asked Sandra Miles in Planning to locate a file for you two days ago..."

"Yes, the Whitewall Farm file." Naomi made her way behind her desk and sat down.

"Quite. What we, that is the Mayor and I, would like to know, is who requested to see it?"

"Oh, I see hang on a minute." She opened her desk drawer, removed several files, flicked through them until she had the one she wanted, opened it up and said, "A Mr. Samuel Chance."

This was the last name that Giles wanted to hear; the connotation of possible incidence magnified enormously and affected his concentration.

"Chance eh?" he said needing absolute confirmation, "Are you quite sure about that?"

Naomi confirmed the name.

Falteringly Giles said, "Er, this Chance chap, do we er, know anything about him?"

"Should we?"

"I mean, do we know where he's from and... what he wanted with the file?"

Naomi saw the look of concern on Giles' face and said, "Only that he was researching his family history and..."

"Yes yes, they all say that," said Giles cutting Naomi off mid-sentence, "but do you think that he was being entirely honest with you? And can people just wander in off the street and ask to see this sort of stuff? Data protection and so on..."

Hesitantly Naomi said, "Yes they can. It's not out of the ordinary to..."

Giles' mind was working overtime and he suddenly changed tack cutting Naomi off a second time.

"Have you heard anything from Sandra Miles yet?"

Naomi remained silent for a few seconds and then said, "Mr. Eaton, do we have a problem here?"

The directness of the question unnerved Giles and he wasn't happy. The name Samuel Chance had thrown his mind into wild disarray and he was aware that the Mayor would be demanding he take control if a situation was to develop.

"Mr. Eaton," said Naomi cutting across his thoughts, "I said, is there a problem with this?"

"What? Yes, as a matter of fact there is."

Naomi paused awaiting an answer, but when none was forthcoming she raised her eyebrows and asked, "In what way? What kind of a problem?"

Giles suddenly felt as though he was being interrogated and needed to get away from the intolerably small office and the damnably pushy woman occupying it. He could feel her staring at him intently and the experience was highly unpleasant.

"Mr. Eaton...?" repeated Naomi.

"Yes, what?"

"What kind of a problem do we have with the Whitewall file?"

"We can't find it!" blurted out Giles. This was the best that he could come up with; he figured that it would give him a breathing space.

"We can't find it and we may even have lost it when we moved offices last year."

He looked up and saw Naomi studying his face. It was like being on trial, it was unbearable.

Naomi nodded a little too slowly for his liking and said, "Right..."

Giles had had enough; he drew himself up from the chair and said, "O.K., that's settled then, must go. Thanks for your time and I hope I haven't disrupted your timetable or anything." He smoothed down his clothing, cast a last sideways glance at the researcher and departed.

As Naomi warily watched the retreating figure through her glass partition she suddenly experienced a sharp pain on the top of her left shoulder. She reached up, rubbed it and then suddenly heard a woman's voice say, *"Don't...don't..."* She frowned, got up from her desk, went to her door and stepped into the corridor. She looked both ways but nobody was there; she listened for several seconds trying to establish where the voice had come from but found nothing. Following one or two puzzled glances she eventually gave up and returned to her desk.

As the lift ascended to the second floor Giles silently castigated himself. *'You idiot!'* he said to himself, *'You blithering, bloody idiot! All she has to do is talk to the Miles woman, and that's the whole shebang pissed up against the wall!'*

He exited the lift and quickly headed towards the Planning Department; it was time to exercise some damage control.

Back in Historic Research Naomi had just started to turn her mind to the day's tasks when there was a knock on her door.

"Good grief! Mr. Wilkes!" she said. This was some day; two senior officials in the basement, and it wasn't even 9:30am.

"Yes good morning Mrs. Draper," said Carlton, "do you mind if I call you Naomi?"

Naomi was experiencing a serious case of déjà vu and said, "No, not at all."

"And do you mind if I ask you a couple of questions?"

"No, of course not." Naomi sat back in her chair and then decided that the increased attention would be better enjoyed with a cup of tea.

"Before you start," she said, "I had been planning on getting myself a cuppa. Would you care for one too?"

"Oh, yes, that would be very nice thank you. White and no sugar."

Naomi walked to the drinks dispenser collected two cups of tea and returned to her desk. The interruptions were seriously disrupting what she had planned for the morning but despite her predilection for routine this was much more enjoyable, it was like a soap.

"Now, please fire away." She tendered the tea and settled back into her chair.

She had seen Carlton Wilkes on several occasions before but had never really had anything to do with him in the past, so to be sitting face to face with such a senior person in her small office was quite an occasion.

"About the Whitewall Farm file," said Carlton, "who requested sight of it?"

"That's just what the Town Clerk asked me ten minutes ago."

"What? Giles Eaton? What on earth was he doing down here?"

"The same as you I presume. He wanted to know who had requested the Whitewall file."

Carlton's warning lights abruptly switched on. The Town Clerk never visited other people's offices; he always sent his secretary Kathryn unless it was important or something that he didn't want other people to know about.

"And did you tell him?" he said.

"Yes. It was a guy named Samuel Chance."

"And then what?"

"And nothing much more except that he seemed to get a bit agitated once I'd told him.

He then asked me if I knew anything about Mr. Chance and why he'd asked to see the records. I told him that he was researching his family history and that was that."

"And did Mr. Eaton say anything else?"

"Only that the file couldn't be found…"

Carlton sat back in his chair. '*Couldn't be found?*' He was now convinced more than ever that something was afoot.

He decided to not involve Naomi anymore and changed the subject.

"How are you on mottos?"

"What kind of motto?"

"I'm not sure," said Carlton, "I think it's French, but I can't seem to find any reference to it anywhere."

"And what is the motto?"

"Cestui que Vie."

Naomi frowned and thought for a second then said "Hmm, interesting; sounds French to me too, but I haven't come across it before. Where did you see it?"

"On the back of an old envelope..."

"An old envelope…" It was out before he could stop himself. He hoped she hadn't made the connection, but she had.

"Wouldn't have anything to do with the Whitewall file would it?"

Carlton carefully considered his response and said, "Let's just concentrate on Cestui que Vie for the present shall we?"

"You don't need to be cagey with me," said Naomi conversationally, "I know that we've been looking at it recently."

"I'm not being cagey," said Carlton.

Naomi looked at the Planning Head and said, "I'm only asking because *where,* or *upon what*, Cestui que Vie was written may give us a clue to its possible meaning…"

Carlton picked up his tea, sipped it but remained silent.

"...and I know that the file is still in our care, so I figured..."

"And you know this file do you?" said Carlton.

"Yes. I was the one who placed it in the Planning basement last year when all the files were moved. It's so distinctive that you could hardly miss it; we've all wanted to look inside it at one time or another, so when Mr. Chance instigated his enquiry I knew that it was going to be my opportunity to satisfy my curiosity."

"Fine," said Carlton, "but how do you know that we haven't lost the file as Mr. Eaton said?"

"Because I saw it just two days ago, and if it is lost, you were the one who lost it. I was behind you when you left the office two days ago with it tucked under your arm." She delivered the last sentence like a coup de gras and let the full impact sink in.

"Ah..." said Carlton looking at Naomi with a renewed respect.

"Yes, 'Ah' indeed," repeated Naomi.

He'd been outmanoeuvred and they both knew it.

In the brief silence that followed he looked across the desk and 'saw' Naomi. He had been speaking to her for several minutes, but he hadn't actually *looked* at her. Their eyes met and something inside him changed. It was perceptible and tangible and he couldn't understand it, but the employee disappeared and the woman appeared in her place.

He quickly gathered his wits and said, "O.K., it's obvious that you know something's out of the ordinary.

So that you know, I returned the Whitewall file yesterday and left it in the care of the Town Clerk. He's had it since then and I've no idea what's happened to it or with it, but I am trying to find out. It would appear that Mr. Eaton wants to keep whatever it is under his hat for the present, and for now there's little or nothing we can do about it."

"And what would you like me to say to Mr. Chance when he returns?"

"When is that?"

"This afternoon at 2:30pm."

"Leave that with me," Carlton put down his empty cup and got up, "I'll go and see the Town Clerk and ask him."

Naomi nodded, leaned forwards and placed her left hand on her desk. She said, "Before you leave, do you remember Postcard Percy?"

Carlton looked down and noted the absence of a ring on her third finger and surprised himself that he had even looked.

"I'm sorry, who?" he said.

"You know, the old chap who comes in and tries to show his postcards and clippings to everybody - Postcard Percy?"

Carlton ordered his mind and the penny dropped.

Everybody knew Postcard Percy. He was an inoffensive man who constantly haunted the Town Hall cornering anybody willing to see parts of his collection of memorabilia and his capacity for collecting and retaining snapshots of local history was boundless. Newspaper articles, old menus, theatre posters, photographs and literally hundreds of old postcards had earned him his nickname.

He was an invaluable source of information particularly to the Historic Research Department, but when people saw him coming their way they would routinely remember something that took them in the opposite direction.

"Yes I do remember him, why?"

"He's popping in to see me this afternoon. I'll see if he knows what Cestui que Vie means, and, I thought I might just mention Whitewall Farm in passing?"

"Be careful Naomi. Let's be very low key about this for the moment." Carlton was warming to her and felt a little protective.

"Don't worry, I will!" Naomi flashed an impish smile that seemed to momentarily light up the room.

It took Carlton by surprise and dealt a second blow to his already shaken equilibrium; he smiled back at her, paused for a second then left and headed back to his own office.

As he opened his door, he saw Sandra Miles sitting waiting for him.

"What's going on Carlton?" Sandra was in no mood for niceties. "I've had Giles Eaton in my office for the last half hour insisting that I lie about the Whitewall file to Naomi Draper. He wanted me to tell her that we couldn't find it!"

Sandra was a phlegmatic sort of person under normal circumstances, but it didn't do to ask her to compromise her own principles.

"I emphatically told him that I would not lie, but he then practically ordered me to keep my mouth shut until I was given further instructions!"

"Whoa. Serious!" said Carlton.

"Yes serious! And I want to know what's going on?" She sat wide eyed and waiting for a response.

Carlton looked at his carriage clock, it was only 10:15am but it felt more like late afternoon.

"You want to know what's going on?" he said repeating Sandra's question, "Well, I have absolutely no idea. I have no idea what was in the file, and I have no idea why Giles Eaton wants you to lie to Naomi Draper. He has told her that the file is lost, but it was pointless to do so, because she knows that we have it; she saw me taking it home the other night and is just as intrigued by this affair as we are.

The whole business was initiated three days ago by a chap named Samuel Chance who is simply researching his family's history and he's got an appointment with Naomi at 2:30pm today.

Naomi's seeing Postcard Percy later this afternoon and she's going to ask him if he knows what 'Cestui que Vie' means.

There, now you know as much as I do!"

Sandra raised her eyebrows but didn't say a word.

Suddenly Carlton jumped to his feet.

"Time for some straight talking," he said decisively, "I'm off to see Eaton right now!"

Chapter 6

The Town Clerk's Office

'Lie upon lie'. Giles Eaton was positively squirming with discomfort. *'Lie upon lie.'* The term kept repeating itself in his brain. *'How,'* he thought, *'can I possibly keep on propagating this ridiculous pretence when too many people know the truth already?'*

He didn't think of himself as a dishonest person, a little slippery perhaps, but he was in local government, not a monastery. He knew that his friends and colleagues had always considered him capable of shaping the truth to suit his needs, but that was a little of his mystique, his way of being able to get things done where others failed. Indeed without his 'qualities' he doubted if he would have attained the position of Town Clerk in the first place.

This however was different; this was lying when others absolutely knew he was lying, and that was not what he was about.

'And,' he thought, *'who the hell can I turn to? Certainly not that blustering buffoon Tom Ramsbottom; if it hit the fan he'd be off quicker than a stabbed rat.'*

All of the unspeakably embarrassing possibilities were racing through his mind when somebody suddenly hammered on his door. He spun round at the severity of it and called, "Yes?"

The door opened and Carlton strode purposefully in stopping just short of Giles' desk

"Mr. Eaton," he said, "I'm in no mood for bullshit so don't try it. You are lying to my staff, and instructing them to lie to each other so there had better be a bloody good reason for it.

Now tell me, what's with all the cloak and dagger crap over some guy researching his family history?"

"All right," said Giles, "please calm down and let me try to explain." He looked at Carlton towering over him; there was something very disconcerting about his whole demeanour and he almost felt threatened.

"Well?" said Carlton interrupting his thought processes.

"I will tell you what's going on but what I have to say should be heard by all of those involved, so before I explain would you please be kind enough to ask Sandra Miles and Naomi Draper to come to my office at 12 noon?"

He could see Carlton staring at him and it felt like a physical thing; he could feel his confidence being undermined and it made him very uncomfortable.

"And you aren't stalling for time?"

"No I'm not. I'm expecting one or two important calls this morning and I don't want to be interrupted while I explain what's going on, so this will give me time to deal with them, after which I'll make sure that we aren't disturbed."

Carlton was pacified; he left Giles' office and promised to return as arranged.

A little after noon Sandra, Naomi and Carlton sat quietly in Giles' office whilst his secretary Kathryn distributed tea and coffee in china cups and saucers; once satisfied that everybody had what they wanted she completed her task by placing a small plate of biscuits between them and quietly left.

'*He's got the china out; must be important.*' thought Sandra still bristling from her earlier experience with the Town Clerk.

Giles waited until everybody was settled then cleared his throat and opened up the proceedings.

"Firstly I feel it is necessary to apologise to both Sandra and Naomi for my unforgivable behaviour in asking, and in Sandra's case demanding, that you both lie about the accessibility of the Whitewall file.

I'm sure that you are all aware that the contents were a little mysterious to say the least; but in accordance with the instructions written on the envelope by Surnh Horrocks the District Clerk of Hundersfield, the antiquated name for our own area in 1869; the Mayor Mr. Ramsbottom and I, opened the file in one another's company.

Now, to say that we have been presented with a dilemma is an understatement of titanic proportions and frankly we don't know what to do about it. The revelations held within that locked file for the last hundred and thirty years or so are of such monumental concern to us locally, that if they are not handled correctly the whole Council could go into financial meltdown. The consequence for thousands of local people would be disastrous; the collateral damage would be felt across large swathes of Lancashire and Yorkshire and it would most certainly make the national news."

Everybody was stunned.

Naomi was the first to speak.

"Can you divulge those contents to us here in confidence?"

"This is part of my dilemma Naomi. I wasn't joking when I told you that I didn't know what to do for the best; and it isn't only the content of the Whitewall file that concerns me, it's also the content of the accompanying letter from Surnh Horrocks."

"Was that the one with Cestui que Vie on the reverse?" asked Sandra.

"Yes. Mr. Horrocks had written his letter and tucked it in with other Whitewall documents and then secured the envelope with a wax seal."

"Can you tell us what Surnh Horrocks's letter said then?" said Naomi pushing as much as she could.

Giles looked at her and drew in a long breath; he bowed his head slightly and exhaled slowly through his nose.

"Following my erm, somewhat questionable behaviour with you all, I really do not want to pull the wool over your eyes any further but I am between the proverbial rock and hard place and for the time being I think it would be best if I remain silent until I've taken legal advice.

I can tell you however, that the contents of the file may have been responsible for at least one murder, possibly more and that when he wrote the letter, Surnh Horrocks was desperately concerned for his own safety."

"My God…" said Naomi.

"And that isn't all. After reading about Surnh Horrocks' concern for his own wellbeing I did a little checking of my own. Our current Walmsfield Borough Council was part of the District of Hundersfield in the nineteenth century so we are lucky to have the old Register of District and Town Clerks dating back to then.

The letter from Mr. Horrocks was dated the 24th May 1869; the date shown in the Register for his incumbency ended just five weeks later on the 30th June. There was a brief account of his accomplishments within his time of office and a note expressing regret at the untimeliness of his early death after his body was discovered at the bottom of a rogue pit."

Naomi instinctively put her hand up to her mouth and said, "No! You don't think…?"

"What's a *rogue* pit?" asked Sandra cutting across Naomi.

Carlton turned to Sandra and said, "Back in the nineteenth century the towns and cities were rapidly expanding and raw materials were desperately needed for building. The single biggest commodity was sandstone which in Rochdale, lay beneath everybody's feet, so opportunist miners would sink pits anywhere and dig it out. Many of these pits were up to one hundred and fifty feet deep before they were abandoned in favour of starting a new one somewhere else, often very close by, and upon closure the miners would simply board the pit over and leave it unmarked.

Very few people knew of their locations and over a period of time they became a serious hazard with unwitting people falling down them to their deaths if the boards became dislodged or the timber rotted. This became a matter of such concern at the time, that policies had to be introduced regulating the sinking of mines and placing control of it with the local council.

Naturally it took time to curb the illegal activities of the opportunists and the mines they sank were branded 'rogue' pits."

"And do you think Surnh Horrocks fell down one of these, or was pushed?" said Naomi.

"It's impossible to say," said Giles, "We have no details of how or why he ended up down there."

"So where does this leave us now?" said Carlton cutting to the chase.

"Frankly, I don't know. The Mayor is coming in again tomorrow morning and we're going to discuss the whole thing in depth after which I should be able to tell you more."

Giles looked around the room and saw that everybody looked appeased.

"Now," he said, "I would suggest that we keep this business strictly between ourselves for the present and if possible," he turned to face Naomi, "somehow procrastinate with Mr. Chance and his enquiry?"

Naomi was still a little shaken following the revelations about Surnh Horrocks and didn't respond at first. Instead she said,

"Given the gravity of what you've just told us, you don't think that we could be in any danger now do you?"

Giles thought for a second and then said, "Not if you remain blissfully ignorant of the contents of that file."

"And if we don't?" said Sandra.

Giles shrugged his shoulders.

"Let's not jump the gun guys," said Carlton, "nobody's suggesting anything, and under the circumstances I do concur with Mr. Eaton that we should temporarily inform Mr. Chance that we cannot locate anything relating to Whitewall Farm."

Giles nodded at Carlton and then turned to the others.

"Following my meeting with the Mayor tomorrow we'll re-convene and I'll advise you on how to proceed. In the meantime thank you for your patience and understanding.

Now," he said smiling and looking at his watch, "I think that that brings us neatly up to lunchtime."

Carlton, Sandra and Naomi thanked Giles for his time, stood up and made their way towards the office door when Naomi suddenly experienced a second sharp pain on top of her left shoulder; a pain that felt as though somebody was pressing a thumb down into the muscle above her left collarbone. She involuntarily said *"Ooh!"* and reached up to rub it.

Carlton noticed Naomi's discomfort and said, "Are you all right?"

Naomi nodded and was about to respond when she heard a woman's voice say, *"Don't... don't let him..."* She turned to face the others and said, "Who said that?"

Silence ensued for a few seconds until Sandra said, "Said what?"

"Don't let him."

Once again a silence descended until Naomi realised that they were all looking at her oddly.

"Sorry," she said shaking her head, "it must be me. I'm going loopy; I've been stuck in that basement too long! Come on, let's go to the pub across the road I'm starving."

As the trio exited Giles' office Carlton kept an eye on Naomi; he wasn't sure what had just happened, but realised that there was a lot more to her than he first thought.

Outside the walls of the council offices, the 21st century roared back into the lives of the three colleagues as they headed for the local pub; the hurly-burly of modern day life rushed around them and it was raining, but it was May and the prospect of summer was just around the corner.

Carlton looked at the two women with him; they couldn't have been more different.

Sandra had the kind of self-confidence that came with age and experience. She'd always been self-deprecating when it came to the issue of her weight but she was a clever and classy dresser preferring labels. Her make-up and jewellery were always tastefully applied and she had perfect white teeth; her stylishly coiffured hair and her near perfect complexion made her very attractive and though she was just on the wrong side of her mid-forties, she looked good.

Naomi on the other hand had the benefit of young womanhood and beauty. Not the plasticized version that was paraded on the catwalks and in the media, but natural beauty. She was in her thirties, was tall, slim and full of fun; her skin was pale yet flawless and her teeth were straight and white. Her clothes were stylish and attractive but unlike Sandra, they were devoid of designer tags or labels. She was also blessed with that curious mix of being a fully grown woman whilst retaining the appealing vulnerability of a young girl.

A mix that was not lost on him.

The trio made their way into the welcoming atmosphere of 'The Ryming Ratt', one of the modern designer pubs that were springing up all over the place. It was Naomi's choice of venue; there was something warm and comforting about the place and even the quirky name transported her back to happy days with her mum and dad.

They ordered their food and drinks from the bar and made their way to an empty table.

"Mr. Wilkes?" said Naomi.

"Please call me Carlton when we're out socially; Mr. Wilkes makes me sound like an undertaker or a stuffy old shopkeeper!" he said smiling.

"Why thank you Carlton I will. Now, regarding this Whitewall business, do you think that we could be unnecessarily exposing ourselves to anything untoward?"

Carlton felt that he needed to pour a little oil onto the water following the past couple of day's events despite harbouring a few misgivings of his own.

"No of course not." he said confidently, "This is the twenty first century not the nineteenth and it's just a bundle of old papers in that case not a phial containing the Black Death!"

"Yes, but a murder? Possibly more?"

"Oh for goodness sake," said Carlton, "that was a long time ago and Giles Eaton loves a bit of drama and intrigue. Try to forget it for now and don't let it play on your mind."

Naomi smiled and said, "My family is forever accusing me of being too melodramatic but I've always been the same; I think the worst in dodgy situations and I suspect everybody! As a little girl there were always ghosts or bogeymen just around the corner; or big dogs with slitty evil eyes and sharp teeth waiting to leap from under my bed and savage me!"

Carlton smiled at Naomi and relaxed back into his chair; her eyes weren't slitty and evil, they were deep brown and beautiful, and being with her was a treat.

A little light banter ensued between the two of them until Sandra excused herself and said that she was going to the bathroom.

Upon hearing her voice, Carlton realised that she hadn't spoken except for ordering food since she'd left the office. He told Naomi that he also needed to 'pay a visit' and caught up with her as she walked across the bar. Out of Naomi's earshot he said, "You're unusually quiet, is everything O.K.?"

Sandra didn't answer for a minute, then slowly turned to face him and said, "What the hell is in that file Carlton?"

Back in the Town Clerk's office, Giles was nursing a small malt whisky and congratulating himself on how well he'd handled the Whitewall situation. He'd always felt that he'd been wasted at Walmsfield Borough Council, that his talents were worth much more than those needed to be in local government.

He dreamed of mixing in the same circles as the top social elite, of being feted for a dazzling achievement and of having the

wealth that would allow him all of the extravagances…
He raised his glass up in the air and said, "To me!"

Chapter 7

How differently Maria felt as Silas transported her up Wordale Moor on this visit to the Whitewall Estate. It wasn't the change in the weather, though the day wasn't particularly pleasant, it was because of the contents of Margaret's letter. She'd read it more than a dozen times but couldn't resist looking at it once more before she arrived. She reached into her handbag and extracted the envelope now bearing one of the recently introduced postage stamps with her Sovereign Queen Victoria' s head upon it. From inside she extracted the letter, opened it up and read;

From; Mrs. M. Johnson,
Whitewall Estate,
Wordale Moor,
Hundersfield.

6th October 1867.

My Dear Maria,

Since the occasion of our last meeting, I have as promised visited Messrs. Hubert and Sons, Solicitors, in Hyde, and have examined the papers relating to the ownership of the Whitewall Estate.

I would be most obliged if you could visit me in October, during the afternoon of the 27th, where you will learn the results of my endeavours. I feel sure that you will be greatly heartened by what I have to tell you.

Please convey by post if it is not possible to meet me on the above date, otherwise I shall deem it acceptable.

I remain your friend,

Margaret.

To; Miss M. Chance, Mottram Road, Hyde.

Maria was distracted from her thoughts as Silas tapped on the roof of the cab and called, *"Drive's in view Miss Maria, shall I turn in today?"*

"Yes please Silas."

She looked across the familiar vista as Silas turned his horse and cab deftly through the stone gateposts and proceeded at a gentle walk down the drive. She could hardly believe that this day had arrived; this was the sixth visit with Margaret since August and on each of her previous trips to the estate, she'd felt like a visitor. On this occasion she felt like the owner.

She was so convinced that Margaret's innate honesty would prevail and the truth be revealed, that she'd put on her very best black silk dress and shoes for the occasion.

The top of her outfit was adorned with a round necked black velvet collar around which she had placed a single, open ended string of pearls. These had been her grandmother's favourites and were clipped behind a large mother of pearl brooch, itself surrounded by pearls. Of the two strands hanging below the brooch, one was attached to a small silver watch and chain which hung freely over her breasts, whilst the other hung slightly lower and swept to a small left-hand breast pocket. Below the six inch black velvet cuffs which finished off the fashionable three quarter length sleeves, she wore two black velvet elasticated bracelets, each adorned with small pearls.

The dress was her pride and joy, a reminder of the days when the family had wealth, and though she'd offered to sell it following the demise of their family fortunes her mother and particularly her father, had insisted that she keep it to wear on the day that Whitewall was restored to the Chance family. She knew that she was possibly being premature in wearing it, but she believed that Margaret's words, '*I feel sure that you will be greatly heartened by what I have to tell you*' could not possibly be mistaken for anything other than a confirmation of her family's true ownership.

Following the visit in which she'd first met Margaret, the pair had met on five further occasions. Twice at Whitewall, twice in Hyde (where Margaret had been introduced to her sister Charlotte and brother Charles), and on another in a well respected café in Rochdale where they had concluded their business and enjoyed each other's company for the rest of the day visiting some of the newly opened shops in the ever expanding town.

Over their time together she'd learned that Margaret had an estranged husband and stepson named Abraham and Caleb; but each time any mention of them had been made, Margaret had changed the subject. She'd come to accept that they were a taboo topic and had made no further references to them.

As originally agreed at their first meeting, she had shown Margaret copies of the documents, lineage enquiries and general correspondence appertaining to the Whitewall Estate and she knew that Margaret had become convinced of her honesty.

What she hadn't expected however, was the speed at which they'd drawn closer in what both hoped would be a lifetime of friendship.

She saw Margaret waiting in the open door as Silas halted the cab in the courtyard; she alighted, walked across to her, held up her hands and smiled. It felt as though she'd known her for years.

"My dear Maria," said Margaret taking the offered hands, "please do come in and sit down. I have ordered some tea to refresh you after your journey."

She led Maria into the parlour, sat her down and said excitedly, "Now to business! I have seen the deeds of the Whitewall Estate and it is perfectly clear that it did indeed belong to your family!"

Without warning Maria suddenly felt faint; she felt herself falling from her chair and was unable to stop it. She heard a startled cry from across the room and all went black...

"Maria, Maria! Are you all right?"

Maria came to and realised that she had been placed on the chaise-longue; she stared into the face of her friend and said, "Please forgive me, I've never been taken like that before."

"Would you like some water?

"No thank you. I... I... it must have been the shock of hearing the truth at last."

Margaret looked caringly at Maria and said, "Would you like to rest for a while before I continue?"

"No, no, please carry on."

"Very well, if you think you are up to it." She paused and saw Maria nod. "All right then, I have also seen the original tenancy agreement."

Maria was dumbfounded; she hardly dared to breathe. This was the moment of truth; this would decide the fate of the Chance family for generations to come. The tension was almost unbearable.

"Well?" said Margaret, "Don't you want to know what I discovered?"

Maria nodded her head and closed her eyes.

"It was as your father had said; the term of the lease was for ninety nine years and one day after which the estate reverted back to the Chance family. There was a provision for renewing the lease if required, but that time had passed and the lease had terminated in 1846.

The end product is my dear; we are now situated in your home and not mine!"

Maria was utterly overwhelmed. A multitude of questions poured into her mind.

'What would the rest of the family say when she informed them that she had finally succeeded? What would her father have said? How would this revelation affect their lives from this day forward? And oh dear God, how much are we owed in unpaid arrears from 1762 until now...?'

The last unspoken question had a sobering effect on her. She immediately wondered how on earth she could tender this subject to the good and honest lady who had just restored them to their rightful ownership.

Margaret broke the silence and said, "Come, take your tea."

Maria leaned up and was surprised to see the tea before her then realised that it must have been served whilst she was feeling faint. She took the proffered cup and saucer.

"You must have so many questions needing to be answered," said Margaret, "that I would suggest you take some time to gather your thoughts."

"Yes of course," said Maria, "you are correct; I truly don't know where to begin."

Margaret took a sip of tea and said, "May I make a suggestion?"

"Please, I would be most grateful for any help."

"Right now give yourself time to think. For example, two of your considerations may be my situation and the financial recompense owed to you in the form of tenancy arrears."

Maria said, "You've been so honest and selfless with me that even the thought of broaching this subject is abhorrent and I certainly wouldn't want you to be indisposed in any way. Indeed, if there is anything that I can do to assist *you* now, you need only ask."

Margaret looked at Maria and believed in her goodness as a human being. She decided to be open and honest with her even if it would be to her detriment at a later date.

A line from 'Othello' flashed into her mind that reflected her feelings;

"Perdition catch my soul but I do love thee, and when I love thee not, chaos is come again."

"I haven't told you about all of my endeavours since our last meeting." she said solemnly.

Maria immediately looked into the face of her friend. Her last sentence had been spoken with such gravity that she instinctively knew something was amiss.

"Is something wrong?" she said.

Uncharacteristically, Margaret continued to look at the floor and said, "We have only known one another for a very short time and I certainly don't wish to impart my woes upon you, but I would be very grateful for a friendly ear."

"Then please speak, mine are such,"

Margaret smiled and said, "It is about my estranged husband and stepson."

Maria saw Margaret turn her head to one side and divert her eyes.

"Has something befallen them?"

Margaret faltered for a few seconds and then said, "I haven't spoken about them previously because my husband was a violent and vicious brute who used to beat me.

Naturally I saw no sign of this evil before we married but within a few months of being wed the abuse and humiliation began."

Maria opened her mouth to speak but was stopped by Margaret raising her hand.

"No my dear please don't, that which has been done cannot be undone and there is no point in raking over the coals of such an appalling fire; suffice to say that I had to endure unspeakable degradation at the hands of that loathsome man until he was paid off by my father in 1859."

Maria was completely stunned; she looked with incredulity at Margaret and wandered how it was possible for such a decent and God-fearing woman to be associated with anybody so vile.

Margaret continued, "I am ashamed to say that I was later heartened when I heard that he had been gaoled within a few months of leaving me for the attempted murder of a young prostitute thinking that that would be the last I saw of him, but it was not to be." She paused for a second and looked directly into Maria's eyes, "He was released earlier this year and is now free."

Maria inhaled deeply.

"I had no knowledge of this until I visited the solicitors in Hyde; and I have to tell you that although I have been steadfast in my resolve, I am greatly troubled about the possible consequence of my actions."

Maria was stunned; it felt as though she'd entered a world of fiction; she'd only ever encountered such things in print. She pulled herself together and said, "Why, what have you done?"

"I threatened to expose Mr. Hubert, the last remaining Hubert of that company, with a legal action if he would not come clean about my rightfully inherited assets; he agreed to co-operate and finally told me that my father had bequeathed the Dunsteth Estate to me. He also admitted that he had been receiving a very handsome annual stipend, paid monthly, by Abraham and Caleb to withhold that information from me."

"But why would they do that? And more importantly how could they do that?" said Maria.

Margaret considered imparting all of the sordid details to her friend but they were long and complicated and could be discussed in detail at a later date. Instead she said, "The full details of how are of little consequence now, please just accept that they had damaging knowledge about my father's past life that enabled them to blackmail him.

And why, you ask? They did it so that they could take Dunsteth for their own."

Maria frowned and said, "So why should you fear consequences now?"

"Because I have written to them informing them that I know all about their scheming and fraudulent actions and that I intend reinstating you as the rightful owner of Whitewall. I've also informed them that I will be taking control of my rightful inheritance Dunsteth and that they now have two months to vacate; if not I will have the law upon them and see to it that they are evicted and prosecuted."

If total safety was the bottom rung of a ladder and mortal danger the top, Maria believed that Margaret had moved at least three quarters of the way up. She now felt desperately uncomfortable and the walls of the suddenly claustrophobic parlour in a farm miles from anywhere seemed to edge a little closer towards her.

"Forgive me for saying so," she said, "but that was either a very brave thing to do, or very foolhardy."

"You may be correct," said Margaret with misplaced bravado, "but those two men ruled my life and made it a misery for years. I am older and wiser now and I have the law on my side."

Maria held her counsel but seriously disputed the 'older and wiser' comment. She thought for a few seconds then said, "When was the last time that you actually spoke to Caleb?"

"On the day that he and Abraham disappeared out of my life in 1859; why do you ask?"

Maria paused for a moment then said, "Perhaps Caleb has grown up differently. The gaoling of his father may have alerted him to the rights and wrongs of life and brought him to his senses. Indeed he may now be the voice of reason, if there is one."

Margaret shook her head and said "Pah!"

"You haven't really spoken of him," said Maria, "was he

similarly subjugated by his father?"

Margaret's whole countenance changed. She narrowed her eyes and said, "*Nothing* could be further from the truth!"

Maria was shocked by the severity of Margaret's reply and realised that she had unwittingly opened a floodgate.

"Ha! Abraham and Caleb!" said Margaret acerbically, "Two biblical names for two of the most Godless creatures to walk this earth.

Caleb was never oppressed by his father; he was a very willing participant in all of his despicable activities!

We lived together in a small cottage in the country and on certain nights they would play a game. 'Redwashing' they named it, so called because it was a perverse derivative of whitewashing.

Abraham had the ugliest, most vicious cross-bred Irish wolfhound you ever saw. It was named Sugg. He permanently mistreated it and kept it underfed; he had to keep it muzzled most of the time because he was scared that it might even attack him in an unguarded moment. *And my dear Maria*," she paused long enough to give gravity to her words, "that dog was like nothing you ever saw before! Heavenly Saints preserve us; it was like something out of your worst nightmare. Cerberus guarding the gates of hell would probably have backed away from that hideous looking beast. It was huge, grey and shaggy and stood way above waist height, and because of appalling cross breeding its back legs were shorter than its front giving it the appearance of a gigantic slavering Hyena. Even the sight of its huge yellow fangs was enough to make folk go weak with fear.

I swear, too, that the dog hated both Abraham and Caleb; it would stare at them venomously and incessantly, seemingly awaiting its moment. Even Abraham didn't like it when he saw that, he'd take his stick to the creature and beat it mercilessly."

Maria was now hearing about a side of life that was so far beyond her comprehension that she was lost and dazed; she sat open-mouthed and in awe.

"They kept the creature chained in an outhouse with the chain from his collar feeding through a hole in the wall to the exterior. This allowed them to shorten it from the outside and pull the dog's head against the wall so that they could remove or replace its muzzle. Once released, the chain was long enough to allow the dog access to all corners of the room.

On the 'redwashing' nights, one or the other of them would have picked up several small animals, generally rabbits, rodents or their particular favourite, wild farm cats, which they'd keep in a sack. They would tighten Sugg's chain, extract one of the poor creatures from the sack, slice its belly until its entrails protruded below, and then throw it into the room with the dog. The sight of the blood and the shrieking of the wounded animal would drive Sugg into frenzy. They would then let the chain loose, and one by one, throw the animals into the room with the dog. The 'redwashing' was the blood of the poor unfortunate creatures upon the wall of the outhouse after Sugg had finished with them."

She paused momentarily and closed her eyes.

"And even after all these years, I am still haunted by the hideous sounds that used to emanate from that God forsaken place."

Maria was mortified. She was rendered utterly speechless and just sat with her hands up to her mouth. She couldn't for one second imagine what pleasure anybody would derive from seeing small animals suffer so, nor could she begin to understand what drove the unspeakably perverse and cruel men that enjoyed it.

She looked at the slight figure of Margaret and was racked by an overwhelming feeling of dire portent.

All she could think was, *'What in God's name have I done? Because of me, these evil despicable brutes will soon be back in Margaret's life..."*

Chapter 8

May 2002. Wordale Moor

ALAN HAWTHORN
AGRICULTURAL SUPPLIES
WHITEWALL FARM
Open 10am – 6pm weekdays

There was no ambiguity about the sign, he was there. Sam Chance turned his car into the driveway of Whitewall Farm and stopped; the sense of presence was crushing. How many Chances had walked down this drive? How many times had Maria walked down this drive? It was almost surreal; he was there, where it had all happened over one hundred and thirty years previously and where generations of Chances had lived and died. He stopped the engine of the car and got out; his feet touched the same ground, the view was exactly the same as the one his forebears had seen and in all of his fifty-five years' existence, it was one of the most moving experiences of his life.

In the Chance family Maria was a legend, everybody knew who she was. The old fashioned pronunciation of her name 'Mariah' helped of course, but even without it they all knew about *the* Maria. They had grown up with the tales of her struggle to reclaim the Whitewall Estate, and had all marvelled at what a stalwart she must have been, a mill girl who refused against all the odds to give up, ever. But that of course had been all of those years ago, and so much had changed since.

Maria's papers had been brought back to light in 1921 by Frank Chance his father, following a bicycle ride he had taken with his chum Merlin when they were both nine years old.

Whilst riding in the town of Dukinfield, Frank had remembered that he had a Great Aunt Charlotte who owned a local Inn close to where they were, so hoping for a free glass of orange juice they'd located it and announced to the bar staff that they'd come to visit his Great Aunt.

Following their introductions and being given orange juice and sandwiches, Great Aunt Charlotte, who was 90 years old and just two days away from meeting her Maker, had instructed Frank to go up into her loft and retrieve an old bundle of papers wrapped around by cloth and tied together with string. She asked him to give the bundle, which she called 'my sister Maria's papers' to his father Bill, and told him that the documents contained within the wrappers could make him, or his children rich.

This had made a huge impression on the nine year old Frank, but when he'd got home and shown his father what he had, his father had told him that he had '*no idea of just how much trouble and heartache, to say nothing of cost, the papers had caused*'; and that he wasn't interested in them at all. He'd told Frank that the papers were his to keep, but that he had to put them somewhere safe until he was older.

Maria's papers had been consigned to yet another loft and had not seen the light of day until he and his brother Terry had insisted on seeing them, following his father Frank's announcement of their existence to his own family in 1967.

He could still, even after 35 years, recall the excitement on the day that his father had opened the old bundle of documents; it had contained numerous letters, scraps of paper, burial notices, an old blood-stained pocket book and a leather wallet amongst many other things.

Over the next few months various interested members of the family had studied them until ultimately they had been consigned to their cousin John to catalogue and preserve.

And now with his daughter living so near, it gave him all the excuses he needed to re-acquaint himself with a major part of that family history.

A visit earlier in the day to the Historic Research Department of Walmsfield Borough Council had been a fruitless affair, but not so Wordale Cottage Museum. The Curator, Daphne Pettigrew, had been very proud that her little museum still retained documents and artefacts that other larger and more prestigious museums would have liked, but she'd made it quite plain that she had no intention of letting them go; subsequently she'd been able to provide him with more than enough information on the old estate than he'd actually needed.

There'd been no mistaking the site of Whitewall Farm on the maps that she'd shown him for when overlaid, the later maps clearly depicted the 'Farm' in exactly the same geographical position as the 'Estate' on earlier ones. But the most intriguing map dated back to the 17th century and showed neither 'Whitewall Farm' nor 'Whitewall Estate', but the simple legend 'de Chaunce'.

This had been the original French spelling of their family name dating back to the time of the Norman Conquest and was proof positive of at least historical tenure.

He took one more look across the moors, got back into his car, drove down into the courtyard and stopped. He could see several likely looking candidates for a front door so he picked one and knocked. The door opened and he was confronted by a homely looking lady with a ready smile. He got right to the point.

"Good afternoon, are you Mrs. Hawthorn?"

"Yes I am."

"My name is Sam Chance and…" The effect was startling.

Mrs. Hawthorn's smile immediately disappeared; she took a step backwards and partially shut the front door.

"You're not here to cause trouble are you?"

Sam was taken aback and said, "Of course I'm not. Why would you think such a thing?"

"Because of your name."

Sam couldn't believe his ears, he was truly shocked. He wondered if it was at all possible that the legacy of Maria was still being felt even after one hundred and thirty years. That would be unthinkable…

"What exactly do you mean, 'because of my name'?"

"You did say Chance didn't you?" said Mrs. Hawthorn abruptly.

"Yes I did, but I'm researching my family history, nothing more."

"And you *really* aren't here to cause trouble?"

"No, I'm not. I'm just interested in seeing where my family used to live, and honestly, nothing more."

Mrs. Hawthorn studied Sam's face for a few seconds trying to see if he was being genuine and having decided that he probably was invited him in.

She led him into a large kitchen, sat him down and offered him a cup of tea and some biscuits. As they drank and nibbled she listened carefully to Sam's reasons for calling, and despite her earlier misgivings took a real interest in the tale of Maria's struggle to reclaim the estate. A story made all the more fascinating because it was associated with where she now resided. Indeed she became so enthralled with the story that upon conclusion of their tea, she volunteered to show him around the older parts of the farm buildings.

Outside, Mrs. Hawthorn led Sam to where the original front door had been.

Sam stared in wonderment and thought, *'Oh my goodness, this is where Maria first met Margaret Johnson all those years ago.'* Once again he experienced that very real feeling of presence; he could easily envisage Maria nervously approaching the door and wondering what type of reception she would receive…

And then, as if fate wanted to confirm to him that he was indeed standing in the right place, he noticed something carved into the stone lintel. It was difficult to make out at first, but as he angled his position correctly there was no mistaking it. A triangle was formed with an 'L' at the top; below it the letters 'J' and 'M'; and at the base, 1748. James Montague Lincoln – 1748. The very same carving that had so incensed his Great Great Aunt all those years ago.

He could only speculate what the estate would have looked like to Maria, but as he gazed around he considered that it looked very much like any other largish farm. According to Mrs. Hawthorn a new house had been erected some time around 1890 on the opposite side of the yard to where the original living quarters had been, and they had been entirely gutted and converted into storage sheds. Only the seventeenth century exterior walls remained leaving very little in the way of architecture, and there was no discernable evidence of the internal layout. This was a huge disappointment to him for in all of Maria's papers there had been no description of the interior parts of the estate, except for sparse references to 'the parlour and dining room'.

Mrs. Hawthorn dutifully showed him around various parts of

the farm before retreating back inside to let him wander around on his own.

He found himself staring in all sorts of odd corners and at different vistas trying to imagine what it must have looked like to Maria, trying to capture some of her inner frustration; her belief in her right of ownership, yet failing through the illegal and scandalous machinations of supposedly honest folk, year after year. For the second time that day he found himself admiring his now long gone Aunt.

As he approached the bottom of the farmyard he noticed a padlocked door that Mrs. Hawthorn hadn't shown him. It appeared to be an extension of the old barn so he first checked to see if there was an unlocked access door from within, but there was none. He walked back into the farmyard and saw that the room sported a glazed window with bars on the interior; he made his way up to it and peered inside. The window was very dirty so he removed a tissue from his pocket, spat on it and rubbed it on the glass.

The result was immediate and terrifying, for as soon as the tissue made a squeak on the glass a huge dog hurled itself at the bars, snarling and barking like something deranged. He recoiled into the yard with his heart hammering as the animal went berserk and repeatedly threw itself at the door; He stood transfixed, not daring to look away in case the door should give, but after two or three of the longest moments in his life the dog quietened down and he was able to let out a huge sigh of shaky relief.

He wasn't a swearer by nature, but that experience dragged a very popular expletive it out of him.

Following the highly stressful experience with the dog, he decided that he'd seen enough and went back to say goodbye to Mrs. Hawthorn.

He sauntered across to the house and was about to knock, when the door opened.

"I've made you another cuppa to see you right for your journey," said Mrs. Hawthorn.

Sam thanked her for her kindness and still feeling decidedly rattled; he accepted the offer and went back inside.

It was at this time that Alan Hawthorn arrived home. He walked into the room where the two were drinking and asked Sam who he was.

Sam instinctively stood up and offered his hand.

"My name is Sam Chance and…"

Alan Hawthorn recoiled at the mention of his name and became instantly aggressive.

"You'd better not be here to cause trouble!" he said in a threatening tone.

This was the second time that Sam had experienced that kind of reaction and he said, "No I'm not! I explained to Mrs. Hawthorn that I'm simply researching my family history. So much of it has been centred on Whitewall that I felt compelled to come here and then see the place for myself; so tell me, why the hostile reaction when I say my name?"

Alan studied Sam's face in complete silence until his wife spoke.

"It's all right love," she said, "I believe him."

"O.K. then, Annie's a good judge of character and if she says you're on the level, I'll take her word for it. But I'd better not find out different…"

Sam couldn't believe the level of mistrust shown by the Hawthorns and decided to try to get to the bottom of it.

"Well?" he said, "Why on earth did you both react like you did when I told you my name?" He fixed his gaze on Alan and waited for a response.

Eventually Alan said, "I'll explain if you promise me now that there isn't going to be any trouble afterwards?"

"I faithfully promise," said Sam.

Alan pulled out a chair from under the table and sat down.

"All right," he said, "the Hawthorns have worked this land as tenants for over a hundred years now. *A hundred years no less!* We've been here as man and boy since my grandfather first took it in 1894; so in 1987 we made enquiries about purchasing Whitewall instead of leasing it.

Our solicitors promised to look into it but then we heard nothing from them. Months went by until I finally went to their offices in Bury where they told me that it would be possible to purchase the Farm, but that there was a problem with the freehold. They said that the testacy of an old will that supported a claim to ownership of the land was in question and that the whole issue was being held in chancery for nine hundred and ninety nine years and a day or, until the validity of the testacy could be determined.

In English that meant that there was a basic problem with the freehold and that it wouldn't be released until it was sorted out."

Sam felt as though a belt tightened around his temple. *'My God,'* he thought, *'don't tell me it's not over! How could more than a hundred and thirty years pass and it still not be resolved? Not one single member of the Chance family has set foot on Whitewall land in all of that time, and yet here I am at the beginning of the twenty first century finding that the issue of ownership is still being disputed...!'*

Alan continued, unaware of the flurry of activity going on in Sam's brain, "They told us that if it ever came to a court battle over legal ownership not only would they represent us, they were also convinced that they would win; so armed with that reassurance we went ahead with the purchase.

We now own Whitewall and we'll defend our right to own it to the end."

Sam still needed clarification that it was *his* family causing the problem and said, "I can understand your passion about this place, but that still doesn't explain your reason for reacting so adversely when I told you my name..."

Alan leaned back in his chair and said, "I'll tell you why. When I asked the solicitors why they couldn't provide us with the freehold, they said that the Land Registry Office was in receipt of documentation dating back to their forebears the old Lancashire Local Registry Office, which threw into question the legal ownership of the land. And the name of the family contesting ownership was Chance!"

Sam was reduced to total silence. He could see Alan looking at him and waiting for a reaction but this was almost too much for him to take in. He didn't know how to respond, he turned to look at Mrs. Hawthorn who appeared to be beside herself. She was staring incredulously at her husband.

Alan looked over to his wife, saw her look of utter dismay and realised that he had revealed far more information than he needed to and that he could have potentially released a dog of war.

He turned to face Sam and said, "But you did say there'd be no trouble didn't you? *Didn't you?"*

"And I meant it," said Sam, "a promise is a promise, and I

never go back on my word."

Alan turned back to his wife and said, "There, you heard him. You heard what he just said!"

Mrs. Hawthorn didn't utter a word. She just sat in stony silence staring at her husband.

Chapter 9

The Historic Research Department, Walmsfield B. C.

At approximately the same time that Sam was enjoying his visit to Whitewall Farm, Postcard Percy waddled into the Annexe of Walmsfield Borough Council's offices and slowly made his way down to the Historic Research Department. Despite the sometimes odd reluctance to stop and talk by some other members of staff, he knew that he would get a warm welcome from Naomi. He always had a soft spot for her and he thought that she was something of a looker too.

It wasn't his seventy years of age or growing paunch that forced him to proceed slowly, it was because he wanted to. The way that the young girls dressed turned his head and the very sight of a shapely leg or two just made going there that much more enjoyable.

He'd always been a ladies man; he was proud that he could remember the name of virtually all of his conquests and most of their vital statistics but he didn't think about that too often latterly, he didn't want to stir up any unwanted feelings whilst he was having to deal with 'the trouble' in the lower ground floor department.

As he slowly closed in on Naomi's office he smiled to himself because he was ready; he was armed and loaded! His new fund raising idea had been a great success at the old folk's home (with the ladies of course), and he was now determined to show the young slips of gals that he still had a bit of the old charmer left in him.

Naomi caught sight of him through her glass partition and jumped up from her desk to open the door.

"Hi Percy," she said, "I've been looking forward to your visit today but first I'm going down to the drinks machine, would you like a cuppa?"

"Yes please," said Percy enthusiastically, "tea, white and no sugar - I'm sweet enough!"

This was a first for him, Naomi had always made him feel welcome before, but today she'd seemed almost anxious to see him. He watched her shapely little bottom wiggle down the hall through the open door.

'Cor,' he thought, *'if I was only thirty years younger...'*

Naomi returned with the drinks and before she could stop herself said, "How are you today? Have you been up to anything interesting?"

"I certainly have!" said Percy, his big moment now at hand, "I've come up with a new idea for raising cash for local charities."

Naomi's enthusiasm instantly crashed and burned. She wanted to talk about Whitewall Farm.

"Oh, what's that then?" she said politely. She did her best to sound enthusiastic but she knew Percy of old...

"I sing songs for a pound a go!" he said triumphantly. The silence that ensued would have been enough to deter most people, but he was on a roll.

"Come on," he said eagerly, "it's just a pound and it's for a good cause!"

Naomi was trapped. The office suddenly felt a lot smaller and she desperately tried to think of *anything* to get herself out of the situation...

"Come on Naomi," said Percy, "surely you can afford a pound?"

He loved it, it was a brilliant idea. Not only were most people too embarrassed to refuse such a small amount for charity, he was now able to show them what a good voice he still had.

Naomi looked at her watch and reluctantly reached down to her bag.

"You don't need to sing Percy," she said, hoping that her plea for mercy would be acknowledged, "I'm happy enough just to give you the pound for charity."

"No. A deal's a deal!" he said, taking the coin and putting it in a plastic bag with several others.

'Gordon Bennett,' thought Naomi, *'how many others has he inflicted this upon?'*

"Have you ever heard of Dorothy Fields and Jimmy McHugh?"

"No," said Naomi, starting to lose the will to live.

"Well they wrote a beautiful and enduring melody in 1935. I hope you enjoy it."

Then in an embarrassingly loud voice he sang the entire lyrics of 'I'm in the mood for love'.

Colleague's faces appeared within Naomi's vision popping up like Meerkats in the desert; she could see that they sympathised with her torment, but they all hastily retreated to the confines of their own secure little space should the nightmare that was Percy turn around, see them, and descend upon them like Dracula on a creamy white neck…

With a flourish Percy finally stopped singing.

Naomi smiled and said, "Very nice Percy, I didn't know you had such a good voice."

"Thank you, would you like me to sing another?"

"NO!" said Naomi just a little too forcefully, "No thank you." Once again she looked at her watch '*Good God,*' she thought, '*was that only three minutes?*'

"I want to pick your brain," she said, trying not to let her anguish show, "Do you know the meaning of Cestui que Vie?"

Percy composed himself and said, "Cestui que Vie? No, I can't say that I do, but if you could write it down for me and be careful about the spelling, I have a book at home that's full of old phrases, I'll be able to check it out tonight."

"And do you know anything historically about the Whitewall Farm on Wordale Moor?"

She had just pushed Percy's button.

"Now you've just asked about one of my favourite pre-occupations. I've made it my business to learn as much about that place as possible 'cos it's not just the history, it's the mystery that gets me!"

"Mystery?"

"Yes of course! Surely you've heard about the goings on up there?"

"No, don't forget that I'm relatively new to the area, I only moved here eighteen months ago."

"Yes, forgive me, you did tell me. Now, Whitewall Farm or

Whitewall Estate as it used to be known in the 1800's is full of mystery and intrigue. Several local historians have written quite extensively about the place but they have concentrated more on the families that occupied it and the businesses they ran."

"Surely farming is farming isn't it? What can you say about that?"

"Well it is," said Percy, "but because you own large swathes of moorland, it doesn't mean that you automatically have to farm it. For example you could lease it to smallholders; you could use it for horticulture, agriculture, or as in the case of Whitewall, open up a mill on some of the land. In its history it has been farmed of course, including dairy and wool farming; but to label it just farming is too imprecise."

"I see," said Naomi, "so what took your interest then?"

"Just about everything else; it is one of the most colourful places in our district. It was rumoured to be the scene of disappearances, animal mistreatment, staff intimidation and debauched parties; it was said to be the headquarters of a group of notorious and brutal thieves, and even home to a ghost."

"A ghost?" said Naomi instantly perking up.

"Yes, and not just experienced by one or two people, but by almost all of those who worked there. It is even alleged that some folk have seen or heard the ghost in broad daylight!"

Naomi was in her element; she loved all of this stuff. She glanced at the clock on her wall; it was 4:05pm, she had plenty of time to listen to Percy and best of all, she was being paid for it! She felt quite smug as she settled back into her chair to enjoy it.

"Who was the ghost supposed to be?" she said enthusiastically.

"Not *who* my dear," said Percy in his most dramatic tone," but *what*!"

"What?" repeated Naomi.

"Yes, what! The ghost is said to be that of a monstrous and fearful dog named Sugg. Its appearance is supposed to be so hideous that it's frightened off workers, postmen and delivery drivers from as far back as folk can remember and the rumours of its presence exist right up to today; and it seems that most of those who've experienced it have utterly refused to set foot back up there."

"Ooh! Scary!"

"Yes, and if I remember rightly," said Percy now getting into full swing, "there is a local legend stating that the dog is up there haunting the estate and endlessly waiting for someone to return..."

"Wow Percy, you're getting me seriously hooked now!" said Naomi smiling.

"Yes indeed!" Percy's theatrical expertise at relating such events was clearly evident from the look on Naomi's face. He paused for the briefest of moments then continued, "But there's a lot more to the story than just the ghost, there's the murders and torture..."

"You're kidding me?" said Naomi excitedly.

"No I'm not." Percy stopped speaking and thought for a second, "Look, I'll tell you what, rather than spoiling the story by missing bits out or getting detail wrong, I'll go home, dig up my material on the place and bring it back here tomorrow. How does that sound?"

"Sounds all right to me!" said Naomi slightly disappointed at not being able to conclude the conversation there and then, "Could you make it around two-thirty?"

"Yes two-thirty it is."

Percy picked up his tea, finished it and then got up. He slowly made his way to the door and stopped; he turned to face Naomi and said, "Are you perfectly sure that you don't want to donate another pound for charity? I know this enchanting melody that I used to sing to..."

Naomi instantly panicked.

"No! Really, no thank you Percy!" she said desperately, "I have loads to get on with and ... and..."

Percy smiled, nodded and gave her a small wave.

"...and don't forget about Cestui que Vie."

"Oh yes, of course, I'll do my best, and I'll see you tomorrow afternoon." He nodded in the direction of the general office and said, "I'll just take a walk down to the main office and see if I can persuade anybody else to part with a pound for charity..."

"Yes, good idea," said Naomi wickedly, "I'm sure they'll be delighted to see you."

Percy smiled, closed the door and waddled slowly away towards his next victims.

Naomi watched him closing inexorably in on them and

couldn't help smiling, he was like a Sherman tank; you could see it coming, but there was nothing you could do to stop it!

Some time later and sitting alone in the comfort of her small office, she could hardly describe how animated she felt. It had truly been one of her most enjoyable, and following the singing episode, memorable days.

She sat back in her chair and thought about what Percy had said, about the 'history and mystery' surrounding the Estate and although she had never visited the place she tried to visualise what it must have looked like in the nineteenth century, in those cold Victorian winters with no electricity and no 'phones. At a time when the most efficient methods of communicating were carried by men, horses and railway trains. When offenders could escape the police by simply being able to run faster...

As she sank further into the realms of historical speculation it suddenly felt as though the thumb pressed onto her left shoulder again.

She'd been experiencing more and more of late including images that seemed to flash across her vision like a fly or spider, but each time she tried to focus on whatever it was, the picture eluded her; and paradoxically, the harder she tried the less successful she was.

However, this was something different, she shivered involuntarily as clear unbidden images started to flood into her mind, scenes of untold cruelty and bestiality; awful, cloying, claustrophobic scenes that thoroughly disturbed her. At first she thought that it was her imagination, but this was more, much more.

She sat shocked and confused by the experience; she could see into dark and forbidding places, beneath floorboards and even under the ground. She could see dirty faces looking at her appealingly, arms were stretched upwards towards her; she heard the sounds of anguish, terrible anguish...

But one sound dominated; a dreadful canine sound, a sound at once awe inspiring and terrible, the sound of a desperately vicious and angry dog.

She sat bolt upright at her desk, every hair on her body seemed to be on end. She shook her head and told herself not to be so stupid. She looked around at the recognizable objects in her office and tried to rid her mind of the awful scenes until finally, after several agonising minutes, she managed to shake herself out of the terrifying ethereal world and back into the present.

For a long time afterwards, she sat quietly trying to rationalise what she'd seen, she knew that she'd always suffered with an overactive imagination but the things that she'd witnessed were like nothing she'd ever seen before; they seemed so real, so tangible.

But what disturbed her the most wasn't the appalling imagery, it was the familiarity. It was as though she had seen it all before and had somehow simply forgotten about it.

Chapter 10

20th November 1867. 11:00pm Wordale Moor

It was a perfect night, "a hunter's moon" his old pater had called it, "bright enough to find your way, but dark enough to evade prying eyes". A hoar frost was starting to turn the grass a crispy white and the wheels of the trap crackled on the hard dry earth.

Abraham looked across the moors and saw that they had an eerie stillness about them; hardly a breath of wind carried away his expelled breath and both he and his horse appeared to leave a trail of steam behind them as they plodded slowly up Wordale Moor towards Whitewall. The higher he got, the colder it felt and as he instinctively wrapped his jacket a little tighter around his chest he felt his favourite knife press into his side through his right hand coat pocket; he reached down and adjusted the position of it so that it wouldn't cut any stitching then gave it a comforting squeeze.

"I'm coming for you bitch!" he muttered quietly, and then he resumed silence as he watched for the telltale gateposts.

At Whitewall Margaret prepared for a good night's sleep. Prior to retiring themselves, her house servants Michele and Derek had given her a cup of tea, preheated her bed with a hot bedpan and then retreated to their own quarters.

She finished the tea, put down the empty cup, snuffed out the candle next to her and then slipped her feet down into the delicious warmth. She fluffed up her pillow, laid down her head and closed her eyes.

As the drive to Whitewall came into view Abraham halted the horse, climbed down from the trap, secured the reins and walked to the rear where his monstrous dog Sugg lay coiled inside a wooden makeshift cage. He'd been careful to muzzle the beast with a leather strap tight enough to keep his mouth firmly closed and silent, but even as he opened the cage, Sugg started to make a strange threatening and unnerving sound from deep within his throat. He saw the hound looking at him with a dark malevolent stare; a stare that was becoming increasingly intimidating. He stared back and narrowed his eyes in an attempt to make the dog avert its gaze first, but that didn't happen so he yanked at the short leather lead and pulled it out onto the road. Next he picked up his oak walking stick with a thick bulbous handle and his leather tool bag.

As he walked down the long drive, he wondered if his wife had changed much; it had been several years since he'd last seen her and every time he thought about her he could see her body. He remembered that she was slim with shapely legs and that her skin was slightly olive coloured; her breasts were small and firm with protruding nipples that stuck out even when he was taking his belt to her.

He relished the idea of seeing her naked again but knew that if all went to plan, this would be his last chance.

Quietly he entered the courtyard and saw that the buildings were just as the delivery boy had described; the couple of pennies that he'd invested in buying the information had been well spent.

The main house was in darkness, but there was a light in an upstairs window just where the boy had said that the servants' quarters were. They would have to be his first priority.

At times like this he missed Caleb, not because he needed his help but because he would have enjoyed it. They'd become close working the sandstone pits; the need to keep secrets had bonded them, and they'd made good money selling the stone. And then of course, because nobody else knew the whereabouts of each shaft, they'd made handy places to lose anybody who needed silencing. "Holing them." Caleb had named it; he smiled, he liked his son's sense of humour.

Another thing that he admired about his son was his level-headedness, nothing seemed to scare him or deter his single-mindedness to carry out what he had started, particularly when it came to matters such as 'holing' people. He never got emotional or angry, just cold and determined; in fact he was a perfect example of how a good son should be, a regular chip off the old block.

Caleb had all but begged him to come along to Whitewall that night, but he was needed at Dunsteth and had to stay. He'd argued that he only wanted to help his pa, but deep inside he knew that his son actually wanted to see the outcome of what they'd carefully planned.

He stood in the courtyard looking for a suitable place to put Sugg and then noticed a room with a split-level door next to the barn. He quietly went inside and looked around. Apart from one or two hessian sacks in the far corner the room was empty. Closer inspection revealed several ringbolts on the wall below the window. It was perfect.

He opened his bag, extracted a length of sturdy rope and fed one end through the ringbolt nearest the door; he then took the other end back outside and attached it to a similar ringbolt conveniently situated on the outside wall. Once completed, he took Sugg inside the room, attached the loose end to his leather collar and pulled on it from the outside forcing the dog's head against the wall on the inside. He then tied a slip knot on the outer ringbolt leaving the dog restricted and muzzled in case he made a sound before he was ready.

Having finished his initial preparations, he quietly and cautiously made his way around the building. He inspected each door and window in turn, first at the front and then at the rear where he got lucky. The Tudor-style windows were impossible to enter without breaking glass but further down the building near the servant's quarters, it was different. The windows there were the sash type and though all the others were locked, he found one small one overlooking a vegetable garden partially raised.

He gently eased it up, dropped his leather bag below the outside of the window and climbed in with just his stick and knife.

Once inside he slipped his knife into his trouser belt and then quickly removed his boots, socks and jacket. He was fit and strong but was bulky about the chest and arms and he'd learned that flapping coat tails and sleeves could snag unnoticed objects and expose his presence just as surely as a pair of heavy boots on a wooden floor.

Being aware that most places had at least some creaky floorboards, he edged his way around the outside of the room as deftly as a cat, sticking close to the walls until he reached the door to the main hallway; he slipped through and then followed the same procedure until he reached the foot of the stairs.

He stopped and listened, straining his ears in the darkness for even the faintest sound but could hear nothing. In fact it was so quiet that he wondered if he'd been rumbled, and that someone was waiting to fall on him from a dark corner. He stood perfectly still not making a sound, breathing very slowly through his mouth until he was satisfied that he could proceed, and then keeping his feet to the extreme edges of the stairs he made his way up in total silence and crept along the landing to the door with a light shining below it.

He could feel his heart beating faster and was aware that the palms of his hands were becoming clammy, so he gripped his stick between his legs, wiped both hands on his shirt, then re-took a hold of it approximately one quarter of the way down leaving the thick, hard bulbous top ready to use.

He listened intently and could hear the distinctive sounds of two separate people asleep. He surmised that there would be one male and one female so he had to make a choice; he guessed that the man would be on the right-hand side of the bed and the woman on the left.

Quietly he lifted the latch, opened the door and saw that he was right about the placing. He instantly darted to where the woman was lying and jumped on top of her. In one smooth action he clamped his big shovel-sized hand over her mouth, leaned over and brought the stick crashing down heavily onto the man's forehead.

Derek emitted an unnatural animal sound as his head slumped to one side and gushed blood onto his pillow.

Michele was now fully awake and staring up at him; for a second he toyed with the idea of making her suffer a little but this wasn't the time for games, he had a job to do.

Slowly enough to let her know what was happening, and so that he could see the fear build in her eyes, he raised his stick in the air, hovered for a second then smashed it down onto the top of her head. The cracking of bone and the involuntary twitching of her body told him that she was finished.

Quickly he jumped off the bed, went across to the window and saw that it overlooked the courtyard. As quietly as he could he lifted the bottom half of the sash until it was as far open as it would go, he then pulled each limp body out of the bed and manhandled them into a position where they were draped halfway across the window sill with their top halves hanging out of the window.

Leaving nothing to chance he removed his knife from his belt, pulled their heads back by the hair, slit their throats and pushed both bodies into the courtyard.

In the outhouse, Sugg heard the noise of the bodies falling into the courtyard and started to pick up the scent of warm blood. He pulled at the collar around his neck; the powerful, broad muscles of his shoulders flexed under the strain and his breathing became shorter and louder.

Further down from the servant's quarters, Margaret lay with her eyes open trying to discern what the strange noises had been; her heart was beating very quickly and she knew that something was amiss. She slowly sat up, pulled the bedclothes up to her chin and strained her ears for anything identifiable.

Suddenly, and to her utmost horror, there was a creak on the landing outside her door. She thought that her heart would burst with fear; she screwed her eyes up tightly and stopped breathing in case it gave away her location. Then, as if hit by a galloping horse, her bedroom door was brutally kicked open and the burly figure of Abraham Johnson filled the doorway.

The light from the moon illuminated enough of his face for her to see that he was unshaven and wild looking. He was sweating too, and she could smell the odour from where she sat. She opened her mouth to speak but he was across the room in seconds.

He grabbed her by the throat, brought his face right up to hers and hissed, "Hello Meg, remember me?"

Margaret tried to scream but Abraham was holding her throat too tightly.

"I'm the hubby you're trying to evict from Dunsteth you evil bitch!"

He saw that Margaret was having difficulty breathing but that just served to heighten his pleasure. He squeezed her throat a little tighter, enjoying seeing her pain, and then with his free hand flicked the tip of her nose so hard that it made her eyes water. He yanked her head closer and said, "It's obvious that you've forgotten who the master is here isn't it? I evidently didn't give you enough good wallopings to make you remember did I? And now you think you can grow yourself a pair of balls and start telling me what's what...?"

His voice grew louder with each sentence and Margaret's panic level rose.

"Did you really think you could take Dunsteth off me you fucking whore?"

He paused, but Margaret couldn't possibly answer.

"Ha!" he yelled into her face, "I thought so you useless bitch! Trying to outsmart me indeed! You were never more than a glorified cook with a fuckhole to poke when I couldn't find anything better!"

The mention of her body stopped him speaking for a second; he pushed her backwards, looked down and said, "Let's see if you're still worth having before I teach you a few lessons..."

Margaret felt weak with fear and lack of air; she could feel her head swimming as Abraham reached down and ripped the front of her nightgown wide open exposing her breasts in the moonlight. She was utterly and profoundly terrified and knew that if she wasn't totally submissive it would only heighten Abraham's enjoyment and invite more torment and pain.

Following several seconds of grunting scrutiny Abraham remembered why he was there and yanked her head forwards again; he placed his face right in front of hers and spoke so savagely that his saliva splashed onto her mouth and nose.

"When I think of all the trouble that I've had with that bastard father of yours you must have been stark staring mad to imagine that I would let *you* tell me what to do! And did you think that we'd just roll over, say sorry and leave Dunsteth like two whipped dogs? Just because *you* decided so! *Are you so fucking stupid?*"

Margaret stared back in half conscious terrified silence.

Abraham reached down to his belt, extracted his knife and held it up in front of her eyes.

"Remember what I used to do with this?"

The sight of the knife briefly focussed Margaret's brain, she could see that it was bloody and sticky but she was way beyond being able to respond.

"Don't you remember me and Caleb's little game? The one with the little farm animals?" Abraham moved his mouth to

Margaret's left ear and whispered, "Well I've got something very special lined up for you like that."

In the darkness of the room adjacent to the barn, Sugg heard the crashes and the sounds of his master's raised voice; he struggled to turn his head in the right direction. He pulled some more at his collar, but not in an effort to get to his prey, he wanted to be free. Over and over the big powerful muscles of his shoulders rippled with effort as he pushed his paws backwards trying to break away, but the fixings remained intact.

Deep inside of him a hate was seething; not a hate of other animals despite the number of confrontations he'd had to deal with, but a hate of men. A hate derived from suppression and beatings and malnourishment. A hate that was predominantly focussed on the two men that treated him the worst; one of whom he could hear nearby.

Up in the bedroom Abraham drew the knife along Margaret's forehead, tracing a line very gently just above her eyes; he saw the fear in his wife's eyes but that just made him more contemptuous. He leaned a little closer and said, "You do remember our little doggie, Sugg don't you?"

Margaret let out a pathetic whimper and nodded her head.

"Yes I thought you did," said Abraham, "Because *wifey dear*, he's waiting to get re-acquainted with you in the barn."

The horrendous thought of what Abraham was hinting at was too much for Margaret and she collapsed into unconsciousness.

Abraham let her fall face down onto the bed. He then rolled her onto her back and with the aid of his knife, cut off the rest of her nightclothes leaving her naked and exposed.

He looked down and could see what had tempted him in the past. She still had the same smooth skin, nice breasts and flat stomach. He reached down, parted her legs and looked at her. He ran his hands up her legs, across her thighs, over her stomach and up to her breasts, cupped each one and squeezed her nipples. He then ran his hands back down and into her thick black pubic hair; it was warm, bushy and luxuriant. He slowly parted it to expose her and then inserted the middle finger of his right hand as far as he could into her. She felt good. He could feel movement in his breeches and wanted her more than he had ever done before, but as he reached down for his belt she let out a groan. He reluctantly remembered why he was there and stopped what he was doing. He had business to attend to.

To make doubly sure that she wouldn't awaken too soon, he kneeled over the top of her limp body and punched her as hard as he could on the forehead. Next he rolled her over, gagged her, extracted some twine from his pocket and bound her wrists and ankles. He then left her where she was and went back downstairs to retrieve his jacket, socks and boots.

Seconds later he returned to his still unconscious wife, heaved her up over his shoulder and carried her across the courtyard to where the dog was held.

Sugg immediately strained at his collar in their direction.

Abraham wanted her awake for this, but she wasn't stirring; he slapped her across the face then took hold of her hair and violently shook her, but to no avail. It was of no concern however, he was confident that he could wake her in time for the 'game'.

He walked across the room to where the dog was restrained, got his face right down level and said, "Right you ugly bastard, I hope you're hungry."

He removed the muzzle from Sugg's mouth and the dog went berserk; the hair stood up on his back and froth emanated from his snapping and snarling mouth as though he were a rabid wolf.

Abraham stared in awe at the monster in front of him. In their entire lives both he and his son had never come across another hound to match this one in both size and ferocity. When they'd acquired him, it had been their intention to enter him into dogfights, but that had proved fruitless because neither the owners of the other dogs, nor the other dogs themselves would come anywhere near him; they cowered in abject fear at the very sight of him.

He wandered into the stable, found a bucket, filled it with water from the pump then returned to the out room and threw it over the pathetic looking figure of his wife.

The coldness of the water awoke her and the horrific realisation of where she was dawned, she could see and feel that she was naked and that somehow she was in a darkened room, but worst of all she could hear the one sound that she never wanted to hear again, Sugg growling and barking like something demented from across the room.

She tried to scream but the gag was pulled too tightly into her mouth. She writhed violently on the floor frantically trying to free herself from her bindings but they were too tight and she could feel them cutting into her flesh.

Starkly she realised that she was heading for some kind of depraved hell and she desperately tried to blank out all thought.

She watched her husband walk out of the door and return a few seconds later with two lighted oil lamps.

Abraham hung them in opposite corners of the room, walked slowly over to his wife and kneeled down. He grabbed her by the hair and lifted her head up to face him. He could see her terror as he looked into her eyes and said, "I should have done this a long time ago."

Margaret shook her head, imploring him with her eyes to stop.

"Time for me and Sugg to have some fun," he said coldly.

He remained where he was for a while staring into his wife's face and then slowly stood up and crossed the room; he walked outside, closed the bottom half of the stable door then leaned down and released Sugg's restraint.

"Kill!" he shouted.

Incredulously, the dog did nothing. It stopped barking and stood in the opposite corner of the room without moving.

Margaret stared in blind panic at the motionless dog; she hardly dared breathe as she waited for the dog to attack.

Abraham was dumbstruck.

"Come on you stupid bastard!" he yelled, but the dog remained motionless. He leaned over the door and tried to strike it with his stick but Sugg saw it coming, jumped to one side and then resumed his stance without movement or sound.

"What's the matter with you, you stupid bugger?" he shouted; but still the dog did nothing. He couldn't believe it.

"What do you want, blood?" he bellowed, *"Fine, I'll give you blood!"*

He hauled on Sugg's restraint until his head was tight against the wall and secured it once more. He walked across to his wife, removed his knife from his belt and without looking at her face, dispassionately slashed it across her right groin severing her femoral artery.

This was too much for Margaret; she let out a small gasping sound and passed into unconsciousness.

The blood from his wife's wound sprayed across the room hitting his coat, shirt, neckerchief, face and hands; he quickly jumped up, spat some of it from his mouth then went back outside and released the dog's restraint once more.

Still Sugg did nothing.

Abraham stared in disbelief as Margaret's life blood sprayed across the room and onto the dog; but it just dropped down onto all fours and lowered its head onto its front legs.

He was beaten. This hadn't worked out anything like he had imagined it would. He stood looking at his wife until the blood stopped flowing and he knew that she was dead. Then in a moment of thoughtlessness he opened the stable door and stepped inside to look at her.

Sugg was up like something possessed; he lunged, snapping and snarling for his tormentor's leg.

Abraham was panic stricken; he lashed out with his right foot and caught the dog clean on the snout. He saw Sugg reel back in pain; ran back out of the room, grabbed the restraint and pulled the dog's head back to the wall. Once secured, he went back into the room, re-fitted Sugg's muzzle and then laid into him with his stick.

Following a brutal beating he stepped out into the courtyard, looked up into the night sky and took a deep breath.

"Sorry boy," he said out loud to the absent Caleb, "I thought I'd have had a better show to tell you about than that."

He slowly took in the view of his newly acquired estate and then caught sight of the bodies below the open window of the servant's quarters. His spirit lifted.

"Still," he said with a renewed enthusiasm, "the night's not over yet, let's go and see what yon lass has got under her nightdress…"

Several miles away in Hyde and despite the late hour, Maria was still awake; she had shown her cousin Dorothy the latest letter from Margaret inviting her to return to Whitewall to 'conclude their business' and informing her that by the time of her visit she 'would be in possession of those documents, to which she had craved sight for so many years'.

This was so wonderful! Not only to be setting foot once more on her own landed family estate, but to be seeing her new friend once again to make all the necessary moving arrangements.

She hadn't closed the curtains that night and could see the waxing moon through her window. She lay back with her head resting on the softness of her pillow and wondered if Margaret was staring at it too and looking forward as much as she was, to her return visit in three days' time.

Chapter 11

Giles Eaton and Tom Ramsbottom were getting nowhere fast; the suave and dapper Town Clerk was starting to get truly hacked off with the foul-mouthed and coarse Mayor. He knew that the two of them were like chalk and cheese; many a time Tom had likened him to the Cheshire Cat, of 'being high and mighty and grinning like an idiot'; whilst he likened Tom to a bad case of haemorrhoids – a complete pain in the arse.

"Well we can't just sit looking at the bloody things," said Tom, "we've got to do something! That bunch of dusty papers could bankrupt this Council and probably half of Lancashire and Yorkshire County Councils too! It's a bloody nightmare."

"But we don't have to do anything, I keep telling you!" Giles was getting more irritated by the minute, "The Chance fellow who asked to see them won't be shown anything and Naomi Draper who works in the HRD…"

"What's the *HRD* supposed to be when it's at home? For fuck's sake use plain English!"

"Oh for Christ's sake Tom! Are you the Mayor of this place or not? HRD; *Historic Research Department*…"

"Don't you bloody patronise me Giles Eaton." said Tom angrily, "I'll thank you to remember that I'm the Mayor, not one of the arse-licking flibbertigibbets who brings your tea and biscuits. I <u>don't</u> work here remember?"

"Yes all right… if we can get back to the matter in hand? Naomi Draper in the *'Historic Research Department'* told me that the Chance fellow lives on the south coast and that he'll only be here for a few days, so once he's finished prying about he'll go and we probably won't ever hear from him again."

Tom was seething inside about the way Giles had said *'Historic Research Department'*; he felt an overwhelming desire to punch him hard on the nose. *'Cocky, bloody jumped up prat,'* he thought.

He walked across the office and headed for the narrow green chair because his new brogue shoes were beginning to pinch, but as he approached it he recalled his last episode; he eyed it suspiciously and opted to perch on the edge of the desk instead. He turned around, heaved up on the toes of his left foot and deposited a big heavy buttock smack onto a sharp metal desk toy that he hadn't seen below the flap of his jacket.

The toy disintegrated beneath his weight and drew blood from his capacious derriere with one of its sharper edges.

"*Shit*! Fucking thing!" he said, irritably dragging his buttock and the demolished toy off the desk.

Giles watched the Mayor flounder about in front of his desk as he imagined folk used to watch dancing bears in the 19th century; grimly fascinated and mildly distracted, but mostly appalled. He continued to hold his peace until he saw Tom concede defeat and sit down in the narrow green chair.

As before, Tom flopped down and sank so far into it that it looked as though the springs had given up the ghost. And as before the halt of his descent was accompanied by a huge rasping sound.

Giles' top lip curled in disgust and he backed away several paces, this time convinced that it wasn't the chair making the sound.

"But that's hardly the point is it?" said Tom oblivious of Giles repugnance.

"Hardly the point of what exactly?"

"Stop being so bloody obtuse!" Tom could feel his ulcer starting to peck away at the wall of his stomach, "You know exactly what I mean."

"Do I?" said Giles, now prodding the open wound that was the Mayor's tolerance level.

"Yes you do!" said Tom heatedly, "It isn't just about whether the Chance guy sees those bloody papers or not, it's about us having positive, historic evidence of blatant dishonest wrongdoings by this Council's predecessors, and us now having proof enough to put those things right."

"It's nowhere near as simple as that and you know it! It isn't only the monetary value of the potential debt that we'd have to consider, though God knows that would be bad enough, it's the other implications. For crying out loud, we have at least one, maybe two whole council estates built on land that according to those papers we never legally owned!"

Tom remained silent.

"If we even *dared* to consider doing the right thing by acknowledging the truth about our District Clerk's dishonest dealings, what the hell could we be laying ourselves open to? Could the rightful owners claim unpaid land rental for 130 years? Could they possibly demand that we knock all those properties down if we refused to pay? Could they claim payment for rights of way? Bloody hell Tom, the possibilities are endless and we only learned the truth a few days ago, it could potentially cost us millions of pounds if not billions!"

He stopped speaking briefly and then let out an exasperated gasp as he thought of something else. "And what if the rightful owners employ a firm of top rate QC's to represent them... it's enough to give you nightmares even thinking about the permutations for disaster..."

He walked behind his desk, flopped down into his seat and looked at the Mayor.

"Naturally we would contest any reclamation bid and we would invoke rights of settlement and so on, but once we open the can of worms I doubt that we'll ever be able to contain it from that day forward. And who could possibly predict the outcome?"

For once, Tom was at a loss for words. He'd only given cursory thought to the problem and hearing the Town Clerk elucidate was no comfort at all.

He thought for a few seconds and then said, "And what about the other illegal sale?"

"That's nothing to do with this Council; we've got enough problems of our own without worrying about other people's."

"But do you intend contacting them and making them aware of our findings?

"No, I'm not doing anything until I've met with our legal people; after that it's up to them to decide what should be done but I warn you now Tom, if one word of this gets out to anybody from the press before we've formulated a plan we'll be sunk before we start."

"And what happens if this Chance bloke gets wind of anything?"

"Then it's up to us to make sure that he doesn't, that's why I cautioned you to say nothing."

Tom thought for a few seconds and then said, "Look, if a bloke is researching his family history he could only be doing it one of two ways; he could be looking because he's found himself by coincidence near some known historical family site or he could have brought himself here for that very purpose, in which case who knows how long he'll be here and what he'll find out."

"But…"

"No, let me finish," said Tom cutting Giles off, "And then if the bloke doing the digging in any way finds out that we have been concealing the truth or have been shifty in any way, it could make things infinitely worse for us. Plus, we could potentially antagonise the press because of our devious behaviour."

Giles heard another suspect noise come from deep within the chair and had suddenly had enough of the uncouth windbag, regardless of how sensible his arguments were.

"Well I don't think that we will hear from him again," he said curtly.

Something about the way Giles spoke went against the grain with the now desperately uncomfortable Tom.

"Yes, but what if we do 'hear from him again'?" he said, trying his best to mimic Giles' patronising tone.

Giles ignored the obvious dig and said, "Then if we do, we'll have to think of something else."

Tom pursed his lips, reached up to the arms of the chair, let out an animal snort and pulled himself to his feet.

"You know what," he said, "I don't know why I even bother talking to you; with you it's either 'my way or the fucking highway'!"

Giles couldn't resist and said, "Good; as long as that's sorted then."

Furiously incensed, Tom pointed to the metal wastepaper bin and said, "Right then tricky fucking dicky, why don't we just sod decency, sod morals, sod protocol and not give a sod about anybody else but ourselves; let's take that bin and a box of matches up to the roof and burn those papers; then no doubt you'll rest easier tonight!"

Giles wanted to strangle the self-righteous, pompous

overblown moron. He took a deep breath but knew that once he started talking it would be like a runaway train…

"And what if there are copies out there? - Hmm? How do we know that these papers aren't copies? - Hmm? And what about Carlton Wilkes and Sandra Miles and Naomi Draper? Shall we ask them to come up to the roof too and then throw them on the fire while we're at it?

Perhaps when it gets hot enough we can toast some crumpets on their smouldering bodies and sing *'Ging gang gooly gooly fucking gang together!'*

He was nearly apoplectic by this time.

"All right, all right!" said Tom, "Point taken! We'll do as you say for now, but if that Chance bloke so much as looks in our direction again I want to know about it pronto, do you bloody comprendez?"

"Yes I *bloody comprendez* for Christ's sake…" Giles was now completely unable to control his exasperation.

Tom knew that the situation between them was spiralling down uncontrollably and with his ulcer giving him serious gyp, he decided to get away.

"And let me know what our legal bods have to say about this shit storm."

He walked across to Giles's ornate hat stand, removed his coat from the peg, threw it over his arm and headed for the door.

Giles nodded and said, "Naturally, I'll keep you fully abreast of any developments."

"Right, be sure you do. I'm out of here."

He snatched back the office door and strode out down the hall, purposely leaving it wide open.

A furious Giles walked across to his door and slammed it shut behind the retreating Mayor. He didn't know what it was about Tom Ramsbottom that cranked him up so much, but as sure as eggs it happened every time they met.

With a wildly beating heart he walked across to his drinks cabinet, poured himself a steadying glass of Old Pulteney malt whisky took a sip and returned to his desk. He let the calmness and relative peace of his office wash over him and then picked up the telephone, called his secretary Kathryn and instructed her that he didn't want to be disturbed for the rest of the afternoon.

He looked at the Whitewall documents spread out on his desk and considered how much simpler life would be if he *could* just burn them, but that was never going to be an option.

In a high state of indecision, he decided to go through the file once again to see if he could derive any inspiration from it.

According to Surnh Horrocks, the documents had been passed on to the old Hundersfield District Council by Hyde Police following the mysterious death of a solicitor named George Hubert in the spring of 1869. At the time of his death the solicitor had no heirs and nobody to succeed him in his business, so for several weeks the office from which he'd worked lay undisturbed.

It then became the responsibility of Hyde Police to sort out what to do with the contents; they took the easy option, noted the addresses to which each of the files related and then handed them over to the appropriate Town and District Clerks to let them sort it out.

In 1869 Surnh Horrocks had become aware of the disastrous impact the documentation from the Whitewall file could have if it ever become public knowledge; so until he could work out what to do with it, he had done nothing and secreted it.

Giles sifted through the swathes of paperwork and saw that amongst the host of general and legal documentation the file contained letters and receipts relating to payments for 'Whitewall Estate Management'. This was paid by the Lincolns and then the Johnsons to Hubert & Sons Solicitors from 1768 until 1869 and ceased two months before the mysterious death of George Hubert.

There were two documents relating to the sale of land; one of fifteen hundred acres from the East to the neighbouring Brandworth Estate in 1868, and another of two thousand five hundred acres from the South to none other than Hundersfield District Council in the early part of 1869.

At this point Giles could see blatant evidence of corruption, for although the two land purchases had been successfully concluded there was absolutely no proof of a freehold document being issued to either the Darke family or Hundersfield District Council upon completion of the sale.

There were however, fully detailed records of huge sums of

money exchanging hands in order to, *'facilitate the procurement and subsequent sale of said land from the Whitewall Estate to the party of the second part'*, and letters from the solicitors to both purchasers informing them of, *'a situation of considerable confusion existing in the Local Registry Office apropos ownership of the Whitewall Estate that would, once resolved, result in an expedient conclusion to the business'*.

He marvelled at the audacity.

Next were the two 'killer' documents. Both were contained in the envelope with the Cestui que Vie inscription on the back. He was aware from the contents that the scribbled out part that Carlton Wilkes hadn't been able to read referred to John Chance, but there was still something totally illegible between the John and Chance that he couldn't make out. It therefore read; *"**John (something) Chance - Cestui que Vie**"*.

He satisfied himself that the missing part was more than likely a second Christian name and gave it no further thought.

The envelope was not the concern though, it was what it contained.

The first document was a copy of the deeds to the Whitewall Estate clearly describing Chance family ownership. There was no ambiguity, no possible misinterpretation; it was plain and simple irrefutable proof of title.

The second was the original tenancy agreement signed by John Chance, somebody with an illegible signature and James Montague Lincoln. The agreement commenced in March 1747 and ran for a period of ninety-nine years and a day after which either a new agreement was to be approved, or the Whitewall Estate returned to Chance family tenure.

The legal validity of both documents was without question.

Amongst other documents, the leather folder contained copies of letters that had been sent by Hubert & Sons to the Local Registry Office in Lancashire. It was obvious that they were attempting to procure the freehold of the Whitewall Estate for the Lincoln family by providing proof of ownership with a completely fabricated mortgage document supposedly commencing in March 1747 and terminating in 1762.

Astonishingly, clearly unambiguous references to 'the fabricated mortgage document' could easily be seen in retained copies of correspondence that had been delivered to the Lincoln family.

Once again he was astonished at the sheer brazenness of the corruption.

Then there was the letter from Surnh Horrocks; even reading it haunted him. He tried to imagine the paralysing omnipresence of anxiety, perturbation and mistrust as Horrocks nervously walked the streets in fear of his life. And worst of all, his suspicions had proven to be completely correct.

He opened up the letter and read it once more.

HUNDERSFIELD DISTRICT COUNCIL
Civic Offices, Mill Street, Rochdale.

24th May 1869.

<u>*To the incumbent Mayor and District Clerk*</u>

If the seal on the envelope of this missive is unbroken you will be the first persons to learn about, and to be able to put right a good deal of wrongs unjustly visited on Joseph Chance 1748 - 1822, his subsequent family and heirs and owners outright of the Whitewall Estate situate on Wordale Moor within the District of Hundersfield. If the seals, locks and padlock on the document case were intact, I have also been successful in secreting these incriminating papers from the evil and scheming men who would destroy them in order to save their unjust and iniquitous necks from the gallows. And, if after making enquiries you find that history can prove the perpetuation of these wrongdoings, you will know that I have not succeeded in bringing these rogues to trial and justice and that some ill may have befallen me. My life and limb are under threat from these co-conspirators and I live in an all engrossing fear of them; ever turning my head as I walk the streets and wondering if the next corner is shielding my aggressor. For me these are indeed, dark and satanic days.

I have enclosed with this letter all the necessary documents and files you will need to bring these scoundrels, thieves and murderers to justice and I pray that God and fate has presented you with these papers within a very short period of time from the date written above.

I first came by them from Hyde Police following the cessation of trading by a company of solicitors named Josiah Hubert & Sons of Hyde when the last of them died in mysterious circumstances and their office was forced to close. You will note as I did that there is clear evidence of conspiracy, corruption and general wrongdoings between a former employee of this Council; Abraham Johnson the current occupant of the Whitewall Estate and Hugo Darke of the Brandworth Estate in Spotland.

Here let me re-iterate that Abraham Johnson is but the current occupant and not the owner of the Whitewall Estate as the enclosed documents will testify.

Upon receipt of these files from Hyde Police I made it my business to investigate the numerous and varied nefarious activities of those involved and soon established that my predecessor Jasper Clough, Hundersfield District Clerk from 1866 to 1869, was complicit in the illegal purchase of land for Hundersfield District Council from Abraham Johnson in 1869. It should be stated here though, that at the time of the transaction Clough was completely unaware that Johnson was not the owner of the land. This was a separate deception perpetrated by Johnson which should have been investigated and exposed by the District Clerk prior to all negotiations in respect of the forthcoming purchase. However, no such searches or checks in respect of ownership were made and my predecessor accepted the highly implausible account of the existing situation at the Local Registry Office without question; greatly assisted of course, by the payment of a substantial amount of money into his private banking account. Additionally, and according to the enclosed records a similar ex-gratia payment was made to Hugo Darke.

I visited my predecessor Clough and told him that I was aware of the personal payment made to him by Abraham Johnson to facilitate the unencumbered procurement of land for Hundersfield District Council, whereupon he became exceptionally agitated and told me that if this became public knowledge, he would be in mortal fear for his life. This proved to be well founded, for within ten days of my visit it was reported in the local newspaper that he had been killed whilst being robbed on his way home one night.

Next I visited Abraham Johnson at the Whitewall Estate and told him that I had proof absolute of two illegal land sales; one to Hundersfield District Council and the other to Hugo Darke of the Brandworth Estate in Spotland. I told him that I was aware that he was not the legal owner of the Whitewall Estate and informed him that I would be publicly exposing all of his illegal activities through the justice system. He became very malicious and threatening; warning me that if I informed the local police about my findings I would not live long enough to see it to its conclusion. And as a by-the-by, I am also of the opinion that had I not so obviously been seen by several labourers entering into heated discussion with Johnson on his very doorstep, such was his anger that he might actually have taken his walking stick to me there and then in an attempt to carry out his threat. I believe this to be a very dangerous and evil man capable of all the degradations this life has to offer.

I also warned Johnson that I would be visiting Hugo Darke and informing him of my intentions, but this never happened; for I would not go to the Brandworth Estate following the receipt of threats upon my life should I ever venture out alone either by day or night.

I now know not what to do except commend my fate to my Maker and pursue this case from behind locked doors.

You are now fully acquainted with the facts of these wrongdoings; and if by the time you read this they have not been put right, you are charged by your honest and God fearing predecessor to do what is right and just and to honour my memory by informing those who should know, that it was with the assistance of my endeavours that you were finally able to right these dreadful wrongs.

I am Sir,
Yr. obt. Svt.,
Surnh Horrocks,
District Clerk.

Giles sat back in his chair and took another sip of whisky. The injustice of it all was palpable; he read again what Surnh Horrocks had written, '*evil and scheming men*', '*unjust and iniquitous...*', *'scoundrels, thieves and murderers...'*

Certainly the legacy bequeathed by Surnh Horrocks to him as his successor was a lighted torch that had been handed to him from the past, a brightly burning beacon of truth that had not died and did not deserve to be extinguished, not after Horrocks had given his very life to preserve the documents that would see justice prevail.

The obvious next step was to pass the entire file to the Walmsfield Borough Council Legal Department and let them handle it. But was it?

He sipped his whisky in total silence knowing that he had the power right there and right then to expose the wrongdoings of evil men, to restore stolen land to its rightful owners and to show the world that Surnh Horrocks had not died in vain.

But something else was ticking away in his brain, the third deadly sin - avarice. He was sitting on a time bomb that somebody might pay good money to keep quiet. Good money that might elevate his personal position and not have him see his days out as the Town Clerk of a mediocre northern town.

Even the briefest thought of girls, cars and maybe even a boat had the notion of justice melting away like snowflakes on a camp fire.

"The trick," he said quietly to himself, "is to hang on to the documents and find out who would benefit from my silence the most..."

Chapter 12

May 2002

"Are you perfectly sure that it's O.K. for me to stay for another three days?" said Sam.

"Perfectly sure." said Sam's daughter on the other end of the phone, "I see little enough of you as it is. But why have you decided to stay for longer?"

"I'll explain fully when I see you tonight but my meeting with the Hawthorns threw up more questions than answers and it's peaked my curiosity even more now so I want to check out another couple of things before I go home."

"All right I'll see you later then. Love you; bye."

"Love you too pet, bye!" Sam ended the call, sat back in his car seat and decided upon a plan of action.

Alan Hawthorn's amazingly frank admission was still reverberating around his head and it made him eager to pursue the investigation, but two minor things niggled him and he wanted to clear them up.

Firstly he wanted to know how big Whitewall Farm was and secondly, and probably ridiculously, he wanted to know how big an acre was! The former because he wanted to establish just how 'landed' his forebears had been and the latter because he had no notion of that size in real terms.

One would require a return visit to Wordale Cottage Museum and the other an answer from a search engine on the internet.

The next day, following a hearty breakfast Sam headed back up Wordale Moor to get himself re-acquainted with Daphne Pettigrew the delightfully pleasant but distinctly quirky Curator of Wordale Cottage Museum.

He'd come across characters like her before and mused whether or not their names were the most important thing on their Curriculum Vitae. He couldn't imagine for one second a poor erstwhile architect applying to a Cathedral Works Committee for a senior position if his name was Ted Shufflebottom, or a girl applying to The National Trust for the position of conservator if her name was Ada Pratt. No, they had to be Barrington Timperley-Jones's or Samantha Partington-Browne's; it just went with the territory. He amused himself with the thought that perhaps their professional calling had been sealed as their parents submitted their names to the Registrar just a few short weeks after birth!

He pulled into the gravel car park of the museum, stopped the car and got out. As he looked around at the stark beauty of the Northern English countryside he couldn't help drawing in a deep breath. It was a necessary thing to do, it was as if the act of filling his lungs with local air was informing the Northern Gods that one of their sons was back on home territory and despite having lived thirty five years of his current fifty five on the south coast, he still felt that he'd returned home whenever he came back.

He locked the car, sauntered over to the museum and at once entered a world of musty archaism.

This was a museum of the 'old school', dark and full of glass cabinets containing long dead weasels, badgers, foxes, owls, and field mice, all set into a micro-cosmic section of English woodland; and all a lasting testament to the skills of a taxidermist who probably departed the earth in the first quarter of the twentieth century.

There was a genuine ducking stool in the corner of the room complete with a rhyme from the early 1700's extolling its virtue, and unlike many of the artefacts found in contemporary museums this was hands-on. He suspected that many a man walking past this particular item had given it a wistful look and an endearing stroke…

The polished wooden floorboards creaked and echoed his footsteps as he moved from display case to display case peering in like a child outside a toyshop at Christmastime.

"Mr. Chance isn't it? Of course it is. I recognise you from your last visit!" Daphne Pettigrew stood smiling up at Sam as he peered into the back of one of the units.

He wheeled around to see where the voice had been coming from and at first looked over the top of her head.

"Down here!" said Daphne chirpily.

Sam looked down and said, "Sorry, I…"

"That's perfectly all right," said Daphne smiling, "Napoleon was only small too, but he didn't have my dress sense!"

She was petite, shapely and in her late 30's. She had a full head of blonde, lightly permed hair that looked appealingly windswept; she wore a lightweight tweed suit, high heeled shoes and a white blouse with a ruffled collar. Her small spectacles hung around her neck on a black cord.

"And what can we do for you today?" she said rhetorically, "You'd like a little more information on the Whitewall Estate I expect."

Sam remembered this odd little characteristic from his previous visit. She had a peculiar way of talking to him that left him speechless, for she answered almost every question she asked, leaving him to simply acquiesce to what she said…

"Er, yes please," he said.

"I expect that you find it fascinating? Well of course you do or you wouldn't be here. Now, following your last visit I had a good rummage around in my drawers and found two more maps of the area both clearly showing the changing face of the Estate and…"

Sam's smile stopped her talking; she raised an eyebrow and waited patiently for him to speak.

Sam couldn't help himself and jokily said, "You don't look big enough to have such sizeable drawers…"

"Document drawers Mr. Chance!" said Daphne semi-seriously.

Sam apologised with a smile still on his face but was convinced that as Daphne turned her head, she too had a smile playing at the corners of her mouth. He quickly changed tack.

"You said 'changing face of the estate'? What do you mean *changing face*?"

"I mean how the shape of the Estate has altered as various pieces have been sold. You have to remember that most estates and large farms started life as gifts from Kings or Nobles to favoured subjects or loyal friends. This practice dates back from William the Conqueror, through the period of The Reformation and on to the Carolingian era. Within a few years of the restoration of Charles the Second to the throne, most estates were settling into the embryonic ones we know now and surprisingly little has changed since."

"I see," said Sam. "But…"

"Did you know for example, that most of the hedgerows bordering established fields have been there for literally hundreds of years? Well of course you probably did, you look like an educated man. In fact there have been recorded instances where modern day artists have tried to find the landscapes of Turner, Constable and other historically prominent British artists, only to discover that the scenes they painted all those years ago are virtually identical now! Unless of course they have been built upon etcetera etcetera stroke developed if you take my meaning."

Sam made the mistake of taking a breath before he spoke and only managed, "Yes, but…"

"Which takes me to the point do you understand? Of course you do."

"Er, yes, I think so," said Sam looking at Daphne and wondering if she had an 'off' switch.

"Good. You see the landscape may have remained the same, but that doesn't necessarily mean the ownership has, does it? Of course not."

"If you say so."

"I do. Over the years it has been necessary to develop some of the land for other things than farming. Industry, habitation, recreational sites such as cricket grounds stroke football clubs stroke sports stadia…"

'Stone the crows!' thought Sam, *'I'm going to have a stroke at any minute!'* He wasn't sure if it was possible to stop Daphne once she was in full twitter mode.

"*Daphne! Miss Pettigrew!* Could I see the maps again please?" Sam's voice was verging on stentorian and his question seemed to echo around the room. There was the briefest of pauses as they both let the museum return to reverent silence.

"Yes of course," said Daphne.

Sam waited for more but none was forthcoming. He saw Daphne staring up at him and not moving; it looked as though she was frozen in time. He opened his mouth to speak but was suddenly cut off when she shot a finger up in the air.

"Yes I remember…" she said, then turned on her heel and headed for a door behind one of the glass cabinets, "…come along Mr. Chance, you don't want me to have to carry them out to you do you? No of course you don't."

Sam followed Daphne into a small ante-room packed with artefacts and curious-looking objects all atop work surfaces over document drawers.

"My drawers!" said Daphne pointing down with mock reproval and raised eyebrows.

Sam smiled and cleared his throat as he watched Daphne delve into one of the drawers; within a few seconds she put on a pair of soft cotton gloves, carefully extracted several maps and opened them up on a muslin covered tabletop. She then overlaid them with the one showing the 'de Chaunce' legend on top.

"The maps are almost to the same scale," said Daphne, "Look, you can see the boundaries of the estate quite clearly as I turn, some are oriented differently but nothing really changes until here."

She let Sam digest the similarities until she turned to one dated 1895. It was glaringly obvious that two large sections of land had been sold off; one from the East and another from the South. She then overlaid the remaining maps onto the 1895 one and it was plain that nothing had changed since.

"So," said Sam, "this is what the present farm boundaries are like today?"

Daphne nodded and smiled at him. She did have an off switch!

"I can work out the perimeter distances from the scale on the map legend," said Sam, "but do you have any idea of approximately how many acres we are talking about here?"

"Ah! We need another tome for that; one moment please." A few minutes later Daphne returned with a piece of paper containing the name of an author, the name of a local history booklet and an ISBN number.

"You'll find a lot of detail in that book Mr. Chance and it's available in most good bookshops. I can't let you have my copy because it's the only one I have and I need it for reference purposes you understand? Of course you do.

However in direct answer to your question, the estate measured approximately four and a half thousand acres prior to the 1895 map. Two sections were sold, one of fifteen hundred acres in 1868, and one of twenty five hundred acres in 1869 leaving five hundred acres in total afterwards."

"Marvellous," said Sam, "could you possibly copy the latest

map and one of those before 1895 so that I can show my family when I get back home?" He pointed to the maps on the table and said, "Perhaps the one with 'de Chaunce' on?"

"Well I can, but not here and not personally. I'll have to send them away to a historical printers and it will probably be up to a month before they're ready."

"That's fine, there's no rush, and the cost isn't a problem either. I'll only research this history once so I might as well do it properly the first time.

I live on the South coast and I'm only here for a few days but my daughter lives and works locally so I'll give you her details and she can pick them up from you when they're ready."

The arrangements were concluded and they made their way back into the main body of the museum.

"Thank you for your help once again Miss Pettigrew." said Sam smiling, for despite her tendency to twitter he did genuinely like her.

"Please call me Daphne I do think Miss Pettigrew sounds rather hoity-toity don't you?" Then with a wink and smile she said, "Of course you do!"

Sam couldn't help himself from laughing.

"There," said Daphne, "I knew you did." She offered a tiny hand and Sam readily shook it.

"I do hope we meet again," said Sam, "it was a real pleasure spending time with you."

They smiled at each other with genuine affection and parted company.

Outside it was delightful, the weather was mild and sunny and spring was in the air. It was such a contrast to the museum; that was then, this was now; that smelled old and fusty, this smelled new and vibrant.

He turned his attention to the second task of the day, acreage. He had found out that an acre was four thousand, four hundred and eighty square yards and that there were six hundred and forty acres in a square mile, so he determined to try and see what fifteen hundred acres would look like.

He returned to his car and drove until he found a conspicuous looking landmark from where he could see the road for several miles ahead. He stopped and set the trip meter of his car to zero and then re-commenced driving, watching the digital indicator as it climbed up until it hit 2.3 miles. At this point Sam stopped the car, got out and looked back to the landmark and was able to judge what it looked like in terms of distance. He then turned his gaze ninety degrees to the left and tried to estimate the same distance in that direction. It was big. It was also approximately what fifteen hundred acres looked like.

With the second task done he looked at his watch and decided that there was ample time for an early pub lunch before undertaking his third task - a return visit to Walmsfield Borough Council Offices, Naomi Draper and someone with the odd name of Postcard Percy!

Chapter 13

"The drive's in view Miss Maria, do you want me to stop or turn in?

"Stop please Silas; the weather will soon be too cold, but for the present it is quite delightful so I'll walk."

Silas stopped the cab, hopped down and held open the door.

"Very well Miss," he said politely, "I'll be here when you return."

"There is no need for you to wait here," said Maria as she stepped out, "If you would care to take your horse and cab down the drive I'm sure that Mrs. Johnson will see to it that you are both adequately refreshed."

Silas walked forwards and stroked the horse's neck; he smiled and said, "That is more than kind of you, but as you rightly point out it's a lovely day so me and old Henry will be perfectly happy waiting here."

"As you wish," said Maria, "I expect to return within two hours." She smiled at him and set off down the drive.

Just before disappearing from Silas's view, she turned around to look at him. He appeared to be in his forties, was well built and strong looking with a kind and honest face.

She hadn't really noticed him before, but the increased visits to Whitewall had brought her more into contact with him latterly and she couldn't help harbouring a growing attraction towards him.

She'd established from previous trips that he and his wife had split up through her infidelity and that he lived alone in a small house near the railway station. He'd had a daughter who'd died when she was young and her death had been the catalyst for the marriage breakdown. The slow trips up Wordale Moor had afforded them enough time together to be able to converse, and as the time had passed she'd looked forward to seeing him more and more. Indeed a very real part of the pleasure of visiting Whitewall had become meeting with him.

Even more pleasingly, during this trip Silas had asked her to let him know in advance of any proposed visits to the Estate so that he could make sure that he was at the railway station when she arrived.

And she knew that his interest wasn't just the cab fare...

She was suddenly aware that she'd been staring at him a little too long and that he was looking back at her. Her cheeks flushed a bright red, she gave a little wave and turned to face where she was going.

This visit was to be the reward for all her hard work. The glorious result of seventeen years' struggle to regain tenure of the estate. Her brothers, sisters and cousin Joyce had been rendered almost speechless when she informed them about her success and they were awaiting the outcome of her meeting with baited breath. And a complete bonus to the whole affair was her growing friendship with Margaret to whom she had warmed so much in such a relatively short time.

There was a spring in her step as she made her way across to the house and even the detested carving on the lintel didn't dampen her enthusiasm; she tapped on the door with her parasol and awaited the smiling face of her friend.

The door opened and her smile vanished in an instant; instead of the slight and feminine figure of Margaret a man literally filled the doorway. She looked at his swarthy, unshaven, unwelcoming face and took a step backwards. There was something at once unnerving and intimidating about him and she felt the irrational urge to turn and go.

"Yes, what do you want?" said Abraham in an aggressive tone.

Maria composed herself and looked straight into his eyes; they were supposed to be the windows to the soul but his were dead; stone cold dead.

"Please inform Mrs. Johnson that Maria Chance has arrived as per her invitation."

She watched as the figure in the doorway appeared to study her; his cold reptilian eyes then looked down and settled on the curve of her breasts long enough to make her instantly regret leaving Silas at the end of the drive. Every alarm bell she possessed instantly switched on.

"Well," she said in an overtly confident manner, "are you going to inform her of my arrival or not?"

Maria's tone had an immediate effect on him; he narrowed his cold piercing eyes to slits and leaned down to bring his face level with hers. His rancid breath cut through her senses like a knife.

"Just who do you think you're talking to in that puffed-up tone? No man, let alone *woman* talks to me like that unless he wants to feel cold steel in his gut, so unless you want me to open you up where you stand you'd best shut your mouth and scarper."

Maria recoiled in disgust as much as nervousness but she wasn't a person to submit to intimidation without giving an account of herself.

"I'll do no such thing," she said defiantly, "I'm staying here until I see Mrs. Johnson."

"Well - haven't you got big hairy balls under that dress?" Abraham looked her slowly up and down then said, "Mind you, you're an ugly bitch so you're probably a bloke anyway."

He waited for a response from Maria but none was forthcoming. He leaned a little closer and said, "Right, you heard me. Fuck off."

Maria remained rooted to the spot and said forcefully, "Go and get Mrs. Johnson immediately!"

"Are you deaf as well as ugly?" said Abraham, "Clear off now or I'll clear you off!"

Maria simply said, "No."

Abraham stared at the slight woman in front of him and was slightly taken aback by her single-minded determination. He hardened his resolve and said, "All right missy, I'm going to give you ten minutes to get back up the drive and then I'm going to set my little doggy free," he took a step forwards, brought his face down level with hers again and said, "and you really, *really* don't want to be around when he's off the lead…"

Maria was having none of it and equally forcefully said, "Don't you dare talk to me in that impudent tone you good for nothing ruffian! I am the owner of Whitewall and I'll have you put in prison if you try to intimidate me."

"Ha!" Abraham almost barked in her face. He turned his head to the right, looked over her shoulder and shouted, *"Caleb! Caleb, get your arse over here and listen to this doxy!"*

Maria heard the byre door open and saw an equally large man appear in the doorway.

"What do you want pa? I'm up to my elbows in blood and shit down here, can't it wait?"

"No it can't boy! Do as I say."

Caleb nodded his head obediently and started walking to where they both stood.

"I forgot," said Abraham with slits of eyes boring into Maria, "The boy's been castrating piglets, cutting their gonads off with his razor; who knows, if you upset him enough he might cut yorn off too…"

Maria was made of much sterner stuff than Abraham gave her credit for and said, "I take it then that you're Abraham, the despicable and loathsome creature that Margaret referred to in our past discourses."

"…in our past discourses…" imitated Abraham stepping even closer to Maria.

"But now I see that Margaret was wrong. Despicable and loathsome was entirely erroneous." She squared up to Abraham and said, "Because I doubt that a sub-human brute like you could aspire to such dizzying heights."

All sense of toying instantly disappeared; Abraham's face contorted into a snarl but before he could speak Caleb appeared at his side.

If it was at all possible, Caleb looked even more intimidating than his father. His only redeeming feature was his pure white teeth. He, too, was bulky and strong with a square but evil looking intolerant face, his hair was thick brown and unkempt, he was unshaven and stank heavily of body odour. His eyes were very pale, almost albino in appearance and they were the coldest, most dispassionate ones that Maria had ever encountered.

Abraham give Caleb a dig with his elbow and said, "This pasty looking strumpet reckons she's the owner of Whitewall boy."

Caleb slowly turned and looked at Maria, and like his father before him, studied her from top to toe.

"Is that so pater?" he said slowly, "Perhaps you an' me better learn us some manners then. Perhaps we ought to be treating the mistress with some respect…"

Maria started to feel distinctly uneasy, she felt that she could deal with Abraham, but there was something very unnerving about his son.

"Perhaps," continued Caleb, "we'd best take her into the parlour and show her what true gen'lemen we are. Perhaps we could show her how to lose some of that formality and how to relax…"

Maria recoiled as Caleb suddenly grabbed her left breast and then squeezed it.

"How dare you, you brute!" she said instantly spinning around and striking Caleb on the left side of his face with her parasol, "As I told your father, I am the owner of this place and I won't have guttersnipes like you two telling me what I can or can't do! Now apologise or it will be the worse for you!"

Caleb stood unflinchingly with a smile on his face, but something had changed in Abraham; the playing was over, he'd had enough.

"Owner indeed," he bellowed, *"you arrogant bitch. I'm the owner of this estate, so shut your bloody prattle and be grateful I gave you time to leave. You now have nine minutes…"*

"You the owner?" said Maria, "Where is Margaret?"

"Never you mind where she is. It's none of your business."

"It most certainly is my business. *I demand* to see her and I'm not leaving this spot until I do."

Abraham came close to Maria and towered over her like a huge cathedral gargoyle, he looked menacing and grotesque; as though he was about to visit some dreadful fate upon her.

"By my reckoning you have about seven minutes left then we'll see whether you leave this spot or not." He turned his head to Caleb and said, "I think it's about time we introduced this witch to Sugg don't you boy?"

Caleb smiled at his father and then shouted out loud, *"Are you listening Sugg you ugly canine bastard? Are you ready for some fresh meat?"*

Such a terrifying and vicious outburst emanated from a nearby room that it instantly filled Maria with panic; she felt the colour literally drain from her cheeks.

Caleb looked at her and said, "You'd better start running now perky tits or you aren't going to make it."

This was no time for heroic gestures; Maria *knew* that they meant it. She turned on her heel and started to run across the courtyard towards the drive; her long black dress caught the front of her shoes and tended to make her trip so she lifted it at the front to allow her more freedom of movement.

As she gathered speed she cast a glance over her shoulder and saw Caleb striding down the courtyard towards a small stable door.

"Five minutes!" Abraham yelled, *"And you aren't going to make it!"*

Maria heard Abraham shout something to Caleb and then saw him break into a run towards the door. In blind panic she pumped her legs for all they were worth.

The rough ascending drive slowed her down and the heat of the afternoon made her heavy dress feel like a lead weight around her shoulders; she felt her legs weakening with both fatigue and fear, and then as if to drain the last of her reserves she heard the sound of pursuit. She turned around and saw Caleb about one hundred and fifty yards behind her running with the most fearsome looking hound she'd ever seen. Both were silent but running easily and they were gaining with every step.

She estimated that she was approximately half way up the drive when it started to level out; she caught sight of the tops of the gateposts and began to wonder if she could make it. With every ounce of adrenalin coursing she ran for all her worth and gained precious ground; and then in a second of carelessness she misjudged her step and tripped headlong over a projecting stone.

She went down like a bundle of washing, scraping the skin from her hands and knees and banging her face with such a force that it temporarily stunned her. Unmindful of the pain, she rolled into a sitting position and fixed her pursuers with a steely glare.

Fifty yards behind her, Caleb and the fearsome monster stopped. Neither man nor beast appeared to be out of breath, they just stood and waited for her next move.

Never once averting her eyes from the frightful pair Maria backed up on her hands and then slowly stood up. For the briefest of seconds she wondered if Caleb was going to let her go, then whilst still facing them she saw him reach for the dog's collar.

'*Oh God preserve me!*' she thought. She turned and ran as fast as she could towards the gate; she could see it, but she knew that she wasn't going to make it. She turned once more, saw that the dog was closing in rapidly and then tripped over the hem of her dress.

She knew that that was the end. In true Maria style she rolled over to face her attacker head on.

The dog was coming straight at her; its huge slavering mouth was wide open and its tongue hung from one side as it ran; then lowering its head it came in snarling for the kill.

Out of nowhere Maria suddenly heard a hissing sound followed by a deafening crack.

Sugg instantly recoiled in front of her barking and snarling.

Another hissing sound preceded an even louder crack and Maria swung around to look at the source. Silas was standing just behind her wielding his long horse whip and inflicting considerable pain each time he lashed it into Sugg's flesh.

"Get behind me Maria!" he ordered, and then turning to Caleb called, *"Do you want some of this, the same as the dog?"*

Neither Caleb nor Sugg made another move towards them.

"I didn't think so, you cowardly curs!" yelled Silas, *"Count yourselves lucky I didn't have my army pistol with me 'cos I'd have shot you both where you stood with ne'er a second thought!"*

He bent down and pulled Maria to her feet whilst keeping his eyes on the man and dog; then with her safely behind him, he edged back up the drive towards his cab.

"You ever set foot on our land again," shouted Caleb, *"and you'll see! We'll fucking bury you here…"*

Neither Maria nor Silas responded, nor did they remove their eyes from the hideous pair staring malevolently from the drive.

They reached the safety of the cab and Silas ushered Maria aboard. As quickly as he could he made her comfortable and then tenderly touched her cheek with his right hand.

"Are you all right Maria?" he said, then suddenly realised that he was being too familiar. He said, "Sorry, *Miss* Maria."

Maria gently put her left hand over his right and said, "A bit battered and bruised maybe, but yes thanks to you - and calling me Maria is just fine…"

Silas smiled, closed the cab door and then climbed up to the driving seat. His whip cracked once more and Henry cantered away down Wordale Moor.

Maria turned to see Whitewall retreating into the distance and a cold shiver ran down her spine. Despite her own considerable discomfort and the horrific episode she'd just endured, a terrible sense of foreboding gripped her when she thought about Margaret.

Caleb watched the retreating cab with a half smile on his face and then turned to pat Sugg in approval. But this was no time for self-satisfied smugness; this was a time for stark and horrifying realisation. Sugg was off the chain, unmuzzled and in pain.

The smile disappeared off Caleb's face as he saw the dog looking at him.

"Come to heel!" he ordered, but Sugg didn't move.

"*Heel you canine bastard*!" He shouted with as much authority as he could muster but he saw the dog's mouth start to quiver and tighten; he was no longer cowed and submissive, but cold and calculating.

Bristle by bristle, the hair started to stand up on Sugg's back; his lips parted enough to reveal his teeth without opening his mouth. A deep and guttural snarl started to emanate from down in his belly and he slowly started to circle Caleb.

Years of abuse and mistreatment had moulded him into the beast he now was and one of the causes of most of his suffering was now standing before him alone and defenceless.

Caleb tried to remain as calm as he could; he slowly bent down, picked up a hefty stone and then took a couple of steps backwards down the drive.

Sugg saw his brutal keeper's retreat as a sign of submission and started to gain confidence, he increased the speed at which he circled and bared his teeth in a full-blooded snarl.

Step by step Caleb edged backwards, he shouted abuse at the dog and tried to sound confident, but he knew that it was just a matter of minutes before Sugg came in for the attack.

It happened in a flash; Sugg lunged low and snapped his huge teeth around Caleb's left leg, but his thick leather gaiters prevented him from gaining a grip.

Caleb struck out with the stone and missed the dog by inches.

Sugg whirled around the back of Caleb and lunged at his calf. This time his teeth caught in the lacing of Caleb's left gaiter and with one or two violent shakes of his head, he wrenched the gaiter completely away.

Fear and blind panic now had a hold of Caleb as the dog started to circle again; his heart was beating very quickly and he was gripped with terror. He had also stopped shouting knowing that it was useless, and that this was a fight for his life.

He watched as Sugg circled increasingly quickly in an anti-clockwise direction. The speed of the dog's movement started to make him feel disorientated and then in an instant, Sugg changed direction and caught him blind-sided.

The dog sunk his huge teeth into the soft exposed flesh of Caleb's left calf; he twisted his head ferociously to the left and tore away a chunk of flesh and muscle.

Caleb screamed in agony as the blood-stained dog reappeared in front of him; he knew that he was going down and as he started to topple he saw Sugg run open-mouthed straight for his face.

In one last supreme effort he swung the stone in his right hand hard around to the left, but Sugg saw it coming and stopped. Carried by the momentum of the swing, he twisted around and fell flat on his back in front of the dog. For what seemed like an age, he saw Sugg looking at him; he knew that he was beaten and he lay on the drive awaiting the inevitable...

The sound of the shot nearly deafened him. He heard Sugg squeal as he was knocked sideways off his feet. He rolled over, looked up and saw his Pa standing several yards away with a double barrelled shotgun.

Abraham watched as Sugg slowly made it to his feet and started to limp his way towards a stile in the dry stone wall. He knew that the dog was badly injured and he allowed it time to think that it might reach the safety of the other side of the wall, but within seconds he raised the gun again, aimed and pulled the second trigger. He saw the fur lift briefly behind the dog's head before it fell over and laid still.

He quickly reloaded the gun, ran over to Sugg and saw that he wasn't breathing; his eyes were half open and he appeared lifeless. He gave the dog one or two light kicks, but it remained motionless.

Satisfied that Sugg was finished he quickly ran across and looked at his son. He was still conscious but only just, and the horrific wound was bleeding profusely. He quickly removed his waistcoat wrapped it tightly around the injured calf and secured it firmly in place with his leather trouser belt.

He then strapped his shotgun over his shoulder, scooped Caleb up in his arms and returned to the house as quickly as possible.

Several hours later and with his son's wound treated as best he could, Abraham went back up the drive to retrieve Sugg's body. He knew that word would soon get around that he was a goner, but he didn't want to advertise it by leaving his carcass lying around for all to see.

As he neared the stile he stopped dead in his tracks. The dog had gone. He immediately adopted a defensive posture and cursed his own stupidity for not bringing his shotgun. His heart started beating wildly and an irrational fear swept over him; he'd been convinced that Sugg was dead but now he was nowhere to be seen.

In rapidly failing light he scoured the surrounding countryside desperate for any evidence that might give away the hound's location, but there was none. There were no tracks or signs of blood either where the dog had fallen, or leading away to potential cover.

A cloud passed over the last of the setting sun; darkness descended and a cold gust of wind blew ominously across the fields. Nervously he cast a last glance around and then set off hastily down the long drive; with every step he took he imagined that the hound was about to leap on him and with mounting panic he finally broke out into a run.

Wordale Moor was bad enough on a moonless night, but with the possibility of an injured and resentful Sugg on the prowl, it became the place of nightmares.

Chapter 14

28th May 2002. Walmsfield Borough Council Offices

As the telephone rang on Sandra Miles' desk she looked at the clock on her wall and saw that it was just after 10 o' clock; it was going to be one of those days, she just knew it. She picked up the receiver and said, "Sandra Miles!" She always made an effort to sound happy in the mornings and indeed there were occasions when she felt it, but today wasn't one of them...

"Yes, good morning Sandra, Giles Eaton here; I'm in the throws of dealing with the Whitewall problem and in order to clarify certain aspects I wondered if we were in possession of any maps relating to the farm and its associated lands?"

'Oh good,' thought Sandra, *'a nice easy one - not!'* The last vestiges of 'happy' just left town.

"I expect that we've got something here in Planning," she said, "but the farm probably dates way back before Walmsfield Borough Council's time and may even cross two County borders."

"Yes I understand," said Giles trying to sound disinterested, "but if you could let me have copies of what we do have, I'd be very grateful."

"All right," said a distraught Sandra, "I'll do some searching and let you have what we've got."

"Oh, and this morning if you could please Sandra?"

"Very well, I'll see what I can do." She replaced the handset, leaned back in her chair and rubbed the back of her neck.

Being the Office Manager in Planning meant that she at least had a small glass partitioned office within the main open-plan workplace and she had a window to the outside world.

The sun was shining and she could see that a gentle breeze was blowing the tops of the Poplar trees on the hilltops in the distance. She let her mind wander for a few minutes and wished that she could be up there with them, alone and with no need to work; with nobody dependant upon her, and free.

She refocussed her mind and decided to try the easy option

first. She opened her office door and called out, *"Does anybody know if we have any maps of Wordale Moor and the surrounding area?"*

There was a brief pause and then one female voice called, *"I'm working on a planning application from the Whitewall Farm and I have one or two maps, but I don't know if they cover all the areas you want."*

Sandra couldn't believe her luck! She headed in the direction of the voice and saw that it belonged to one of the newer members of staff.

"Jacqui isn't it?" she said as she approached.

"Yes Mrs. Miles. I've got two maps here, are they any good?"

Sandra looked at the maps on Jacqui's desk and saw that they were perfect.

"Yes," she said, "they're just what I want but I need them copied, so if you would be kind enough?"

Jacqui nodded her head and said, "O.K. I'll do it right now."

Sandra smiled, started to walk away and then had an afterthought. She turned back and said, "What exactly is the planning application for?"

"Oh standard stuff as far as I can make out; the current owners want to install some new farm equipment into one of their outhouses and it won't quite fit, so they've applied to us for permission to extend one wall, remove some existing flooring and sink footings. I'm not expecting it to meet with any objections"

Sandra smiled again and said, "All right, thank you."

As she slowly made her way back to her office, she thought that it was strange how things worked out; up until recently she hadn't had anything to do with the Whitewall Farm, yet now it seemed to be in her face at every turn.

She sat down, looked back out of the window and cast her mind back over the last few days. Something about the whole Whitewall affair didn't seem to add up, she puzzled for a few minutes longer and then did what she always did when she wanted to clarify things in her mind. She took an A4 pad and pencil from her drawer and wrote down what she knew;

Whitewall Farm

1. _A locked file unopened since 1869._
2. _The murder of at least one unknown individual. - Who and why?_
3. _The possible murder of Surnh Horrocks - Why?_
4. _A dilemma of titanic proportions - What?_
5. _Revelations of monumental concern that would make the national news..._
6. _A need for secrecy - Why?_
7. _What would happen if the secret was out?_
8. _Giles Eaton's request for plans of Whitewall Farm - ????_

She stared at the list for a few moments and then shook her head; it plagued her but made no obvious sense. She decided to take it to The Ryming Ratt and run it past Carlton and Naomi at lunchtime to see if they could make any more of it.

Half an hour later Jacqui presented her with the copies of the maps covering Whitewall Farm and the surrounding areas; she studied them for a while still trying to find clues, but nothing looked particularly unusual, so as requested she dutifully delivered them to the Town Clerk.

Giles now had what he wanted. Not only did the maps show the boundaries of the farm, but also the topography and names of other properties surrounding it. He could clearly see the two areas of Whitewall land that had been sold in the 19th century because the boundaries were rectilinear compared to the original; he also noted that the large and highly populated Summerton Housing Estate, one of Walmsfield Borough Council's more lucrative assets, was situated smack bang in the middle of the land fraudulently purchased in 1869. The other smaller section of land sold in 1868 now formed a part of Brandworth Farm on the adjacent Hobb's Moor; the old 'Brandworth Estate' referred to by Surnh Horrocks.

As he stared at the map trying to commit the various boundaries to memory, something kept drawing him back to the area sold to Brandworth; for some reason it looked familiar, but the harder he tried to recall whatever it was, the more it eluded him.

He reached for his telephone and dialled the number of the Council Tax Collector's Office. He was pretty sure that he knew who the owner of Brandworth Farm would be, but he wanted confirmation.

Within a few minutes he had it. He replaced the receiver, picked up the Whitewall file, kissed it and went to his drinks cabinet. Despite the early hour, he poured himself a large glass of Old Pulteney.

"*Yes!*" he said out loud, "Adrian Darke! *The* Adrian *bloody* Darke!" He was almost delirious.

Adrian Darke was probably the wealthiest man in the North of England. His face was never out of the newspapers; he was in his mid forties, was good looking in a Latin American sort of way and was on the board of several public companies.

He had a string of very public love affairs with prominent and not such prominent but always beautiful women and he had a long-suffering but equally beautiful wife.

He had cars, high-powered motor cycles, a boat, a hot air balloon and even the ultimate status symbol, a private helicopter.

In short, he had it all.

Giles walked around his office holding onto the leather folder, sipping his whisky and digesting the information. He could hardly believe his luck.

He knew that Darke's ownership of the fraudulently sold land was potentially significant, but how, and how to exploit it, was going to be something of a puzzle.

He finished his whisky and decided to have a top up; he casually threw the leather folder onto his desk, walked over to the drinks cabinet and replenished his glass. Still deep in thought he wandered back to his desk and sat down.

When he looked at the folder he saw that it had come to rest on the smaller scale map and that it had temporarily blanked out Wordale Moor. Something about the changed appearance caught his eye and he twisted it around to take a closer look.

It struck him like a hammer blow. Involuntarily he said "Oh my sweet Lord Jesus…" He snatched up the phone and dialled Sandra once more.

"Sandra Miles." The chirpiness had long since evaporated.

"Yes Sandra," said Giles desperately trying to keep the excitement out of his voice, "sorry to trouble you again, but do we have a map showing the proposed route of the new M6631 across Hobb's Moor?"

"Yes we do," said Sandra.

"Would you be an angel and bring it up to my office now please?"

Five minutes later he had it and it could not have been better! He overlaid the map of the proposed motorway route onto the small scale map that he'd been studying earlier, and the route cut clean through the rectilinear section of the Whitewall land that had been illegally sold to the Darke family in 1868!

He was now in possession of the perfect bargaining piece. Now was the time to wipe the smile off the smug bastard's face. Now was the time to call whom the newspapers dubbed, 'the North's smartest businessman'. Mr. Adrian 'I've bloody got it all' Darke!

He picked up the Whitewall file, kissed it and said, "Thank you Surnh! Thank you from the bottom of my heart!"

With a smile still on his face he reached across his desk for the phone but the earlier cups of coffee and whisky suddenly conspired to call him to a more pressing appointment. He didn't want a full bladder spoiling the enjoyment of his next call, so he headed out of his office and down the corridor to the Executive Rest Room.

Having satisfied the call of nature he washed his hands, checked his appearance in the mirror, smiled at himself and swept out of the door straight into the bulky figure of Tom Ramsbottom.

"Bloody Hell Giles!" said Tom recoiling from the blow, "Where are you going in such a hurry?"

"Oh sorry Tom, busy busy busy; you know…"

The Mayor frowned and said, "Right, well I was on my way to see you." He was considerably calmer than the previous day.

"And what exactly did you want?" said Giles.

"Before you let our legal bods have that Whitewall file I want to show it to an old pal of mine who might be able to help us personally with this situation. We don't want to look like a couple of completely nonplussed chumps when we're dealing with the legal eagles so he might be able to give us one or two pointers to go in armed with. He's a retired solicitor who's totally reliable and he has some considerable knowledge of land ownership and the like."

Giles was mortified. In his excitement he'd completely overlooked Tom's involvement in the proceedings and the last thing he wanted now was for the Mayor to walk away with his prime bargaining piece. He had to think quickly.

"I'm sorry Tom," he said as matter-of-factly as he could, "you've had a wasted journey because I've got appointments this afternoon and I took the papers home for safekeeping; they're in my personal wall safe."

"Blast it!" said Tom, "I hate wasted journeys!" He looked at his watch, nodded towards the office and said "Well the least you can do is treat me to a glass of that malt you have in there."

Giles knew that the file was on his desk and in full view.

"I can do better than that," he said, thinking on his feet, "Why don't you let me buy you an early lunch as my way of burying the hatchet following yesterday's little disagreement?"

Tom looked at his watch again and said, "It's only eleven thirty, and what about your appointments…"

"They aren't until mid-afternoon and so what that it's only eleven thirty, we can have a couple of nice malts and order at our leisure; and it's all on me."

Tom raised his eyebrows and said, "Well, I won't say no to that!"

"Good, then that's settled, I'll just pop into my office and retrieve my mobile. You go and call the lift."

Tom nodded his agreement and walked towards the lift doors.

Giles returned to his office, went in and closed the door. He quickly placed all the Whitewall documents back into the leather case then picked up the telephone and dialled his secretary's number.

"Kathryn," he said in a hushed tone when she answered, "I'm popping out for some lunch with the Mayor. There's a distinctive looking case on my desk, please file it somewhere safely until I return."

"Very well Mr. Eaton," said Kathryn, "but don't forget…" Before she'd finished speaking, the phone clicked down at the other end. She looked at the receiver and said, "All right then, be like that!"

Now satisfied that he had all the bases covered, Giles went back down the corridor and rejoined Tom Ramsbottom for their early lunch.

A few minutes later, Kathryn walked into Giles' office and immediately saw the case. She looked around in bewilderment for a few seconds wondering where best to conceal it. She checked all the likely drawers and cupboards, but wherever she tried it didn't fit.

Suddenly she had a brainwave. There really was only one good safe place, a place that she knew the Town Clerk would approve of.

She sat down, wrote him a note and left it on his desk. It informed him where she'd deposited the case, and reminded him that she was off work that afternoon.

Chapter 15

The Historic Research Department

At 2:30pm Postcard Percy returned to Walmsfield Borough Council Offices loaded with his files on Whitewall Farm and a barrowload of self satisfaction. The new direction his 'songs for a pound' fund raising scheme had taken was a huge success and he could feel the plastic bag full of pound coins weighing heavily in his trouser pocket. He reached the end of the corridor on the lower ground floor and saw that Naomi was already with somebody. He checked his watch and although it was just a little after 2:30pm as they had arranged, he realised that these things happened and he was happy to wait.

He thought for a second and decided to purchase a tea from the drinks dispenser. He walked slowly past Naomi's office and waved as he went by to acknowledge his presence.

Naomi caught sight of him and immediately jumped up from behind her desk and opened the door.

"Percy! Hi, please do come in."

"If you are busy, I'm happy to wait." Percy nodded in the direction of Naomi's other visitor.

"No, there's somebody I'd like you to meet." She pulled another chair towards her desk and indicated to Percy to sit down.

He made himself comfortable and then turned to the smiling face next to him.

"Percy," said Naomi, "this is Mr. Sam Chance."

Not many things caught Percy off guard, but this one did.

"Mr. Chance!" he said, offering his hand, "I'm perfectly delighted to make your acquaintanceship."

"Do please call me Sam," said Sam shaking Percy's outstretched hand, "I've heard a lot about you and I couldn't wait to meet you." He cast a sideways glance at Naomi and winked.

"Really!" said Percy, "I expect that Naomi has told you about my fund raising activities too?"

Naomi knew that there was no point in avoiding the issue and took the bull straight by the horns.

"So how's the fund raising going then; have you made much today?"

"Excellent!" said Percy enthusiastically, "Look at this!"

He undid the button on his jacket, pulled it to one side and then lifted up his jumper to access his left trouser pocket. His trousers were held in place by braces and the waistline was so high that he had difficulty bending his arm high enough to get it in; and then once in, the pocket appeared to be about three feet deep.

Naomi and Sam watched with mounting amusement as Percy's arm disappeared up to his elbow and then weaved around and about looking like a snake in a sack.

"Ah! Here we are!" he suddenly announced, and with a flourish he dumped a bag full of pound coins on Naomi's desk.

"Wow! You have been busy," said Naomi, "it's a wonder that your voice isn't raw after all that singing."

"Aha! That's where you're wrong." said Percy beaming all over his face, "I didn't make this from singing; I made this from keeping quiet!

Would you believe that more people paid me *two* pounds not to sing, than one pound to sing?"

Sam and Naomi looked at one another smiling and nodding, knowing that they too would have gladly paid the two pounds for silence.

"Ingenious Percy," said Naomi, "ingenious." She paused long enough for Percy to feel their genuine appreciation of his guile and then she changed the subject.

"Now, what have you brought us?"

Percy reached down and extracted a scrapbook from his plastic carrier bag and opened it up before them.

"As I told you yesterday Naomi, I have gathered a lot of historical data about many of the local places of interest, but the Whitewall Estate has been one of my favourites. It is shrouded in mystery and the stories that have emanated from there range from the bizarre to, well frankly, the scary." He turned to Sam and said, "Being a member of the Chance family I'm sure that you can tell me things that I don't know, so if I start to recount anything that is already known to you please stop me."

"No, not at all," said Sam, "please do carry on. Most of what I know is based upon papers that were passed to my father many years ago; I knew absolutely nothing about the Whitewall Farm until I visited it yesterday, so anything you can tell me would be most appreciated."

"What sort of papers?" asked Percy.

"Letters and documents handed down from a Great Great Aunt dating from the mid-nineteenth century."

"But that's precisely the period that interests me most!"

"Well I can let you have a copy of the papers if you think they'll add to your research"

"Oh yes please," said Percy enthusiastically, "I'd love to see them!" He saw Sam nod his agreement and then continued.

"Now, to return to what I know. Most of the mystery surrounding the place comes from a small date window starting around 1867 and ending well before the turn of the next century.

The owner of the estate was by all accounts a very nasty and dangerous man named Abraham Johnson…"

Sam couldn't help uttering an audible "Hmm…" which stopped Percy in his tracks.

"Isn't that correct?" he asked.

"Not strictly," said Sam, "but please don't stop, the papers will explain later."

"O.K., I have print-outs of newspaper articles dating from late 1867 reporting the local police force's efforts to locate three people who mysteriously disappeared from the estate. One was actually Abraham's estranged wife Margaret and the other two were her servants, Michele and Derek Horton, a man and wife team of maidservant/housekeeper and estate manager.

According to the article the police interviewed Abraham Johnson who informed them that he had never met the Hortons because they had left before his reconciliation with his wife.

When questioned about his missing wife he told the police that she had left to visit relatives in Shropshire and that he had not heard from her again. He also told the police that he didn't report her absence directly to them because he was used to her going away on lengthy visits to elderly relatives.

The police made extensive enquiries in an effort to locate the missing persons but none of them were ever seen again. Naturally suspicion fell on the Johnsons but following weeks of careful investigation no evidence of foul play was found so the case was dropped.

The next thing we have is another article dating from December 1868 involving Abraham, his son Caleb and an apparent friend of theirs from a neighbouring estate named Hugo Darke. The police were called in to investigate the disappearance of three young prostitutes and a young man who went missing after a party up there…"

Naomi suddenly felt the pressure on her left shoulder and started to feel uneasy, the name Hugo Darke seemed familiar to her; so much so that she believed if she shut her eyes and concentrated hard enough she'd be able to recall his face.

She could hear Percy talking but she couldn't hear what he was saying; she tried to pull herself back to the conversation, but something had a hold of her mind and wasn't letting go. Around and around images started to flash, a mantle shelf, a wallpaper pattern, a distinctive looking candlestick, a wooden table…

"NO! Stop!" she said out loud. "I can't see what…"

The ensuing silence brought her back to temporary reality.

"Can't see what dear?" said Percy.

Naomi sat quietly looking at both men for a while until Sam leaned forwards and asked if she was all right. Once again she remained silent, puzzled by what she'd seen, but mostly because she could hear a voice.

"This way," it was saying, *"this way Maria…"*

"Naomi," said Sam, "are you all right? You look a little disorientated, do you feel dizzy?"

"This way Maria, this way…" Naomi heard it again but this time she saw a small hand pointing downwards.

"Naomi!" Sam stood up and started to walk behind her desk whilst Percy watched in bewildered silence.

"Naomi!" He reached out and took a hold of her left arm, "Speak to me. Are you O.K.?"

The physical contact brought Naomi back to reality; she said quietly, "I could see some odd things, and I heard a voice saying *'This way Maria, this way'*"

Sam said, "What do you mean you could see and hear things? What sort of things?"

Naomi suddenly became self-conscious and apologised.

"I'm sorry," she said shaking her head slightly, "It was nothing really. Please ignore me, I'm always experiencing odd things like this and I shouldn't have let it interfere with our meeting."

The old fashioned way in which Naomi had pronounced the name Maria made Sam frown; he opened his mouth to speak but thought better of it.

Percy didn't know what to make of the puzzling episode but was aware that Naomi had temporarily stolen his limelight; he waited for a few seconds and then re-took the initiative. He said, "Shall I carry on dear?"

"Yes please do." said Naomi, aware that Sam was still scrutinising her.

"All right then, as I said the next thing we have is another newspaper article dating from 1868 concerning Abraham, his son Caleb and this friend of theirs from the neighbouring estate."

"Hugo Darke." reiterated Naomi.

"Precisely; the police were called in to investigate the disappearance of three young prostitutes and a young man who never returned home from a party up there.

The usual searches and investigations were carried out, but once again no proof of foul play was ever found and that case was dropped through lack of evidence too.

However, the strange disappearance of all of these people hadn't gone unnoticed by the local townsfolk and encouraged by one or two relatives of the missing girls a new enquiry was launched in..." He flipped over the page of his scrapbook and studied the small print for a second.

"...ah yes, here we are, in January of 1869. There was a bit of a public scandal attached to it because the police were granted permission by the Courts to excavate several places at Whitewall in an attempt to unearth some form of evidence hinted at by unnamed sources, but apparently it was an exceptionally cold winter that year and the ground was so hard that it couldn't be dug properly. The two weeks given by the Courts to carry out this work expired without result and despite calls for extra time, and a request for another attempt in warmer weather, no further access was granted by the local Magistrate.

Many people at the time wondered if the Magistrate a Mr. Joseph Cutler had been bribed, and their suspicion was fuelled even more when it was revealed several months after the case was closed that he was indeed the brother-in-law of Hugo Darke. The time however had passed, and nothing further was ever investigated."

Naomi and Sam looked at each other but didn't speak.

Percy continued to sift through his scrapbook, sticking his fingers between the leaves like bookmarks until finally he said, "There are lots of other little snippets in here but they are not all detrimental. For example, there are reports of Whitewall flourishing because of Abraham Johnson's decision to build small cottages on the estate to accommodate tenant crofters who worked the land; and another about the sale of his Dunsteth Estate to make way for a civic reservoir. And there's an interesting one about their dog Sugg going missing in 1867."

"Why would anybody write an article about a missing farm dog?" said Sam.

"Ah, well I'll tell you," said Percy, "It was because this was no ordinary dog; apparently everybody associated with Whitewall from the staff to trades people actually celebrated when it happened. It was reported to be an absolute fiend; in fact let me read this quote from a tradesman who encountered it a couple of weeks before it disappeared.

The man, a baker, said;

"...this was no ordinary dog; this was a hound from hell itself. It was huge, ugly and vicious and tried to attack anybody without provocation. The whole time I was there I never once removed my eyes from the beast, fearful that it should slip its leash and be free.

It ceaselessly strained and heaved at its bonds, forever wheeling its head around and around in an effort to escape. Then from time to time it would issue such a frantic howl as to freeze the blood in your veins..."

"Good grief," said Sam involuntarily, "I've had one or two brushes with nasty dogs in my time, but nothing that sounded as bad as that."

Percy nodded and said, "There are other bits and pieces here, but not really of much interest until…"

"What about the ghost?" said Naomi.

"Ghost, what ghost?" asked Sam.

"I was coming to that." said Percy. "Following the disappearance of Sugg, numerous people have reported hearing a fearful sounding dog up there but very few have actually seen him. Most of those who experienced it believed that it was locked in one of the storerooms and admitted to being absolutely petrified in case it got out."

Sam felt the hairs go up on the back of his neck but said nothing.

Percy looked at Naomi and theatrically said, "But now it gets weird... When the people who'd heard it reported it's presence to the current owners, they'd be shown inside the room and be confronted only by various bits of farm equipment and no sign of a dog!

As you would expect, the rumours and stories about its presence grew over the years and the ghostly dog, believed to be Sugg, has become the stuff of urban legend."

Sam said, "You may not believe this but I think I heard it too."

"Never!" said Naomi, "You can't be serious!"

"Well I can't be absolutely sure unless I return and see for myself, but when I was looking around I saw a storeroom with bars on the window..."

"...next to the barn! said Percy.

"Yes exactly." said Sam. "I went to look through the window and what I thought to be some huge and vicious dog literally threw itself against the door from the inside. I don't mind admitting to you, I was nearly wetting myself in case it got out!"

"Did you see inside the room?" said Naomi.

"No, once the dog had quietened down I returned to the main house and didn't mention it because I had absolutely no desire to go anywhere near the place again!"

"Did the farmer hear it?" said Naomi.

"It was his wife, and if she did hear it she didn't say so."

"It sounds like you've joined the club," said Percy. "and you'd be surprised how many there are of you!"

"Has anybody ever speculated about *why* the dog haunts the place?" Sam asked Percy.

"Legend has it that Sugg is waiting for someone to return and that it won't rest until they do."

"That must be a real joy for the Hawthorns." said Sam earnestly.

A silence descended upon the office, until Percy caught sight of the clock and said, "Sorry folks I think that's about all I have to offer right now and I have to leave. I've promised to sing for some ladies at a local club and I don't want to keep them waiting."

He turned to Sam and said, "I'll leave you my scrapbook; you can give it to Naomi when you've finished with it and I'll collect it from her when I next call."

Sam thanked him and shook his hand.

Percy stood up and retrieved his bag of coins from the desk; he smiled at Naomi and Sam then slowly walked across to the door. Suddenly he stopped and turned.

"I very nearly forgot, do you recall that you asked me to find out the meaning of 'Cestui que vie'? Well I have, 'Cestui que Vie' is *the person for whose life any lands or hereditaments may be held*. I hope that makes sense to you."

Naomi made a quick note on her desk pad and sat looking at it in puzzled silence until she heard Percy suddenly shake his bag of coins in her direction.

The panic level instantly rose; she opened her mouth to protest but then saw Percy smiling at her.

"Only kidding!" he said wickedly. Then with a big smile still on his face he bid them goodbye and left.

Chapter 16

30th June 1869. The Whitewall Estate

The big day had arrived for Abraham, Caleb and Hugo Darke of Brandworth Manor and everything was in place.

"Come on Caleb!" shouted Hugo from the confines of his personal coach and four as he waited with Abraham in the courtyard of Whitewall, *"Give that gammy leg of yours a shake and let's get going!"* He looked around the buildings and his eyes alighted upon the outhouse next to the barn. He quickly looked the other way, almost fearing that if he looked at the room long enough someone might see him and become suspicious. It also did nothing for his peace of mind in the middle of the long dark nights being reminded of the place and the dreadful…

'No,' he thought, *'best not to think about it at all.'*

Caleb, supported by his stick, hobbled across to the coach and pulled himself in.

"Bastarding leg; bastarding dog!" This was always his first comment of the day and invariably his last. He'd not been able to walk properly at any time since Sugg had attacked him but it always troubled him most early and late.

"Are you ready for the day's business?" asked Hugo.

"Ready as I'll ever be." Caleb wiped his mouth on the sleeve of his coat. "I seem destined to be plagued by bloody hounds, so first we get rid of that dog Horrocks and then we do for that bitch Chance."

Abraham smiled; he loved his son's wry sense of humour.

"Then to business!" said Hugo as he banged the underside of the roof with his cane.

The driver slapped the reins and the horses started pulling the coach up the long drive for their first appointment in Rochdale.

Abraham looked across his land and reflected upon how well Whitewall had been doing since he'd had more cottages built for tenant crofters. The rents were his main source of monthly income, but since the District Council had purchased the whole of the Dunsteth Estate so that the valley in which it lay could be flooded to make way for a new civic reservoir he and Caleb had become wealthy men. Life had been good to the two of them and the only real daily burden had been the injury to Caleb's leg.

One and a half years had passed since he'd shot Sugg and for the first few months he'd scanned the open fields and pastures every day for signs of him. Neither he nor Caleb had ever dared to venture out without a shotgun, nor had they gone near any thickly wooded areas as darkness had fallen in case he'd been patiently awaiting his chance. And although they'd not seen or heard any sign of him, neither of them had really considered him dead and gone; they'd both known him of old, they'd known what a cunning and eminently patient dog Sugg had been, and neither would have been surprised to see him again one day.

He also recalled the incident with the Chance woman and how much trouble she'd caused him with the police, but despite her best efforts it had worked out satisfactorily with them in the end.

Caleb's months of painful recovery had at least been blessed by no demands or threats of legal action from her and he'd hoped that she'd been scared away for good. But he'd realised that he'd underestimated her strength of character when within six months of the attack, the first letter had arrived. At first he'd ignored them, but then they'd become more copious and more persistent, threatening not only legal action but exposure in the newspapers, too.

His turning point had come when the local District Clerk had threatened to uncover his wrongdoings, too. With the Chance woman constantly threatening legal action he'd decided that something decisive needed to be done before any of his questionable activities could be brought to light.

He'd informed Hugo that they were both exceptionally vulnerable and could end up being jailed and dispossessed; and following lengthy discussions they'd come up with a plan to eliminate both problems.

He looked across at his friend of the past year and a half and could hardly reconcile the bond between them given the vast differences in their family backgrounds.

Hugo was a tall man in an age of short people; the average male height was about five feet three inches but he towered over everybody at a full six feet in height. He was wealthy, self-assured, clean-shaven and handsome. He was a successful landlord and farmer and was married to his third wife.

They'd met when he'd purchased part of the Whitewall land to expand Brandworth Manor in 1868 and they'd hit it off ever since. He'd found that they'd shared the same taste in entertainment but following an occasion at Whitewall where things had gone too far for Hugo's liking, the more extreme activities had been substituted by drinking, gambling and womanising on a regular basis.

One particular extreme episode had resulted in them all having pretty close shaves with the law and in order to avoid any repeat of that, they'd been very careful to restrict all of their activities to places well away from where they lived.

He casually glanced across the carriage and wondered how Hugo would cope with the day's planned activity.

He'd paid a local footpad named Arthur Bullington to follow Surnh Horrocks every working day for a month to establish his daily routines, including the routes he took to and from work; but it was Horrocks' sparse lunchtime ventures that had been the most interesting, for weather permitting, each Wednesday he would walk to the local park and eat his lunch in the open air. Once Bullington had established a steady pattern they'd decided upon the location of the nearest rogue pit and the scene had been set.

The pit that they'd chosen had been nicknamed the Twist Pit. It was one that he and Caleb had sunk for extracting sandstone; the bedrock had required the mining process to curve and twist into an unusual shape so that the bottom could never be seen from the top however much light was introduced into the opening. Additionally, the base had been left full of angular cuts sticking up like blunt stalagmites absolutely ensuring that when anybody 'fell' in, they would not survive the experience. This had made it perfect for disposing of the odd person though they'd only actually 'holed' two others down there and that had been several years hence.

He looked out of the carriage window, saw huge towering clouds in the sky and hoped that any potential rain would not impair their carefully cultured plans.

Something else niggled him too, he turned to Hugo and said,

"Are you sure we can make it to Hyde on time in the coach? I mean, what if we are delayed here with 'events'?"

"Stop worrying Abe," said Hugo, "it's only about twelve miles and we'll have plenty of time. Even if we are delayed the attendants have been paid enough; they'll wait."

Abraham was placated and resumed looking out of the window, then almost as an aside he said, "I haven't taken the railway train yet have you?"

"No." said Hugo, "I don't trust anything I can't control." He removed his timepiece from his waistcoat pocket and looked at it.

"Nearly twelve of the clock Caleb; we'll drop you off at the pit, you get it uncovered and we'll go and get Horrocks. We should be back within the hour if all goes according to plan."

"I'll be ready." said Caleb pulling on his cap and greatcoat.

Wiggins the coach driver stopped where instructed and Caleb jumped down.

"Bastarding dog!" he said as a pain shot up his left leg.

The coach departed and he hobbled across to the pile of stones that he and his father had arranged after their last visit; he manhandled them to one side and exposed the thick planks of wood that covered the entrance. The damp conditions made them difficult to remove, but following a concerted effort and a lot of cursing, he finally opened up the entrance.

The stench from the pit was ghastly; a reminder of his and his father's previous visit. He peered into the stygian darkness and remembered what his mother's face had looked like just before his father had pushed her in. Her mouth had been gagged but he still recalled that imploring look; a look tinged with sorrow and bewilderment even as she had disappeared over the edge...

He saw some wild flowers by his feet, plucked them up and threw them into the pit.

"There you are mater," he called, *"don't ever say I didn't get you flowers..."*

Surnh Horrocks looked at the sky as he walked from his office to Rochdale Park; the huge cumulus clouds towered above him and he, too, knew that it could rain, but he enjoyed his early lunches in the open and he knew that he could take temporary shelter under the canopy of the bandstand if necessary.

The park was one place where he felt safe, and since receiving threats from the heinous Johnsons he'd avoided all areas that could conceal potential attackers. Indeed before he'd finally allowed himself the weekly pleasure of taking his bread and cheese in the park, he'd been very careful to pick the route opting at all times to go only where numerous people frequented.

As he turned the corner on the final approach to the park gates he saw a fine looking coach and four stopped directly outside; the well-dressed occupant appeared to be in heated conversation with the driver and both were waving their arms in apparent frustration.

"Of course we can take the coach in!" said the well-dressed occupant.

"But we can't sir!" said an equally insistent driver, "Yon's a closed park to wheeled vehicles."

"Balderdash!" said the occupant.

Horrocks watched the noisy altercation in fascination as he approached, then just as he turned to enter the gates he heard a cry.

"You sir!"

Horrocks turned and saw that the occupant was looking at him; he pointed to his own chest and replied, *"Me?"*

The occupant strode across to Horrocks and said, "Yes sir, you sir; my driver steadfastly refuses to take the coach into the park saying that it isn't allowed in there. Do you know if that is the case?"

Horrocks said, "I'm afraid he's perfectly right, the park is closed to wheeled vehicles."

"Why that's preposterous!" said the occupant, "What's the point of contributing towards public amenities if the public can't take full advantage of 'em?

And how am I going to tell my aged uncle that we can't take the coach in?"

Horrocks shrugged his shoulders and said, "Sorry, rules are rules."

"Look," said the occupant gently ushering him towards the coach, "it's obvious that you know what's what, so please be a good gentleman and try to explain the rules to my recalcitrant old relative will you?"

Horrocks opened his mouth to object but realised that it would only take a minute of his time; with a resigned sigh he walked with the occupant across to the coach and watched as he opened the door.

It swung back and there sat Abraham Johnson. Before he could respond Hugo pushed him forwards and Abraham brought a heavy cosh crashing down onto the top of his head.

Hugo quickly caught the falling Clerk and bundled him up into the coach; he cast a quick look around to make sure that nobody was watching, then climbed aboard and shouted to Wiggins to proceed.

Caleb saw the carriage approaching at speed; the wetness of the soft ground caused the wheels to send sprays of water to the left and right as it raced along the sodden valley track. Within seconds Wiggins brought it to a halt in front of him, he stepped forwards, opened the door and saw the limp body of Horrocks propped up in the corner.

"Is he dead?" he said.

"No course he's not," said Hugo, "Your Pa just had to 'persuade' him to step inside."

Caleb nodded and said, "All right, tie his hands behind his back, gag him and then wake him up; we don't want him out cold for this." He looked at his father and said, "It looks as though it's going to piss down."

Abraham looked up and said, "Rain's good boy, it keeps prying eyes away."

As Hugo finished doing as he was instructed, Horrocks slowly regained consciousness; at first he was disorientated, but bit by he bit realised who he was with and started frantically straining his bonds.

Abraham turned to face him and brutally slapped him across the face.

"We've been waiting for today Horrocks; we've got unfinished business."

Horrocks knew that something bad was going to happen and started making a loud whimpering sound.

"Taking us seriously now are you?"

Horrocks stared back, not knowing what to do.

"Get him out of the coach boy!" said Abraham.

Horrocks turned and to his utter despair saw Caleb Johnson

there too.

Caleb reached in, grabbed Horrocks by the coat and yanked him out. He slowly circled the nervous Clerk then suddenly leaned close to his left ear and said, "You meddling bastard!"

Horrocks remained impassive.

"What did you think we'd do you fucking tomnoddy, just say sorry Mr. Horrocks sir and give Whitewall back to the Chance woman?" He stared hard into Horrocks' eyes but saw no response. Ignoring the gag tightly round his captive's mouth, he contemptuously said, "What's up, cat got your tongue?"

Horrocks stared at the ground.

Caleb watched him for a while and then said, "You fucking people, poking your noses in other folks' business." He leaned closer to Horrocks' ear and said, "Well now I'm going to batter it right off your fucking face."

He turned and called, *"Wiggins, get my stick!"*

Wiggins, who'd been watching the proceedings with a growing sense of unease didn't respond at first.

"Wiggins! Get my fucking stick!" shouted Caleb.

Wiggins jumped down from the driver's seat and looked around.

"Over by yon pit."

The words 'by yon pit' had a galvanising effect on both Wiggins and Horrocks. Wiggins immediately ran to where he could see Caleb's stick; Horrocks through an immediate and stark realisation why he was there.

"Nnn...! Nnn...!" Horrocks eyes widened; he shook his head from side to side trying to say *'No!'* through the tightly bound gag.

Wiggins appeared by his side and held up the heavy looking stick.

Caleb snatched it from him, turned his head and nodded for him to back away.

In that instant Horrocks saw his chance and took it. He caught everybody off guard and ran like a jackrabbit towards the bushes at the valley side.

Caleb spun around and shouted, *"Fuck!"* He turned to the startled Wiggins and yelled, *"Well don't just stand there, get after him!"*

Horrocks knew that he was at a disadvantage; he couldn't run properly with his arms tied behind his back and the gag hindering his breathing, but he was an ex-cross country runner running across the slushy ground with all the determination of a man fearing death.

Wiggins set off in hot pursuit but within seconds could see that he wasn't making any headway; he pumped his legs for all they were worth but couldn't gain ground.

Suddenly a shot rang out and a bullet swished by his ear making him duck to the left; his foot caught a sod of earth and he fell heavily over onto his side.

As he regained his feet he looked up and saw Horrocks stagger in front of him; he wheeled around and saw his master standing in the open doorway of the coach holding a pistol. He looked back at Horrocks and saw him topple face forwards into the wet grass.

For a few seconds time stood still. The sound of the shot echoed around the valley and all birdsong ceased. He alternated his gaze between the prone figure of Horrocks and Caleb who appeared to be in some sort of shock.

Suddenly he heard Caleb shout *"Fuck!"* and saw him throw his walking stick to the floor. He decided to keep well away from the raging man and ran to the figure lying in the grass.

It was clear that Horrocks was dead; all the colour had drained from his face and his eyes were half open. He bent down, tentatively prodded the lifeless body with his right forefinger and then took stock. He hadn't been sure what would result from the day's activities but as sure as hell he hadn't expected to witness a murder.

Resignedly he grabbed the neckline of Horrocks' coat, stood up and pulled his body slowly back to the coach.

Caleb was absolutely blazing; he didn't know which way to turn through pent up frustration.

"What the fuck did you do that for?" he yelled at Hugo, *"Wiggins could've caught him and we could've done him how we intended!"*

Abraham intervened and said, "All right, all right! Cussing's getting us nowhere. Let's get him holed in case that shot attracted attention."

Caleb released one final irritated snort then beckoned to Wiggins. Between them they manhandled Horrocks's body to the edge of the pit until it was ready to go over.

Caleb quickly went through the dead Clerk's pockets, removed some cash and a signet ring from his finger and then stood up. He spit on the body then aimed a last vicious kick into Horrocks' torso and sent him hurtling into the abyss.

A few seconds later he heard the familiar impact sounds from deep below and shouted, *"Bastard! I hope that hurt!"*

He slowly regained self-control and then turned to face Wiggins.

"Right," he said pointing to the open pit, "I opened this up; you and buggerlugs can cover it back up." He hobbled over to the coach and physically pulled Hugo out.

"Go on," he said, "you spoiled my day today, now do something to make up for it!"

Hugo looked into Caleb's ice cold hard eyes and didn't argue.

"Well," said Abraham leaning over and helping his son into the coach, "that didn't go as planned did it?"

Caleb grunted.

"Aw come on boy," said Abraham, "Hugo might have spoiled it for you, but at least we can rest in peace now."

"Not until we've done for that interfering bitch as well."

"One at a time boy;" said Abraham, "one at a time."

Caleb plonked himself into a corner and begrudgingly accepted that so far all had gone reasonably to plan; he relaxed slightly, turned to his father and said, "Aye, and I suppose we shouldn't spring more than one guest on mater at a time, she couldn't cope..."

Abraham burst out laughing and patted his son on the back.

Four hours later, the coach rattled into the yard of The King's Head Inn near Hyde old market place; the occupants alighted and made their way to the tavern's interior.

Wiggins handed the reins to the stable boys and instructed them to keep the horses tethered. He found the head ostler and took him into a quiet corner of the yard.

"Did a large crate arrive addressed to Mr. Hugo Darke?"

The ostler said "Aye, in yon corner..." he turned and looked nervously at the package, "what on earth..."

"Never you mind," said Wiggins cutting across him, "we have

an appointment within the hour, but we'll be back here for the night. You just make sure that it's very carefully loaded into the luggage compartment of the coach tomorrow morning."

"But…"

"But nothing; do as I say and there's a good drink in it for you."

"As you wish." The ostler knuckled his forehead and departed to impart instructions to his staff.

Wiggins watched for a few seconds and then made his way into the public bar to await orders.

The three co-conspirators sat in silence in the lounge bar; each man hugged a large whisky and waited.

Hugo took a gulp and tried to blank out the imagery of the past few hours. He kept seeing Horrocks stagger and fall, over and over again the images replayed in his mind; he'd known that they were going there to kill Horrocks, but for some inexplicable reason he hadn't reckoned on the cold stark finality of the actual deed. Worse still, he'd been the one to do it.

He knew that the nightmares would start again. They'd only just subsided from the incident with the girls and boy at Whitewall and he dreaded the thought of more sleepless nights.

He took another gulp of whisky and resolved there and then to sever all ties with the Johnsons.

At precisely 7:00pm, the outside door to the lounge bar opened and in stepped Maria Chance.

Hugo quietly remarked that she appeared to keep good time and reached into his waistcoat pocket to retrieve his pocket watch. It wasn't there. He did all the customary things; he checked all of his pockets including the ones that he never placed his watch in, but it had gone.

Maria looked around the room and caught sight of Abraham and Caleb. She lifted her head high, braced her shoulders back and defiantly started to weave her way through the tables and chairs towards them.

As she approached, Hugo leaned over to Abraham and whispered, "I've lost my time piece…"

Chapter 17

28th May 2002. The Executive Suite, Darke Industries H.Q.

Adrian Darke sat flicking through his Sunseeker Yacht diary when the telephone rang on his desk.

"Adrian," he answered in his informal style. Nobody dared to address him other than Mr. Darke, but he thought that by answering "Adrian" it made him sound more approachable. He, however, was very definitely hoi oligoi not hoi polloi, and was as different from the ordinary man as it was possible to be.

"A Mr. Giles Eaton, the Town Clerk of Walmsfield Borough Council would like to speak to you." said Jayne Dickens, Adrian's Personal Assistant.

"Haven't I paid my Council Tax or something?" he asked.

"I don't know about that, but he does say it's personal."

Adrian looked at his gold Rolex, it was just after 4:10pm; he said, "Tell him to ring me back at 4:35."

"Very well Mr. Darke."

Adrian replaced the receiver and leaned back in his red leather chair; he wasn't busy enough to keep the Town Clerk waiting, he just wanted to. He also wanted to see how keen the man was to speak to him, figuring that the closer he rang to 4:35pm, the keener he was.

He re-commenced looking at his Sunseeker diary and let the minutes tick by until the phone rang again. He looked at his watch and it was exactly 4:35pm; the corner of his mouth turned up in a half smile as Jayne put through the call.

"Darke." This was his altogether more formal response

"Ah, yes Mr. Darke, my name is Giles Eaton…"

"Yes, I'm perfectly aware of your name and who you are. What do you want?" He was always uncompromising with bureaucrats.

"I want to talk to you about the section of Brandworth Farm that is being considered by the Highways Agency for the proposed route of the new M6631." He waited for a response but none was forthcoming. A couple of seconds ticked by until he said, "Did you hear me Mr. Darke?"

"Of course I did but you said you wanted to talk to me, not have me talk to you..."

'*Go on,*' thought Giles, '*wind me up. You'll pay for it later you arrogant b...*'

"Yes of course," he said, trying his best not to sound flustered, "but what I have to say would be better said face to face and not down the telephone line."

Adrian was enjoying the Town Clerk's discomfort and gave it another squeeze.

"Well why didn't you just telephone my secretary and ask for an appointment? That way we wouldn't have wasted time talking but saying nothing..."

"Yes, I, er... yes I'll do that then," said Giles losing impetus, "I just wanted to make sure that you'd see me first..."

"Why wouldn't I?" said a now totally smug Adrian, "An important man like you..."

The sarcasm wasn't lost on Giles. He said, "Yes, quite. Very well, goodbye for now."

Adrian put the phone down without saying goodbye, leaned back in his chair and smiled to himself; he'd always been interested in mind games and controlling people, he revelled in it every time.

He recalled a seminar he'd once attended, a high-powered professional selling skills course which was entirely aimed at controlling conversation and turning situations to the user's advantage; he'd soaked it up and embraced its ethos so enthusiastically that he'd picked up the course prize at the end of the week. And that had been when he was a novice, now he was the grand master.

The telephone rang again.

"Adrian." He was 'Mr. Nice Guy' again.

"I've booked an appointment with Mr. Eaton to see you at 10:00am tomorrow if that is satisfactory."

"Tomorrow?" said Adrian, "He must be desperate."

"He did say that it was a matter of some urgency and you are free until 12.30pm."

"O.K. that's fine. I'll see him as per."

"Thank you Mr. Darke."

Adrian settled back in his chair to mull things over. He liked to get inside the head of people before they came and an appointment within eighteen hours of initial contact had the potential to make the visit more interesting than he might first have thought.

At Walmsfield Borough Council Offices Giles was still berating himself for being such a jellyfish with Adrian Darke; the episode on the phone added to his already considerable distaste of the man and following the forced lunch with Tom Ramsbottom earlier, his supply of obsequiousness had totally run out.

He inwardly smiled at the sheer power of his bargaining piece and knew that the contents of the Whitewall file would wipe away Darke's smugness. He looked around for it and then remembered that he'd asked Kathryn to put it somewhere safe.

He picked up the phone and dialled her. There was no answer so he replaced the receiver and dialled again; once again there was no answer. Frowning, he got up and went into her office but found it empty. The chair was placed neatly behind her desk and there were no signs of her usual daily activities.

Feeling puzzled, he returned to his office and as he approached his desk he caught sight of a piece of paper beneath it on the floor. He bent down, retrieved it and read what it said.

Mr. E.

The Whitewall file wouldn't fit into anything safely in our offices so I've returned it to Sandra Miles for safekeeping.

Please don't forget that I'm off this afternoon as we arranged.

See you tomorrow.

Kathryn.

Giles gasped. He clenched his fists and shut his eyes so tightly that it hurt. He blurted out, "Idiot!!" He could not believe his own stupidity. He repeated, "You bloody idiot Eaton!!" His mind was racing, he needed to act quickly. He picked up the phone, dialled

Sandra's number and waited, but she didn't answer.

'Shit, what if she's looked at it?' All sorts of thoughts raced through his mind as panic started to set in; all his dreams of wealth were in the balance.

He jumped up from his desk, raced down to Sandra's office and let himself in without knocking.

Sandra was staring at some papers on her desk and had a perplexed look on her face; she looked up, saw the Town Clerk and quickly stuffed them into her desk drawer.

'Fuck! She's got them...' thought Giles. He tried to keep calm and said, "I just tried calling you."

"Oh sorry," said Sandra, "I've just returned."

Giles nodded and said, "And er, what have you been up to?"

"The usual, this and that."

"Mmm," he tried to read her mind, "anything interesting?"

"Not really."

Giles pondered for a second and then said, "Kathryn left me a note informing me that you have the Whitewall file, is that correct?"

"Yes it is."

"May I have it?"

"You may." She reached down to retrieve the case and saw that one of the catches was still open; she coughed loudly and clicked it shut but knew that she hadn't been able to mask the sound.

Giles heard it and shook his head.

Sandra smiled sweetly as she brought the case into view and said, "Sorry about that Mr. Eaton, I must have knocked the catch open with my shoe; still, no harm done eh?"

Giles just stared at her face for a second then said, "Yes right, no harm done." He held out his right hand and Sandra gave him the case.

'Kiss my hairy ass...' he thought.

"I had asked Kathryn to look after it for me, but I'd forgotten that she was off this afternoon. Have you had it long?"

"Why do you ask?" said Sandra.

"I didn't want you to be inconvenienced in any way."

Sandra knew that he was fishing, but she wasn't about to take the bait.

"It was no trouble at all Mr. Eaton. Now, if there's nothing else I have some pressing matters to attend to before I go home."

Giles had had enough; all his artificial pleasantness vanished.

"All right, let's not beat about the bush. You've copied the files haven't you?"

Sandra's eyes narrowed; she said, "And why would you think I'd do that?"

Giles wanted to say, *"Because you're a sneaky bitch!"* but he tried to remain calm and said, "Frankly I don't know. But I warned you..."

"*Warned* me now is it?" flashed back Sandra.

"I warned you that the documents were highly sensitive..."

"Right..." said Sandra sitting forwards, "and you and the Mayor are the only people allowed to see them! Very convenient!"

"Just what the hell are you implying?"

"Well, how do I know that you aren't lying? How do I know that the file didn't contain valuable documents or maybe some, some, penny black stamps or something, and that you and the Mayor aren't planning to sell them privately?

And who regulates you two? Have you taken advice from our Legal Department? I wonder. Have you even told them about the file and its contents?"

"You cheeky bi..." Giles stopped himself just before the word was out.

"Nice!" said Sandra, "I'm a bitch now am I?"

Giles was now totally convinced that she'd at least seen, if not copied the files. He figured that all too soon her cronies Wilkes and Draper would be a party to the contents too and then he could whistle for his money. He decided to go in hard.

"All right," he said, "stop pussy-footing around and hand them over!"

"Yeah, right!" said Sandra sarcastically. She sensed that the gloves had come off at last. This she could deal with.

Giles' voice got even sterner, he leaned over her desk and said, "Listen to me Miles, hand them over now before you get into serious trouble!"

"I've *not* copied the files," said a now fully angry Sandra, "and even if I had, I wouldn't bloody well give them to you!

I'm beginning to wonder if there isn't some sort of hidden

agenda going on here…"

"How dare you insinuate such a thing?" shouted Giles, *"I could have your job for that!"*

Sandra sat back in her chair and calmly said, "Yes, and then all of this would come out in the wash wouldn't it?" She paused and looked straight into the Town Clerk's eyes. She saw his uncertainty and sensed that she suddenly had the upper hand.

"And I'll bet that you wouldn't want that would you? In fact I'd bet that this little episode won't even leave this room!"

Giles was fuming, but utterly nonplussed; he stared at her face for a second and then turned around and stormed out of her office.

'You nosey interfering cow!' he thought as he made his way back up the stairs to his office, *'I'm not going to be on the verge of making the big score, and then lose it because of the likes of you, you fat bitch…'*

He was absolutely livid. He felt sure that she'd photocopied at least some of the file contents but didn't know how much; his mind was ablaze with dark thoughts.

There was no way that his plan would work if other people were a party to the contents of the file. Ramsbottom he could deal with but Sandra Miles was an altogether different kettle of fish.

By the time he made it to his office the seeds of a plan were forming; there were only two other people who would be interested in the contents of the file so he needed to know if Sandra had spoken to either of them. He telephoned Carlton first and then Naomi on the pretext that he was looking for Sandra. Both confirmed that they had neither seen, nor spoken to her that afternoon.

'So far, so good!' he thought. He checked his watch, it was 5:15pm; she would be leaving at 5:30pm and he had to be ready.

He accessed the Walmsfield Council employee's car parking permit numbers via his laptop and quickly established that she had a red Ford in the multi-storey car park adjacent to the main office in bay number 41, third floor.

'Perfect,' he thought, *'the same floor as me.'*

He almost sprinted across to the car park, raced up the stairs and got behind the wheel of his Range Rover.

He'd never noticed before, but he could see Sandra's car through his rear view mirror and to his delight, bay 41 was the first in the row next to the lift and stair lobby.

5:37pm. His pulse was racing and he let out a long breath through his mouth; she had to be alone for this to work.

'What if she...' The familiar whine of the lift cut through his thoughts like a knife. *'Oh God...'*

His pulse rate soared as he switched on the engine of his Range Rover and selected reverse gear. He couldn't hear the lift because of the throaty growl emanating from his vehicle, but his eyes were glued on the lobby door.

It opened and Sandra walked out towards her car carrying the object of his desire, her briefcase.

He waited for a second to see if she was accompanied, then realising that she was alone, released the footbrake and accelerated straight back at her.

The violence of the impact sounded horrendous and threw Giles's head back against the headrest with an almighty blow. He didn't want to look, but knew that it would only be seconds before somebody arrived. He quickly composed himself, jumped out of the driver's door and went to the back of the Range Rover.

The sight before him purged his mind forever. In his wildest imagination he could not have envisaged what he was now looking at.

Sandra was pinned behind the vehicle in an upright position with her head leaning forwards against the back of his tail door. Her distended tongue hung out like a grotesque gargoyle and she'd sprayed blood all over the tailgate window. He clapped his hand over his mouth and looked down. He saw that the spare tyre on the rear door had hit her half way down the rib cage and crushed her entire middle section against the wall. She looked like one of the dreadful images from Dante's Visions of Hell; he felt his stomach heave but had to get her briefcase.

It was lying on the floor next to her feet; he bent down and, *'Oh sweet Jesus Christ!'* He clapped his hand over his mouth again as the sight below the vehicle came into view.

He'd once witnessed an accident where a lorry had hit a large dog and virtually split it in two. The poor unfortunate animal lay in the road disembowelled and whimpering; he recalled feeling a mixture of revulsion, horror and helplessness. Within seconds he'd jumped behind the wheel of his car and driven straight over the dog's head killing it instantly.

But this was profoundly different, this was Sandra Miles; a mother, a wife and a work colleague and he'd split her open just as surely and horrifically as the lorry had the dog.

He felt sick but had to act. He quickly diverted his eyes and snatched open the case.

They were there, photocopies of the Whitewall deeds and tenancy agreement. In seconds he stuffed them into his coat pocket, banged the case shut and dropped it back in the place he'd found it.

He suddenly became aware of footsteps racing up the stairs; he stood up, placed his hands over his mouth and feigned choking back vomit

The door burst open and a guy from the floor below ran in, froze at the sight before him and said, "Oh shit! – Oh, bloody Nora…"

He turned to the distraught figure of Giles and said, "Are you O.K. mate? Here, come with me." He put his arm around Giles' shoulders and pulled him away from the butcher's shop scene in front of them.

Giles was genuinely sobbing when he said, "It slipped. My foot, I thought I was pressing the brake, the car shot back, I panicked…"

"It's O.K. mate," said the stranger trying to comfort him, "it was an accident. Try to stay calm while I call the emergency services."

Chapter 18

23rd July 2002. Walmsfield Borough Council Offices

Eight weeks after the death of Sandra Miles normality had ostensibly resumed at Walmsfield Borough Council.

Giles Eaton had returned to work following an extended period of compassionate leave and counselling; a police enquiry had found nothing overtly suspicious about the accident and a Coroner's verdict of 'Accidental Death' was expected at the forthcoming hearing.

And Naomi and Carlton didn't believe a word of it.

The Mayor and his wife Peggy were on a previously unplanned holiday in America, Sam Chance had returned home to the South Coast of England and nothing further had been heard about the Whitewall documents.

Carlton had made numerous attempts to see the Town Clerk, each without success and he and Naomi had taken to spending every lunchtime together. They had found themselves drawn together in a bond of mutual mistrust and had vowed to leave no stone unturned about the circumstances surrounding Sandra's death. Naomi had practically ordered Percy to find out as much as he could about Whitewall Farm and wanted to know *everything*, however small or seemingly unimportant.

She had also become more concerned about her visions too, for as each day had passed they had come more easily, more unbidden and in the case of some, more clearly; and as before each one had been preceded by the feeling of a thumb pressing on the top of her left shoulder. She'd spoken to her mother and father about them, and though both professed to know of no other family members experiencing that kind of unusual activity she'd become increasingly certain that her father knew more than he was letting on.

She was also convinced that her insights were the small parts of a bigger picture or bigger story, like the single pieces of a jigsaw puzzle. She believed that if she could somehow mentally back away from what she was immediately seeing, more of the picture would come into view; but she had not been able to master that and the snippets seen in the visions were so diverse and disjointed that it would have been akin to positively identifying John Constable's painting of 'The Haywain' from an oak leaf or single cartwheel.

Three experiences seemed to dominate; she had seen them over and over again, sometimes in the day but mostly at night when she was at home and relaxed.

The first one was the small left hand pointing down accompanied by the voice saying *"This way Maria, this way..."* She could clearly see the hand, and though it was only small she was convinced that it belonged to a woman rather than a girl; she could also see a ring on her middle finger, a gold ring decorated with a white cameo against a black background.

The second experience always started with her staring at a huge portrait of Queen Victoria set against a wide expanse of pale green painted wall. She felt that she was in a large uncarpeted high ceilinged room; she could hear indistinct and muffled voices echoing around her and then within seconds she would hear an urgent feminine voice whisper, *"This way quickly... '.* She would turn and start to run towards a door, and though she didn't know how, she believed that the woman was helping her to get away from something.

Her most dominant vision was her most disturbing. In it she wore a full length, white cotton nightdress and was being pulled down a hallway to a room containing a bath full of cold water. She was then roughly grabbed by the back of her hair and pushed face first into it...

At this point she would invariably return to reality and however hard she tried, she was unable to reconnect to it. This particularly unpleasant experience always left her with a feeling of despair and helplessness, mostly because she could never see beyond the ducking.

She wanted to confide in Carlton but as the days had turned to weeks, she'd grown fonder of him and didn't want to scare him away. Indeed it had been a frustrating period of time for her all round because everything seemed to be at a hiatus - that was until fate intervened from an entirely unexpected quarter.

In the middle of the afternoon the telephone rang shrilly on Naomi's desk.

"Good afternoon," she said, "Naomi Draper, Historic Research Department."

"Good afternoon Mrs. Draper, my name is Chief Inspector Crowthorne of Lancashire Police."

This was a first for Naomi; she said, "Yes Chief Inspector, how can I help you?"

"Would you be free to visit Whitewall Farm on Wordale Moor tomorrow?"

Naomi instantly felt the thumb press down on her left shoulder but neither saw nor heard anything unusual. It was the one question that she'd hoped nobody would ask; she couldn't explain it, but something about Whitewall seriously bothered her. It felt as though she'd experienced something dreadful up there and didn't want to return.

"Mrs. Draper, are you still there?"

"Yes, I'm sorry Chief Inspector, I was a little distracted for a moment. Why do you want me to go there?"

"I take it that you didn't see the news this morning?"

"No, should I have done? Has something happened there?"

There was a brief pause and then Crowthorne said, "Planning permission was recently granted to the present owners of Whitewall Farm to install some new equipment in an outhouse adjacent to the barn and while their contractors were digging under the floor yesterday they discovered some bones."

The thumb pressed harder on Naomi's shoulder and voices started; she ignored them and continued listening to the Chief Inspector with mounting apprehension.

"We haven't yet established whether they're animal or human, but our forensic people and a team of archaeologists are now on site to investigate the findings."

Naomi felt her heart rate increasing and said, "Do you think that the bones are relatively modern?"

"It's too early to say, but we expect to have some answers later today."

"And why exactly do you want me to visit the site?"

"We understand that you've recently been researching the history of the place and have a pretty good knowledge of the past

154

owners and incumbents. Therefore, if the findings do prove to be historical and dateable you may be able to assist us by establishing who was in situ at the time."

Naomi's mind was racing; she didn't want to go to Whitewall, it was becoming more worrying than interesting and every time she heard something different about the place there seemed to be a death connected to it.

"It's true that I've been researching Whitewall, " she said more calmly than she felt, "but why can't you question me here at Walmsfield Council Offices rather than have me ride all the way up there on my motorbike?"

"Have you ever visited Whitewall Mrs. Draper?"

"No I can't say that I have."

"Well I think that it would be very useful if you did, and of course there would be no question about you riding up there on your motorbike, we will collect you from your office and return you once we've concluded our meeting."

Naomi was cornered; the thought of going there upset her, but it was no time for airing such things.

"All right then," she said reluctantly, "what time would you like to pick me up?"

"Would 9:30am suit you?"

Naomi agreed and the date was set.

Almost as soon as she'd replaced the telephone receiver she gathered up as much information as she possessed in preparation for her visit. She telephoned Carlton and Sam to see if either man could add to her knowledge; she rang Postcard Percy to ascertain his latest findings and then she placed all the information into a file and laid it on her desk ready for the next day.

Just one thing bothered her; should she tell the police about the mysterious file currently held by Giles Eaton?

She got up from her desk and went to see Carlton.

Carlton's inner core was a seething pool of anger and irritation because he was convinced that Sandra's death was linked to the opening of the Whitewall file.

His inability to be able to speak to the police about it frustrated him beyond measure but as an employee of Walmsfield Borough Council he was bound by their confidentiality rules.

What he needed, what he craved, was evidence of foul play. It didn't matter how small or obscure, but it had to be concrete not conjecture.

A secondary cause of his exasperation was his inability to be able to see the Town Clerk; he was convinced that Giles was avoiding him and that just one single look into his eyes would tell him whether he had deliberately run into Sandra or not. But to date he'd not been able to get anywhere near him.

His thought processes were interrupted by a knock at his door.

"Come in," he called.

Naomi entered and said, "Did you see the news this morning er, Mr. Wilkes?"

"Oh come on Naomi," said Carlton whose previous penchant for protocol was softening by the day, "in here I don't expect you to call me Mr. Wilkes."

"Sorry Carlton, I was just, you know…"

"Yes I do. But in answer to your question, I didn't see the news. Why?"

"Some bones have been unearthed at Whitewall Farm and the police want me to go up and liaise with them on their research."

Carlton was taken aback and said, "I trust that their request for your involvement means that they're not recent bones?"

"The police haven't confirmed it yet, but I believe so."

She went on to describe her conversation with Chief Inspector Crowthorne and explained how he would be asking her for as much information as she had on Whitewall, but once having imparted all that she could, the big question remained. Should she tell him about the Whitewall file?

The two companions discussed the various aspects of the situation and ultimately concluded that the file should remain temporarily off the radar in accordance with the instructions of the Town Clerk.

There was something else too. Carlton didn't want to reveal Giles' request to withhold information; he wanted to be able to disclose it at a time of maximum and decisive effect. If it was to be Giles' Achilles heel, he wanted to make damned sure it did the trick.

Having determined their course of action Naomi settled back in her chair and conversationally said, "It's no wonder that I'm hesitant about setting foot on Whitewall Farm, there are so many awful conundrums associated with that place that Sherlock Holmes would have found it difficult to resolve. I mean just look at all of the deaths; and not just in the past, there's…" She didn't finish the sentence, she knew that they were both thinking about Sandra.

Carlton lowered his head and shook it slowly from side to side.

"God I'm so *bloody* annoyed about the whole Sandra thing. If it takes me until the proverbial end of days I'll get to the bottom of it. And I swear to you now Naomi, if I ever find out that Eaton hit her on purpose there'll be no corner on earth that he'll be able to hide from me."

He recalled a small piece he'd read somewhere and thought how apt it was.

"And turnest not thy turbid mind to imprudent scheming things,
Look not upon my countenance, if vengeful thought it brings.
For thee know not, what be unleashed when rancorous act ye contemplate,
And thine be hell, with all its demons should thee open up this gate.
No time too long nor distance great if then thee turn to flight,
For Nemesis is at thy heel to turn thy days to night."

Naomi said, "If Sandra was murdered by Eaton why would he do that? What on earth could she have found out that warranted such an extreme measure?

"I don't know, but do be careful with speculation like that, it's all right in here with me but don't ever voice such an opinion where others could hear you."

"Naturally; but do you remember me asking Eaton if we were in danger? He responded by telling me that we weren't as long as we were completely unaware of the contents of the file. Well what if Sandra had seen the contents and that was why something had happened to her?"

"But how could she?" said Carlton, "as far as we know it never left the presence of Giles Eaton. Even his secretary Kathryn would have had easier access to it than Sandra."

The mention of Eaton's secretary Kathryn polarized both of

them; they immediately looked at each other and Carlton reached for his phone.

"It couldn't be this simple surely..." he said as he dialled.

"Mr. Eaton's secretary," said Kathryn on the other end of the line.

"Yes Kathryn, Carlton Wilkes here. Is Mr. Eaton available this afternoon please?"

"No, I'm sorry; he has an appointment at Darke Industries in Manchester this afternoon and isn't expected back until tomorrow morning."

"I see," said Carlton, trying to sound as casual as possible, "How about tomorrow morning then?"

"No I'm sorry Mr. Wilkes, I'm not trying to be evasive but Mr. Eaton has asked me not to book any appointments for him until he instructs me to."

"Very well, in that case would you be kind enough to let me know when he does start accepting appointments?"

"Yes of course," said Kathryn pleasantly, "Will that be all Mr. Wilkes?"

"Yes, thank you." Carlton left the briefest of pauses; just enough time for Kathryn to remove the phone from her ear, then he called out loudly, "*Oh Kathryn...*"

"Yes Mr. Wilkes?"

"Just one last thing before you go, did either you or Mr. Eaton return the Whitewall file to Sandra Miles for safekeeping at any time?"

"Yes. I did as a matter of fact. On the very day that she, well you know..."

Carlton clapped his hand over the mouthpiece and whispered, "Sandra had it!"

He removed his hand from the receiver and said to Kathryn, "May I ask why you returned it to Sandra?"

"Mr. Eaton asked me to put it somewhere safe for him while he was out to lunch with the Mayor. He'd forgotten that I was off that afternoon, and not wanting to leave the file anywhere indiscreet I returned it to Sandra then left him a note telling him what I'd done with it." She paused and said, "There wasn't a problem with that was there?"

"No, absolutely not, you made a very sensible and considered choice. Thank you for your candour." Carlton quickly diverted her attention by saying, "And you will remember to call me when Mr. Eaton's free won't you?"

"Yes I will."

Carlton thanked her and put the phone down. He was beside himself.

"Damn it!" he said, "Sandra *did* have it!"

"You don't think that she had it when she was hit do you?"

"There were no reports of anything like that being found on the scene, either with her or Eaton. Some guy had run up from the floor below and found him just standing there looking horrified, but there was no mention of him being in possession of anything at the time; and that file would have been pretty obvious. Additionally, Sandra's briefcase and handbag were found with her and neither appeared to have been tampered with."

"And how do you know that?"

"From conversations I had with the police."

"So if she didn't have the file with her, why would he want to kill her?"

Carlton paused and then said, "Perhaps it was something she knew...?" Things started to click into place in his mind; he said, "Did you receive a call from Eaton that day asking if you'd seen or spoken to Sandra during the afternoon?"

"I did."

"So did I." Carlton sat forward in his chair and stared into Naomi's eyes, "So let us presume that he has established that Sandra is aware of some sort of damning information and that she hasn't yet divulged it to either of us. The only logical thing to do would be to silence her immediately wouldn't it?"

"That would make sense," agreed Naomi. "but if Sandra *had* seen the file, and had found out something of major importance, why wouldn't she have just called one of us?"

Carlton sat back and said, "I don't know." He paused for a while longer and then said, "We know that she had the file for some time, but we don't know what she did with it. Did she venture a peek inside? Did she find something that was disturbing enough to get her killed and if so, like you said, why didn't she call one of us?"

"Or drop us a quick email. She could have scanned whatever

she'd found and…" Naomi suddenly stopped talking.

Carlton looked across at her and said, "Go on…"

"Or what if she'd photocopied the files? What if she'd realised that the files would only be in her possession for a limited time and she hadn't wanted to chance emailing copies? Photocopying would have been her only other option wouldn't it?"

"Good grief, you could be onto something there; and what if Eaton had actually caught her copying the files?" Carlton paused in thought for a second and then said, "My God all of that fits; the first person on the scene of the accident was the guy from the floor below. When he arrived Eaton was standing near Sandra's body and her briefcase was at her feet. There would have been enough time for him to open it and remove any incriminating evidence before the man from below had time to get there."

Naomi put her hands up to her mouth; it felt *too* right to be wrong. She said, "Should we tell the police about what we suspect?"

"No, we need proof. We can't turn up with a half-cocked story and nothing to back it up."

The pair sat in total silence for a while until Carlton said, "Wait a minute, we can check if Sandra had been copying anything from the user log on the photocopier nearest her office.

You go and find out her user code and I'll run a print-out of user activity for the day of her accident."

Fifteen minutes later they had clear proof that Sandra had indeed copied four pieces of A4 paper at 4:18pm on the day of her death.

For security reasons the photocopier didn't keep reproductions of the documents copied but they had enough.

Carlton said, "Now we need to look for what she photocopied. We need to discreetly find what she'd been working on and see if it required any copying; we also need to establish whether or not anybody else could have asked her to do any photocopying for them. Then if we find nothing, we can begin to theorise that she may have copied something from the Whitewall file, but I should warn you – if we find out that she has, we could be getting involved with something much blacker and infinitely more dangerous than anybody currently believes."

Naomi said, "Yes I agree." She paused for a second and then said, "It's good that we have something positive to aim for for a change, but I can't help feeling a bit worried about the possible consequences if we're right."

"Of course," said Carlton cautiously, "we must be extremely careful how we handle this. We don't want anybody second guessing what we're doing and we certainly don't want to alert Eaton about any of this, because if he has killed once for whatever motive, we'd be stupid to assume that he wouldn't be capable of doing it again."

Naomi nodded and then in a moment of surreal déjà vu, looked up at Carlton and echoed Sandra's words, "What the hell is in that file Carlton?"

"I don't know love," said Carlton being uncharacteristically familiar, "but we'll find out. And so help me, if Eaton attempts to harm you or even looks at you sideways after what happened to Sandra, I'll hunt him down and finish him off myself."

Naomi smiled and said, "You just called me love."

Carlton stopped for a second and then said, "Sorry I…"

"No don't apologise," said Naomi, "I liked that."

Time froze as they stared into each others' eyes. Neither knew what to say but something had changed.

Naomi quickly looked down as a blush tinged her cheeks and a tremor of excitement ran through her body.

Chapter 19

30th June 1869. The King's Head Inn, Hyde

Maria felt her heart beating wildly as she made her way through the tables and chairs to where the despicable Abraham and Caleb Johnson were sitting with another man. The very sight of the cold and lifeless eyes of Abraham Johnson took her straight back to Whitewall and the events of November 1867.

It had been a full eighteen months since her last encounter with the Johnsons and in all of that time she'd heard nothing from Margaret. She was totally convinced that some ill had befallen her and she had told Rochdale Police so on numerous occasions.

Upon her insistence the police had visited Whitewall at diverse times between December 1868 and February 1869 but had found absolutely no evidence to substantiate her claim that either Margaret or her servants Michele and Derek Horton had been harmed.

The investigating officer had accepted the account given by Abraham Johnson that the Hortons had left before he'd returned to Whitewall to try to reconcile his marriage, and that Margaret had departed within a few weeks of their re-union to visit sick relatives and had never returned.

Naturally she didn't believe a word of it but she had been so persistent with her claims to the police that in the end it felt as though they had become less tolerant of her and more understanding with the Johnsons. Regardless, no proof of foul play had been found and the case had been dropped.

During the last twelve months she'd resorted to writing threatening letters again but it had been to no avail. She hadn't received a single reply.

Then to her amazement, she'd received a letter from the Johnsons requesting a meeting; the venue was open to the public and the suggested time was early evening, so feeling reasonably safe she'd cautiously agreed.

"Miss Chance I presume." Hugo stood up and offered his hand.

Abraham and Caleb remained seated and said nothing.

Maria hesitantly shook the proffered hand and said, "And who do I have the dubious honour of meeting?"

"Why Miss Chance, please reserve your judgement and you will see that 'tis not a dubious honour at all. I am Hugo Darke of Brandworth Manor." He gestured towards a chair and said, "Please, won't you take a seat and let me purchase you a little light refreshment?"

Maria ignored the offer and cast a wary glance in the direction of the Johnsons; both seemed to be malevolently disinterested.

"Oh don't mind them," said Hugo, "we've had a busy day and they aren't feeling very sociable."

Maria squared up to Hugo and said, "And let me absolutely assure you sir, just in case it was ever in question, that socialising with these black-hearted, brutish cowards of men is the very last thing that I want to do."

Caleb immediately reacted. He tried to jump up with clenched fists but Abraham grabbed his sleeve and restrained him.

"Steady boy!" he hissed, "Let's not be hasty in front of all these good folks."

Caleb cast a glance around the room and though very few people were present, he thought the better of it and slowly sat back down. He stared venomously at Maria through slits of eyes.

Maria felt her knees weaken but remained rooted unflinchingly to the spot.

"Come come Miss Chance," said Hugo eagerly trying to diffuse the tension, "let's at least try to be civil with one-another. After all I hope, or should I say *we* hope, that you will be pleased with the outcome of the day's proceedings."

Maria cautiously sat down whilst watching the faces of the Johnsons.

"If we are to proceed," she said pointing to Abraham, "I want him to explain to me why I haven't heard from his wife for this past one and a half years."

Abraham stayed silent.

"I warn you sir," said Maria determinedly, "that I shall leave this very instant if I do not get a satisfactory answer."

Hugo looked questioningly at Abraham, but saw that he, too, was now starting to appear as sullen and aggressive looking as Caleb. He had to think quickly.

"I'm sorry to have to be the bearer of bad tidings," he said, "but I thought that you knew of her untimely demise in the colonies earlier this year."

"In the colonies?" said a shocked Maria, "What are you talking about?"

"In New York madam, that's where she departed this earth. Following a breakdown of their marriage and irreconcilable differences, she took herself off on an extended trip to America where she resided in comfort for a goodly period of time before being struck down with cholera which she ingested from a polluted water supply."

Maria's mind was in turmoil. She didn't know Hugo Darke; his explanation seemed natural enough and tinged with a little sadness, but she didn't truly know what to believe.

"I am very sorry to hear about that," she said, "And you will forgive me for not wishing to linger on that issue, but for now I will reserve my judgement as to its veracity."

"As you wish," said Hugo, "though I hope time will prove to you that I am an honest and trustworthy man. Now, may I offer you that light refreshment?"

"No thank you," said Maria, "I just wish to know why you have come here to see me."

Hugo looked at Abraham and asked, "May I explain?"

Abraham grunted.

"Following the very sad loss of Margaret Johnson, some time ensued before we were able to have her Will read..."

"Wait a minute," said Maria, "you said 'we' were able to have the will read; what has any of this got to do with you?"

"Ah yes of course," said Hugo obsequiously, "Abraham and I have become like brothers since I helped his son recover from a terrible injury incurred by that fearsome and unruly hound of his..."

"Ha!" said Maria delightedly pointing towards Caleb, "So the hound turned on him? Dear Lord above, it's a wonder the poor beast didn't die from food poisoning!"

Caleb screwed up his fists and tried to stand once again but Abraham restrained him.

"What delicious justice that is!" said a joyful Maria, "Why I haven't heard such a good yarn in a donkey's age!" She stopped speaking for a second and then feigned concern. "Oh dear," she said solicitously, "how thoughtless of me to express joy. Why that poor unfortunate animal now probably suffers with a canker of the teeth after a repast of such unwholesome meat."

"You bitch..." said Caleb as he leapt to his feet.

Maria recoiled and instantly remembered what dangerous and unstable company she was in.

"*Sit down boy!*" said Abraham sternly, "Remember where you are!"

Caleb looked at his father and begrudgingly sat back down.

Once again Hugo took the initiative and said, "Please gentlemen, Miss Chance, be good enough to let me explain."

Maria calmed and decided that it would be safe enough to hear what Hugo had to say. She tentatively said, "Very well, proceed."

Hugo looked at the Johnsons, Abraham nodded and he continued from where he'd left off.

"Over this past twelve months I have undertaken most of Abraham's legal dealings because he is not as well educated as I, so naturally I was invited to be present when the terms of Margaret's Will were finally made known to us. In it she clearly stated that she wished you and your kin to be reinstated as the rightful owners of the Whitewall Estate."

Maria could not believe her ears; she narrowed her eyes and said, "And you are not toying with me?"

"Not in the slightest. We have arranged for you to see the documents yourself, and this very evening at the office of Josiah Hubert & Sons here in Hyde."

Caleb shot a frowning glance at Hugo that wasn't lost on Maria.

"The solicitor's office is close by; he is at this very moment awaiting your presence and we would of course be happy to take you there in my carriage. Once you have seen the papers for yourself and satisfied yourself that they are not a fiction, we shall be happy to return you to your home."

Maria cast a glance in the direction of Abraham, there was

something about his face that she couldn't put her finger on; he appeared to be confused and listening almost as intently as she was. Her mind was working overtime, so she aimed a question directly at him.

"You knew all along that your wife wanted my family to be reinstated to Whitewall, she wrote and told you such. I then visited you and told you again before you set that brute of a dog on me; since then I have written numerous letters informing you that we are the rightful owners of the estate and you have steadfastly ignored all of my claims. So what has changed now?"

Abraham didn't know how to respond, he looked at Hugo who sat watching impassively.

"Well, answer me!" Maria put more pressure on Abraham.

Hugo waited until he could see that Abraham wasn't going to respond.

"Miss Chance, it is no secret that Abraham did not want you to re-take the Whitewall Estate, and it is also true that he and his wife were not on the closest of terms…"

"Ha!" said Maria for the second time, "There's an understatement of epic proportions!"

Once again Caleb's eyes flashed and went into slits as he stared at Maria with unadulterated malice. His left calf throbbed badly; he blamed not only his wound, but also the loss of the best dog he had ever known on the bitch sitting opposite him and she was sorely testing his patience. Every instinct in him was urging him to lean over and rip her throat out with his bare hands.

"That maybe so," continued Hugo totally oblivious of Caleb's punitive thoughts, "but it alters nothing; Margaret made her intentions quite clear in her Will, and though my good friends here may wish it otherwise there is little or nothing that they can do about it."

The finality of the statement left the trio in silence until Maria said, "And you wish me to travel with you this very night to the office of the solicitor whereupon I may view these documents?"

"Precisely." said Hugo.

Maria Chance was now forty eight years of age and unmarried; she was four feet eleven inches in height and weighed seven and a half stones. Although her body remained in good shape her face had become hard and lined following years of solid graft at the cotton mill.

From the age of thirty she had fought unwaveringly to regain possession of the Whitewall Estate, and having undergone all the trials that the worrisome endeavour had put her through, she had become as wily as a weasel.

She knew that she was in the company of a virtual stranger and the most dangerous and evil men that she had ever come across and they wanted her to travel alone with them to an unknown destination somewhere in Hyde.

She looked across at Caleb who seemed to be awaiting her response with all the eagerness of a wolf that had just sighted an injured rabbit.

"Well you can think again." she said contemptuously, "Do you believe that I am completely stupid? Nothing this side of hell would entice me into a carriage with those sick creatures beside you."

She had gone one step too far.

Caleb immediately turned around and saw that only two distant tables were occupied. In a flash he jumped up in front of Maria and shielded her from view, he punched her hard on the side of the head and then feigned tripping over her feet by crashing into the table.

Hugo didn't know what had happened. In one second he'd been talking, in the next Caleb was up and apparently falling over the prone body of Maria. He jumped to his feet too and the glasses on the table fell over with a crash drawing attention to the sudden chaotic behaviour between them.

A man approached from another table as Caleb started picking himself up from the floor and apologising for his apparent clumsiness to the now badly stunned Maria.

"Can I help you sir?" said the man from the nearby table, "The lady looks in considerable distress…"

Hugo's wits were with him again.

"Thank you for your concern," he said, "but I am a doctor, and I can attend to this."

"What happened?" asked the stranger.

"My colleague here is crippled in the left leg and tripped as he

167

alighted from the table. He caught our lady friend here on the side of her head with his elbow and has temporarily stunned her, but my surgery is nearby so we shall take her there and attend to her injury."

"Would you like some assistance?" said the man.

"No thank you, we are three; I have a carriage and a driver and we shall manage very well."

The stranger was placated and returned to his table.

They needed to act quickly; Caleb was dispatched to fetch Wiggins with the carriage whilst Hugo and Abraham carried the limp figure of Maria outside into the coaching yard.

Maria started to show signs of regaining consciousness so Hugo called to Abraham who placed his hand tightly over her airways and constricted her breath until she fell silent once again.

After what seemed like an interminable length of time the carriage clattered into the yard. They speedily positioned Maria inside, climbed aboard and departed the Inn. Within seconds they were heading up the High Street.

"What the blazes did you do that for?" said Hugo to Caleb, "You could have ruined everything!"

"I wasn't going to sit there and let that bitch talk to us like that…"

"That impulsive temper will be the undoing of you boy." said Abraham. "That wasn't how your pater told you how to do things."

"The end result was the same wasn't it?" snapped Caleb.

"Watch your tongue when you're talking to me boy!" said an equally snappy Abraham.

Caleb became instantly subdued, sunk his head and said, "Sorry pa."

Presently he lifted it and turned to the unconscious Maria.

"I'd like to finish this bitch now…" His cruel streak took a hold; he grabbed a handful of Maria's hair and yanked her head forwards, then with his other hand squeezed her cheeks tightly below each cheekbone.

"You fucking ugly sow!" he shouted into her face.

Abraham grinned at Hugo and said, "It's good to see the boy enjoying himself…"

Maria started to show signs of coming round; which was all the excuse Caleb needed to strike her a brutal blow with his fist straight into her forehead. She immediately slumped back into unconsciousness.

There was something about really hurting the soft face of a woman that Caleb liked; it made him feel powerful and masterful. It made him want to rut. The stirring in his breeches made him think about it for a few seconds but he surreptitiously looked at his father and put it out of his mind.

Hugo, who was in no mood to see Caleb enjoying himself said, "That's enough! You know what we agreed."

"*The other coach is in view.*" Wiggins' voice cut through their exchange focusing them all.

"*Are you sure that it's the right one?*" called Hugo.

"*I can see the name on the back of it.*"

"*Very well, pull up alongside it.*"

Wiggins did as he was bid and the rear door of the opposite coach opened.

A huge, grim-looking man clad in a long white coat appeared. He walked lugubriously to their door, peered in and enquired, "Which of you gentlemen is Mr. 'ugo Darke?"

Hugo leaned forward and nodded. "I am."

The enquirer looked more intently into the rear and caught sight of the still figure of Maria.

"And this is your poor unfortunate sister is it?"

"It is." said Hugo.

The white coated man saw the obvious discolouration on Maria's forehead and said, "I take it that she needed pacifying."

Hugo didn't answer at first; he extracted his wallet, removed two shillings and said, "This is for you and your colleague. Take care of her as we arranged and there will be plenty more where that came from."

The white coat took the coins and placed them into his pocket.

"Oh don't you worry none sir, you can rest assured that we'll take *very* good care of 'er." He reached into the pocket of his white coat, retrieved a bottle of Laudanum and tapped it.

"By the time that she's, 'ow shall we say sir, 'medicated', she won't know 'er hanus from 'er helbow."

"Yes, charming similitude." said Hugo. "She's been such a burden on my poor old mother; maybe now she can take comfort from the knowledge that her daughter will be very well looked after."

The white coat knuckled his forehead and said, "She will that sir." He replaced the Laudanum then turned and called over to the opposite carriage, *"Mr. Twitch! Hover 'ere if you please."*

Simeon Twitch heard the call and replied, *"Certainly Mr. Honeysuckle sir."* He made his way across to his colleague.

"It's Mr. *Honeysucker* I keep telling you, not *Honeysuckle*!"

Honeysucker glared at Twitch then reached into the coach and gently extracted Maria's limp body. He turned and handed it to his associate.

Twitch looked down into the face of his 'patient', closed his eyes and muttered, "Oh my Gawd!"

Honeysucker heard his colleague's comment and kicked him sharply on the ankle.

"Take the lady to the coach Mr. Twitch, there's a good gentleman." He glared once more at his associate then nodded abruptly in the direction of the coach.

"Yes sir right away." Twitch took a deep breath and carried Maria's limp body over to their coach.

Honeysucker nodded to the assemblage then turned and followed his colleague to make preparations for their journey.

Caleb's curiosity got the better of him; he stepped down and walked around to the rear of the second coach. As he approached he heard a muffled sharp exchange between the two men inside but the instant that they became aware of his presence they fell silent.

In the dark interior he could see that they'd placed Maria on a stretcher and had secured her waist, ankles and wrists with leather straps; and over her mouth they'd placed a thick leather gag.

He looked slowly around and saw that the coach had no windows and that the interior was completely padded. Even he was repulsed at the idea of being strapped in there in the total darkness with absolutely no chance of escape.

He returned to the confines of Hugo's comfortable coach, looked at his father and shook his head in repugnance.

"They've got the bitch strapped to a stretcher; there are no windows and the inside's as black as a coal miner's arse."

Abraham raised his eyebrows and smiled at his son, "Black as a coal miner's arse? Where do you get those sayings boy?" He turned to Hugo and said, "Young buggers of today's always coming up with something new to say…"

Hugo wasn't really listening; he smiled and nodded but was lost in his own thoughts.

Within a few minutes Honeysucker re-emerged from the interior of the coach minus his white coat; he turned briefly, nodded to Hugo and then climbed up into the driving seat. Without saying a word he slapped the reins and the carriage moved slowly away.

Emblazoned across the back door were the words; *'Cheshire Lunatic Asylum, Parkway, Macclesfield.'*

Chapter 20

23rd July 2002. The Executive Suite, Darke Industries H.Q.

Adrian Darke leaned forwards in his red leather chair and placed the palms of his hands down on his desk.

"Do you want something to drink?" He shot the question without removing his eyes from those of the Town Clerk. He believed that he could assess men by their appearance alone and he was already convinced that the bureaucrat in front of him was not going to be any kind of challenge.

"A malt would be nice, thank you." said Giles.

"Do you have a preference?"

"Old Pulteney if you have one."

Adrian walked across to his extensively stocked drinks cabinet, poured Giles his choice and then poured himself a Caol Ila.

"I prefer the Islay malts," he said trying to point score, "I believe that they are for the more discerning whisky palate."

Giles raised his eyebrows and said, "Maybe."

Adrian walked slowly back to his desk, sat down and said, "Now then Mr. Giles Stuart Eaton what have you got to say?"

He wanted to intimidate Giles and watched with glee as he got the desired result; he took a sip of his drink, leaned back in his chair and made himself comfortable. He wanted to digest everything that the 'Council pen-pusher' was going to say.

Giles hadn't liked Adrian either knowing or using his full name but it illustrated that his host had taken more than just a passing interest in him.

He looked impassively across the desk and tried to remain as businesslike as he could.

"I have in my possession certain documents dating back to the latter half of the nineteenth century which confirm absolutely and without question, that fifteen hundred acres of land were purchased from the then Whitewall Estate by one of your forebears for the then Brandworth Estate. The deal was concluded between one Abraham Johnson of Whitewall and your direct ancestor Hugo

Darke in 1868."

He stopped and took a sip of his whisky allowing Adrian time to digest this first statement.

"*And*?" said Adrian almost disinterestedly.

"I will be fair and point out that a similar sale was conducted between Abraham Johnson of Whitewall and the then Hundersfield District Council for another twenty five hundred acres of land from the Whitewall Estate in 1869."

"And the point is?" Adrian was already growing wearisome of the council wallah and his bureaucratic jargon bullshit.

"Both of the land sales were illegal."

Adrian gave nothing away; he just stared intently at the Town Clerk without answering.

Giles iced the cake.

"And even more to the point, both Hugo Darke and the Clerk who purchased the land for Hundersfield District Council knew that they were illegal purchases. I have proof of that too."

"Huh!" said Adrian bluntly, "I don't believe a word of it!"

"Be that as it may," said Giles coolly, "I *do* have the proof."

Adrian still felt dismissive and said, "How could you possibly know that either your predecessor Clerk or my forefather knew that the land sales were illegal?"

"Because both men were paid large ex-gratia payments into private bank accounts upon the conclusion of the respective purchases and you will find as I have, that you don't have either a Bill of Sale or a Freehold document relating to that section of land dating back to 1868."

"*Pah!*" said Adrian, "Who the hell could put his hand on any document dating back to 1868 and cite it as proof of honesty? Do me a favour!"

Giles remained silent.

"And another thing, part of what you said makes no sense anyway. What would be the point of paying my 'great great whatever' an ex-gratia payment? If some questionable deal was being sweetened to help it along why didn't this Johnson guy just drop the price of the land instead of supposedly paying my forebear a lump sum afterwards? It's piffle!"

Giles leaned back in his chair and said, "I can't answer that; the machinations of the recipients are a complete mystery to me.

Regardless, it is an absolute and documented fact that they each received a substantial amount of money upon the conclusion of the deals."

Adrian leaned forward, picked up his whisky glass and drank down the contents. He walked over to the drinks cabinet and poured himself another without offering a second to Giles.

Something wasn't adding up; he took a sip of whisky and returned to his desk.

"Even if I did believe this cock and bull, what difference would it make anyway? You couldn't just come in here and tell me that it was 'apparently' purchased illegally over a hundred and thirty years ago and that now it had to be handed back. That's ludicrous."

"It wasn't 'apparently' purchased illegally Mr. Darke, it was a straightforward, no-nonsense downrightly illegal purchase." Giles paused and then added, "And we shall see whether it's ludicrous or not in due course shall we?"

Something about the coolness of the Town Clerk was unnerving Adrian; the annoying bureaucrat knew something more, he was convinced of it.

"All right," he said, "how do you think your Councillors would react if you told them that you'd discovered proof that one of your old Town Clerks had purchased some land illegally for the Council in the 1800's and that you now intended handing it back to the rightful owners? They'd think you'd completely lost it!"

"Would they?" said Giles calmly.

Giles' smug attitude was starting to get under Adrian's skin.

"Of course they would! There are probably council houses and all sorts of other things built on that land by now, so don't try telling me that they'd simply hand it back because they wouldn't!"

"Wouldn't they?"

"No they wouldn't. Now stop wasting my time with this bullshit and spit out what you're really here for."

Giles was relishing every moment. On the wall behind the desk was a huge coat of arms with the Darke family motto below it.

"Aquila non capit muscas"
(The eagle does not catch mosquitoes)

He looked at Adrian's irritated face and thought to himself, *'Looks like the mosquito is about to catch the eagle...'*

Coolly he said, "All right I'll cut straight to the chase, I will destroy all the papers in my possession if you pay me five hundred thousand pounds."

"Five hundred thousand? Half a million!" Adrian was aghast. "You must be out of your tree! I'm not even paying you five pounds let alone five hundred thousand. Now get out of my office or I'll report you to the police..."

"Very well, but you'll be making a big mistake."

"The biggest mistake I made today was giving you credibility, now get out before I change my mind and make the call."

"O.K. - but you do know which piece of land I'm referring to don't you?"

Adrian slowly looked up and narrowed his eyes."

"I thought not," said Giles reading the response.

Silence ensued for a few seconds until Adrian said, "Well?"

"It's the rectilinear piece directly to the west of Brandworth Farm."

If Adrian had run headfirst into a wall he could not have been brought to a dead stop quicker. It felt as though he'd been hit in the face.

"Ah," said Giles, "I see now that you're listening."

To friends and colleagues Adrian Darke was a legend; in the business world he had been showered with all sorts of accolades for business excellence and countrywide his companies employed hundreds of people.

His two leading concerns, Darke Industries and Darke Dealings were the backbone of his empire but during the past twelve months he'd been made aware of a sharp decline in their annual profits. Additionally the share prices of both companies had fallen worryingly low and the Directors of both companies had called for radical shake-ups which carried the threat of redundancies.

The thought of having to announce that news to the public had been bad enough for a proud man like him, but that had been the least of his worries.

There was also another company that was not so well known -

Darke Desires. Conspicuously it traded internationally in 'objet d'art', but it was a cover for an offshore company sourcing and supplying arms purchased mainly from ex-USSR countries to some of the poorer warring African States and whilst the majority of the time his questionable deals had paid huge dividends, within the last few months one had gone to hell in a handcart.

Darke Desires had brokered a deal between an infamous African Warlord and a Chechnyan crime syndicate for seven million pounds worth of military equipment which was going to net the company a one million pound profit.

The Warlord had paid a two million pound deposit which had been forwarded on to the syndicate and the Chechnyans had shipped the equipment to the African country; and because of trust inspired by previously successful transactions they had accepted those terms based on a promise from Darke Desires to pay the outstanding money within fourteen days of delivery.

The militaria had been successfully delivered and the Dictator's agent had promised to transfer the remaining five million pounds to Darke Desires within twenty-four hours of completing the inventory of goods received.

But then it had fallen disastrously apart.

Before the inventory had been completed the African Warlord had been assassinated by his long time opponent; all of his senior officials had been gaoled and all of the equipment had been seized.

Despite every tactic and strategy that Adrian and his team could employ they'd been refused payment point blank and had been told that the equipment had been forfeit. Furthermore, they'd been left under no illusion that any attempt to try to recover it would be considered an act of aggression that would be dealt with in the severest manner.

Effectively, the entire shipment had been lost.

The crime syndicate had been utterly uncompromising in its demand for payment and everybody at Darke Desires had known that it would have been life threatening if they hadn't paid.

This had left the company in the red to the tune of four million pounds.

Adrian had transferred two million pounds of his personal fortune to the company but he had had to borrow a further two million pounds from Darke Industries on the pretext of carrying out major rebuilding works to his home at Brandworth Farm.

The Directors had agreed to his request on the proviso that the money be paid back to Darke Industries from the three and a half million pounds agreed for the purchase of Brandworth farmland by the Highways Agency for the siting of a section of the new M6631 motorway.

And that was the rectilinear section of land to the west of Brandworth Farm. Nothing could be allowed to jeopardise that sale.

He stared at the Town Clerk in total silence until his equanimity stabilised and then said, "Go on, I'm listening."

Giles said, "It is a fact that the Chance family may never be able to regain possession of that piece of land on Hobb's Moor but the documentation that I possess is genuine and very compelling. Furthermore I have spoken to lawyers who specialise in land ownership and have been advised that if the paperwork is authentic, there would most definitely be case to answer. They also advised that the action would attract all sorts of attention ranging from specialist lawyers, similar potential claimants, land owners and so on right through to the media; so in short, the uniqueness of the case would make it impossible to ignore."

He paused for a second and then continued, "And then of course who could possibly predict the outcome? The considerations are so varied and widespread that it would be anybody's guess.

The only thing that I'd be prepared to put money on would be the colossal possibility that the ensuing civil action would freeze any proposed developments up there for years. Maybe even long enough to persuade the Highways Agency to seek an alternative route for the new motorway."

Adrian pursed his lips and then said, "And I suppose that meeting your demands would be a solution to all of my problems?"

"Yes, once I have receipt of the money I will invite you to watch me destroy all of the documents relating to Whitewall land ownership."

Adrian remained quiet for a few seconds and never once removed his eyes from the Town Clerk. He wasn't about to let a Council pen-pusher start dictating terms to him yet he could not allow anything to get in the way of that sale. As he sat staring at the man opposite him an idea started to form.

"Before I pay you anything," he eventually said, "I want to see proof of what you say."

"Please give me some credit," said Giles, "do you really think that I'd come here with a demand like this if I didn't have the documentation to back it up?"

"Nevertheless, I want to see proof."

"Very well," said Giles tediously, "where and when?"

Adrian flicked through his diary and said, "Bring it here the day after tomorrow at 10:30am. If you have what you say I'll consider your proposal."

Giles stood up and extended his right hand, "OK," he said, "it's a deal.

Adrian looked down and said, "I'm not shaking your hand you blackmailing shit. You know what you have to do, get the fuck out of my office."

Giles withdrew his hand, shrugged and walked out.

As soon as the door had closed, Adrian reached across to his intercom and pressed one of the buttons.

"Yes boss?"

"Is Burke still outside in the Jag?"

"Yes boss."

"Right, tell him to follow the guy in the grey pinstripe suit with dark curly hair who'll be leaving the visitors' car park in a few minutes time and to keep him under surveillance until I say. Is that clear?"

"Yes boss."

Adrian thought for a second and pressed the intercom again.

"Yes boss."

"And send for FA Cup."

Chapter 21

24th July 2002. The incident at Whitewall Farm

"Sir, look at that!"

Crowthorne and Naomi leaned forward and looked out of the windscreen of the police car. At the bottom of the long driveway they saw team members running to the perimeters of the farmyard and disappearing through open doorways whilst others retreated behind walls and ducked down.

"Good God." said Crowthorne to the driver, "Pull up before we enter the yard and let me see what's happening." He turned back to Naomi and said, "You stay in the car until I say."

Naomi nodded.

As the driver stopped the powerful BMW beside the imposing eighteenth century gateposts one of the younger forensic archaeologists appeared from nowhere and jumped into the back.

"Holy Christ am I glad to see you…?" he said breathlessly. He cast a glance to his right and saw Naomi, "Sorry I didn't mean to offend…"

Naomi said nothing.

"Yes, yes," said Crowthorne, "what's happened?"

"Something's just gone absolutely berserk in one of the rooms."

"*Berserk?* What do you mean something's just gone berserk?"

"I mean exactly what I say; something just went absolutely mental in the room next to the finds room."

"For pity's sake," said Crowthorne, "you're supposed to be a scientist, explain yourself properly."

The forensic archaeologist looked across the farmyard and said, "Look, how the hell am I supposed to know. All I can tell you is that some, some, bloody huge sounding animal, a dog I think, just had a major conniption fit in what we thought was an empty room and it's scared the shit out of us…" he faltered as he saw the girl and said, "Sorry…"

"No problem," said Naomi. She shot a quick glance at the

occupants of the police car and realised that she was the only one who might be able to explain what was happening. She closed her eyes and desperately hoped that she was wrong.

The archaeologist cut across her thoughts and said, "I'm not usually so crass but whatever made that noise put the fear of God up me."

Crowthorne looked across the deserted yard and said, "And have you checked to see if anything's in there?"

"Absolutely bloody not!" said the archaeologist, "I wouldn't go anywhere near that room. You should have heard it, it sounded totally deranged."

Crowthorne frowned, put his hand up to his mouth and stared at the door in question; for once in his life he didn't know what to do. He hated dogs and thought of dealing with one, let alone a deranged one, filled him with concern. He took in a deep breath and turned back to face the others.

"All right," he said, "here's what we'll…"

"*Sir!*" The police driver pointed through the windscreen.

On the opposite side of the yard the door had opened and Francesca Drake, one of the female team members had staggered out. She lunged forwards, stumbling and falling in an effort to get away from the room.

Without thinking Crowthorne jumped out of the car and ran towards her.

He got half way across the yard when a howl that would have stopped a charging bear erupted from the room in front of him. He didn't just hear it; he felt it. It plunged sickeningly icy fingers into his chest and squeezed his heart. Terror spread through him like a cold primeval wave and stopped him dead in his tracks.

He stood in petrified silence and listened as the sound of the horrendous howl receded across the top of the moors.

"Please help me…" begged Francesca.

Crowthorne heard her pleading but couldn't move, his legs felt like jelly. He remained motionless and stared intently at the door behind her.

"Please, Inspector…"

The second call for help shook Crowthorne into action; he ran forwards, grabbed the distraught woman and yanked her to her feet.

"Come on," he said pulling her towards the police car, "let's get you out of here." He looked up and saw the driver staring at him.

"*Cooper get over here!*" he shouted.

The driver didn't move.

Intent on dragging the stricken woman, Crowthorne didn't notice at first, but when he looked he was stunned to see that the driver hadn't moved.

"*Cooper, get your arse over here now!*" he shouted.

With an enormous bang, a door slammed behind him.

Francesca turned, looked back across the farmyard and said, "Oh God, no..."

Crowthorne could feel his heart hammering; he stared steadfastly at Cooper as he approached the police car but just knew that something bad was going to happen.

Suddenly, Cooper's eyes widened with fear and he involuntarily shifted backwards in his seat.

A black shadow emerged from the room and started to form into a shape.

Cooper swallowed hard and watched as it approached the car; twisting and spiralling it snaked blackly across the yard then suddenly curled up into the air and hovered directly above them.

In his highly agitated state of mind he half expected it to form into a hideous demon and come screaming down upon them, but almost as quickly as it had appeared it thinned and vanished as though it had never been there.

Then whilst all eyes were gazing upwards, the door from whence it had come slammed with such a deafening crash that everybody squealed out or recoiled in fear.

Crowthorne didn't think he could take any more; he felt as though his legs were made of lead. The distraught woman felt like a ton weight in his arms but through sheer dogged determination he finally managed to get her into the rear of the police car.

He then quickly jumped in the front and locked the door.

With utter disregard for his superior officer and the two women in the car Cooper said, "What the *fuck* was that?"

"Flies," said Naomi, "That was a huge swarm of flies." She hesitated and then said, "And the other is... is..."

Crowthorne wheeled around and said, "Mrs. Draper please, if

181

you know something I need you to tell me about it now."

From her seat in the rear of the police car Naomi saw the concerned faces and knew that it was up to her to help where she could, but…

"Mrs. Draper, please!" repeated Crowthorne.

Naomi looked down at her hands and could see them physically shaking, she closed her eyes and took a deep breath.

The thumb was pressing heavily down upon her shoulder and the voices were overwhelming.

It reminded her of turning on a radio and being unable to find the correct channel. As her mind swept across the choice of 'stations', one voice above all others was the most clear, it was the one saying *"This way Maria, this way…"* She kept seeing diaphanous images of the left hand within her mind, but this time the hand had grown into an arm adorned in a cream cotton sleeve with an elasticated cuff. Even more disconcertingly, the hand was no longer pointing down but directly in front of her towards the room that everybody was staring at.

"Mrs. Draper," said Crowthorne, "I know I can't force you, but if you do know anything that could help us to understand what's going on, now would be a *really* good time to tell us!"

Crowthorne's anxiousness cut across Naomi's thoughts. She looked up and said, "All right, listen…"

She quickly told them about the numerous reports of inexplicable sightings and doglike sounds, and how they had been attributed to the long dead Sugg.

Crowthorne listened in silence and then shook his head.

"Look, I'm sorry if this offends you, but I don't believe in all that, that… nonsense and from what I can gather here, it sounds as though we are dealing with something more real and down to earth than the figment of anybody's imagination."

"But, but…" said Francesca.

"Perhaps if you knew as much about us and this place as we do," said Naomi curtly, "you'd realise that we are just as down to earth as you are Chief Inspector, but obviously with far more open minds!"

Crowthorne shrugged his shoulders and said, "O.K., I respect your views and we'll agree to disagree but in my limited experience I've found that most ghostly goings on can usually be explained away quite rationally."

He shot a quick glance into the farmyard and then added, "However, I will grant you that this occurrence does appear to be a little more difficult to rationalise."

Following one or two seconds brooding silence he realised that he was the senior figure of authority and that everybody would be waiting for him to do something.

He took a deep breath and said "All right, let's see what's really going on." He looked at Naomi and said, "You wait here with Cooper and don't come any closer until I'm satisfied that it's safe."

Naomi nodded.

"Chief Inspector…" said Francesca.

Crowthorne ignored her, got out of the car and called across to one of the duty constables.

"You there, follow me and don't let anybody come any closer until I've checked inside that room."

The constable responded with a 'Yes sir,' and nervously took up position a few yards behind his superior.

Crowthorne could clearly see the room in question; it was located to the side of the main buildings and adjacent to what appeared to be a barn. The single, black painted split-level door was still ajar and the interior was in darkness.

He turned and called to no-one in particular, *"Are there any lights in there?"*

"There were," shouted an anonymous voice, *"but they all fused when that sound came."*

Crowthorne turned to the constable and said, "There's a flashlight in the car. Go and get it."

The constable quickly retrieved the flashlight, handed it to his Chief Inspector and resumed a position behind him.

Crowthorne was aware that everyone's eyes were upon him; he quickly checked to see that the torch was working and crept reluctantly towards the room.

He got to within ten feet or so of the door when it suddenly and violently slammed shut again causing him to stop dead in his tracks. This time a high pitched shrieking emanated from the room followed by such a cacophony that it sounded as though all the demons of hell had broken loose.

He dropped the torch, covered his ears and screwed up his eyes as did the constable behind him.

Suddenly something crashed into the back of the door with such violence that the two policemen jumped back in alarm. They started retreating backwards as quickly as they could without taking their eyes off the door; they heard it being repeatedly smashed into from the other side with a sound that was horrendous and utterly terrifying.

Every hair on Crowthorne's body was standing on end, he just wanted to run and keep on running but his character wouldn't allow it and once he'd put enough space between him and the door he adopted a defensive posture and held his ground. He stared wide-eyed at the door in case it should break and release whatever God forsaken thing was inside. And then, just as if somebody had thrown a switch, it stopped.

Everybody outside was frozen with fear and gaped at the door in total silence.

Crowthorne became aware that he could hear no birdsong, no buzzing insects, no wind, nothing, just silence; an eerie and prolonged silence.

Nobody moved a muscle.

Inside the police car Naomi watched in petrified silence. The thumb was pressing heavily down on her shoulder and all the voices but the one with the arm had stopped. She could still hear it saying *"This way Maria, this way…"*, but this time it wasn't stopping there. It was also saying, *"In the parlour, you remember…"*

She could see more of the woman; her shoulder was now in view but nothing else. As she struggled to focus upon what she was seeing, she suddenly realised that the hand hadn't been pointing to the room from which the awful sounds had been coming but slightly to the right, towards what appeared to be an open-fronted storage area.

Her mind was in utter turmoil, she could feel Francesca tugging at her sleeve and trying to convey something, she could see Crowthorne standing nervously in front of the car and she desperately wanted to tell him what she was experiencing, but his earlier contempt for anything out of the ordinary put her off.

She decided there and then that she would tell Carlton about her unusual experiences, and if possible persuade him to come with her to Whitewall at a later date to pursue what the voice was trying to tell her.

In front of the car, and following a couple of minutes of complete silence Crowthorne relaxed his defensive posture and gingerly took a step towards the room.

With an ear-shattering crash he suddenly heard the sound of breaking wood and thought that the door had finally disintegrated under the strain. He turned and ran for his life. He dropped down onto his haunches behind the police car with his back to the number plate and closed his eyes. He'd never experienced anything so terrifying and he was shattered.

Following several of the tensest minutes of his life he peered out from behind the car and saw to his amazement that the door was still intact. He wondered if whatever had been in there had found another way out and looked nervously for the slightest signs of movement.

The seconds ticked tortuously by but only silence ensued.

He felt wrecked; his heart was beating wildly and he was in turmoil.

Nobody else moved.

Suddenly, the black door swung half open.

Crowthorne ducked again and closed his eyes; he no longer cared what anybody else thought.

A huge wheezing, gasping sound erupted from the room followed by such a foul stench that all those near enough covered their noses in an attempt to avoid breathing it in.

Everybody waited for something else to happen but as the seconds ticked by it became obvious that whatever had occurred had finished.

Birdsong could suddenly be heard again, and one by one everyone started to relax, faces nervously re-appeared from behind hiding places and small pockets of nervous and animated conversation started.

Crowthorne instantly quelled all sound by standing up and raising his hand in the air. He tentatively made his way towards the room, picked up and switched on the torch and peered inside.

Everybody waited with baited breath and nobody would have

swapped places with the policeman at that time.

Everything seemed still; and having satisfied himself that the room was indeed empty, Crowthorne called to Professor Catchpole the senior forensic archaeologist to join him.

"Does everything look all right in there to you Gordon?" he said, pointing to the interior.

The Professor nervously edged forwards until he could see inside the room.

"It seems to be, nothing ha... whoa, whoa!" he turned to Crowthorne who'd stopped dead.

"Give me your torch will you please?" He took the torch from Crowthorne and shone it into the far corner of the room.

"Good God!" he exclaimed, "Look at that!"

The two men peered inside and then nervously entered to look at where the Professor was shining the torch.

They could see what appeared to be broken pieces of wood sticking up out of the ground; they looked at one another and then moved in closer.

Slowly the Professor kneeled down and then said, "There's something under here."

"Isn't that just part of your excavation?"

"No. We haven't looked in this room yet."

The Professor cautiously brushed some light soil from around the broken pieces of wood and said, "Crikey Bob it's the top of a large barrel, but the pieces of wood are facing upwards, not down."

"What are you driving at?" said Crowthorne.

"What I'm saying is, if we had indiscriminately beaten open the top of the barrel from here, the pieces of lid would have dropped down inside; but these are facing up not down. Or put more simply, it looks as though something or other has broken out."

Crowthorne said nothing.

Slowly the Professor leaned over the breakage, directed the torch beam down and peered inside the barrel. He instantly recoiled and said, "Shit! Look in there!"

Crowthorne took the torch from the Professor, made his way past him and aimed the light into the top of the barrel. As the interior illuminated he saw a huge stack of bones.

"Oh Good Lord!" he said, "They're human!"

He shone the torch slowly around the barrel and said, "And there's more than one; I can see at least two skulls and fragments of clothing…"

He turned to look at the Professor kneeling down behind him and said, "This is the second lot. What in God's name has been going on up here?"

The Professor shook his head and shrugged his shoulders in the darkness.

"I've no idea Bob, and no doubt I'll be able to shed more light on things in due course, but bones I can handle; what bothers me is, where did that bloody dog go?

Look about you, there are no windows and doors other than those we could see from the farmyard, so where is it?"

Crowthorne quickly scanned the room and found to his own amazement that he hadn't really expected to find anything physical in the room once the sound had subsided and the door had swung open. This of course made a nonsense of his own stated misgivings to Naomi earlier and had him seriously re-evaluating his rationale.

"And," said the Professor cutting across Crowthorne's thoughts, "what caused the barrel to burst open like that? Either I'm missing some vital piece of evidence or something's seriously out of kilter with what we would consider to be normal here!"

Crowthorne shivered involuntarily, looked around in the gloom and said, "I can't answer you Gordon, but right now I've had enough of this place, let's get back outside into the daylight."

Chapter 22

1st July 1869. The Twist Pit

Back in the countryside of the Roch Valley, Caleb was beginning to lose patience with Hugo as Wiggins scrabbled about outside looking for his missing pocket watch.

"What's so important about that timepiece anyway?" he said in an aggravated way.

"It belonged to my father and I don't want to lose it!" said an equally aggravated Hugo, who was by now finding his companion's constant complaints tedious.

Caleb looked out of the window of the carriage.

"If it wasn't so bloody rainy out there I'd go and help him look."

"There is no need," said Hugo, "Wiggins is a good man. If it can be found, he'll find it."

Ten minutes later a very bedraggled looking driver appeared at the door of the carriage and reported his apparent inability to be able to find the missing piece.

"You probably dropped it when you were re-covering the pit after we holed that bastard clerk," said Caleb.

"That's true!" said Hugo with a renewed enthusiasm. He turned to Wiggins and said, "Go and move some of the stones covering the entrance, it's probably amongst them somewhere."

"Very well sir." The driver knuckled his forehead and turned away cursing under his breath.

"Oh, and Wiggins," called Hugo from the comfort of the carriage interior, "do be careful. If it isn't already broken, I don't want you breaking it!"

"Very good sir." Wiggins squelched across to the stones covering the entrance and started to remove them one by one. The rain was so heavy that it had completely soaked through his clothing and he could feel it running over his back and down his legs.

He set about the task and thought about the package in the

luggage compartment; he grinned to himself and couldn't wait to see what kind of reaction it would get when the master opened it up.

One by one he removed the stones, knowing exactly where he'd laid the pocket watch until finally he uncovered it. He retrieved it, wiped it on his coat and placed it in his pocket. He turned around to return to the coach and was shocked to see Abraham in front of him with both arms raised in the air.

He looked up and saw that Abraham was holding the heavy bulbous ended stick and that it was aimed directly at his head.

"What..." he shouted, *"Wait! What have I done?"* He stumbled backwards in a vain attempt to avoid the blow, but it was far too late.

With a deep whooshing sound Abraham brought the stick crashing down.

Wiggins ducked to the left. The stick smashed into his right collarbone and broke it with a loud crack. He screamed in agony as Abraham lifted the stick again, but before he could even think or react the stick crashed down a second time and caved in the top of his skull.

Abraham stood quietly in the rain and dropped the stick to the ground; he watched the twitching body in front of him as the life spirit shook its way out of the weak man-flesh. It was a sight he'd seen on numerous occasions and it always intrigued him.

Inside the carriage, Hugo was mortified; he'd never expected Abraham to kill Wiggins - he had to think quickly.

He looked at Caleb, saw that he was totally distracted by his father's actions and then quietly stood up behind him. He reached into his coat pocket, removed his ex-army revolver and brought it crashing down onto the top of the unsuspecting man's skull. He watched as Caleb collapsed into unconsciousness and fell onto the coach floor.

Back outside Abraham became aware of footsteps behind him.

"What did you have to do that for?" said Hugo, "I liked him, he was a good driver."

"Maybe so, but he was a witness to all that's gone on. Haven't you learned anything of what me and Caleb taught you?"

Hugo said nothing.

Abraham saw his friend's obvious distress and said, "Buck up Hugo there's plenty of good drivers around, now let's not waste any more time we've got to hole him."

He bent down, started to drag the remaining stones from the pit entrance and remembered his friend's pocket watch.

"Your timepiece is in the driver's jacket pocket." he said casually over his shoulder.

Hugo reached down, retrieved his father's watch, checked it and placed it carefully in his own waistcoat pocket.

"Come on then," said Abraham, "don't just stand there in the pissing rain, make yourself useful and give me a hand."

The two men quickly cleared away the stones and once more exposed the thick wooden beams that covered the pit. With several hard pulls there was enough of the entrance open to be able to complete their task.

Hugo made his way over to Wiggins's body, got hold of his feet and dragged him towards the open hole.

Abraham saw what was happening and stopped him; he leaned down, deftly went through Wiggins' pockets and retrieved a few coins for his trouble. With a grunt he nodded to Hugo and the two men manhandled the dead carriage driver to the edge of the pit.

"Do you want to say anything?" said Hugo.

"Like what?"

"I don't know, a few words, a pr…"

"Don't be so bloody stupid," said Abraham, "just push the bugger in!"

He shook his head incredulously and muttered, "Do I want to say anything indeed…"

With one or two more pushes, Wiggins' body disappeared over the edge and into the darkness. Both men listened for the usual impact sounds but to their surprise they heard nothing.

Abraham frowned and said, "Did you hear anything?"

Hugo shook his head.

Abraham was clearly troubled and leaned over the top of the pit in an effort to see inside, but it was too dark.

"Can you see anything?" said Hugo.

"No, nothing." said Abraham straining his eyes.

Both men stood for a moment until Hugo broke the silence.

"Well, I suppose if we can't see him, neither will anybody else."

"That's not the point," said Abraham, "we should have heard him hit. This pit has some old ladder bracings projecting into the shaft walls and he may have snagged one on the way down."

Hugo stood looking blankly at Abraham.

"Don't you understand? If ever the pit's opened up, happen he can be seen in full daylight."

"Maybe so, but we'll be covering it up anyway won't we?" said Hugo.

"Course we will you stupid bugger, but that doesn't mean nobody else could find it and look inside. The Council mine inspectors are always looking for rogue pits and when they find one, they usually just backfill it. They're hardly likely to do just that if they open this up and see your driver dangling down there like a marionette!"

Hugo drew in a deep breath and looked up; the rain appeared to have stopped its incessant pouring but the thought of having to remain any longer than he had to still irritated him.

"So what do you propose?" he said resignedly.

"I propose that we open it up fully to see if we can see what's happened."

He nodded in the direction of the coach and said, "Go and get Caleb, he can help us."

Hugo kept his wits about him and said, "The last I saw he'd nodded off in the coach. He did this on his own last time so we can manage without him now."

Abraham cast a glance in the direction of the coach and said, "All right but the lazy sod can help us cover it when we're done."

The two men removed the remaining beams until the entrance was completely exposed.

Hugo looked in first but it was so dark that he couldn't see a thing.

Abraham skirted around the edge and stared in too, but he was equally unsuccessful.

"That's bloody unusual," he said, "we should have heard something…"

"And are you completely sure that you can't see anything?"

"No not a thing…"

"Good, then my work here is done."

Abraham who was still peering into the darkness said, "*Your* work? Don't you mean *our* work?"

"No, I mean precisely what I said. *My* work here is done."

Abraham looked up and saw his friend standing a little way from the edge of the pit with a pistol in his hand. At first he wasn't sure what was happening and said, "What are you doing?"

"Learning from the master; you always taught me to tie up loose ends when a job was done."

Abraham looked at Hugo for a few seconds and wondered if he was playing some sort of macabre joke, but something about his face told him otherwise.

Menacingly he said, "Are you planning to kill me, Darke?"

Hugo saw the change in Abraham's demeanour but remained calm and didn't answer. He backed up to the rear of the coach, undid the buckles of the luggage compartment and swept the cover to one side.

Inside was a large wooden crate with holes drilled into it. Slowly and deliberately he undid the catches until it fell open with a crash. He then reached in and pulled out the contents.

Abraham's mouth fell open with astonishment as Sugg jumped obediently to the ground and stood looking at Hugo.

"You bastard!" he shouted, *"Where did you get him?"*

Sugg heard the voice and reacted immediately. He yanked his head around and nearly pulled Hugo off of his feet.

Abraham jumped backwards in alarm.

Hugo smiled as he put his pistol back in his pocket and said, "Pleasant surprise I take it?" He leaned down and removed Sugg's muzzle.

Sugg went into frenzy, snapping and snarling at Abraham.

Abraham backed away another few steps and repeated, "Where did you get him?"

"We came to visit you on the night Caleb was attacked and found him lying on your drive. Wiggins saw that he was still alive so we put him in the coach and left. It took months, but we eventually got him back to good health. Since then he's repaid our kindness by being a good and loyal guard dog; and we also knew that if we were ever going to have any trouble from you or Caleb, we'd have the animal to protect us."

The mention of Caleb's name reminded him of his son asleep

in the coach.

"And do you think yon Caleb's going to just sit there and let you get away with this? He'll tear your treacherous head off, you bastard!"

Hugo raised his eyebrows and coolly said, "Oh, didn't I mention, I've already taken care of him…"

Abraham leapt forwards in blind fury but Sugg counter-lunged snapping and snarling towards him. He stopped abruptly; he needed time to calm his mind. If he was to have any chance at all, it wouldn't be by making rash moves.

"Why are you doing this Darke?" he said, "I thought that we were friends…"

Hugo calmed Sugg and said, "We were and I'm genuinely sorry it has come to this but all this killing is too much for me and I don't want to be associated with it or you anymore."

"But you don't have to do this!" said Abraham.

"I do, you taught me so. I want a clean break from both of you and killing Wiggins has given me the perfect opportunity. Given your history with the local police it will be easy to convince them that you stopped the coach in an attempt to rob me and killed my driver in doing so. I will tell them that I shot you both and plead self defence."

"You traitorous bastard!" said Abraham, "And how will you explain yon pit?"

"I'll cover it before I leave and deny all knowledge of it."

"And why did you bring the dog, was he part of your plan too?"

Abraham remembered that his throwing knife was tucked inside his right gaiter and desperately tried to think of a way to distract Hugo. He edged a little closer.

"Partly," said Hugo, "but mostly I brought him for protection."

Abraham was in awe at the sheer deviousness of his erstwhile friend and was stunned to think that he could have been planning this for a long time. He'd thought that they'd been friends and he berated himself for placing so much trust in him. Anger and hate started to bubble up.

The idea came to him in an instant. He suddenly looked over to the carriage door, feigned surprise and said, "I thought you'd finished the boy off!"

Hugo spun around, saw nothing and turned back in time to see Abraham drop down to one knee. In a moment of panic he let go of Sugg's lead and made a grab for his gun...

Suddenly he felt a searing pain in his left breast and looked down in disbelief. A knife was sticking out of his chest. He felt a gurgling sensation in his left lung and within seconds coughed up blood. He clutched at the knife handle, dropped down to his knees and fell onto his side.

Abraham saw Sugg leap towards him snapping and snarling and ducked away at the last moment.

Sugg raced past his right shoulder and then wheeled around and came back at him on the run.

Abraham quickly whipped around but it was too late.

Sugg leapt open-mouthed and snapped his huge jaws around Abraham's face. His fangs sank into flesh and bone; warm blood ran onto his tongue and he heard squeals of agony as he dragged his old tormentor along the ground viciously shaking his head from side to side. He kept it up relentlessly until he heard a cracking sound and felt the man he most hated fall limp.

He stopped walking and held onto Abraham's head for several seconds then dropped it onto the ground with a heavy thud. Almost impassively he looked down, sniffed at the body a few times and then quietly walked back to the injured Hugo.

Inside the coach Caleb slowly came to, he sat up and rubbed the top of his head. He looked out of the carriage door and could hardly credit the scene in front of him.

To his absolute horror he saw Sugg standing next to the prone figure of Hugo and presumed that the dog had killed him. A little further away he could see his father lying motionless on the ground too. He couldn't begin to understand what had happened, but leapt instinctively out of the coach and ran towards Sugg.

He snatched up the heavy wooden stick and swung it at the pre-occupied dog catching him in the side.

Sugg let out a yelp and spun around to face his attacker.

Caleb squared up to Sugg, when a shot suddenly rang out from behind him; a bullet whistled past his right ear and he whirled around to see where it had come from.

Lying a few feet away was Hugo, head up and staring at him

with blood frothing around his lips; a smoking gun was in his right hand and he was trying to cock it again with his left.

Caleb swiftly looked back and saw that Sugg had disappeared. He then ran across to Hugo, snatched the gun out of his hand and said "What are you doing? You nearly shot me you idiot!"

Hugo said nothing, he knew that the end was near and he didn't want any more pain than he already had.

Caleb looked down and caught sight of his father's knife sticking out of Hugo's chest. He frowned as he tried to understand it all. He didn't know where Sugg had come from, what had happened to his father and how Hugo had ended up being stabbed; none of it made sense.

He looked down and said, "What happened? Where did Sugg come from? And who the fuck hit me on the head?"

Hugo said nothing.

Caleb stared at him for a few seconds and wondered if he was unable to answer. He said more forcefully, "Hugo! What happened? Speak to me!"

Hugo remained silent.

Caleb was mystified. He quickly cast his mind back to when he was in the coach and realised that the only person who could have hit him was Hugo. He looked down into the face of his friend and said, "Did you do all this?" He grabbed hold of Hugo's jacket and yanked him partially up. "Answer me! Did you do all of this?"

Hugo felt as though he was drowning, he coughed up some more blood but remained silent.

"You did didn't you? You hit me on the head and set Sugg onto pa…"

The mention of his father's name made him wheel around to look at him; he dropped Hugo back onto the ground and quickly ran across to where Abraham's body was lying.

He looked down at his father's dreadfully disfigured face and let out a howl of anguish. "*You bastard Darke, you did this didn't you?*"

Hugo still said nothing.

Caleb ran back, dropped down onto what he now considered his father's killer and smashed the butt of the gun into Hugo's mouth, breaking all of his front teeth.

"First," he said coldly looking down at the agonised man

below him, "I'm going to kill you. Then I'm going to Brandworth Manor and I'm going to kill every one of your fucking brood. First your sons, then your wife; and after I've had a little special fun with your daughters, I'll kill them too."

Hugo looked pleadingly and shook his head.

Caleb leaned a little closer and said, "And guess what? They're all going to die slowly. Slowly, and *very* fucking painfully…"

He saw the look of horror on Hugo's face and said, "But right now it's your turn."

With his left hand he grabbed hold of Hugo's coat, yanked his head up off the ground, jammed the barrel of the gun into his left eye socket and pulled the trigger.

The back of his ex-friend's head exploded. Blood and soft tissue splashed back into his face then dripped slowly onto Hugo's body as he stared at him.

He let the sound of the shot dissipate then stood up and wiped his face on the sleeve of his jacket. He looked down at Hugo's corpse and shouted, "*You backstabbing bastard, I hope you rot in fucking hell!*"

He put the pistol in his pocket, retrieved the knife from Hugo's chest, wiped it and slipped it into his right gaiter. He then rolled Hugo's body to the edge of the pit, took the valuables from his pockets and unceremoniously kicked him over the edge. He heard the body hit the bottom with a satisfying thud.

Once completed, he stood up and scoured the surrounding trees for any signs of Sugg and then instinctively checked to make sure that the gun was still loaded. He was aware that between them they'd made a good deal of noise and he suddenly felt the urge to get away.

He walked across to his father's body and knelt down by his side.

"I'm sorry I let you down pa," he said trying not to look at his badly mauled face, "but I will do for those bastard Darkes, you just see if I don't."

He reached down and cradled the head of the only human being that he had ever loved; held on for a few precious seconds then said, "I've got to go now but I'm sending you down to ma, she can look after you from now on."

He looked down and tried to obliterate the reality of what he was seeing; closed his eyes and kissed the forehead of his beloved pater.

In a final gesture of care, he fastened the buttons of his father's large overcoat and then gently eased him to the edge of the pit. He sat down at right angles to his body and began to push.

"Hey, mister! What are you doing?"

Caleb spun around and saw a young boy staring at him from approximately fifty yards away. He was mortified; he'd no idea where the boy had come from, nor how much he had seen.

He knew that he could never catch him with a damaged leg, so he snatched the pistol out of his pocket, cocked it and fired straight at him.

The boy let out a terrified shriek and started to run.

Caleb cocked the gun again, took careful aim and fired.

The bullet screeched past the boy and crashed into the foliage at the side of the valley.

Exasperatedly he re-cocked the gun once more, but by the time he'd lifted it the boy had gone.

This was a disaster. The boy had been close enough to identify him, Hugo and Wiggins were at the bottom of the pit with two others, including his own mother, and his father lay dead in front of him.

There was no way that he would not be directly implicated with everything that had happened, and if the boy had seen him kill Hugo, it would be the gallows for sure.

He needed to get away; away from the pit, away from Whitewall and a long way away from anybody who knew him.

He realised that it would be pointless to push his father's body into the pit, so he leaned down kissed his head one last time and said, "Got to go pa."

He ran across to the carriage, unharnessed one of the horses, grabbed the reins and pulled himself up. Without looking back he galloped away as fast as he could.

Seconds after Caleb had departed, Sugg padded back into the valley bottom; he walked across to where Abraham was lying and sniffed around until he was sure that he had his other old tormentor's scent.

Within less than five minutes he'd set off in pursuit.

Chapter 23

24th July 2002

On the return journey from Whitewall Farm Naomi had calmed her mind by thinking of two things; one was Mexican fajitas and the other was Carlton Wilkes.

Her father had surprised her by telling her that he was arriving in Walmsfield the next day on what could turn into an extended visit and naturally she had invited him to stay with her. Fajitas were one of his favourites, so she wanted to make sure that she had some in time for his arrival. That had to be a trip to the supermarket.

Carlton Wilkes, however, was something else. Over the weeks since Sandra's death the two of them had lunched together almost every working day, and as the time had passed she'd felt a growing attraction towards him. During the last two weeks, she'd had to stop herself staring at him whenever he'd looked away for fear of him suddenly turning around and seeing her. She'd found herself daydreaming about him, imagining what it would be like to be a bigger part of his life, and though she'd known that there was an eight year age difference between them, she hadn't cared.

She'd relocated to the north-west of England to be with her ex-husband Andy, who'd had to move due to a promotion from within his company, but six month's after the move and to everybody's astonishment including his own family, Andy had announced that he'd fallen in love with somebody else.

The split up had been painful but speedy and though she'd had the option to return south, she'd decided to stay at her post within Walmsfield Borough Council. It had represented a promotion for her and lots more autonomy too.

For the next twelve months she'd immersed herself in her work and hadn't really thought about anybody else until Carlton Wilkes had started pervading her every thought.

She leaned her head back on the headrest of the police car,

closed her eyes and tried to imagine what it would be like to be in his arms.

A little after 7:00pm the same day Carlton sat alone in his lounge hugging a bottle of Belgian Beer; he looked around and saw that everywhere was pretty much immaculate - immaculate and clinical. The carpet had been vacuum cleaned to within an inch of its life, no dust could be seen anywhere, not even on the screen of his thirty-two inch television, and every ornament remained precisely were his late wife had placed them.

Outside the evening sun was still shining, and as he sat slouched in his chair wearing nothing but shorts and a polo shirt, he suddenly felt lonely.

His wife Mena had died five years earlier as a result of breast cancer. She'd discovered a lump but had remained silent for ten months before informing anybody; and when she finally had, she'd done so because she'd known that it had grown. He'd been devastated and annoyed by his wife's stupidity but his ultimate loss had been shattering. For years he'd left things where she'd put them. He hadn't cared what people had said about clearing out her clothes and personal belongings, he'd been happy to see them; it had reminded him of how much he'd loved her, and would continue to love her.

The house was silent except for the odd creak caused by the slowly setting sun; he gazed around the room and made a mental note that the ceiling would benefit from a lick of white paint in the autumn.

He raised the bottle to his lips, took a sip and looked at his watch for the umpteenth time. He tried to rationalise why he'd started to feel impatient; he'd never usually paid attention to time in the evenings and the silence and emptiness of his lounge had been all right for the last few years, but now it wasn't.

He got up and walked to the open back door. His hundred foot garden was a modest one laid out mostly to lawn with a central path leading to a hard standing on which stood his shed and a small red and white sailing dinghy. He was miles from the sea in Walmsfield, but there were one or two good sized lakes within a few miles and when the whim took him he was able to indulge in one of his favourite pastimes, sailing.

The grass was cut, the bushes trimmed, the exterior of the house was painted, the shed and fences creosoted, his garden furniture was varnished and his small patio was clean and adequately pointed. In short, nothing needed doing.

He looked down at his watch again and found that a whole five minutes had passed since his last check. He took another sip of beer, wandered across to his wooden bench and sat down in an attempt to soak up the last of the evening sun.

As the heat warmed his face, he tilted his head backwards and wondered what Naomi was doing. He had her mobile number and wondered whether to call her, but each time he came up with an apparently valid reason to do so, he realised that it was just dross and that she would probably think that he was unnecessarily disturbing her at home. He put the cordless telephone down on his garden table, sat back in his seat and reached for the bottle of beer. On picking it up, he saw that it was all but gone so he ambled back into his kitchen for another cold one from his refrigerator.

He'd just extracted the bottle when the phone rang. He didn't rush to answer it expecting that it was just an annoying sales call which nearly always seemed to coincide with him taking the first forkful of his evening meal.

Unhurriedly, he opened the bottle and then casually walked back to the garden seat. The phone stopped ringing.

"Ce'st la vie…" he said out loud as he held up the beer bottle in acknowledgement

The telephone rang again.

"O.K.," he said reaching for it, "let's see what's on offer this evening…" He clicked it on and said, "Yes good evening, it is wonderfully peaceful in my back garden, the sun is shining here in England and I have a small beer in my hand. Now, what's this evening's entertainment going to be?"

"Carlton, it's Naomi."

He sat bolt upright in his seat and said, "Naomi! Sorry, I thought that it was just one of those annoying sales calls that you get just before you start dinner."

"I haven't caught you about to eat have I?" said Naomi.

"No, no you haven't, I just meant, that they normally call when…" He realised that he was sounding flustered, "…well, you know what I mean, don't you?"

Naomi couldn't help herself from teasing, and though she knew perfectly well what Carlton was talking about she said, "No, sorry, what do you mean?"

"I mean, when those sales people normally ring, it's usually just when you're going to eat."

"But you said you aren't about to eat didn't you?" Naomi hoped that Carlton couldn't hear her smirking at the other end of the line.

"Yes, er, I mean no…"

"Yes?" cut in Naomi.

"No!"

"No I don't know, or no you aren't about to eat?" Naomi could hear Carlton getting more tongue-tied as the conversation went on and loved it.

"No, I don't mean you don't know, I mean no, I'm not about to eat…"

"Ah," said Naomi unable to control her mirth any longer, "well at least that's as clear as mud then!"

Carlton paused for a moment, and the penny dropped.

"You minx!" he said, "I thought that…"

"You thought that I didn't know whether you knew that I knew whether or not I should know whether you were about to eat or not. Is that about it… or not?"

"*What?*" said Carlton; then down the other end of the line he heard Naomi laughing.

"You just wait until I get to work tomorrow Naomi Draper, I'll have you on the mat for that!

"Ooh, Carlton Wilkes," said Naomi, "that does sound interesting, but you must promise to close the door before you dress me down!"

Carlton hadn't felt so alive in years, he wanted to say all sorts of things to Naomi, but simply said, "Hmm. Now perhaps you'll tell me why you called?"

Naomi paused for a second and then said, "O.K., all joking aside, I'd like to talk to you about Whitewall and some odd feelings I've been having."

"What kind of odd feelings?"

"They're difficult to explain, especially over the phone." Naomi paused hoping that Carlton would take the hint.

"And do I take it that you'd rather talk in private than at work?"

"No, I mean yes"

Carlton jumped straight onto the bandwagon.

"Was that no, you'd rather not talk at work or yes you'd rather talk in private?" It was Carlton's turn to smile.

"Yes I'd rather not talk at work…" Naomi suddenly realised what Carlton was doing and instead of forcefully saying '*Carlton!*' by way of admonishment, she made a slip of the tongue and simply said, "*Cal!*"

"Did you just call me Cal?"

"Yes, it just slipped out - sorry!"

"Don't apologise, nobody's ever called me that before. I rather like it."

"Then I shall call you Cal from now on." said Naomi, "but only if you promise that you'll let nobody else call you that."

"It's a promise." Carlton suddenly felt as though he'd taken a huge step towards her. He smiled to himself and with a boosted confidence said, "About these odd feelings, would you like to talk about them over a drink one night?"

The words had no sooner left his mouth when he suddenly remembered the age difference between them and became embarrassed in case he'd interpreted things wrongly. He quickly said, "Not that it's a date or anything like that, I wouldn't presume…"

"Cal, shush!" said Naomi, "A drink would be lovely, but not for a week or so because my father is arriving for a stay." She had an afterthought and said, "Would you like to meet him one lunchtime while he's here?"

"Yes of course." said Carlton.

"Good, O.K., I'll pop into your office tomorrow and arrange things then."

"All right, I'll see you tomorrow."

Carlton put down the phone, picked up his bottle of beer and took a long drink; he slowly looked around and nowhere seemed quite as empty as it had before.

Chapter 24

One day after the incident at Whitewall, Giles returned to Darke Industries H.Q. for his second meeting with Adrian and as he waited for the lift to take him up to the executive suite he couldn't help thinking that it was a shame that this day had arrived.

On the one hand he would be very happy to be in receipt of half a million pounds, but on the other, he wasn't sure how Adrian would react when he showed him his 'proof'.

He'd considered copying the files and bringing those for Adrian to see and depositing the originals in a bank vault as a form of insurance, but he'd ultimately dismissed that idea in case they were ever discovered and linked to his illegal deal.

He also secretly nursed a regret that given the age of the documents, it truly was going to be a tragedy to have to destroy such an important piece of local history particularly when his predecessor Surnh Horrocks had succeeded in preserving them long enough to be able to see justice finally prevail.

But emotion had had to be set aside; he knew that he had no option but to destroy them as agreed, and in the presence of Adrian Darke. That way nothing could ever be discovered that would associate him with Whitewall at all.

The lift arrived and he stepped inside. The interior was adorned with mirrors and as he stared at each reflected image in turn, he could only see a guilty-looking face over and over again disappearing into oblivion. He shivered and wondered whether fate was giving him a glimpse of the future.

The lift arrived at the top floor and he stepped once again into the opulent splendour of Adrian's personal suite.

Adrian got straight to the point and said, "Did you bring them?"

Giles lifted up his briefcase and patted it by way of an answer.

"Right, let me see."

Giles opened up his briefcase, extracted the leather document holder and opened it up on Adrian's desk.

Adrian quickly spread the contents around, flicked open the odd letter and then looked up at Giles.

"This is nothing; it's just old correspondence and receipts." He quickly looked down again and flicked through more papers but found nothing of any substance.

"This may be what you are looking for." Giles held up a C3 sized envelope.

Adrian snatched it from Giles and pulled out the contents.

"These are photocopies! What are you playing at Eaton?"

"Do you think that I'm stupid enough to bring all the documents here without seeing any cash?

The originals of the papers that you are holding are the documents that prove historic Chance ownership of Whitewall. I'll let you digest the contents and decide for yourself, and once you have made your decision and paid me my five hundred thousand I will destroy the originals, in your company, and our deal will be concluded."

Adrian glared at Giles for a few seconds and then leaned over and pressed a button on his intercom.

"Yes boss?"

"Send FA Cup in."

"Yes boss."

Giles frowned and waited in silence until he heard a knock on the office door.

"Come!" called Adrian.

The door opened and the largest, grimmest looking man Giles had ever seen quietly stepped in. He watched in silence as the man walked across to where he was standing, leaned over and sniffed his face.

He immediately recoiled several paces and stared at the man mountain.

He guessed that he was all of six feet eight inches tall; he was very broad, had a bald head and two large protruding ears, hence he presumed, the name FA Cup. He was dressed completely in black - suit, shirt, tie and thick soled black leather shoes and he appeared to be leaning towards him as though he was trying to see something in detail.

"What is this?" he said, "What's he doing and why have you

sent for him?"

"This is FA Cup and he always sniffs the people he takes an interest in."

"And why would he be interested in me?"

"Because I told him to kill you if you fuck me about."

Giles mouth fell open. He'd thought that he'd been smart photocopying the most sensitive Whitewall documents and in his wildest reasoning he'd never considered a threat being made on his life.

"But, but I thought…"

"I don't give a shit what you thought," interrupted Adrian, "because this is what's going to happen.

I'm feeling very, very generous and I'm going to give you fifty thousand pounds in cash right now. FA Cup is going to go with you to wherever those original documents are, you're going to give them to him and I'm going to destroy them."

"But we had a deal! I told you I wanted five hundred thousand not fifty thousand."

"No, we didn't have a deal. I told you that I would consider your proposal if you brought the papers to me today and you haven't, so consider yourself lucky that you're getting the 50k."

Giles looked at the menacing FA Cup who unnervingly kept staring at him as though he was some sort of unusual bug on the wall. He said, "And how do I know that FA Cup…"

FA Cup suddenly snarled and took a step closer to Giles.

Giles jumped back in alarm and looked at his clearly angry face.

"What have I done?" he said.

"He didn't like you calling him FA Cup because he's sensitive about his ears."

"But that's what you called him!" said Giles.

"That's because I know him and he works for me. Everybody else has to call him by his Christian name or he gets very agitated." Adrian stopped talking without elucidating further.

Giles raised his eyebrows and said, "So what is his name?"

"Leander."

"*Leander?*" said Giles, "That's…" He suddenly heard another noise come from FA Cup and quickly changed tack.

"As I was saying before, how do I know that, er Leander won't just take the money back from me once I've handed him the documents?"

"Because I haven't told him to; and you can go directly from here and place it in your bank account before giving him the documents if you want, but I warn you Eaton…"

Giles stuck his hand in the air and said, "There is no need. I'll do as you say."

"Right." Adrian turned to FA Cup and said, "Use the back lift to the car park, go with him, let him put the money wherever he wants, then go to where he's got those documents and bring them back to me."

FA Cup leaned over Adrian's desk and said something quietly to him.

Giles watched as Adrian imparted something back and then nodded. He suddenly felt very vulnerable and realised that he was way out of his depth. He decided there and then to take the fifty grand and to never get involved with Adrian Darke again.

Adrian walked across to a wall safe, opened the door, removed a bundle wrapped in cellophane and handed it to him.

"Fifty grand Eaton, and don't you ever come near me again or FA Cup will do more than sniff your face. Is that clear?"

"Perfectly." said Giles surreptitiously checking that money was in the bundle.

Adrian walked back to his chair and said, "It's all there. Don't insult me."

Giles quickly stuffed the bundle into his pocket and stared impassively at Adrian; he waited for some kind of acknowledgement but none was forthcoming.

A couple of seconds passed by until Adrian looked up and said, "You still here?"

Giles opened his mouth to speak but saw that Adrian had resumed looking at whatever interested him on his desk; he kept quiet, nodded and followed FA Cup to the lift.

During the entire car journey to Giles' bank where he placed the fifty thousand into his safety deposit box; and then on to his home, FA Cup said nothing. It appeared as though he was staring intently at something on his collar, and he found it thoroughly unsettling. Only once did he say, "I'm not going anywhere

Leander, you don't have to stare." But it was a pointless remark that resulted in nothing.

FA Cup accompanied him into his well appointed bachelor flat and followed him into his bedroom where he removed a briefcase from below his bed and extracted the final Whitewall documents.

He handed them to FA Cup who pocketed them, looked at him oddly and then departed briskly leaving every door open behind him.

Giles quickly shut and locked the doors, returned to his bedroom and put the briefcase back under his bed; he then dropped down onto it and breathed a huge sigh of relief. He sat for several minutes reliving the events of the last two hours and then took himself into his lounge for an Old Pulteney.

He poured himself a generous helping and took a deep swig. The smooth warming drink calmed him and a smile played across his lips; he held the glass up and said, "Cheers Surnh! It may not have been half a million but fifty grand isn't too bad!" He took another swig and casually wandered across to his armchair.

"Not bad for a day's work - not bad at all." he said.

As he sat down he caught sight of a red light blinking on his telephone docking station. He couldn't ever recall seeing that before; he got up, walked over to it, stared at it curiously for a second then leaned over and pushed the button.

Chapter 25

John Chance was basically a quiet man. He was 62 years old, had a slim athletic build, piercing blue eyes and he exuded calm and serenity. He lived with his partner Jo in a splendid house not far from where Giles lived and thanks to his own endeavours enjoyed a comfortable lifestyle. His position in the Chance family was that of patriarch. Despite not being the eldest male relative, he nevertheless was the man that everybody turned to when a family matter needed resolving. Reunions, funerals, caring for elderly relatives, keeping in touch with family members generations removed, family news; nothing fazed him, nor was beyond him. If anybody in or stemming from, the Chance family wanted one single person to turn to for help, it was John. He was the linchpin, the stalwart; quiet, reliable and utterly trustworthy.

He was also the natural successor to Maria; not in terms of direct lineage, but by being the custodian of the all-important documents referred to as *Maria's Papers*, all of which had been placed at his disposal once he'd informed other family members of his intention to explore the family tree.

He'd commenced his research in the 1970's when his professional status had afforded him a reasonable amount of spare time, but the task had been arduous and immensely time consuming. His natural fastidiousness had ensured that nothing had been committed to paper until it had been verified, and all too often that had meant endless visits to parish records offices, museums, churches, graveyards and to any other archive source worth investigating. Nevertheless within two years of commencing, and with grateful thanks for an inordinate amount of support from his second cousin Alan, each of the Chance family members had been presented with a family tree dating back to the latter part of the seventeenth century. And for the better part of thirty years, nothing further had been researched because it had been generally accepted that his family tree had been the definitive work and that it could not be improved upon.

All of that had changed however following Sam's telephone call, informing him that he had found *the* Whitewall Farm. Within days they had met and during one of their animated conversations about family history, Sam had asked him whether he'd ever re-looked into the family history using the internet.

Most of his career had been involved with computer technology but he admitted that since completing the family tree, amazingly he hadn't even considered using the internet to see if his work from the 1970's could be improved upon. A new take on one of his favourite subjects using modern technology from the comfort of his own home had him reopening searches into the past and almost as soon as he'd begun, new and exciting revelations started coming to light. And one in particular was about to make a huge impact.

He reached for his phone and dialled Sam. "Hi Sam," he said to his cousin, "it's John, I've barely scratched the surface of re-looking into the family history, but I've found something that's going to make your hair stand on end. Listen to this…"

Sam suddenly heard a strange sound; he wasn't sure if it was local or from down the phone but within seconds he heard John say, "Good God Almighty…"

"What was what?" said Sam.

"It was an explosion, and it must have been hellishly large because it shook all the windows in my house…"

Chapter 26

"It's her I'm telling you!" Simeon Twitch was beside himself with concern. "I told the missus who we'd brought in last night and she couldn't hardly believe it neither!"

"You 'ad no right giving away confidentialities Mr. Twitch," said Honeysucker, "what goes on 'ere stays 'ere!"

"But that's not the point Mr Honeysuckle…"

"*Honeysucker* I keep telling you!"

"…sorry Mr. Honeysucker but that's not the point! That woman is Miss Maria Chance, most of the staff here knows her especially Senior Sister Florence Parks and she's as sane as you and me!"

"Things change Mr. Twitch, 'oo can tell the workings of the 'uman mind. One minute it's ticking away regular as a church clock, next *'poof!'* and it's the nut 'ouse." Honeysucker quickly looked around in case anybody had heard his insensitive reference to their place of work.

"Not in two weeks they don't."

Honeysucker looked at his subordinate and said, "'ow do you mean?"

"Look Mr. Honeysuck…*er*, Miss Chance had an uncle what resided here for years, her Uncle Albert I seem to recall, she used to visit him every few weeks and over that time she got to be real friends with Sister Florence.

Many's the time they've worked together on charity stalls when the asylum's had an open day, or some kind of fete to celebrate things like Whit weekend, and many a time I've seen them leave here at the end of a day arm in arm."

Honeysucker sat back in his chair in the porter's lodge and listened intently.

"Regardless of what we was told by the toff in the big coach last night, she's neither his sister nor mad. And to make matters worse, she was here just the week before last helping Sister Florence organise the open day next week."

Honeysucker instinctively patted the two shilling coins in his coat pocket and recalled what the toff had said about plenty more like it being available in the future.

"And just 'ow do you know that it weren't the gen'leman's sister?" he said.

"Because her name isn't Darke and it's a well known fact that she's a spinster!"

Honeysucker emitted a long 'Hmm' and then said, "Well I'm sorry if this upsets you Mr. Twitch but we aren't paid to think. We're paid to do what we're told and Matron Pinkstaff and Doctor Cobbold is in charge 'ere not Sister Florence."

Twitch exhaled a loud breath in frustration.

"And it's no use you getting all flustered neither," said Honeysucker, "'cos that'll change nothing. Naturally I'll tell Matron about your concerns, but she'll deal with it 'ow she sees fit."

He stopped speaking for a second and then added, "And don't you go gossiping to all and sundry about 'oo we bring in 'ere no more do you 'ear me?"

Twitch opened his mouth to object but thought better of it.

Honeysucker looked hard at his underling and decided to warn Matron that Twitch could be about to make trouble and that he should be excluded from all further 'private' arrangements...

Up in the Ward Nine ante-room Female Orderly Eudora Snike grabbed hold of a handful of Maria's hair, wrenched her head violently backwards and slapped her hard across the face.

"Don't you ever dare disobey me you wilful bitch!" she yelled into Maria's face, *"'Cos this is what'll happen when you do...."*

Maria tried to recoil but couldn't because of the vice-like grip of her accomplice. The dirty handkerchief that had been stuffed into her mouth didn't help either.

A sadistic smile lifted the corner of Male Orderly Ely Capper's mouth; he half wrestled Maria towards the door and cast a wary eye down the corridor to make sure that nobody was around.

"All clear Dolly." he said.

"The water's good and cold is it?" said Snike.

"Bloody freezing," said Capper cruelly, "most of it was from the old artesian well pump."

"Right, let's go."

Capper arced his head around the doorway before proceeding and then happy that they were alone, released his grip from around Maria's arms and chest.

Snike yanked on the leather restraints around Maria's wrists and pulled her into the corridor leading away from Ward Nine.

The pale green painted walls seemed to rush by Maria as she was hurriedly dragged towards the bathrooms; her long coarse cotton nightdress clung to her legs as she half ran down the hall and she wondered if she would trip.

Suddenly Snike halted their advance, cast a quick glance back and forth and then pushed open the door to Bathroom One. Satisfied that they remained undetected, she dragged Maria in.

Capper quickly followed and shut the door.

"Can I prepare her?" he asked lasciviously.

"Yes," said Snike, "but don't bugger about, we don't want to be here when Staff starts her rounds." She looked mercilessly at Maria and said, "And if you know what's good for you, you'll keep your mouth shut about this little initiation to your world or you'll really pay for it later, do you understand?"

Maria nodded her head.

Snike went over to a corner cupboard, opened it and reached behind a cardboard box on the bottom shelf; she extracted a length of rope that she kept concealed there and deftly tied it around the strap restraining Maria's wrists. She threw the loose end over the pipes above the bath and yanked Maria's arms up until she was almost on her tip toes.

Capper moved in close behind Maria and felt the familiar twitch in his pants as he anticipated what was to come next.

Slowly he bent down and lifted the hem of Maria's nightdress. He gathered the material up and ran his hands up her legs, across her stomach and over her naked breasts until he'd lifted the nightdress into a bundle over her bound wrists. Next he turned her round, slipped his thumbs into the elasticated waistband of her cotton knickers and slowly pulled them off.

All of Snike's secret lesbian desires rushed into her mind as she stared at Maria's naked body. She knew that her captive was middle aged but her pulled up arms accentuated her small shapely breasts and perfectly proportioned pale pink nipples. She glanced down at Maria's slim waist and dark furry mound and a small trickle of saliva formed in the corner of her mouth.

Suddenly she became aware that Maria was watching her hawkishly and she quickly snapped out of her salaciousness.

She double checked that the nightdress wouldn't get wet and said, "Right Ely get her in."

This was the part that Capper had been looking forward to most. He turned Maria to face away from him, wrapped his left arm around her ribcage then slowly and deliberately slid his right hand down the small of her back, over the contour of her shapely little backside and deep down between her legs.

Making sure that his fingers were placed just where he crucially wanted them, he lifted her up whilst Snike slid the rope along the pipe until it was directly over the bath. He then dropped her in.

The coldness of the water was so intense that Maria felt as though she was being stabbed in multiple places. She gasped and tried to pull herself up on the rope but this prompted Snike to release more of it and she dropped heavily back down into the icy depths. She desperately tried to gain her feet but Snike anticipated it each time and manipulated the rope until she realised that struggle was pointless.

With cast iron fortitude she finally brought her considerable will-power to bear; gave a contemptuous look to her tormentors and then sat motionless in the water.

The minutes dragged by until with growing disgruntlement they realised that playtime was over.

A vexed Snike said, "Right, get her out."

Capper grabbed Maria by the arms and pulled her up. Because of the paleness of her skin she had gone lobster red from her armpits down. He looked at her and cast a worried glance over to Snike.

"Christ Dolly, she don't look too good."

Snike looked at Maria's body and then at her defiant face. Their eyes locked for just a few seconds but it was enough to jolt her to the core. She suddenly felt really threatened; it was as though some sort of message had been transmitted to her with a dire warning attached to it. It instantly disorientated her.

She averted her eyes in an effort to conceal her jarred equilibrium and turned to Capper.

"Stop mithering about her, she's as tough as old boots; dry her off and take her back to the Ward."

She cast another furtive glance back towards Maria and saw that she was still staring at her with diamond hard eyes. Once again a feeling of intense intimidation swept over her and she felt rattled for the second time in quick succession.

"Stop staring at me," she yelled, *"or it'll be the worse for you!"*

Maria retained her stare just long enough and then looked down at the floor.

Snike looked at Maria for a few seconds longer and felt the irrational need to give ground.

She turned to Capper and said, "Maybe you're right. Give her a hot water bottle and an extra blanket; and if she doesn't kick up a fuss with Staff let her keep them."

She looked back at Maria and with the briefest of nods knew that they had a begrudging agreement.

"Yes, but what…" said Capper.

"Yes but nothing Ely," said Snike aggravatedly, *"just bloody do as you're told!"*

One hour later Maria lay absolutely still with her eyes closed. Her whole body felt as though it was being purged by pins and needles and she shivered incessantly.

She knew that she was in some sort of hospital but had no idea where it was and why she was there. Nobody had spoken to her except the despicable Orderlies, and the last thing that she'd remembered was being with the Johnsons and Hugo Darke at the King's Head in Hyde. She gathered that she'd been incarcerated at the order of the Johnsons or Darke and that it was their money keeping her there, not ill health.

She'd been a prisoner for less than twenty-four hours and had already endured a grossly sexual assault and to her utmost revulsion she realised that there could be more to come, and possibly worse.

But she was a member of the Chance family; the 'Iron

Chances' people called them, and she would cope.

No spineless bullying excuse for human beings would subjugate her, and if it took until the end of her days she'd make sure that the despicable creatures responsible for her predicament would pay for their evildoings very dearly indeed.

Chapter 27

Giles pushed the button and heard the first message that he'd ever received on his new telephone docking station. It was blunt and straight to the point.

"Giles, Tom here, sorry to bother you at home but I tried your office this afternoon and your girly said you were out.

Anyway, the reason for the call is to let you know that I might have a solution to our problem with that Whitewall business.

I won't go into detail now and I'm busy tomorrow so I'll call you Monday afternoon the 29^{th,} at your office.

O.K., speak soon, bye for now."

Giles sat staring at the answering machine with eyes like a Bush Baby, he removed the hand that he'd clamped over his mouth and said, "Oh my God!" In all of his dealings with Adrian Darke he'd completely forgotten about Tom Ramsbottom.

He drained the contents of his whisky glass, took a deep breath and dialled Adrian's number.

The following morning he was back in Adrian's office feeling as small as a mouse.

"You fucking idiot!" bellowed Adrian as he dropped back into his seat knowing that the Whitewall papers were well and truly incinerated. He covered both eyes with the palms of his hands and said, "You *stupid* brainless idiot! Has anybody else seen those papers for Christ's sake?"

"No, just him." Giles was reluctant to mention Naomi, Carlton and Sandra because they'd only seen the file and not the contents. Furthermore he didn't want any more vitriol from the already raging Darke.

"Oh Whoopy doo! Only the Mayor of Walmsfield - absolutely bloody brilliant!" Adrian was furious, "And I suppose half the

damned council know about them now too?"

"No, only him, he hasn't even told his wife…"

"Yeah right…" said Adrian sarcastically.

"No truly," said Giles, "we were both acutely aware of how the contents could impact Walmsfield Borough Council if they were ever exposed, so we swore each other to secrecy."

Adrian could not believe the naivety of the man in front of him.

"And you really don't think that he would have told something of such magnitude, to his own wife? Are you totally bloody stupid, or just pretending to be?"

"I… er… I wouldn't think…"

"Yes exactly!" scorned Adrian, "Thinking doesn't seem to be your strong point does it?"

He leaned forward and placed both elbows on his desk and held his head in his hands. He remained silent for a few seconds and then said, "Just how do you propose explaining away the loss of the papers if he asks for them tomorrow?"

"He can't, he's on holiday in Florida with his wife."

Adrian suddenly looked up; his mind went into overdrive. He thought about the situation slowly until a plan started to form. He broke the silence by brusquely asking, "When's he due back?"

"Not for another two weeks."

"And do you think he *might* have told anybody else?" said Adrian eyeing Giles suspiciously.

Giles recalled Tom commenting about showing an old friend the papers, but doubted whether he would have mentioned it without having custody of the file first. Regardless, he didn't think that it was the time to bring other people into the equation.

"No," he said decisively, "I know him, I'd place money on the fact that he's told nobody else, with of course, the possible exception of his wife that is…"

Adrian looked into the eyes of the man opposite and shook his head; he got up from his chair, paced around the room for a few minutes, then turned and said, "Do you know where he's staying in Florida?"

"Not right at this moment. But I have an itinerary back in my office; he left details of where he would be staying in case I needed to contact him urgently."

"And are you absolutely positive that he would not have confided in anybody else regarding those papers? 'Cos so help me, if I find out that you've held out on me again…"

"I am absolutely sure that nobody else knows about them." said Giles confidently.

"Right," said Adrian, "You get back to your office and email that list to me and once I've given you my personal email address, make damned sure that only you use it do you understand?"

"Perfectly." said Giles.

"Right, leave now before I change my mind about the fifty grand, and listen to me very carefully; *do not*, I repeat, *do not*, try to contact the Mayor in America is that absolutely clear?"

"Absolutely." said Giles.

Back in his office at Walmsfield, Giles clicked the icon on his laptop, and watched as the 'Send/Receive Complete' notice almost instantly flashed up at the bottom of the screen. Adrian had the Ramsbottom's itinerary in Florida.

He sat back in his chair and stared at the mouse linked to his laptop. It was a simple button that he'd clicked, just the once; it took no effort at all, just 'click' and it was done.

He had no idea what Darke was planning, nor did he want to know, but ominous thoughts ranged through his mind. He looked sombrely at his right forefinger and knew that if he didn't ever see them again, for the rest of his life he would never forget how simple it had been to be the herald of death that day.

'Click' - a simple solitary, effortless *'click'*.

For a long time he stared at his mouse. He should have been happy, he should have been congratulating himself on the successful conclusion to his business and maybe even daydreaming about what his newly acquired fifty thousand pounds could buy; but he wasn't. In fact he was the most *un*happy that he could ever remember being.

Carlton arrived at The Ryming Ratt a little earlier than his and Naomi's usual time because he wanted to make sure of securing a table for four. He'd been informed by Naomi that she was bringing her father and another man, but he had no idea who the fourth person was.

He opted for the restaurant rather than the area reserved for bar meals, selected a nicely located table and sat down. He ordered a drink and informed the waitress that he was expecting three others within the next fifteen minutes.

As he sat waiting and sipping his beer he found himself feeling a little edgy and he knew exactly why; it was because of the fourth person coming to lunch. He was dreading Naomi turning up with another man, and being told that it was her partner.

She hadn't really given him any reason to be possessive about her and he certainly wasn't trying to erase the memory of his late wife, but he couldn't stop himself thinking about her. He was falling in love with her, and he knew that if she was going to turn up today with a 'significant other', he would hate it. He even hated thinking about it!

He made a conscious decision that if the lunch date didn't reveal any nasty surprises; he would pursue her more seriously.

"Hi Carlton!"

Carlton was so deep in thought that he didn't see the others arrive; he stood up and saw that Naomi was accompanied much to his relief, by two older men.

"Carlton," said Naomi, "I'd like to introduce you to my father and my second cousin."

Carlton shook the hands of both men and then cast a glance at Naomi who appeared to be beaming from ear to ear.

They all sat down and made themselves comfortable, but he was distracted by Naomi still grinning like a Cheshire Cat. He looked at her questioningly and said, "O.K., what?"

Naomi remained silent until she could bear it no longer.

"Come on," said Carlton, "what is it?"

"All right." said Naomi turning to her father, "Tell him who you both are."

Carlton turned to face Naomi's father.

"For all my sins, I'm Sam Chance and this is my cousin John!"

Carlton couldn't have been more surprised if he'd tried.

"Never!" he said, "I can't believe it!"

"It's true I'm afraid." said Sam jokily pointing to Naomi, "I've tried to distance myself from this tyke but she keeps on coming back!"

219

Carlton smiled then turned to Naomi and said, "Why on earth didn't you tell me that you were a Chance?"

"Because up until now I didn't want anybody else to know, particularly Giles Eaton. Dad has always warned me to exercise extreme caution when discussing Whitewall and to be mega-careful about whom I took into my confidence."

"But you could always have trusted me." said Carlton.

Naomi recognised a dose of hurt feelings and pampered to it.

"I know Cal. I know it now and I knew it from the beginning, but I also wanted it to be a surprise when dad arrived."

"Well it certainly was that. You could have knocked me over with a feather!"

The four companions got themselves thoroughly acquainted over lunch, each swapping anecdotes and snippets of light interest; sharing jokes and generally enjoying the whole lunchtime ambience.

John let the light-hearted banter continue until the coffees had been served and then asked Naomi and Sam if he could make Carlton fully aware of the situation that existed within the Chance family.

Naomi and Sam both nodded their approval.

John took a sip of coffee, and then carefully explained the family history to Carlton.

Carlton was amazed. All the recent things that had happened at Whitewall paled into insignificance compared to what he heard.

"Now," said John at the end of his narrative, "for some reason, nothing in what we call Maria's papers is dated after 1869. We are entirely in the dark about what happened to her after that and we know that nobody in the family even gave it a second thought until Sam kicked the whole thing off again by finding Whitewall Farm."

Carlton turned to Naomi and shook his head.

"This is amazing, I had absolutely no idea. Have you told your dad and uncle about what's been happening here?"

Naomi nodded and said, "That's one of the reasons for dad coming back."

Sam said, "When Naomi told me about the renewed interest in Whitewall following my visit, I could hardly believe it. She told me about the old Whitewall file that you had; that it had been opened and that nobody but the Mayor or Town Clerk were allowed to see the contents.

This had us puzzling long and hard; we wondered what could possibly have been in there that required such secrecy? What could cause shock waves big enough to make the national news? It didn't make sense to us that something hidden for so long could cause so much fuss now.

John and I racked our brains without getting anywhere until through a lengthy process of elimination we ultimately concluded that it had to be related to the land sold illegally to the old Hundersfield District Council.

We pondered over whether somebody at Walmsfield Council had found out that there was a problem associated with that old estate or maybe had irrefutable proof that the land had, and maybe still does, belong to the Chance family?

And that led us of course to consider what could possibly have been in the file to make them aware of that fact?"

John spoke. "We believe," he said gravely, "that it either had to be the original tenancy agreement proving Maria's assertion, or a copy of the deeds showing historic ownership of the estate, or even better, both.

The existence of the expired tenancy agreement would have proved that the sales of land in the 1860's by the incumbent tenant, Abraham Johnson, would have been illegal."

He looked around to see if anybody had any questions but nobody said a word. His speculation was as disturbing as it was potentially explosive. The possible repercussions seemed endless.

"It's the only thing that makes sense don't you see? If the Mayor and Town Clerk now have unassailable proof that the land rightfully belonged to the Chance family and not Abraham Johnson, and that the purchase of land from the Estate by one of their predcccssors had knowingly been an illegal one, that'd cause one hell of a stir wouldn't it?

Could you even begin to imagine the chaos that would ensue if some court were to ultimately rule that the ground rent raised from every property built on that land since 1868 had to be paid back to the Chance family heirs? How much would that be in monetary terms?

And even worse, what if the courts then ruled that the land had to be returned to Chance family ownership?"

Everybody sat wide eyed; it was mind blowing stuff, far too big to comprehend without serious and considered thought.

Carlton said, "Wow! I could certainly see why they wouldn't want anybody to know about that!"

The four companions fell silent as each mind toyed with different scenarios and outcomes.

"We've got to get our hands on that file at all costs." said Carlton, "We can't let this business go any further until we know exactly what's in it."

"I agree," said John, "it is pointless endlessly speculating, when the answer may only be across the road in the Council Offices."

Carlton looked at his watch and said, "Right. Let's be decisive. Why don't we go to see Giles Eaton right now and sit outside his office until we get to see him?"

There was a nod of agreement between them, the bill was settled and the foursome headed back to the Council Offices.

On the way back to the Council Offices Sam walked beside John and said, "By the way, did you ever find out what caused that huge explosion the other night?"

"Yes," said John conversationally, "it was an old lady's house a few miles away; apparently she'd left the unlit gas on and went to bed…"

Chapter 28

Luck was on their side; as the four companions waited for the lift to take them to Giles's floor, he arrived there too. There was no escape for him, they quickly established that he was free and before any excuses could be offered, they found themselves together in his office for the first time since Sandra's death.

Carlton saw Giles wince as he introduced the two members of the Chance family to him, but was careful not to reveal Naomi's relationship to either man.

Giles had been outmanoeuvred and invited everybody to be seated.

Carlton decided to take a chance and said, "We now know what is in the Whitewall file."

"Oh yes," said Giles, "And what exactly is that?"

"The original deeds to the Whitewall Estate and a tenancy agreement dating back to the 1700's proving that the Chance family were the historical and rightful owners."

Giles was shocked; his instant reaction was such that it would have been futile to deny it.

"How on earth…?" He faltered for a second, then nodded his head and said, "Yes of course, Sandra Miles told you didn't she?"

Carlton's face dropped, this had been the very last thing that he'd expected Giles to say. He felt a rush of anger and wanted to grab the slimy Town Clerk by the throat and beat the truth out of him right there and then.

Giles saw the look change on Carlton's face and knew that he'd made a huge mistake, but it was too late it was out in the open.

The atmosphere between the two men crackled but Carlton reigned in his emotions. He needed confirmation about the contents of the file first; he would resolve the Sandra Miles issue at a later date. He composed himself and said, "Let's just say that we know shall we?"

If Giles Eaton was nothing else, he was quick witted. Years of side-tracking, double-dealing and being an ex-estate agent had made him very capable of thinking on his feet. He knew that the file had been destroyed; he knew that Adrian Darke was going to resolve the 'Tom Ramsbottom problem', and he knew that playing the good guy was now going to be his best option. He needed to show compassion, he needed to show concern for those who had been wronged...

"Very well," he said in a conciliatory manner, "I'll be honest with you."

'*That'd be a first.*' thought Carlton.

"You are of course correct." said Giles, "The file did contain documents showing that the land was historically owned by the Chance family..."

Naomi felt a rush of emotion upon finally hearing proof that Maria had been right; but the penny suddenly dropped about Giles's use of the past tense.

"What do you mean *did* contain documents?" she said, "Don't you mean *does* contain documents?"

Giles looked perplexed for a few seconds and then said slowly, "Ah yes, of course. I was referring to that period of time when I looked at the file; i.e. the file did contain documents when I looked. Not, did contain them then, but doesn't now, if you take my meaning..."

Everybody remained silent long enough for Giles to retain the initiative.

"Good," he said patronisingly, "Now that we have that cleared up. As I was saying the file *did*," Giles made the inverted commas gesture with his forefingers, "contain documents showing that the land had been owned by the Chance family but it isn't quite as straightforward as that.

Bearing in mind that we have had possession of a section of it for so long, the question of ownership would be a contentious one, and like it or not, you have to understand our position here. We, as a Council would always err on the side of honesty and fortitude, but it behoves us nevertheless to act in the best interests of the people we serve.

Now having said that, and in accordance with what we considered to be the honest, yet prudent thing to do, the Mayor and

I sought advice from a solicitor specialising in land ownership. He advised us that despite our legitimate claim to a possessory title, there may indeed be a case for the courts to decide regardless of whether the land was sold or purchased illegally, all those years ago.

Upon hearing this, we decided not to go public until we'd exhausted all the legal avenues and possibilities."

He looked around; everybody was silent and looked calm. He made a mental note that despite it not being his first choice, punctiliousness appeared to be a good card to play when circumstances dictated.

Naomi was the first to speak. She said, "Can we now see the contents for ourselves?"

All heads turned in her direction and Carlton suddenly felt protective towards her. He knew right then, and right there, that he did love her and God help anybody who dared to try and harm her.

"I'm sorry," said Giles with what appeared to be genuine concern, "but you can't. I don't have the file."

"So where is it?" Carlton was far brusquer.

"The Mayor is looking after it. He's on holiday in the States at the moment and we decided that it would be just as safe in his personal care as here at the Council Offices and he's not so adept at making important decisions as I, so he asked if he could use his time on holiday to consider what he thought to be the most sensible course of action to adopt upon his return."

"I've never heard anything so preposterous!" said Naomi defiantly, "Are you seriously trying to tell me that our Mayor, a man given his position by popular vote rather than by professional capability has arbitrarily been given custody of important historical documents? And taken them on holiday with him? Pah!"

Giles's obsequiousness disappeared in a flash.

"I didn't say that he had taken them on holiday with him Mrs Draper, I said that they were in his personal care. And if you are implying any sort of impropriety here I suggest that you think very carefully about what you're implying before voicing it. These may be colleagues of yours in the office, but they are also witnesses to any potentially slanderous comments."

Naomi looked at her father who was frowning at her in a way that she knew meant 'Sshh!'

"Now," said Giles still giving Naomi withering looks, "of course, in the end we will strive to see that injustices are fairly treated; our procrastination is not sinister it is considered. We have a right to mull over the possible consequences of such a portentous discovery before releasing it for public consumption, and frankly I think that we would be behaving irresponsibly if we did not."

It was a compelling argument, and met with no objections.

"So," said Giles haughtily, "now that you *are* aware of the contents, I will inform the Mayor of that fact upon his return, and I feel sure that he, like I, will want to include all of you in our final decision making process."

He was feeling very pleased with himself, the explanation had been a good one and could not be disputed. The plebs had been quelled.

Then the mouth went into gear before the brain engaged.

"Let's just cross fingers that the Mayor *has* put the file somewhere safe eh? It'd be a tragedy indeed if we were on the verge of seeing justice prevail, only to see all hope fade because he'd lost it or something, what?" He smiled, but nobody else did.

John, who had up until this time remained silent quietly said, "Well, maybe not all hope…"

All eyes turned to face him, and with the last vestiges of a smile still etched on his face Giles said, "What do you mean?"

"Well," said John, "the major feature of the Whitewall saga has always centred on a dispute between the Chance family and another family over ownership. Without a doubt the two most important documents have always been the deeds and tenancy agreement which until recently, we thought had been lost forever."

He turned to face Giles directly and said, "Unknown to you, we had a distant Aunt who fought tirelessly to gain access to those documents in an attempt to prove that the Chance family were the rightful owners of the Whitewall Estate but we don't know whether she ever saw them because we have no record of what happened to her after 1869.

However," he said pausing for gravity, "she had missed a very vital piece of evidence."

Everybody was enthralled by what John was saying and the smug smile had totally vanished from Giles's face.

"I did too when I first researched the family tree in the

seventies but with the aid of the internet, more information has come to light."

Naomi could hardly contain herself, "What piece of vital evidence had she missed?"

John gathered his thoughts for a second, and then said, "At the start of the original tenancy in March 1747 we had always assumed, mostly due to Maria's papers…" He turned to Giles and said, "Maria was the distant relative I mentioned earlier."

Giles nodded acknowledgement.

"…that the agreement had been made between one James Montague Lincoln and our distant forebear another John Chance, whom Maria had always insisted was the original owner of Whitewall. But it turns out that he was not the sole owner.

John had a twin brother named Matthew and they were joint owners of the Estate!"

Naomi gasped.

"And according to my latest research," said John, "the brothers were each given a copy of the deeds and original tenancy agreement in an envelope marked with the legend - 'John and Matthew Chance – Cestui que Vie'.

Giles was mortified; he recalled the illegible part of the inscription and had wrongly presumed it to be old John Chance's second Christian name. He closed his eyes and couldn't believe that this was happening…

John delivered the coup-de-gras.

"Apparently, John's copy was handed to a firm of solicitors for safekeeping but Matthew held onto his. So somewhere out there could be another copy of the documents that the Mayor currently has; and if he does accidently lose them as you earlier mooted Mr. Eaton, we'd have to find out whether Matthew Chance had any living relatives and see if those copies were still in existence."

"Good grief John!" said Naomi, "You never fail to amaze me!"

"And have you started to look into Matthew's family?" said Sam.

"I've started." said John with a wink, "It's always best to have a back-up plan…"

Carlton was silent and brooding; he was staring intently at the Town Clerk's deeply troubled face and remembering Sandra.

Chapter 29

Sunday 4th July, 1869. Sister Florence Parks' Cottage, Henbury

"All right Sim," said Florence, "you and Matt come in, I'll put the kettle on and you can tell me what's bothering you." Florence ushered Simeon and Martha Twitch into her small parlour, sat them down and pushed the kettle over the open fire.

"Now," she said, "what's so important that it couldn't wait until tomorrow?"

Simeon looked nervously at his wife and didn't really know how to proceed; he knew that the subject would be contentious and he didn't want to upset one of the few people that he really liked at the asylum. He attempted to start one or two times but faltered each time until finally he looked to his wife for inspiration.

"Go on Sim," said Martha, "just say what you've come here to say. Sister Florence knows you aren't an educated man, so if things come out a bit wrong she'll understand."

Florence frowned as she waited patiently for Simeon to proceed.

"All right," he said, "How much do you know about private ward nine?"

"There isn't one," said Florence.

"But there is Sister."

Florence cast a glance across to Martha who simply nodded. She turned back to Simeon and said, "Are you sure? I know that there are plans to extend the buildings but it's officially a Pauper Lunatic Asylum and wouldn't accommodate private patients."

"I'm positive Sister," said Simeon, "'cos me an' Mr. Honeysuckle brung a patient in late last Thursday night and we was instructed to put her in there."

Florence frowned and said, "And just where is ward nine?"

"In the same building as the Reception Lodge."

"But that's all admin offices."

"Not up on the second floor." said Simeon.

Florence tried to picture the office block and realised that she hadn't ever been in there. She said, "And how do you get access to those wards?"

"You go through the door marked 'Private' on the left hand side of the reception desk, down the corridor to the last door on the left, then up the stairs."

Florence was stunned; she was aware that the asylum was expanding all the time and that she may not have been familiar with all of the rooms, but she was astonished to hear that there were private wards *and* containing patients. She shook her head and said, "Who greeted you?"

"The Super and Matron."

Florence was taken aback for the second time in quick succession and said, "Doctor Cobbold *and* Matron? What time did you bring the patient in?"

"About half past eleven."

The kettle suddenly came to the boil over the fire; Florence hooked the chimney crane with the hanger, swung the kettle out of the flames and proceeded to make everybody a cup of tea in complete silence.

Martha and Simeon could see that she was deep in thought and let her quietly ruminate.

Florence handed her guests a tea each, set hers down on a small table and said, "Did you see how many private wards were up there?"

"Not rightly," said Simeon, "but we there was at least three others after number nine."

"And did they appear to be occupied?"

"There was clothes outside the ones leading up to ward nine."

Florence was fully aware of the asylum routine; the patients rose at 6:00am in the summer and 7:00am in the winter. At 8:00pm it was bedtime. The window shutters were locked, the folded clothes of the patients were placed outside the doors of the respective Wards or bedrooms and then they were locked for the night.

Simeon's confirmation that clothes were outside the doors indicated that the souls occupying those quarters were indeed patients.

"Odd thing though Sister," said Simeon, "there was only one set of clothes outside each ward."

Florence nodded and said, "That would be typical of private patient quarters; their single occupancy rooms could still be referred to as wards - it depends upon the terminology used by the particular asylum."

She sat back in her chair, picked up her tea and whilst taking a sip tried to understand why she as the Senior Nursing Sister hadn't been told about those patients and that part of the asylum.

Her thoughts were interrupted by Martha.

"Sim," she said, "tell her why we came!"

Florence said, "You mean there's more?"

Simeon looked worriedly at his wife and then turned to Florence.

"I didn't come here to tell you that we've got private wards at Parkway Sister, because for all I knew you may have been aware of them...it's, it's..."

"For goodness sake spit it out!" said Martha, "Sister hasn't got all night."

Simeon looked at his wife and said, "That's all very well Matt, but what if I'm wrong?"

"Well you seemed sure enough when you told me!"

"Told you what?" said Florence.

Simeon turned and said, "Who we put into ward nine."

A silence ensued for several seconds as Simeon appeared to make a superhuman effort to overcome his doubt until finally he said, "It, it was Miss Chance."

Florence frowned and cocked her head slightly to the left. The penny didn't drop at first and then a dawning realisation started to creep over her.

"No, you're not trying to tell me that..."

Simeon nodded and said, "That it was *the* Miss Chance? Yes I am."

Florence's mouth fell wide open. She was utterly astounded and said, "What, Maria Chance? No! Impossible, I don't believe it!"

Simeon simply nodded and said, "Yes."

One and a half miles away at Parkway Asylum the Medical

Superintendent Doctor Edwin Cobbold, Matron Ida Pinkstaff and Senior Ward Orderly Arnold Honeysucker sat in the Superintendent's office and nobody was happy.

"Well if you took more of a part in the social side of this place Ida," said Cobbold, "maybe we wouldn't be in this mess now!"

"Don't you dare Edwin!" retorted Pinkstaff, "This isn't my fault and you know it!"

"Matron, Doctor," said Honeysucker, "it isn't going to do none of us any good trying to apportion blame. You two 'ave only been 'ere since New Year an' I've been 'ere less than four weeks, 'ow was we to know 'oo was friends with 'oo and the like?"

"Arnold's right," said Cobbold, "it was much easier for us all at Cheddleton; we knew most of the daily goings on there, here we're still relatively new and don't."

"And I warned you not to set up the private wards until we'd been here at least a year." said Pinkstaff.

"Yes, yes all right!" said Cobbold, "Like Arnold said, apportioning blame now won't get us anywhere, we need to make a plan."

The trio sat pondering for a while until Pinkstaff said, "We only risk exposure if we lose control.

We know that we can rely on the six Orderlies to keep the patients sedated in the unlikely event of an outside visit by a County Medical Officer and we know that the patients themselves will become accustomed to being incarcerated here once they accept that there is no hope of release; so providing that we don't let any medical staff in there except us, and providing that we are very careful about how we proceed from now on, there's no reason to presume the worst."

Honeysucker looked down and uttered a quiet 'Hmm'.

"What?" said Cobbold.

"T'aint my place to contradict, but it strikes me that it may not be too long until 'ward nine' realises where she is and that was never the case with inmates at Stafford."

"He's right Edwin," said Pinkstaff, "as well you know, part of the patient settling process is siting them in completely unfamiliar surroundings."

Cobbold drew in a deep breath and said, "God Almighty, this is a proper bugger's muddle and no mistake; who could have ever imagined that that woman would have ended up in here… a personal friend of our Senior Sister for crying out loud!"

The trio fell into silence again.

"It's not insurmountable," said Pinkstaff, "we just have to be very careful about how we do things."

"And what would you suggest?" said Cobbold.

Pinkstaff thought for a few seconds and said, "All right, here are my initial thoughts. First we never tell the Chance woman where she actually is; we could for example inform her that she's in Cheddleton Asylum, and if she believes that she's in Staffordshire it will help her to settle once she realises that she's alone and we're her new family as such.

We must keep her confined to the private wards and the enclosed airing court for at least the next six months and Edwin and I must never come into contact with her again in case she recognises us from one of her previous visits. Finally, Edwin is in charge here and his diagnoses will not be questioned so we make absolutely sure that she is never released. That way she will never be able to expose anything untoward."

"And if the question of visitors ever crops up?" asked Honeysucker.

"If she asks for visitors we'll tell her that no-one has applied."

The two men sat in silence for a few minutes until Cobbold said, "That sounds like the basis of a good plan. We'll do what Ida says for now and if we meet with any problems as we proceed, we'll adapt accordingly."

Back at Florence's cottage in Henbury the shock of Simeon's revelation had settled.

"I have to get into those private wards and see for myself."

"You'll never get past reception," said Simeon, "During the day you can't get into the admin offices unless you work there and at night they have specially selected monkeys what's in the employ of the Superintendent."

"How do you know this Simeon?"

"Last Thursday was the first time I've ever been involved with anything like this and when I told Mr. Honeysuckle I didn't like it he slipped me three pence and told me not to worry 'cos all the night staff and Orderlies was in on it."

"Unbelievable! said Florence, "Truly unbelievable; and all this has been going on under my nose!"

She paused for thought and then said, "Very well, thank you for bringing this to my notice. I won't involve you any more but you may rest assured that I will somehow get into those wards and find out what's going on."

Martha looked at her husband and frowned.

Simeon nodded back at her and said, "We aren't going to let you do this alone Sister. Matt and me have received so many kindnesses as a result of the charity work you and Miss Chance have done here in the past that it would be a sin not to help you now."

"But I couldn't possibly allow you to do this," said Florence, "what I'm planning could be dangerous and illegal and if I'm caught it could be instant dismissal and prosecution."

"You're not allowing me to help Sister; I'm doing it because I want to."

"Well that's very comforting, thank you Simeon," she looked across to Martha and added, "you too Matt I'd be very grateful for any help in this endeavour but frankly, right now I have no idea where to begin."

Martha looked at Simeon and raised her eyebrows.

Simeon frowned and shook his head.

Martha was having none of it and said, "No Sim, she needs to know!"

Florence caught the exchange and said, "What's going on?"

Martha said, "You may have more of an ally in Sim than you know right now."

"How so?"

Martha looked across to her husband and said, "Will you tell Sister or should I?"

"You tell her." said Simeon.

Martha nodded and turned back to Florence. "Do you remember a few years ago when it was in all the local newspapers about a notorious burglar named 'The Spook'?"

Florence nodded and said, "Yes, but he was never caught was he?"

"No he wasn't," said Martha, "because he married me and mended his ways."

Florence wasn't easily shocked but this revelation did it.

"It was a long time back Sister," said Simeon, "but thanks to Matt and everybody at the asylum I've been able to turn my life around and go straight."

Florence was still in shock and just smiled.

"Right," said Martha, "there's no time like the present; what would we need to get started?"

Simeon thought for a while and then said, "Who do you call when a toilet backs up Sister?"

Len Chapman," said Florence.

"Is he a local contractor?"

"No he's one of the estate maintenance men."

"Right," said Simeon, "I need to meet with him as soon as you can arrange it; I need to know how many staff are on duty at night and whether staff numbers change at the weekends. And if you have a master key to the internal rooms we'll need to get two more cut."

Florence nodded and like Martha couldn't help looking at Simeon; his whole persona had instantly changed, he was no longer the subservient Orderly, he was confident and self-assured and appeared to be about two inches taller.

Simeon was back doing what he did best and Martha knew just how good he was at it.

Chapter 30

Eight days after their meeting with Giles Eaton, Naomi's usual routine was in turmoil; her bedroom was in turmoil and she was in turmoil.

It was 6:45pm; she and Carlton had arranged to go to one of his favourite countryside pubs for something to eat and he was calling for her at 7:15pm and despite having all day to get ready, she still hadn't decided which top to put on. The whole of her wardrobe appeared to be lying on her bed and she stared in desperation at her reflection in her bedroom mirror.

"The local news will be on in a minute love..." Sam called from the living room.

"Thanks dad, I'll be down in a tick." She shut her eyes and reached behind her; her hands closed around a piece of material and she thought, *'Right, whatever this is, I'll wear it.'* She kept her eyes tightly closed and drew the mystery item up in front of herself so that she could gain an instant reaction to how it looked with her new black trousers.

"Come on love, you'll miss it..." Sam called again.

"All right, I'm coming!" She opened her eyes and saw that she was holding a clean pillowcase.

"Oh damn..." she said throwing the hapless pillowcase onto the mini-Mount Everest on her bed.

Sam called up, *"It's on!"*

Naomi quickly made her way into the living room and sat down.

She and Sam had taken to following all the items on the local news in case any references had been made to the situation at Whitewall Farm, but ten days had passed already, and there had been no news from Chief Inspector Crowthorne either.

Within ten minutes of the programme starting the doorbell rang; Naomi looked at her watch and saw that it was 6:55pm.

"My God!" she said in near panic, "If that's Carlton he's

early!" She looked down and said, "And I still haven't chosen a top!"

"It's O.K.," said Sam, "you go and get one on and I'll answer the door."

He stood up, went to the front door, opened it and saw Carlton standing with a bunch of flowers in his hand.

"Oh, Carlton," he said jokily, "how did you know that I liked roses?"

Carlton stood with an awkward smile on his face; it had been years since he'd been on a date and he felt like a dinosaur in the twenty-first century.

"I...er..." he spluttered.

"Come on in you big lump." said Sam as he ushered the tongue-tied man into the living room.

To the amazement of both men, Naomi was standing in front of the television, still clad in only a white bra and trousers with her right hand up to her mouth.

Sam walked around to face her and could see that she was clearly upset about something.

Carlton saw it too and said, "Naomi, what is it?"

Naomi turned to face them both, oblivious of her state of dress and said, "You're not going to believe this, but as I started to leave the room to get a top on..." She suddenly realised that she hadn't got her top on and immediately covered her bra with her arms. "Oh! I'm sorry!" she said feeling acutely embarrassed.

"It's all right love." said Sam, "What aren't we going to believe?"

Naomi said, "As I was leaving the room I heard the local newsreader announce that BBC North West had just learned of the deaths of Mayor Tom Ramsbottom and his wife Peggy in an accident in America."

"No!" said Carlton. He was utterly astounded, "Did they say what had happened?"

"They said they'd been walking back to their hotel in Orlando when a speeding car that was being chased had mounted the pavement, hit them both and killed them instantly. The newsreader said that the Orange County Police had been adamant that the pursuing car had not been a police vehicle and that they were considering the possibility that the cars were involved in some sort of gang related incident.

They said that the Ramsbottoms appeared to be innocent pedestrians who just got unlucky."

Carlton sat down on the sofa and laid the flowers on the adjacent coffee table.

"Oh, these are for you." he said to Naomi.

Naomi thanked him, excused herself and made her way to her bedroom to put on a top. Ironically, she put on the first one she came to without even looking at it and made her way back into the living room.

On the way she heard Carlton explaining to her father that the only living person who'd seen the contents of the Whitewall file was Giles Eaton, and that everybody else had died in suspicious circumstances.

She plonked herself on the sofa next to Carlton and said. "You don't think that they were hit purposely do you?"

Carlton didn't say a word.

"And that Giles is involved?" said Sam with a doubtful look upon his face.

"It's impossible to say," said Carlton.

"It does seem too much of a coincidence," said Naomi quietly.

"Too damned right it does," said Carlton.

Sam turned to Carlton and said, "Will you talk to that Chief Inspector Crowthorne about your suspicions?"

"I don't really know, this whole business has me at a loss."

"Do you recall that remark Eaton made about it being a tragedy if the file was lost at the eleventh hour?" said Naomi.

"Yes."

"Well you don't think that the death of the Ramsbottoms could have anything to do with that do you?"

Carlton looked puzzled and said nothing.

"That doesn't really make sense does it?" said Sam, "I mean, it's not as though this Eaton chap has anything to gain by the loss of those papers does he? If after some lengthy legal battle they'd proved our ownership of Whitewall, how would that cause him to be out of pocket? Think about it; the Council, not he personally may have been obliged to make some kind recompense but that wouldn't have affected him. So why would he need to kill anybody? I'm sorry, but to me that idea is a non-starter."

Carlton conceded that it was a compelling argument but remained convinced that Eaton was involved somehow.

The trio continued to put forward various possibilities until Sam reminded Naomi and Carlton that they were supposed to be going out to dinner.

Three-quarters of an hour later Carlton and Naomi were on their way to a country pub at the base of the Derbyshire foothills and as they got closer to their destination Carlton casually said, "Nearly there."

"Where are you going, The Moorfield Arms or The Little Mill?"

Carlton's mouth fell open with surprise and he said, "The Little Mill, but how on earth do you know about those pubs?"

"You forget that my dad was born near here. Both pubs were his and mum's favourites and they brought Ewan and me here every time they revisited."

"Ewan?"

"Ewan's my elder brother."

"And does he live with your mum and dad down South?

"No," said Naomi, "he works as crew aboard an eighty-four foot luxury yacht on its way to Baja in Mexico."

"Wow!" said Carlton, "I'm impressed! Talk about the life of a millionaire!"

"Well more like skivvy to a millionaire, but he does share that lifestyle and when he tells us about the sort of tips he makes we all turn green with envy!"

"Have you ever been on the boat?"

"Only once when he was in Poole but that was about eighteen months ago, now I believe he's in Fort Lauderdale."

"Very nice;" said Carlton, "have you ever been to America?"

"No, how about you?"

Carlton didn't answer for a second as he negotiated a tight right hand bend and then said, "I haven't been to North America."

"North America?"

"Yes, I went to South America-ish, or should I say The Falklands when I was in the forces, but never did go to the U.S."

He turned his head away, but not far enough to stop Naomi catching him smile.

"And?" she said.

Carlton knew that she wouldn't let it go. He said, "And it's not for the want of being invited."

"And?"

There was no evading what he'd started with the half concealed smile.

"It's who's doing the inviting."

"Cal!" she said in a mock-exasperated tone, "*And*?"

"All right, it's Auntie Rosie and the sewing circle!"

Naomi smiled and put her hand up to her mouth.

"And does Auntie Rosie want you to join her and the ladies for some serious stitching?!! Is that why you won't go?!"

"O.K., laugh it up chuckles!" said Carlton as he turned the car into the pub car park, "But if you ever get to meet him…"

"*Him*?" said an astonished Naomi.

Carlton turned to face her, winked and climbed out of the car; he walked around to the passenger side and opened the door for her.

Naomi climbed out, took his offered arm and said, "Auntie Rosie's a *him*?"

Carlton said, "I'll tell you when we get settled."

They headed into the comforting warmth of the main bar, ordered their choice of drinks and food and then found a table and sat down.

"O.K.," said Naomi, "you've kept me waiting long enough. Who is Auntie Rosie, and why is *she* a *he*?"

"Because he's gay."

Naomi didn't think that she could have been more surprised.

"And the sewing circle? Are you going to tell me that they're all gay guys too?"

Carlton smiled and nodded.

"Carlton Wilkes!" she said, "You continue to amaze me! And just why do they want *you* to go and visit *them*?" She suddenly had a thought, and said, "Oh, er, unless…"

"No! Don't even think it!" said Carlton defensively, "They're always asking me to go and visit because I did a Lone Ranger act in The Falklands and saved three of their lives."

Naomi opened her mouth to speak but was instantly quashed.

"It was nothing that any of the other guys wouldn't have done in the same situation." said Carlton obviously not wanting to pursue it.

Naomi gathered that he wasn't the type to acknowledge that he'd done anything out of the ordinary and decided not to push it. Instead she said, "And did you know about their particular persuasion before you helped them?"

"No, it wasn't until much later that I found out that they were men who were, er... good with scatter cushions shall we say."

Naomi couldn't help smiling at Carlton's analogy.

"Auntie Rosie is an ex-SAS Colour Sergeant named Rob McCloud and the sewing circle consists of four other marines - one corporal and three privates."

Naomi sniggered and said, "One corporal and *three* privates! Now I'd like to meet him!"

Carlton gave her a glance of mock disapproval and said, "Oh you would, would you?" He smiled and then continued, "Three of the guys, Rob, Henry and Lloyd were in the same unit in The Falklands and after leaving the forces they joined the Merchant Navy where they met Pete and Kevin another two ex-marines. They bonded like some sisterhood out of hell. Rob became Rosie, Henry became Hilda; Lloyd, Lola; Kevin became Kitty, and Pete, Randy."

"Randy?" said Naomi smiling, "Do I take it that that's the obvious?"

Carlton gave her that look again and said, "No, it's because his surname is Kincaid and it had to be *Randy* Kincaid after the countless famous old cowboys didn't it?"

Naomi smiled and said, "Right got it, but how on earth did they become known as the sewing circle?"

"That was because of me. Whenever I spoke to Rosie either on the phone or in general conversation I would enquire how he was, then follow it up by enquiring after the rest of the 'sewing circle'. It just fell into affectionate use by us all."

"And how and where did they end up in America?"

"Once they'd exhausted their travelling bug on the cruise ships they settled in Miami."

Naomi shook her head in amazement and said, "How weird is that? In the same two hour period we hear that the Ramsbottoms, my brother and your, your..."

"Yes, spit it out laughing girl, my, my what?"

"Your close friends who are good with scatter cushions" said Naomi barely suppressing her mirth, "are all currently in Florida!"

"Yes, it does appear to push the boundaries of coincidence to the extreme doesn't it?"

"So what do they do now?"

"They run two small businesses, one offers protection and transport to sensitive clients such as politicians, personalities and celebrities etcetera, and the other is running a small but apparently infamous gay revue bar near Miami Beach.

And who knows," he said, "your brother Ewan may have even had a glass or two in their establishment!"

Naomi raised her eyebrows and said, "Not likely…"

"And now that they've put down roots," said Carlton, "they are constantly inviting me over for a visit."

"Aren't you ever tempted or do you feel awkward in their company?"

"I am tempted, and no, I never feel awkward in their company. Auntie Rosie was a field promoted Colour Sergeant with a string of bravery medals and the sewing circle is about as hard a bunch of men as you'd ever want to meet, so there is never any trouble! I just haven't made the time."

As Carlton finished telling Naomi about the sewing circle their meals arrived. There was enough food on the plate to sink a battleship and Naomi gasped as it was placed in front of her.

"Good grief," she said, "I'll never finish that lot!"

"You get it down you," said Carlton sternly, "it'll put hairs on your chest!"

Naomi looked at Carlton for a second and said, "Hmm, firstly you tell me that you're close to five gay marines and next you're encouraging me to grow hairs on my chest. Do I sense a pattern here…?"

Carlton burst out laughing and said, "Absolutely not!"

As the evening progressed they spoke about cabbages and Kings and everything in between thoroughly enjoying one another's company, and then as Naomi was passing on a small piece of trivia about Sir Arthur Conan-Doyle's father being both an accomplished artist and a patient in a lunatic asylum, something triggered in Carlton's brain.

He recalled the famous quotation made by Sherlock Holmes stating, *'When you have eliminated the impossible, whatever remains, however improbable, must be the truth.'*, and his mind started to wander over to Whitewall and Giles Eaton.

Suddenly the veil drew back and he let out an involuntary, "Ha!"

Naomi, who was half way through an anecdote stopped and looked at him questioningly.

Carlton apologised for his outburst, reacquainted Naomi with the famous line and said, "I think that that's where we've been going wrong. We haven't even eliminated all the possibles yet, let alone the impossibles. We've only really thought about the one possibility, the land purchased by the old Hundersfield District Council and that Eaton would have had nothing to gain by suppressing the truth.

But do you remember what your dad said? He told us that *two* pieces of land had been sold illegally, so what if Eaton's silence was worth paying for if he was to suppress the truth about the other sale?"

Naomi sat thinking until she heard Carlton quietly say, "Cui bono?" She looked up and said, "What did you say?"

"Cui bono Naomi; it means 'who benefits?' - in other words who could possibly profit by buying Eaton's silence to retain the status quo?

They both sat in silence finishing their meals and ruminating over Carlton's theory until Naomi decided to change the subject.

"Right, now that you're in a thoughtful mood, I have something else to tell you, and I want you to promise that you won't laugh at me."

Carlton looked at her curiously and said, "It sounds serious, what is it?"

Naomi carefully explained all of the unusual psychic experiences that she'd been having, starting with the female voice, right through to the ones where she could feel her head being pushed under water and that of the female arm pointing to a storage area at Whitewall.

She explained her reluctance to bring up the topic to anybody apart from her family because of the reaction she'd had from Chief

Inspector Crowthorne and told him that she was concerned that her professional rationale could also be questioned if she spoke about her revelations whilst trying to deal with historic matters.

Carlton listened to Naomi's experiences and when she'd finished said, "Personally, I would discount nothing. I am too long in the tooth to think that I know everything and frankly, the older I get the more I realise I don't know.

I would never mock you or poo-poo the idea because I've seen what happens to people in life or death situations and I don't think that psychic imagery is just for the mysterious-looking women who adorn themselves in black clothing and ankle length skirts, but I can see how outsiders might think that your objectivity could be compromised if they think that you're making judgements based upon the ethereal, rather than the factual."

"I would never do that," said Naomi.

"No quite. But you told me how Crowthorne reacted when he heard the tales of apparent psychic activity and it would do your credibility no good at all now, if you are anything other than totally professional." He paused for a second and then said, "But having said all of that, if somebody from the past really is trying to help you and it actually turns up new evidence, how good would that be? What a fantastic card to have up your sleeve. And who knows what else could turn up?"

"And what about the arm pointing to the storage shed?" said Naomi.

"We'll wait until you're asked to go up to Whitewall again and I'll find an excuse to come with you, if you experience that or any other feelings, we'll try to deal with them on the spot."

"And do you think we should confide in the Chief Inspector if I get a feeling?"

"Let's see if you do first."

Naomi sat back on the sofa and couldn't have felt happier, the softness of the cushions tended to push them together and she could feel the strength of the man next to her.

One of her biggest fears, that of not being taken seriously about her unusual experiences had been allayed and Carlton had totally accepted her for who she was.

Not for the first time that night, she turned to look at the man next to her and really liked what she saw, but this time he was looking at her with the same look upon his face.

Their eyes met and time stood still, she felt her mind start to swim in a glorious rush of emotion, and then as if her head had been magnetised, she felt her face drawing towards his.

She closed her eyes, their lips met and his kiss lifted her off the planet and out into space.

Chapter 31

6th August 2002. Whitewall Farm

Thirteen days after the unnerving episode at Whitewall, Chief Inspector Crowthorne was back. He was not the sort to be put off by inexplicable incidents but he couldn't help feeling uneasy; he was aware that he was listening for even the faintest noise from outside and each time he heard one, he would turn in that direction and momentarily stop speaking.

"I can see that this place is affecting you Chief Inspector." said Alan Hawthorn as he looked across the kitchen table, "Mind you, you got a bit bloody close to Rover-over last time you were here didn't you?"

Crowthorne smiled uneasily at Alan, "I take it that you mean the dog or whatever it was, and yes it was a little too close for my liking."

The Chief Forensic Archaeologist, Professor Gordon Catchpole, Forensic Archaeologist Doctor Barbara Wayne, the Finds Director Doctor Maureen Williams, Naomi, Carlton, Crowthorne and the Hawthorns, this time with their daughter Joyce, made up the nine people sitting around the table.

"Do you know that most of the original team have refused to come back?" said Gordon to Crowthorne.

"Yes, I had been told but fortunately the incident had exactly the opposite effect on other folk; following the breaking of the story in the local news, and then especially in the national news, we were inundated with offers of help."

"Did you ever find out who told the news people?" Annie Hawthorn placed a tray with biscuits and large mugs of tea for everybody on the table.

"No, but if had found out I would have had their guts for garters."

Everybody took sips of their respective drinks and turned almost as one when Crowthorne noisily cleared his throat and said, "Let's get to business shall we?"

He pointed towards Carlton and said, "For those of you who don't know, this is Carlton Wilkes; he is the Head of the Planning Department at Walmsfield Borough Council and has been involved with these proceedings since the outset."

All heads nodded towards Carlton and he acknowledged them with a smile and nod back.

"And," said Crowthorne, "may I also introduce Joyce, Annie and Alan's daughter."

"I'm the chief tea maker!" said Joyce smiling at everybody.

Once again everybody responded back with a smile.

"Now Gordon, would you please start us off and tell us what you've found?"

Professor Catchpole opened up a document folder, smoothed the contents with his right hand and looked at everybody in turn.

"Right." he said, "First things first. I'm sure that you'll all be relieved to know that we haven't had any further strange sounds or occurrences emanating from any of the rooms since the occasion of the Chief Inspector's last visit."

"More's the pity," said Alan, "we've lived with his shenanigans for as long as I can remember, and Rover-over used to keep unwanted visitors at bay. I expect that now he's stopped barking and putting the sh..." he cast a quick glance in the direction of the ladies, "...sorry, the willies up people, we'll start getting all sorts of ne'er-do-wells knocking at the door."

"That's the second time I've heard you call him Rover-over?" said Doctor Wayne, "Is that what you called the dog we heard the other day?"

"It's what Alan and I called him when he started making a din," said Annie, "We'd just look at one another and say, 'It's only Rover over there.' That got shortened to Rover-over."

"Well," said Crowthorne, "I can't say that I'm sorry Rover-over's stopped making a din as you say."

"That's not strictly true though is it dad?" Joyce looked across to where her father was sitting.

Alan frowned at his daughter and said, "Leave it Joyce."

A pregnant silence ensued before Annie Hawthorn said, "Alan..."

Alan shot a darting glance over to his wife and said, "I said, leave it be!"

Nobody said a word; they just stared intently in his direction.

Joyce broke the silence and said, "Come on dad, we're not keeping secrets from anybody and so much weird stuff has happened here that one more bit won't make a difference."

"All right, all right!" said a clearly exasperated Alan, "I think I've heard him again. There, are you satisfied now?" He paused long enough to invite comment, but when none was forthcoming he continued, "At the back of the storage buildings there's a dense copse. I'd gone up to call the herd yesterday morning when suddenly I heard this bloody awful racket coming from within the trees. Wasn't just my imagination either, 'cos it spooked all the cows and had 'em running across the field in panic. Naturally I was hesitant at first, but when nothing more happened I thought it must have been a large dog that had finally gone away. Anyway, I called the herd in and thought no more about 'til this morning.

The cows were out to pasture in the same field and as I approached them, this bloody howl went up from within the trees that nearly had me mess my britches. The herd scattered again, so this time I came back for my gun and went back to the copse for a look see.

End result is, I found nothing. No animal, no footprints in the mud, no nothing, so I headed back out into the pasture and had no sooner cleared the last trees when another bloody howl came from right behind me. I don't mind telling you, I very nearly let go that time. I whipped round with the gun ready to shoot, but there was nothing there. Not a bloody thing."

The atmosphere within the room could have been cut with a knife.

Alan looked from face to face then slowly said, "Whatever was in that room didn't go away; we haven't got rid of him, we've somehow opened the door and let him out."

Naomi sat back in her chair as a thought process started to gain momentum in her mind; she looked back at the seated assembly, opened her mouth to say something, and then decided against it at the last moment.

"And did it sound like the same animal we all heard in that room across the yard?" asked Gordon.

"It didn't *sound the same*," said Alan forcefully, "it was the same."

This was all becoming too much for Naomi, the thumb was pressing heavily down upon her shoulder and she could hear the voice saying *"Maria, Maria, this way... Maria..."* She shook her head and tried to clear her mind. Suddenly she sat up with such a jerk that Carlton immediately asked her if she was all right. She nodded and said, "Sorry, just a nerve..."

Carlton continued to stare at Naomi and knew that something was wrong.

She looked at Carlton, briefly shook her head and mouthed quietly, "It's O.K. - I'll explain later."

Following a few seconds of close scrutiny, Carlton heard the Chief Inspector speak and turned to look in his direction.

"Perhaps we'd better let Gordon continue," said Crowthorne. "We can speculate as much as we like about the sounds we heard coming from that room, but we have no evidence to suggest that it was er, er..."

"Ghostly?" said Alan.

"Yes, quite," said Crowthorne.

"So what do you think was in that room Chief Inspector," said Alan cuttingly, "Scotch bloody mist?"

Crowthorne shrugged his shoulders uncomfortably and said, "At this point in time I don't think that we have enough evidence to say one way or the other. I think..."

"I think you nearly shat your pants when you thought that *lack of evidence* was going to get out and bite your arse..." said Alan acerbically.

"Alan! That's enough" said Annie.

"Well," said Alan, "can't say one way or the other indeed!"

Gordon decided to divert attention away from the luckless policeman. He took a deep breath and said, "Right then, if you'd all care to pay attention; we have managed to establish that we are dealing with the remains of at least four people."

"Four people?" said a shocked Annie, "That's dreadful!"

"Four people," confirmed Gordon, "Three women buried in the room to the left of the barn, and one young male buried in a barrel, or to be more precise, large water butt, in the room immediately to the right of it."

Annie Hawthorn removed the hand that she'd clamped tightly over her mouth and said, "One male buried in a barrel for God's sake? What on earth…"

"Forgive me for interrupting Gordon," said Crowthorne, "but when I looked into the barrel I could see the remains of two people in there, not one."

"No," said Gordon, "you saw two skulls, which led you to believe that there were two bodies in there, but in fact there was only one."

"Oh, this just keeps on getting better doesn't it?" said a mortified Annie.

"So where did the other skull come from?" said Crowthorne.

"From one of the bodies recovered in the other room."

"Oh good Lord above!" said Annie, now totally incapable of controlling her emotions, "That's horrific! Are you telling us that somebody cut the head off one of those young women and buried it with the young man in the barrel?"

Gordon paused for a second and then said, "Would you prefer us to continue without you Mrs Hawthorn? I realise that this is very distressing, and I don't want to expose you to unnecessary trauma…"

"No," said Annie, "I've been a farm girl all my life and I'm made of sterner stuff than that, I just couldn't help expressing my feelings when you said what you did."

"Well, if you're sure?"

"I am!" said Annie, "please continue."

Gordon looked around the room, satisfied himself that everybody was calm and said, "It would also appear that the young man may have been buried alive with the head of the young woman."

Annie let out a gasp and said, "O.K. I'm sorry, I take it back, I'm not such stern stuff after all. I have a daughter of my own and this is too much for me; I'm going outside for a breath of fresh air. Don't stop on my account, Alan can bring me up to date later."

There was a pause in the proceedings as Annie excused herself and left the room.

"Now," said the Professor, "none of the bodies found are recent burials and there is dating evidence on the barrel. When we finally unearthed it and cleaned it up, we were able to see a cooper's stamp dated 1867. There is no guarantee that Carbon 14 dating will provide definitive proof, but several samples of material have been sent away for analysis. The associated evidence however, seems to indicate that all of these activities dated from around the same period, which of course may in turn point to all of these crimes having been perpetrated by the same person, or persons."

Once again Gordon stopped in order to allow questions to be asked, but as before everybody remained silent.

"Thanks to Naomi we do know positively that seven people were reported missing from here in mysterious circumstances…"

"There are more bodies…" Naomi's comment stopped the proceedings dead. She saw Carlton frown and then stare at her in disbelief.

"What do you mean, there are more?" said Crowthorne, "Have you uncovered some new evidence?"

Naomi knew that she'd spoken prematurely, and against the advice of Carlton, but it was out in the open. She mentally kicked herself for having made a statement based on subjectivity rather than objectivity, the very mistake that she had specifically identified as being the worst thing that she could do. She needed to recover the situation quickly.

"No I haven't," she said, "I mean that there are more reports of people missing from here in the same period of time, and that if we have found only four, it would be fair to assume that we could potentially find more."

She saw Carlton visibly relax; she seemed to have recovered her position without exposing herself to potential ridicule.

Crowthorne wasn't so easily appeased.

"Are you quite sure that you aren't withholding anything germane to these investigations Mrs. Draper? You did sound as though you were making a statement of fact."

"No of course I'm not, why would I?"

Crowthorne looked at her quietly for several seconds then said, "Very well. I am aware that there are other reports and we are currently checking our rather sparse records for missing people from that era, but for the present we shall not concern ourselves with speculation."

"Does that mean that despite having found bodies in two of the rooms from the old building, you won't be checking out any others?" said Joyce.

Crowthorne started to feel as though he was being interrogated rather than chairing a meeting.

"No, I didn't say that we wouldn't be examining other rooms on site, I am simply pointing out that for the present, we have no evidence leading us to believe that we may find anything else here."

"Does being bloody evasive form part of your copper training?" said Alan just as Annie walked back into the room.

"No not at all," said Crowthorne, "and let me assure that we will bring in specially trained sniffer dogs to check other locations, but police resources are finite and we cannot haphazardly dig holes without at least suspecting that there's something to find."

Alan opened his mouth to speak but was quelled by a withering look from Annie.

Gordon decided to throw Crowthorne a lifeline and said, "I've spoken with the Chief Inspector in private and I can confirm that once we have completed our current investigations we'll turn our attention to other parts of the farm; but he is perfectly right in saying that we will only dig holes where we believe we are likely to find something."

Joyce turned to Naomi and said, "Who do you think the bodies are?"

"That's a very difficult question to answer factually," said Naomi.

"But I thought the Chief Inspector said that you knew who they were."

"No," said Naomi, "he said thanks to me we know of seven people reported missing from here. That's an entirely different thing to actually knowing whose bodies we've found. These four may be other people altogether."

"And do you think there are more people buried up here?" asked Joyce.

"That," said Carlton fending off Naomi's answer, "would as Chief Inspector Crowthorne said, be pure speculation.".

"Precisely," said Crowthorne, "Now, I suggest we let Gordon finish his report."

"Before we go any further," said Annie, "do you think that all the people found over there were murdered?"

"I know so," said Gordon.

"Oh Lord above!" Annie put her hand up to her mouth, "And we've been living here completely oblivious to it all these years."

"How do you know?" asked Naomi.

"Dr. Wayne can answer that better than me." Gordon turned to face her and said, "Barbara?"

"Because apart from the obvious decapitation, the three females recovered from below the flags in the original finds room had marks between their ribs consistent with stab wounds from an unusually shaped knife.

We found no such marks on the bones of the body recovered from the barrel, but I concur with Gordon that the male placed in there may well have been alive when he went in."

Almost in unison, Annie, Naomi and Joyce gasped in horror.

Carlton said, "How have you arrived at that conclusion?"

"Because we found faint but distinguishable scratch marks on the underside of the barrel lid and traces of the same wood under the male's fingernails."

"So the lad was buried alive with the head of one of the women?" said Alan.

Dr. Wayne looked at Alan and said, "I said that he may have been alive when he was buried, not that he was. Certainly he was alive when he was placed in the barrel, but it is possible that he died before the barrel was buried."

"Nevertheless," said Annie, "what must that poor soul have gone through?"

"Do the fragments of clothing found in there tell us any more?" asked Crowthorne.

"They too have been sent away for analysis, but of course DNA testing would be pointless because whoever committed these crimes will have been dead for a long time too."

The pressure of the thumb on Naomi's shoulder was now so powerful that it physically hurt her and she started to gently massage the area whilst stretching her neck from side to side.

Carlton saw her discomfort and said, "Excuse me folks, but are you all right Naomi?"

"It's just a stiff neck," she said, "I must have slept on it wrongly but thank you for asking."

Carlton was now utterly convinced that something was wrong.

"Over the next few days," said Crowthorne, "we shall be

working closely with Mrs Draper in trying to establish the identity of the bodies found here, and as I said earlier, if we find even the remotest hint that other bodies may be buried in any of the other buildings, we shall fully investigate it."

Everybody remained silent.

Crowthorne looked slowly around the assemblage then opened one of the files in front of him; he turned several pages and said, "For your information, the local police visited Whitewall on several occasions between 1867 and 1870, the time period that we believe we are dealing with, but according to our records, and despite numerous reports of foul play, no evidence was ever found to substantiate it and nobody was brought to trial."

"Unbelievable!" said Naomi.

Upon receiving no further comments Crowthorne turned to Gordon and raised his eyebrows.

Gordon nodded and said "Now, the dog. Firstly there is no denying that we all heard some kind of canine sounds emanating from the room next to the barn and we are not the only people to have heard them as there are countless reports stretching back for years. However, in cold hard facts we've found absolutely no evidence of a dog having ever been in that room. We found no footprints, no fur, no scratches, no anything.

When Bob and I first went in there we found the top of a barrel burst open and wondered whether that could have accounted for anything to do with the sounds, but not so. A closer examination revealed that lid had somehow been forced open from the inside but we can't assign this to anything and apart from the human remains, we found nothing else in there; not even anything that could have explained the huge swarm of flies either.

We've carried out exhaustive tests since the occurrence and we're still at a complctc loss to explain any of it.

"But what about the woman who was inside the room when the racket started?" said Naomi, "Surely she must have seen something?"

"Ah yes," said Gordon, "Frankie – she's no longer with us."

"I'm not surprised," said Naomi, "she must have been traumatised!"

"Yes she was, but she never saw anything; and apparently she tried to tell everybody in the police car so on the day, but she said that she was ignored."

Naomi felt a bit culpable knowing that she had been one of the guilty parties. She glossed over it and said, "That seems impossible, we saw how she staggered out of that room, she was scared stiff."

"I agree, but we questioned her very thoroughly and she was adamant that she saw nothing in there. She said that as soon as she'd stepped inside the lights had fused, the door had slammed shut and some huge animal had started growling and barking at her from the corner. She said that she'd been so petrified by the ferocity and intensity of what she heard that she'd collapsed onto the floor and had expected to be set upon at any moment, but when nothing had happened she'd dragged herself to her feet, staggered outside and been helped to safety by Bob."

"Now do you believe in ghosts Chief Inspector?" said Alan.

Crowthorne twisted his head uncomfortably to one side and said, "We are not for one moment considering that this occurrence was anything not of this world.

I agree that the animal sounds are difficult to rationalise, but the barrel could have been forced open by something like a pressure build-up; maybe created by a chemical reaction of some sort which could have vented itself once we started creating ground disturbances nearby."

All eyes turned to Gordon who was frowning at Crowthorne. He opened his mouth to speak, but thought better of it.

Everybody was stunned by Crowthorne's ridiculous explanation but his dogged determination not to accept that it might have been something out of the ordinary was difficult to argue with logically.

Following a few seconds of uncomfortable silence Crowthorne re-took the initiative and said, "Right ladies and gentlemen, another reason for bringing you all together like this is to inform you that the *factual* things we have spoken about this morning will form the basis of a press bulletin to be released later today.

We will not be speculating about sounds or talking about anything that could be construed as ghostly and if any of you are individually approached by members of the press, we would advise you to do the same."

Nods of approval came from everybody around the table.

"Finally," said Crowthorne, "until all of the investigations are complete, you are to divulge no further details of our findings to anybody. Is that understood?"

Everybody nodded but remained silent.

"Very well then, it just remains for me to thank you for your co-operation and patience, particularly Mr. and Mrs. Hawthorn and Joyce, and to tell you that if you want to see the bulletin it will be shown on tonight's early evening news."

As the assembly parted company Carlton made his way across to Naomi and said, "Are you all right? You had me concerned about you several times today."

Naomi said, "We've got to go into the yard as soon as possible."

Carlton didn't argue, he simply said "Wait here for me."

He walked over to Crowthorne who was talking to Annie and asked if they could be allowed to have a look around some of the older parts of the farm for interest's sake. Annie immediately gave permission but he could feel Crowthorne staring at him as he slowly moved back to Naomi.

"O.K. let's go," he said. They nodded and waved goodbyes, thanked the Hawthorns and moved into the courtyard.

"All right, what's this all about?" said Carlton quietly.

Naomi could hardly speak, the thumb was pressing hard into her shoulder and the voice was clearly saying, "*In the parlour Maria, in the parlour...*"

"Yes I heard you, but where is it?" said Naomi out loud.

Carlton turned to her and said, "What do you mean, where is it?"

"*You remember when you first visited me...*"

"But I haven't visited you," said Naomi.

Carlton stopped dead in his tracks and looked hard at Naomi. She appeared to be in a world of her own as she walked to the opposite side of the farmyard.

"*Of course you have my dear Maria,*" said the voice, "*how could you possibly forget...*"

Naomi carried on walking until she found herself inside an open fronted storage shed. The walls were the local sandstone and had no render or plaster on. The back of the shed had four Tudor style windows let into the centre, whilst on each side of her, were blanked out walls. Directly overhead was the bare underside of the roof.

"I'm not Maria," said Naomi, "What do you want? And who are you?"

She could clearly see what had made her jump during the meeting. In front of her wasn't just a hand or an arm, but a full length small, slim, attractive looking lady dressed in an ankle length dress. She had dark hair tied up in a bun and was pointing to the ground beneath her feet.

"*Why of course you are! I'd recognise you anywhere,*" said the voice, "*And you know me too, I'm…*"

"Naomi, are you all right?"

Carlton's voice cut across her senses like a knife, she turned and saw him standing behind her just inside the shed.

"Shush Cal. Please stay there and keep quiet." Naomi closed her eyes and tried to recall what she had seen, but whatever had been there had gone. The thumb had stopped pressing on her shoulder too.

For several minutes she stood quietly trying to reconnect, but to no avail. Presently she turned and said, "It's not just an arm anymore, it's a full woman I can see and at one point I thought she was going to tell me her name."

"Good grief," said Carlton, "that's amazing. Doesn't it disturb you?"

"No not really," said Naomi slowly walking back to Carlton and linking his arm, "but amazingly she keeps on calling me Maria and…"

"*Down here Maria! Down here!*"

Naomi whirled around with such speed that Carlton jumped back in surprise. The woman was back and pointing straight down to the ground below her. Naomi looked at the spot and then looked back at the woman and nodded.

"*Splendid!*" said the woman, "*And how could you possibly forget your friend Margaret?*"

"Margaret?" said Naomi; then the penny dropped. "Oh my God, not…?"

"*There now, I knew you'd remember.*" She smiled at Naomi and said, "*Goodbye my dear, and oh, Florence wishes to be remembered too."*

"Florence?" said Naomi, but the vision had vanished as quickly as it had appeared.

"Margaret, Florence?" said Carlton, "You're starting to worry me now. What are you talking about?"

Naomi ignored Carlton's questions, walked across to where 'Margaret' had been pointing and said, "We've got to dig here and I've got to speak to Alan Hawthorn - *now*."

Carlton said "Naomi!"

"Please Cal, trust me and do as I say."

Carlton took a deep breath and said, "O.K., if you're really sure…"

"I am. Now I'm going back inside to speak to Alan, will you speak to the Chief Inspector?"

"I will," said Carlton, "but how on earth am I going to explain my request, I…" He saw Naomi looking at him with a determined look upon her face. "All right," he said, "don't worry, I'll speak to him now."

Naomi thanked Carlton and returned to the kitchen where Alan was still receiving a mild roasting from Annie for his intolerant behaviour with the Chief Inspector. As she walked into the room Annie stopped much to his relief.

"Alan," said Naomi, "would you be kind enough to take me up to the copse where you heard the barking?"

Alan frowned, looked at Annie and got up from his chair.

"I hope you don't expect to find anything up there," he said, "'cos you won't. But if looking's all you want to do well fine, I'll take you."

As they made their way across the field towards the copse Naomi suddenly felt the thumb press down upon her shoulder; she closed her eyes and rubbed it and walked straight into the back of Alan.

Alan whipped around; put a finger up to his mouth and said, 'Sshh'. He stood silently staring into the trees for what seemed like an eternity then turned and quietly said, "I thought I saw something move in there."

"Like what?" whispered Naomi.

"I don't know but perhaps we'd best get the shotgun."

Naomi was so distracted by the pressure from the thumb that she said, "What do you want?"

Alan looked at her oddly and said, "I said we'd best get the shotgun!"

Naomi regained composure and said, "Sorry, of course, you go and get it, I'll wait here."

Alan said, "No lass, I'm not leaving you here on your own."

Naomi nodded and started to follow Alan back to the farm then suddenly said, "you'd better bring a spade too."

"*A spade?*"

"Yes, a spade, but please be discreet and don't tell anybody else."

"All right," he said resignedly, "nothing about this place surprises me anymore…"

As Naomi waited for Alan at the edge of the farmyard she tried to reconnect to the voice, but the thumb had stopped pressing and try as she may she neither felt, nor heard anything more.

Five minutes later Alan returned with an uncocked shotgun over his left forearm and a spade in his right hand.

"Right," he said as he approached, "let's get on up there. Time's a passing and nowt stops for owt on a farm."

As they reached the edge of the copse he put down the spade and cocked the shotgun. For a while he watched and listened until he was satisfied that they were alone then he turned to Naomi and said "Where do you want to go?"

Naomi opened her mouth to speak but the thumb pressed down again.

"*Follow him…*" said the voice.

Naomi wasn't sure what the voice meant but she didn't want to arouse any suspicions in Alan, so she remained silent.

"Well?" said Alan.

"*Follow him…*" said the voice again.

"Why don't you show me where you were standing when you heard the barking?"

Alan grunted, picked up the spade and led Naomi a little way into the copse. The whole time he kept constantly alert, looking left and then right for any unusual signs of activity.

"It was about here," he said.

"And were you on this same spot, when you heard it on both

occasions?"

"Roughly."

"And from where did you hear the barking?"

Alan turned and pointed to a spot several feet behind him.

"Just there," he said.

Naomi walked over to the spot and the pressure from the thumb became almost unbearable, she reached up to her shoulder and massaged it.

"*Here...*" said the voice.

She looked down at the ground and said to Alan, "I know that this sounds odd, but will you please carefully dig up one or two spades full of earth for me?"

Alan nodded, activated the safety catch on the shotgun, stood it up against a nearby trunk and started digging.

The voice in Naomi's head suddenly made an "*Aah*" sound as Alan stopped digging.

"Ayup," he said, "what's that?"

Naomi walked over, looked into the shallow hole and instantly recognised the top of a human skull. She kneeled down gently brushed some damp soil to one side and said, "We'd better get the Chief Inspector up here, there's a girl in there."

"How do you know it's a girl?" said Alan.

Naomi realised that she'd spoken again without thinking first and made a mental note to be more cautious in the future. She looked at Alan and guessed that he wouldn't know the full extent of her professional knowledge.

"It's my job to know such things," she said.

"And how did you know where to dig?"

"Just a hunch based upon what you said about letting Rover-over out. I figured that if we'd found things where he'd been barking for years, and then he'd started barking somewhere else nearby, maybe he was alerting us to some other finds."

"Bloody 'ell lass, that's creepy!"

"Nevertheless..." Naomi pointed into the open hole.

"Stone the bloody crows," said Alan clearly taken aback, "what if yon dog turns up barking all over the show?"

"Then based upon what we've seen today, we'd better start looking there too."

Alan leaned on the spade and said, "I knew this place had

some weird history, but this just about takes the biscuit." He thought for a little longer then added, "And how are we going to tell that bloody copper how we've found this?"

"I shouldn't worry too much about that for the moment," said Naomi, "I think he'll be having an interesting enough conversation with Carlton right now."

Chapter 32

Florence walked smartly into the Reception Lodge, swept past the counter and headed straight for the door marked 'Private'; she grabbed the handle, turned it and found that it was locked.

The male receptionist leaned through the glass partition over the counter and said, "Sorry Sister that door stays locked for security purposes."

"I understand," said Florence, "will you unlock it for me please?"

"What exactly do you want Sister?"

"I want to go into the admin offices."

"If you're just delivering something, I can take it for you; I've a pile of other stuff to go down."

"No thank you," said Florence, "That's very kind of you but I have a query about my remuneration that needs sorting out."

"Very well Sister, just a mo."

Florence watched as the man unlocked a small wooden cupboard on the back wall of the reception office and removed a single key from the first hook on the left of the top row. He then walked back to the counter, slid the partition shut, unlocked his office door and walked across to where she was standing.

"Allow me Sister." He unlocked the door and held it open.

Florence thanked him and hoped that he wouldn't escort her down to the admin offices. Her luck held.

"Tap on the small window to my office just inside the door when you've done, and I'll let you out."

Florence thanked him and walked in.

It was just as Simeon had described; there were four plain wooden doors on the right hand side of the corridor numbered one to four, one door directly facing her at the end, number five, and door number six was the one that led up to the private wards at the far end on the left.

She cautiously walked down to number six and turned the

handle; it was locked. She pressed her ear against it and heard nothing; she quickly reached up and felt along the top of the door frame but nothing was there.

She turned to her right and looked at door number five; it appeared to be a cupboard but she wasn't sure, she carefully turned the handle and pushed. That was locked too. She tapped lightly on it but drew no response.

She looked anxiously down the length of the corridor for any sign of a cupboard or even hook that may house a key but in keeping with the décor of the other buildings, the walls were painted the same pale green and devoid of anything except the small window to the reception area. She didn't know what to do next; should she brave it out and enter the admin office or not? Her heart was beating quickly; she'd never done anything like this before and whilst it was exciting, it was nerve-racking too.

Suddenly she heard footsteps coming down the stairs from behind door number six. She had to get away quickly. She hurried across to door number four and tried it; it was locked.

The footsteps drew closer.

She moved up to door number three, turned the handle and pushed, it too was locked.

She heard a key go into the lock of number six.

With a hammering heart she rushed to door number two, turned the handle and pushed. It stayed shut.

She heard the handle start to turn on number six and then the sound of keys being dropped. A female voice uttered a quiet curse.

In near panic she let go of the handle to number two and in doing so pulled it slightly. To her utmost relief it swung open; she went inside and quickly closed the door.

It was a cupboard and it was pitch dark. She stood perfectly still as she heard the footsteps walk up to where she was, hover for a second and then walk past.

She hardly dared to breathe. For one or two agonising seconds she stayed perfectly still listening as another door opened and then shut. She presumed that the person had gone into number one and couldn't now risk going in there for fear of being seen by somebody from the private wards, particularly Matron.

She had to leave.

All sounded quiet outside; she gingerly opened the door and

stepped smartly out. She hurried to the exit and tapped on the window.

The receptionist unlocked the door and smiled and said, "All done Sister?"

"Yes thank you."

"Did you sort out your problem satisfactorily?"

"Yes I did, thank you."

"One thing you can say for those girls," said the receptionist conversationally, "they're efficient; why, you haven't been in there but a couple of minutes!"

Florence hadn't considered how long she'd been in the corridor, it had felt like a lifetime and she just wanted to get away. She smiled and nodded and then hurried out of the lodge into the warmth of the afternoon sun.

With a settling heart and shaky legs she walked back towards the female epileptic wards until she reached a garden seat overlooking a flower bed and sat down.

She was now at the rear of the admin block. She turned her head to the left and looked up to the second floor. For the briefest of seconds she could have sworn that she saw somebody looking at her from an unfrosted window, but in an instant the face was gone.

She'd achieved what Simeon had asked her to do first; next she had to block a toilet and send for Len Chapman.

In less than an hour from Florence's visit to the admin block Pinkstaff was in the Medical Superintendent's office with Cobbold.

"It was Sister Parks Edwin, I saw her through the window. Charlie from reception told me that I'd just missed her, I went into the admin office and nobody had seen her so I rushed back up to the ward office, looked out of the window and saw her sitting on a garden seat staring up at the second floor."

"And you're sure that she didn't go into any of the admin offices?"

"Perfectly; I asked everybody and nobody had seen her so she had to be hiding in the store cupboard when I walked past."

"That's preposterous Ida, she must have already left."

"Not according to Charlie. He was adamant that she'd left just seconds before I spoke to him so she had to be somewhere when I came down and the only place apart from the offices was the cupboard."

Cobbold said, "I don't like the sound of this. It's just too much of a coincidence that Sister Parks' friend is up there and she's suddenly sniffing around."

The two colleagues sat in silence for a while until Cobbold said, "I'll get Arnold to arrange some help and we'll get the nine private patients down to Stafford. If Sister Parks is going to go on a crusade let's let her find nothing but empty rooms.

We know that Sir Trevor, the Chief CMO and Henry at Cheddleton are all in on the scheme so it shouldn't be too difficult to arrange temporary accommodation for our patients until all of this blows over."

"All right," said Pinkstaff, "but it's Tuesday afternoon now, I won't see Arnold until tomorrow so it's going to be at least Friday before we can move them."

"That'll be fine, let's just get it done."

A little after 10 o' clock the same evening Florence was startled by a loud hammering on her front door. Her husband Cornelius was still travelling with the circus and she didn't particularly like opening it at that time of night.

"Sister, it's me, Sim! Open up!"

Florence rushed to the door, opened it and said, "Whatever's the matter Simeon?"

"They're moving them all this Friday night!"

"Who? What?" said Florence with a puzzled expression on her face.

"All of the private patients, they're taking them to Cheddleton Asylum in Staffordshire!

I saw Mr. Honeysuckle talking to a couple of the other lads in the messroom but he shut up when he saw me and left not long after. I spoke to my mate Jim who told me that Mr. H. had been asking for volunteers to take some patients to Stafford on the late train Friday night."

Florence was stunned; she invited Simeon in, sat him down and said, "But it might not be the private patients that they're moving…"

"But that's the only thing what makes sense isn't it Sister? And even if we're wrong it won't do no harm to get Miss Maria out as quick as we can just in case."

Florence agreed and the two of them set to work on a plan that had to be executed within forty-eight hours.

As the time approached 11:15pm Simeon said, "Are you positive that Len Chapman will help us Sister?

"Yes, I've known him for years and we get on very well; I told him what had happened to Maria and what I was planning to do and hoped that he'd be sympathetic. Fortunately he's another man who likes her and he was just as shocked as we were at what had happened; he immediately offered to help.

He also told me that he'd heard rumours about patients being up on the second floor, but that he'd never been asked to carry out any maintenance work there."

"It's one thing saying you'll help Sister, actually helping is something else."

"Don't worry Sim; I'm sure that we'll be able to count on him."

"All right," said Simeon, "Please tell him that I want to see him on Thursday morning in the staff canteen at 8:30am, and ask him to bring a plan of the asylum sewers and service tunnels."

Florence grimaced but nodded and said, "Very well."

"Now," said Simeon, "that still leaves us a man short if we want to carry out the plan we've come up with."

Florence sat back in her chair and racked her brain for a man who could and would help them with such a questionable and risky operation.

"This is impossible Sim," she said, "don't you know anybody who could help us?"

"I do, but they're mostly bad 'uns, and I don't want to get involved with them no more, nor do I want them knowing where I work." He paused for a minute and then said, "And we need transport too."

The mention of transport triggered a memory in Florence's brain.

"Silas!" she said, "Silas Cartwright!"

"Who Sister?"

"Silas Cartwright; he's a cabby who's been courting Maria for this past year or so. She's spoken to me a lot about him; he has a

Hansom cab, lives in Walmsfield and works from the rank at the railway station."

"Walmsfield?" said Simeon, "That's miles away! He can't bring a Hansom cab all the way from Walmsfield to Macclesfield!"

"No, he doesn't need to. I can arrange for a small carriage to use; we just need to get him here because I'm sure that he'd help us if he knew what had happened to Maria."

Simeon thought for a few minutes and said, "I'll have to talk to Matt but I can't see any reason why I can't catch the train up there first thing tomorrow. I should be able to find him 'cos if he isn't on duty the other cabbies will know where he lives, and if he agrees, we could be here by tomorrow night."

"Excellent!" said Florence, "I'll talk to Len tomorrow." She paused for a second and then said, "But what about the keys? We need to get those copies you asked for."

"I'll get Enoch my locksmith mate to meet us here with his key cutting equipment at nine o'clock tomorrow night if that suits you?"

Florence agreed and the plan was hatched.

One or two other minor details were discussed until Simeon announced that he was about to leave.

Florence walked over to him and kissed him lightly on the cheek.

"Thank you Simeon," she said, "I don't know how I'd have managed without you."

"T'aint over yet Sister," said Simeon a little bashfully, "but God willing we'll give it a bloody good go."

"Yes, God and good luck willing," said Florence.

Chapter 33

"I've asked you all to come here at the request of Chief Inspector Crowthorne because of the tragic events that overtook our sadly missed colleagues and indeed dear friends, Mayor Tom Ramsbottom and his lovely wife, Peggy." Giles looked at the people sitting in front of him; they consisted of Crowthorne, Naomi, Carlton, Sam, his newly arrived wife Jane, and Sam's cousin John. He said, "We will of course be calling a press conference when we make a formal statement regarding their tragic deaths, but with the exception of Mrs. Chance who singularly hasn't been involved in the Whitewall affair since it first broke, we thought that it was important to acquaint you with certain facts before we go public."

Jane Chance interrupted Giles.

"Excuse me Mr. Eaton," she said, "I have been involved in the Whitewall affair right from the beginning - Sam is my husband and we *do* talk!"

Giles was taken aback by her abruptness and said, "I'm sorry Mrs. Chance, I meant no offence."

Jane nodded her acceptance of his apology. She was a straight-talking woman who had been told about Giles Eaton before meeting him and she hadn't liked what she'd heard.

The mildly chastised Town Clerk turned to Crowthorne and said, "Yes, now, Mr. Crowthorne will bring you up to date re. the current situation and provide you with an approximation of what we will tell the press."

Crowthorne cleared his throat and said, "Tom and Peggy Ramsbottom were killed outright by a large black saloon car which mounted the pavement as they walked back to their hotel in Orlando and to date the Orange County police have not apprehended anybody for their deaths but they do stress that their investigations are still under way.

They are keeping an open mind with regard to the possibility that this may have been a deliberate act of murder, but with no apparent motive for such a crime they are having difficulties in pursuing that line of enquiry."

Naomi shot a darting glance at Carlton urging him in to say something, but he remained quiet and impassive.

"Both the Lancashire and Orange County Police Forces are engaging in exchanges of information, but we like them, are at a loss to put a motive to such an apparently motiveless act."

Once again Naomi stared hard at Carlton and wondered why he wasn't feeling her eyes boring into him.

"The Ramsbottom's next of kin have been informed;" said Crowthorne, "and once the post mortems have taken place arrangements will be made to return their bodies to the UK for burial."

He stopped speaking for a second, looked around to see if there were any objections or criticisms and then said, "And that more or less covers the basis of the statement we will be giving to the press later today."

He paused and looked at the assemblage and knew from the looks on one or two faces that he had done the right thing in requesting the meeting. He took a deep breath and said, "Look, I know that some of you harbour deep misgivings about this business but until we have factual proof about what's happened all of your suspicions would be pure speculation.

Therefore I urge you, should any of you be contacted by members of the press, not to elaborate on the statement that we will be releasing."

Naomi was desperate to speak but saw Carlton looking at her negatively; she decided against it.

Crowthorne allowed a little time for his statement to sink in and then added, "Personally, I'm not a man who believes in too many coincidences and in the relatively short time that has ensued since we were made aware of the circumstances associated with Whitewall Farm far too much seems to have happened in far too little time for those coincidences to be, in my opinion, unrelated.

Therefore, following discussions with my superiors, I am happy to announce to you that Lancashire Police will not be treating this as an open and shut case and we will continue to pursue all avenues of enquiry until we are fully satisfied that foul play is not involved. Furthermore we will actively encourage anybody who can help us to come forwards with whatever information they may have, regardless of however tenuous it may seem."

Naomi could have jumped up and hugged him.

"I would ask therefore," continued Crowthorne completely unaware of Naomi's emotions, "that you contact me or any members of my team, if you think you have any information, however small, that may be germane to these enquiries."

The nods of approval and general agreement with the official police stance did nothing to appease Giles's growing discomfort as he resumed talking.

"Yes thank you Chief Inspector," he said, "I'm sure that I speak for us all in commending your resolute determination to uncover the facts surrounding this affair."

More nods of approval.

"Now, onto other matters;" said Giles, "I have informed our local police that the Mayor had in his safekeeping certain case-sensitive documents relating to the Whitewall Farm and that we are most anxious to retrieve them.

I took it upon myself to call the police in Florida…"

Naomi saw Crowthorne spin round and look at the Town Clerk with a deep frown upon his face.

"…and they informed me that they had found nothing fitting the description of that old container, nor had they found any obvious loose documents which may have been removed from it."

"Has anything turned up at the Ramsbottom's home?" asked Carlton.

Giles turned to Crowthorne and raised his eyebrows.

Crowthorne who was still frowning at the Town Clerk composed himself, checked his notes and said, "The next of kin have informed us that they have not found anything matching the description of the file, but they're not sure that they've fully exhausted finding all the places in which their parents may have secreted personal items.

I am referring of course to such places as bank vaults, solicitors offices and so on."

Naomi simply couldn't contain herself any longer; she knew

that she could potentially incur the wrath of her superiors at a later time, but said, "The contents of that file are very, *very,* important Chief Inspector Crowthorne."

All heads swivelled around to look at Naomi, but only Giles gestured for her to keep quiet.

"No, I'm sorry Mr. Eaton, I will not keep quiet!" said Naomi, "The Chief Inspector should be made aware of certain facts!"

Crowthorne's initial look of interest turned to one of concern. He said, "I think you'd better explain Mrs. Draper."

Carlton immediately jumped in and said, "If I may be permitted Chief Inspector?" All heads turned to face him.

Crowthorne nodded in his direction and said. "Yes."

"Naomi as you know, is in charge of our Historic Research Department and is responsible for the welfare and safekeeping of all of our historic artefacts, documentation and files, and is therefore concerned that once found, this particular file should be treated with the utmost care and consideration due to its age and condition."

"Oh, I see," said Crowthorne thoughtfully.

Carlton saw Giles sit back in his chair with a relieved look upon his face whilst he shot a quelling glance at Naomi.

Against her better judgement, Naomi remained silent and nodded in the direction of the policeman.

"Well in that case please let me assure you," said Crowthorne, "that we will call you personally the minute we locate the file and we will of course let you supervise its handling and safekeeping from then on."

Naomi thanked him and fell silent as Giles spoke again.

"Good," he said, "I think that we have all the bases covered for now, unless anybody has any further questions either for me or the Chief Inspector."

There was a brief pause and then Jane Chance spoke.

"Mr. Eaton, does Chief Inspector Crowthorne know what was in the Whitewall file?"

Crowthorne turned to look at Giles.

"No he does not."

"Wouldn't it help him get a clearer understanding of things if you told him?"

"It may very well," said Giles, "but I am the Town Clerk of

Walmsfield; I have a duty to the people of this Borough and I am restricted by the confines of the Data Protection Act. If the police establish that criminal activity *is* involved, we will happily impart as much information as they require, but until then all private and personal files will remain fully confidential."

Everybody in the room remained silent, but Naomi saw Crowthorne look at Giles with a frown upon his face again.

Giles looked slowly around the gathered company and finally said, "Very well then, I'd like to conclude by thanking you all for your time today, and for the Chief Inspector's help in trying to trace our missing file. I feel sure that it will only be a matter of time before our splendid boys in blue do locate it.

Now, I have arranged for light refreshments to be served in the boardroom, so," he pointed towards a door in the corner, "shall we?"

Everybody moved into the adjacent room.

Carlton sidled up to Naomi and said, "That was silly and impulsive."

"Yes I know. I'm sorry but I agree with mum, if Crowthorne did know the contents of the file he would have a completely different view of things."

"Maybe so," said Carlton quietly, "but you don't play poker well if everybody else can see your hand. An old army instructor of mine once told me to keep my friends close, but keep my enemies even closer so let's not do anything impulsive that may put Eaton on guard. We need to engender self-confidence, smugness..." he looked down into Naomi's big brown eyes, they looked so beautiful that he felt himself waver, he paused momentarily then said, "Do you remember the saying, 'give a man enough rope and he'll hang himself'?"

Naomi looked up at Carlton, moved in closer and whispered, "I want to kiss you."

Carlton was stunned; he looked back at her and realised that that was what he wanted to do more than anything in the world. A look passed between them; a seal of fate look, a bond, an unshakeable, unbreakable bond and both of their lives changed in that one minute.

"Mrs. Draper!"

Naomi turned to look at who was calling. Giles' secretary

Kathryn was leaning around the boardroom door.

"Yes Kathryn?"

"Are you all right to take a telephone call?"

"Can you take a number and I'll call them back?"

"I could," said Kathryn, "but," she covered the mouthpiece of the phone and said in a lowered tone, "it's a call from America and if you can speak now, he'll be paying!"

"America? Wow! I'll come right away." Naomi excused herself and disappeared out of the boardroom.

Fifteen minutes later she returned looking flushed. She immediately made her way across to Carlton and said, "You've *got* to hear this!"

Before Carlton could stop her she called out, "Mum, dad, John, you're not going to believe this."

Everybody stopped talking and turned to face her.

"Whoa! Whoa; wait a minute!" said Giles, "What do you mean, '*mum, dad*'?"

Naomi turned to face Giles and said, "Oh, did I forget to mention that my surname was Chance before I got married?"

Giles was utterly astounded.

Crowthorne was equally shocked.

"But I had no idea…" said Giles, "I didn't…"

"Well, never mind Mr. Eaton," said Naomi, "now you do! And there are more of us Chances around you than you know."

Giles immediately cast a suspicious eye around the room, half expecting another one to jump out from behind a curtain.

"Now," said Naomi in a voice that reduced the room to silence, "I've just been speaking to a Mr. Alan Farlington who resides in Dunnellon, Florida.

Yesterday he downloaded a copy of the news item that was leaked to the press about the unexplained sounds heard at Whitewall Farm in July this year. It seems that with the aid of the internet, he has been sporadically collecting data relating to Whitewall Farm because he believes that he is a distant member of the Chance family with a claim to the estate.

He has traced his lineage back over two hundred and fifty years and can provide irrefutable proof that he is the direct descendant of," she turned to look at John and said, "you're going to love this John - Matthew Chance!"

John's mouth fell open in surprise. He said, "And did he indicate whether or not he had any proof to back up his claim?"

"That's the best bit!" said an excited Naomi, "He said that he has just taken possession of a small sealed chest which was left to him by his recently deceased grandmother.

Apparently she had always told his family that the chest contained some very old documents proving a claim to an estate in the North of England called Whitewall!"

"And have they opened the chest?" said John getting more excited as the story unfolded.

"No, but they are planning to open it for the first time in anybody's living memory!"

"So why did he want to speak to you?" said Carlton.

"For two reasons; firstly he wanted to know if we could supply him with any history relating to the estate; and secondly, to see if we knew of any living descendants of the Chance family who were themselves interested in, or in any way involved with Whitewall!"

Sam was the next to speak.

"And did you tell him who you were?"

"I certainly did, *and* I told him that I was in charge of the Historic Research Department here in Walmsfield." She paused for a second then almost bursting said, "*And guess what*? He became so excited that he was speaking not only to a distant relative, but a professional historian to boot, that he has offered to pay for me to go to Florida to meet him and to personally supervise the opening of the chest!"

There was a stunned silence in the boardroom.

"Well, somebody say something!" said an excited Naomi.

"That's amazing pet!" said Sam, "Do you intend going?"

"And can I come with you?" asked Jane jokily.

"Too damn right I'll go!" said Naomi excitedly. She glanced over towards Carlton and was surprised to see him looking concerned and deep in thought.

A general buzz of excitement spread throughout the room and nearly everybody started firing questions at Naomi all at once.

Giles was one of the two exceptions; he had a look similar to Carlton's upon his face. His heart was beating quickly and he felt weak and vulnerable. He kept seeing visions of Adrian Darke's face in front of his and wondered how on earth he was going to break the news to him.

Completely oblivious to Giles' deepening discomfort, Naomi made her way over to Carlton and said, "I know that you're concerned, but can we talk about this in the Ryming Ratt later?"

"Not today love," he said, "I've got to see someone."

Chapter 34

Every time that Adrian Darke spoke to Giles Eaton he hoped that it would be the last time. It had been bad enough having to sort out the problem with the Ramsbottoms in Orlando and expensive too, but like the proverbial bad penny Giles had turned up once again and with another problem in America.

"And just exactly what do you want *me* to do?" said Adrian to the bowed figure opposite him.

Giles' time with Adrian always felt oppressive because it only ever represented periods in his life when he was either being yelled at or made to feel like some sort of bungling incompetent.

"I don't know," he said exasperatedly, "You're usually the one with all the answers!" He paused for a moment then said, "I don't have the contacts or the experience in dealing with these sorts of things like you have." He got up from his chair, walked across to the window and looked into the distance.

"Thinking about it," he said, "I suppose that there are all sorts of possibilities; for example, the chest may not contain anything after two hundred and fifty years, time alone could have destroyed anything in there; or damp, insects, whatever.

I only know that this Farlington chap claims to be a direct descendent of Matthew Chance the twin brother of old John Chance whose copy of the Whitewall documents you destroyed and to me, it seems that we should be hedging our bets.

I'm not suggesting for one minute that we have a repeat of the Orlando incident, that would be far too extreme; but if you could arrange via your associates that the chest simply goes missing, then that would seem to solve all of our problems."

Adrian leaned back in his leather chair and studied the Town Clerk's face; they'd had their spats, but he was devious and he could work with that. He stood up, walked over to his drinks cabinet and said, "Whisky?"

Giles nodded.

Adrian extracted the Old Pulteney and Caol Ila and poured their respective choices. He stood pondering in silence for a while and then sauntered over to his desk.

"We'll have to wait until your Historic Research girly has possession of it."

Giles looked up and listened attentively.

"I can't send my people to break into someone's home without knowing that the chest will actually be there. For all we know it could have been placed into a bank vault for safekeeping until she arrives."

"And will you be able to find this Farlington guy?"

"There can't be too many people with the name of Alan Farlington living in somewhere as small as Dunnellon can there?"

"No, I suppose not."

"No," said Adrian, "finding him is the easy bit, when to strike is something else altogether."

The two men sipped their drinks in silence for a while until Adrian said, "Right, here's what we'll do for now. I'll start my people looking for Alan Farlington; you go back to your office and play the nice guy by offering to have Walmsfield Borough Council fund your research girlie's trip to America. That way we'll know exactly where, *and* when, she'll be arriving and leaving. That'll give my guys in Florida something to work on schedule-wise O.K.?"

Giles nodded.

"Now think on," said Adrian, "you need to do that as soon as possible and before she makes her own arrangements, got it?"

Once again Giles nodded.

"Then somehow, and I don't know how at the moment, we've got to grab that chest whilst it's in transit.

We can't simply have your girl go to the Farlington family home or to a bank vault or somewhere else and have her do the job there. By hook or by crook, we have to arrange it so that the chest ends up being transported somewhere - and before it's opened."

"I don't envy you the task of trying to work that one out," said Giles.

"No," said Adrian showing a spark of his old contempt, "I seem to remember telling you once before that thinking wasn't your strong point."

A little after 3:00pm the same day, the telephone rang on Naomi's desk; she picked it up and said, "Naomi Draper, HRD."

"Naomi, it's Cal; listen to me very carefully. I want you to leave the office via the front door and make your way down to a silver Ford saloon that is waiting outside.

The driver is a plain clothes policeman who will show you his warrant card to prove his identity; then you must get in without any fuss or questions and he will bring you to me. Do you fully understand?"

Naomi was amazed and taken aback by the mysterious instructions and feebly said, "What about my afternoon's work?"

"Make any excuse you have to, a forgotten dental appointment, a sick Aunt, whatever, just please do as I say."

"O.K., I'll leave right away."

Naomi said goodbye and made her way down to the front entrance. As Carlton had said, there was a silver Ford parked outside with a man standing casually by the driver's door.

Upon seeing her approach, the driver stepped forward and said, "Mrs. Draper?"

Naomi nodded and the man discreetly flashed a warrant card. Satisfied that he was a policeman, she stepped into the rear of the car and they sped away from the Council Office buildings.

"What's going on officer? And why all the cloak and dagger stuff?"

"I'm sorry Mrs. Draper," said the driver, "I can't answer your questions, I've just been asked to deliver you to your destination."

Naomi realised that it was pointless questioning the driver so she remained silent until the unmarked car turned smartly into an underground car park below the Central Police Headquarters and stopped.

The driver hopped out and opened the door for his passenger.

Naomi thanked him and was escorted to the third floor of the building. As she walked through the open plan office she saw Carlton sitting in a partitioned office with Chief Inspector Crowthorne.

"Do come in and make yourself comfortable," said Crowthorne as she knocked and entered.

Naomi sat down and said, "What's this all about Carlton?"

Carlton said, "I'll let the Chief Inspector explain."

"Before we talk to you about our reason for bringing you here like this," said Crowthorne, "I'd just like to say that we've received word from Whitewall farm that three more bodies have been found. One female and one male from the copse and another female from under the second outhouse floor pointed out by Mr. Wilkes."

"Two bodies from the copse?" said an astonished Naomi.

"That is correct."

"And has anybody heard Rover-over since our last visit?"

"Nobody has said anything to me about that; but then again, I'm probably the last person anybody would want to speak to about bizarre hunches! My attitude to date has left more than a little to be desired and the highly unusual circumstances surrounding the discoveries at Whitewall make me seriously wonder if there is more to this stuff than first meets the eye."

Naomi was waiting for Crowthorne to ask how she knew about the bodies and was madly trying to think of a way to explain it.

She saw Crowthorne look at her and held her breath.

"It's all right Mrs. Draper, you don't have to elucidate. I imagine that your explanation would be far too fanciful for me anyway, so let's just say that we are adopting a multi-faceted approach to our investigations."

Naomi breathed a sigh of relief and smiled.

Carlton relaxed too and said, "Shall I tell Naomi why we brought her here?"

"Yes, please do," said Crowthorne.

Carlton swivelled his chair around and said, "Do you recall me telling you that I had to see somebody after the meeting in Giles Eaton's office?"

"Yes."

"Well it was the Chief Inspector here. I went to see him because I think that your life may be in danger."

Naomi was shocked and said, "My God! Why?"

"Because you announced that you were going to America to supervise the opening of that chest."

"But what was wrong with that? And why would anyone want to kill me?"

"Why would anyone want to kill Sandra or the Ramsbottoms?"

said Carlton gravely.

Naomi shot a glance in the direction of Crowthorne and said, "So you think that they were deliberately killed?"

Crowthorne didn't respond.

"My God, you can't…"

"If," said Carlton interrupting Naomi, "I could possibly have stopped you announcing your intention to go to America last Friday, I would have. But as usual, and I mean no criticism here, your excitement got the better of you and you just blurted it out."

"I'm sorry," said Naomi feeling a little hurt by the 'blurted it out' comment, "I really didn't think that I was doing anything wrong."

"And under normal circumstances you'd be right; but we don't think that these are normal circumstances anymore."

"He's right Mrs. Draper." said Crowthorne, "As far as we can make out, it seems that somebody is very anxious indeed for the old Whitewall documents to remain unseen and following lengthy deliberations about the possible contents with Mr. Wilkes we have come up with one or two scenarios that would make their disappearance a very desirable thing."

"But there's no need to deliberate," said Naomi, "because we know what's in the file."

"No. I'm afraid that you do not," said Crowthorne emphatically, "You know what you were *told* was in that file, but that is entirely different to seeing the contents for yourself.

According to Mr. Wilkes the Town Clerk admitted that you were right in your assumptions; but he may have lied. Your evidence is purely circumstantial."

"But several of us heard him admit what was in there," said Naomi.

"Nevertheless," said Crowthorne, "you didn't actually see anything, and he could deny saying it."

Naomi let out an exasperated sigh and said, "O.K., so why did you bring me here if we can't do anything?"

"I didn't say that we couldn't do anything Mrs. Draper. On the contrary, there is a great deal that we can, and will be doing.

"All right," said Naomi, "but first, why on earth do you think my life may be in danger?"

"Because Mr. Wilkes and I suspect that the Town Clerk may

already have destroyed the Whitewall documents, and if he has, and is in any way responsible for the deaths of the Ramsbottoms and Mrs. Miles, he will be equally determined to prevent you from getting your hands on any copies."

Naomi was shocked and distraught, "The Whitewall documents destroyed? No, please tell me that that's not true…"

"I'm sorry," said Crowthorne, "but Mr. Wilkes and I do believe so."

Carlton nodded in agreement. He said, "I'm sorry Naomi but all the evidence seems to point to that."

He explained to Naomi how through a process of elimination he had arrived at his conclusions and how in the end he'd felt compelled to talk to Crowthorne.

"Do you remember when I mentioned the Sherlock Holmes quotation?" said Carlton, "and I told you that we hadn't even exhausted the possibles yet?"

Naomi said, "Yes."

"Well I did some searching of my own before I came to see the Chief Inspector and it seems that the other sale of land made by Abraham Johnson was to Hugo Darke of Brandworth Manor in 1869, and that that land could be the cause of all this mystery and intrigue, not the one purchased by the old Hundersfield D. C.

I believe that Eaton found out, the same as I have, that the section of land illegally sold by Johnson all those years ago was the very same section of land that the Highways Agency now wants to purchase from Adrian Darke for millions of pounds to make way for the new M6631."

Naomi was shocked.

"And do you remember in July after Sandra's death how we tried to see Eaton and were told by Kathryn that he had an appointment at Darke Industries?"

Naomi nodded.

"Well now I think I know why; I believe that Eaton was aware of the proposed land sale to the Highways Agency, and that he was blackmailing Adrian Darke by threatening to disclose the contents of the Whitewall file which had the potential to put a block on the deal."

Naomi let out a gasp of surprise.

Crowthorne felt that he should introduce a little

circumspection and said. "Of course all of this is pure conjecture Mrs Draper, but something about Mr. Wilkes's Sherlock Holmes theory isn't such a bad one and I am happy to continue with our enquiries along those lines."

"And do you think that he actually succeeded in blackmailing Adrian Darke?"

"We have no proof of that, but we shall be watching Mr Eaton and his bank account for any unusual activity; but even I don't think that he would be stupid enough to deposit a large sum of money into anywhere so obvious."

"The Chief Inspector can't be as speculative as me," said Carlton, "he has to work on facts. I, on the other hand, can give vent to my suspicions rather more easily, and to me the blackmailing of Adrian Darke, particularly if it was for a substantial amount of cash, would make the deaths of Sandra and the Ramsbottoms, then the subsequent destruction of the documents all fit very nicely together."

Naomi was shocked into silence until several pennies dropped all at once.

"I can't believe that you think Giles Eaton actually *murdered* Sandra? And that he somehow arranged for the Ramsbottoms to be murdered too?"

The two men remained quiet.

"That's ridiculous," said Naomi, "Giles Eaton a *triple* murderer?"

"We have no proof of that Mrs. Draper," said Crowthorne, "but he knows that you are planning a trip to America to retrieve what may turn out to be a copy of the very documentation that he may have gone to so much trouble to conceal."

"But what if the original documents are eventually found by the Ramsbottom's next of kin?"

"Then none of this makes sense and we shall have to think again. However, for the present I am happy to proceed on the hypothesis that Mr. Eaton may be complicit in foul play, and in the manner that Mr. Wilkes has suggested."

Naomi was flabbergasted. It was so surreal; to know that these were ordinary people and not the cast of a Hollywood murder/mystery film. She couldn't adequately explain how she felt inside; she didn't feel particularly vulnerable or threatened; in fact she didn't know what to feel.

The two men gave her a little time to compose herself and then Crowthorne said, "Now, about your planned trip to America, apart from us two, only your family and Mr. Eaton know of your plans to go, so if Mr. Wilkes' theory is right we need to protect you should any attempt be made to steal that chest. Accordingly we've come up with a strategy that should foil his attempts and expose him if he tries."

"This is crazy," said Naomi, "it doesn't seem possible that we are talking about our own Giles Eaton for goodness sake! And he certainly doesn't strike me as the kind of guy who could order stuff in America..."

"No," said Carlton, "I don't think so either."

Crowthorne looked at Carlton sideways and frowned, "Are you trying to tell me something?" he said.

"Only that I tend to agree with Naomi," said Carlton, "Which of course begs the question, who could he be working with if indeed he is?"

Crowthorne lapsed into silence for a while and then said, "Yes, interesting; it certainly would be prudent to consider all the possibilities..." He hurriedly scribbled down a few notes then looked up at Carlton and said, "All right Mr. Wilkes, does your speculation end there or are you keeping any other little gems up your sleeve?"

"No I'm afraid not," said Carlton smiling, "But if the plan we've hatched does turn up trumps not only should it prove our theory about Giles Eaton, it could also expose whoever else is involved too."

Chapter 35

Simeon and Silas bundled the dirty-looking, overweight, semi-conscious woman into the Reception Lodge and shouted, *"Shop!"*

The night receptionist Chinny Nesbitt, who'd been snoozing with his feet up on the office desk nearly fell of his chair and exclaimed, "What the f…"

He jumped to his feet, lurched across to the glass partition and said, "What's going on? Nobody told me we was taking anybody in tonight!"

"It's all right Chinny," said Simeon, "you remember me from the other night when we brought that other woman in…"

Chinny stared at Simeon with a frown on his face and said, "Maybe but…"

"But nothing Chinny," Simeon sidled up to the counter. He cast a furtive glance left and right and then slid a silver threepenny bit across the desktop.

"…Arnold said to give you this for your trouble."

Chinny looked down at the coin, hesitated for a second and then pocketed it.

"Wait here," he said, "I'll get the admissions pad."

"Arnold said there's no need to do it tonight; he'll sort it out in the morning with Matron. He wants us to drop the lass off and get to bed 'cos we've all got a late one tomorrow night – remember?"

Chinny still looked suspicious but finally nodded and said, "I'll get the keys for you."

A few seconds later he handed the keys to Simeon, looked across at Silas and said, "He new?"

"He is;" said Simeon, "he was released from Strangeways Prison last month so he'll be useful to have on the team."

Chinny nodded and said, "Go on then, be sharp about it but don't waken anybody up, the Orderly likes his kip and gets bloody tetchy if you wake him."

Simeon quickly unlocked the door marked 'Private', waited until Silas bundled the woman through and then locked it again.

Chinny called, *"You didn't need to lock it, I'm here!"*

"Sorry mate!" called Simeon, *"I'm still new to this."*

He heard Chinny grunt and shuffle back to his chair.

Silas leaned down to the woman and whispered, "Are you all right?"

Florence looked up and nodded.

Simeon hurried down to door number six that led up to the wards and unlocked it; he then turned to his right, unlocked door number five and then motioned for Silas and Florence to proceed.

They all entered door six and closed it behind them. Before ascending to the second floor they all quickly removed their shoes and left them in the short corridor at the foot of the stairs.

As quietly as church mice they crept up. They couldn't be sure if the Orderly was asleep, but they hoped that Chinny was right.

They reached the opening onto the second floor landing and Simeon removed a tiny mirror from his pocket; he positioned it so that he could see a reflection of both ways and then mouthed, "All clear."

They crept along the landing until they reached Ward nine.

Florence removed her master key and quietly said, "Let's hope it fits…"

She was just about to push it into the lock when something triggered in her brain. She quickly turned to Simeon and whispered, "Go to Ward ten and see if it's locked."

Simeon frowned and pointed down to the neatly folded bundle of clothes at their feet; he whispered, "There's no clothes outside of ten, so why waste time?"

"They may have moved her just in case…"

Simeon closed his eyes and then nodded. He crept along the landing quietly turned the handle to Ward ten and found it locked. He motioned to the others.

Florence and Silas quietly moved up to where he was standing.

"What if she's not in here?" whispered Silas.

"I don't know, I guess we'll have to keep trying until we find her."

"And it'd better not be too long," whispered Simeon, "Cos

Chinny'll start to wonder where we are."

Florence looked at the others and received nods of readiness. She inserted the key into the lock and turned it. It opened.

The three friends quickly stepped inside and shut the door.

Florence motioned for the men to remain still; she quietly crept over to the bed, gently pulled down the covers and was surprised to see Maria staring wide eyed up at her.

"Florence!" she said quietly, "What are you doing here?"

"We've come to get you out, but you must hurry. Take off that nightdress and put these on." Florence reached under her voluminous dress and pulled out a pair of men's breeches, a thick pair of socks; a brown cotton shirt and flat cap, and then quickly pulled off the dress to reveal that she was wearing male clothing virtually identical to Simeon.

Once completed the two women walked across to the men and only then did Maria see Silas. Her mouth fell open in surprise and she flung her arms about his neck.

Before she could speak Silas said, "We'll speak later love, now do as Simeon bids."

Simeon imparted instructions to Maria, all four quietly left the Ward and Florence locked the door behind them.

They crept along the landing hoping that they wouldn't disturb the Orderly until they reached the stairs. Step by step they crept down until they reached the ground floor where Simeon, Silas and Florence quickly put their shoes back on.

Simeon checked to see that the corridor was still clear and happy that it was, he said to Maria, "Here we part company. You'll come with me, and God willing we'll see Silas and Sister later."

Maria wanted to say something but just nodded then turned and hugged Florence and then Silas.

"Take care, both of you," she whispered.

The four friends stepped into the ground floor corridor. Florence and Silas quietly waited until Simeon and Maria disappeared through door number five, then locked it behind them and walked back towards the entrance door.

Silas unlocked it, let Florence through, stepped through himself and locked it back up.

Much to their relief, Chinny was dozing in the chair once again so Silas indicated for Florence to go outside. He waited until she was out of view and then threw the keys across the reception counter and onto Chinny's desk.

Chinny wakened with a start and nearly fell off the chair again.

"Sorry to startle you," said Silas, "I thought you were awake!"

"I was!" said Chinny indignantly, "I never nod off on duty!" He composed himself, picked up the keys and said, "I take it you're all done then? Where's your mate?"

"Waiting outside, he's anxious to get off home."

"I don't bloody blame him," said Chinny, "can't wait to get off myself."

Silas nodded and waved and stepped outside into the cool night air.

Maria heard the key turn in the door behind them.

"Where are we going?" she quietly said to Simeon.

"This leads to the basement, but stay close, I've never been in here before so it could get tricky."

Simeon removed a small lamp from his pocket and lit it. He shone it around until he saw another door and said, "Over there."

In the gloom Maria could see the rectilinear shapes of cupboards and tables covered in boxes and packets; there appeared to be spare chairs and desks and other bits of unidentifiable office paraphernalia. She gathered that she was in a store room.

Simeon stopped in front of the door and tried it. It was locked. He extracted the master key that he'd had cut from Florence's original and tried that, but it didn't open the lock.

Maria whispered, "What are we going to do now?"

Simeon put his finger up to his mouth and made a shushing sound. He replaced the key that he'd tried and extracted a ring with three contemporary door lock skeleton keys on it given to him by Enoch.

The second one worked; they stepped in, closed the door and locked it behind them. Simeon shone the lamp in front and saw that he was at the top of a stairway. He gestured to Maria to follow and quietly descended.

Safely down, he quickly removed a piece of paper from his inside pocket and spread it out on the floor beside him. It was a hand-drawn plan of the basement given to him by Len. He studied it for a few seconds and then shone the lamp around the basement trying to orient the plan properly.

"It should be somewhere over there near the corner…" he said quietly.

Maria looked to where Simeon was pointing and said, "What?"

"There's a trap door in the floorboards that leads down to a service tunnel." He folded the plan up and put it back in his pocket and quietly set off in the direction he'd indicated.

Maria followed quietly and then abruptly stopped when she heard Simeon let out a groan.

"What's wrong?" she said.

"Look." Simeon directed the lamp over towards the corner.

Maria leaned around Simeon and saw dozens of heavy metal radiator guards piled on top of one another in the corner.

"Our trap door is somewhere under there."

"Well," said Maria resolutely, "standing here won't do any good, we'd better move them."

One by one they commenced moving the heavy guards, making sure that they wouldn't topple and alert anybody above.

As the minutes ticked by Maria could feel herself weakening under the strain of moving such heavy objects but she was aware that Simeon was becoming increasingly agitated as no trap door appeared.

She reached forwards, tapped him on the shoulder and said, "Do you want to stop for a few minutes?"

Simeon extracted a small pocket watch from his jacket, looked at it and shook his head in despair.

"No," he said, "I thought we'd be out of here by now, we've got to keep going."

Maria nodded and they set about removing more guards.

Ten minutes later they had it. Simeon removed one more guard, set it to one side and exposed the elusive trapdoor.

He put his fingers into the ring and pulled. Slowly and creakily the door lifted. He shone the lamp down and saw that they only had a four foot drop onto a brick ledge running alongside an open sewer.

He quickly directed Maria down, dropped down himself and then closed the trapdoor above his head.

"Which way now?" said Maria trying to stare down the tunnel into the dark.

"This way Miss," said a deeper sounding male voice, "and watch your step, it's quite rough down here."

Maria wheeled around in alarm as Simeon directed the lamplight in the direction of the voice. She caught sight of a man's face and nearly stumbled backwards into the sewer.

Simeon grabbed her arm and said, "It's all right Miss Maria, this is Len; he's a friend of the Sister's and he's here to help us."

Maria smiled and tried to regain her composure.

"I was beginning to wonder if you'd been caught until I heard you moving stuff," said Len, "then I guessed that the trapdoor had been covered over."

Simeon said, "We'll tell you about it later, let's just get out of here."

"All right, follow me and keep your heads down."

He led Maria and Simeon through a confusing labyrinth of low ceilinged narrow tunnels, turning at once left and then right until they emerged into a larger tunnel that allowed them to stand upright.

Maria's feet were beginning to feel cold and sore through the socks but she kept quiet and hoped that their ordeal would soon be over.

They followed Len until he turned a final right hand bend and stopped. In front of them was a service shaft with metal rungs leading upwards.

"I'll go first and make sure that the coast is clear. If you see me get out and then close the grating, follow this tunnel for another seventy-five yards or so and you'll come to another service shaft. Try there, but wait at least ten minutes before attempting to get out."

Maria and Simeon acknowledged Len's instructions and then watched and waited as he headed up.

Len reached the top of the shaft, twisted the handle on the underside of the grate and gently pushed it up. He peered out and quickly scanned the area, found that it was all clear then called for Maria and Simeon to ascend.

Once they were up he checked that everybody was ready and then gave the grate a final push. It dropped with a gentle clunk onto the surrounding grass. He cast a last final glance around, quickly climbed out and then helped his two companions out.

Maria saw that they were in a small patch of lawn surrounded by trees approximately one hundred yards from the Reception Lodge and close to the access bridge that led to the public highway.

Len quickly closed the grating, inserted his locking tool into it and secured it.

"Quick," he said, "follow me."

He led the Maria and Simeon across the bridge, constantly checking to see if anybody was watching, through the main gates, and then left onto the road where they ran to a horse and cart that was waiting.

As they approached Florence and Silas jumped down to help Maria and Simeon aboard.

Len said, "I'll walk from here. I'm no but a few hundred yards from where I live so you go, and take care."

The four friends bid him a very warm goodbye and promised to meet with him at a later date.

Without saying another word all four alighted, Silas jumped into the driving seat and set the horse off.

One hour later they all sat safely in Florence's cottage sipping hot tea and trying to assess what would happen once Dr. Cobbold and the Matron received news about the audacious break out.

"You'll forever remain an escaped patient," said Florence to Maria, "you will be arrested by whichever police find you and returned to the asylum if you are caught, and though we know that it was payment that occasioned your incarceration, the practice is widespread and very deep-seated and the diagnosis of the Medical Superintendent backed up by the Matron will not ever be questioned. All they have to do is remain steadfast in their opinion about your state of health and they will be untouchable."

"Then what am I to do?" said Maria.

"You must move away from Cheshire to a different County, you must change your name, and you shouldn't attempt to contact any other members of your family for at least a year."

Maria nodded and tried to digest the information; she took a sip of hot tea and closed her eyes. It was a daunting prospect, but for the present she was just happy to be amongst friends and safe.

Across the room Silas was deep in thought. The contents of a recent local newspaper article had given him the wildest idea that he had ever had, and he was seriously starting to consider whether it might just work.

Chapter 36

Ewan Chance sat hugging a 'Bud' at Monty's Bar opposite Miami Beach Marina. Through the security gate he could see the sleek white bow of the Sunseeker super-yacht 'Las Ventanas' that he'd so meticulously cleaned earlier, rising and dipping slowly as various other vessels weaved slowly in and out of the pontoons.

As the second mate/crew he was the ship's dogsbody but that was fine, he was the one sitting in the sunshine at Miami's South Beach unlike most of his pals back at home in England.

The three man crew comprised the skipper Paul Bolton, the hostess/cook (and Paul's wife) Jo-Anne and him. They had all been with the vessel since it had come off the production line at Poole in Dorset and had been responsible for fitting her out to the multi-millionaire owner's exacting requirements and for being with her throughout her trials.

'Las Ventanas' maiden cruises had been in the Mediterranean where they'd all spent months pandering to the tastes and whims of the very wealthy and high tipping charterers, but at the end of the summer season the owner had announced that he wished to cruise the waters of the Bahamas, the Caribbean and the Florida Keys.

She had subsequently been despatched via a vessel transporter to Florida and moored much to the crew's delight at the prestigious South Beach Marina.

As a person Ewan was so laid back that he was almost flat, nothing ever seemed to faze him. He was eighteen months older than his sister Naomi, was slim and wiry, invariably dressed in the latest clothes and his height, square shoulders and handsome face with an angular jaw almost guaranteed that he was never short of female attention.

Paul the skipper was also very laid back but he was a bull of a man. He was tall, red haired, big chested and as strong as an ox.

Jo-Anne who was dark-haired, slim and attractive had a temper so hot you could roast chestnuts on it and nobody in their right mind dared to be chauvinistic in her company.

The combination, though sounding diverse worked very well and the three of them had gone on more than a few legendary benders in the various ports around Miami, but as Ewan sat sipping his beer at Monty's he could honestly say that the bar he had been asked to go to by his sister, was not one that he'd ever heard of before.

"Your round Chancey!"

Ewan spun round to see Paul and Jo-Anne approaching from the marina gate, he acknowledged their arrival with a smile and then called for Geoff the barman to set up the round. As his companions perched down at the circular bar, he said, "Have either of you guys ever heard of a bar called Camp Stanley?"

Paul and Jo-Anne looked questioningly at each other and then shook their heads.

Geoff the barman, who'd overheard Ewan walked back with their drinks and said, "Did I hear you say Camp Stanley?"

Ewan nodded and said, "Yes, do you know where it is?"

"I certainly do!" said Geoff with a wry smile on his face, "You guys aren't planning to go there are you?"

Ewan frowned and said, "My sister has asked me to meet a couple of guys there at nine o' clock tonight."

Geoff smiled and turned to the other regulars.

"Hey guys," he called out, *"Ewan's planning to meet a couple of guys at Camp Stanley tonight!"*

"Did you say guys or gays?" said one smiling local.

From the way that the other regulars joined in the laughter, Ewan clicked immediately and knew that he was in for a rough ride.

"Hey Ewan," called one of the other bar stool jokers, *"when you said 'meet a couple of guys' could you just clarify the spelling for us? Is it with a double 'e', or an 'ea'?"*

Everybody burst into laughter.

"O.K., laugh it up knuckleheads," said Ewan, "but just think, if I do make good friends there I could be inviting them over here for cocktails tomorrow!"

"Cock and tail did you say?" said another, much to everybody's amusement, "Ooh, we'd all like that wouldn't we girls!"

Spontaneous laughter ensued once again.

Ewan raised an eyebrow and shook his head dismissively; he let the laughter and one or two other jibes pass by and then asked Geoff for directions.

Paul, who'd remained relatively quiet said, "Chancey, what the hell do you want to go to a gay bar for?"

"Not just me," said Ewan, "we're all going..."

"Whoa, whoa, steady on cowboy!" said Paul, "You're not getting me in one of those places..."

"Oh come on Paul," said Jo-Anne, "it sounds like fun."

"No way!" said Paul indignantly, "And that's final!"

Jo-Anne shot her husband a withering look and said, "Care to bet the next round on that?"

Paul began to feel his resolve crumble and turned to Ewan.

"Why do you need Jo-Anne and me to go with you anyway?" he said desperately.

"Because Naomi has asked me to help her with a problem before she arrives here in Miami..."

"Naomi's coming here?" said a surprised Jo-Anne.

"Yes, in a few days' time as far as I can make out."

"And how will us all going to a gay bar help Naomi?" said Paul.

"Because she thinks that if we go to this bar together, it will look more like an impulsive decision by all of us to go in there, rather than a conscious one by me."

"I still don't get it," said Paul, "who cares if you want to go in a gay bar anyway? Nobody in this town gives a shit where you drink or who you drink with, so why do you need us to go with you?"

"I don't know," said Ewan, "but Naomi has specifically asked that we all go to together."

Paul, who harboured something of a soft spot for Naomi faltered at the mention of her request, but then seemed to gather resolve that any gay bar would be out of bounds for him.

"I'd really like to help," he said, "but a bloody gay..."

Jo-Anne jumped in and said, "Paul, we're going! And if you still don't believe it, bet me the next round that we aren't going. No, in fact bet me the next six rounds!"

Paul groaned and shook his head. On the boat he was the

undisputed skipper, on the land he most definitely was not!

By the time that the trio arrived at their destination, Paul couldn't have cared less where he was. The 'Art Deco' section of Miami was awash with all sorts of interesting bars and Camp Stanley was just another to be enjoyed.

They made their way through the colourful interior where 'Barbra Streisand' was belting out a number from Yentl and pushed up to the bar.

One of the barmen caught sight of Ewan resting his arm on the counter, walked across to where he was standing, leaned over and touched him lightly on the cheek with his fingertip.

"Nice bone structure!" he said.

Ewan couldn't help blushing and the barman picked up on it immediately.

"Ah!" he said, "and she blushes beautifully too!"

Ewan, who wasn't often caught off guard said rather too meekly, "Er…is Auntie Rosie about?"

The barman's eyes narrowed; he leaned over and said, "Who's asking?"

"My name's Ewan Chance."

"And who sent you Ewan Chance?"

"I was told to tell you, Carol."

The barman's demeanour changed; he looked carefully at the figure before him, cast a glance at Jo-Anne and Paul and asked, "They with you?"

Ewan nodded.

The barman said curtly, "Wait there," then turned to another bartender and said, "Lil, I'm just popping round the back for this young man…"

"I wish you would for me!" said Lil with a puckish stare.

The first barman looked at Ewan, raised the back of his left hand to his mouth and said loudly enough for the other barman's sake, "*She's anyone's for a large G and T…*" He then disappeared through a doorway at the rear of the bar and left Ewan smiling sheepishly at Lil.

"I think you've pulled," said Paul raising his eyebrows and nodding at Lil.

Ewan looked at Paul awkwardly and said nothing; he was fully aware that Lil was listening.

Several minutes later the first barman reappeared, lifted up a panel in the counter and directed Ewan to an office on the first floor.

Lil waited until Ewan had disappeared through the doorway and then sauntered over to Paul; he looked him up and down for a second and said, "My word, you're a big boy! You look just like that legendary, pillaging and raping Viking, Eric the Red."

He then caught sight of Jo-Anne, looked at her disapprovingly and said, "Make my day, tell me that she's your sister..." he cast another critical look in her direction and then added, "...or mother..."

Ewan followed the directions to the office and knocked on the door.

"Entrée!" said an obviously over-the-top effeminate voice.

He composed himself and walked in.

The figure behind the desk jumped up, minced across the office floor and said, "So you're Carol's new friend?"

Ewan smiled and extended his hand.

"Ooh, so formal," said Rosie, "come and give us a hug."

Ewan didn't know how to respond, he felt completely out of his depth.

Rosie threw his arms about Ewan, gave him a squeeze and said, "Right, because you're a friend of Carol's I'm your Auntie too, so let's have a look at you." He stepped back, gave Ewan the full once over, and said, "Yes, very nice! I've decided to call you Yolanda!"

Ewan was totally overawed, he didn't have the heart to say that he hadn't even met 'Carol' let alone become friends with him/her? He just stood in amazed silence.

"All right Yolanda," said Rosie, "Sit your little bum down there and tell me, do you know why you are here?"

Ewan explained that he'd simply received a telephone call from his sister asking him to trust her, to go and see Auntie Rosie, do whatever was required of him and to say that he'd been sent by Carol. Apart from that he was no wiser.

"Very well young man," said Rosie after digesting the information, "tomorrow you are in for a treat, you'll be having a ride with your favourite Auntie!

We will be picking you up from the marina at 08:00 hours and we are going to a small place called Dunnellon. We'll be staying there overnight so clear it with your skipper and tell him that we'll be back in Miami by 17:00 hours the next day.

Is that clear?"

Ewan nodded, posed one or two questions, and then agreed for his sister's sake to go along with Rosie's instructions.

With business settled, Rosie relaxed, leaned forwards and flicked a switch on his desktop. A television screen lit up on the office wall and they saw Lil talking to Paul whilst an amused Jo-Anne stared at them with a tall drink in her hand and a smile on her face.

"You'd better go and rescue your buddy before Lil decides who she wants for breakfast..."

Ewan smiled and said, "Don't let Jo-Anne fool you Rosie..."

"*Excuse me Yolanda!*" said Rosie indignantly, "It's *Auntie* Rosie to you!"

"Sorry, *Auntie* Rosie, but like I said, don't let Jo-Anne fool you, if she thought for one second that Lil was a threat you'd have world war three down there."

Rosie leaned forwards and looked more closely at Jo-Anne on the television screen.

"Hmm," he said thoughtfully, "perhaps girls are a bit more interesting than I thought..."

At 8:05am the following day a silver Hummer H1 swept quietly and powerfully across the MacArthur Causeway and joined the I-95 heading north. The darkened glass obscured Ewan and Rosie in the rear and two other guys in the front; one of whom the driver, Ewan recognised as the first barman he'd spoken to the previous evening.

They were all dressed like typical tourists, but seemed composed and exceptionally focussed on what they were doing; even Rosie was different when he spoke.

"O.K. Ewan, this is the serious bit after which we can all lighten up."

The use of his correct name confirmed to Ewan that the situation inside the Hummer was wholly different to that inside

Camp Stanley.

"Firstly, let me make the introductions. As you know, I am your *Auntie* Rosie..." He leaned around and stared hard into Ewan's face clearly reiterating his insistence of the title 'Auntie' from the night before.

He continued, "I am also known in another life as Rob McCloud and I am in charge of this operation. At the wheel is Lola, aka Lloyd Masters our first driver and next to him is Kitty, aka Kevin Langdon our co-driver and we are all ex-marines."

At the mention of their names each of the men in the front seat nodded slightly, but never once removed their eyes from the roads around them.

This was surreal for Ewan; apart from their feminine nicknames there was nothing effeminate whatsoever about his travelling companions. They were barely recognisable as the guys from Camp Stanley; they looked hard, very hard in fact, and certainly not the type of guys the average man would want to cross.

"Apart from one stop en route for coffee and a pee break," said Rosie, "we shall be driving directly to a motel in Marion Oaks near Ocala where we shall spend the rest of the day carefully planning the morrow's activities and keeping ourselves otherwise respectably entertained.

We will not touch one single drop of alcohol until we return to Miami tomorrow.

At 19:30 hours we will enjoy a convivial dinner in a nearby excellent steakhouse after which we will go to our separate rooms at 23:15 hours sharp. We will shower and go to bed, and 'lights out' is at 23:45.

At 08:00 tomorrow we will go to an address in Dunnellon, collect a sealed chest from a Mr. Alan Farlington and return it to Camp Stanley.

You will be the person who actually takes receipt of the chest from Mr. Farlington but once it is put in the vehicle, I will be responsible for its safekeeping.

In the event of an emergency you will do *precisely* as you are instructed; you will not question what we say, nor will you stop to think about it. If something happens to me, Lola will take over and you will follow his instructions."

He paused briefly then said, "Now, do you fully understand and do you have any questions?"

Ewan was a little overawed by the curt professionalism and found it almost as difficult to deal with as gay men, particularly as the two were so closely entwined; but he was legendarily phlegmatic and was able to take it in his stride.

He acknowledged that he understood and said, "Are we expecting any trouble?"

"No we are not," said Rosie.

For mile after mile in relative silence the Hummer sped effortlessly up the I-95 until Lola picked up the R-528 north of Cocoa and headed west before joining the Florida Turnpike.

Just south west of Orlando Lola turned the Hummer into a rest stop and the four companions disembarked.

They headed for the facilities and gift shop and Ewan was amazed once again to see the transformation in the men; there was absolutely no hint of curt professionalism or effeminate behaviour in any of them. Lola and Kitty had become animated and apparently light-hearted, almost as though they had just arrived on vacation, whilst Rosie remained silent but smiling and attentive.

As they walked from the car parking area a large black Jeep pulled into a bay several spaces away from the Hummer and two men in business suits stepped out into the sunshine. They seemed to be taking no notice of the foursome, but Ewan knew that Rosie had seen them.

The quartet openly enjoyed their rest stop and each had a light snack followed by a non-alcoholic drink; they availed themselves of the washroom facilities and wandered around the gift shop whilst Lola purchased a genuine pair of soft leather Indian moccasins which he paid for in cash.

Within the space of an hour they were fully refreshed, and ready to leave for the next leg of their journey.

They left the coolness of the air-conditioned interior and Ewan noticed that the suited businessmen from the Jeep were heading for their vehicle too. As casually as he could, he walked across to Rosie and opened his mouth to speak.

"I know - I've already seen." said Rosie anticipating his comment.

Without further ado they climbed back into the Hummer and with Kitty at the wheel headed back out to the Turnpike. Much to Ewan's surprise he saw the Jeep exit the rest stop, turn south east and drive away from them.

Within the hour they picked up the I-75 heading north until it was crossed by the SW CR-484 where they turned left and headed west into Marion Oaks for their stay at the Days Inn Motel.

A little after 7:30pm the four companions ate a hearty meal at a local steak-house; the food was first-class, the conversation was light and good humoured and from being initially unsure of how to behave in the company of overtly gay guys, Ewan soon learned to relax and enjoy being with his new found friends. He also noticed once again that no alcoholic drinks were consumed.

Throughout the evening he kept his eyes peeled half wondering if the two suits would turn up, but they did not.

Following the agreeable and alcohol-free mostly hetero night, they retired to their respective rooms, showered and were in bed with lights off by 23:45 hours.

At 1:35am a black Jeep quietly pulled into the motel car park and stopped in one of the bays. The two men Ewan had seen earlier, got out and made their way silently across to another room.

Neither of the new arrivals saw the briefest of movements as the curtain to Rosie's room was put back into place.

At 8:00am the following morning having already breakfasted on eggs, pancakes and fresh coffee the quartet made their way back to the Hummer and Lola once again resumed his position in the driver's seat.

Before departing Rosie made a mental note that the Jeep he'd seen arriving in the early hours had already departed.

Lola turned the vehicle west along the SW CR-484 until he picked up the Ned Folks Highway east of Dunnellon Airport, then having located his destination with the aid of his satnav, he turned right into SW 136th Court Road and stopped the Hummer at the Farlington house.

Ewan reached for the door handle but was stopped by Rosie.

"One minute please," he said.

Ewan looked in front of him and saw Lola and Kitty scan the local vicinity through unusual looking binoculars. They were no more than 200 yards off the main SW CR-484, but the road surface had turned to compacted earth, and the house was surrounded by outlying trees.

Presently they nodded to each other and said, "All clear boss."

Rosie allowed Ewan to exit the vehicle.

As instructed, he walked across to the front door and rang the bell. Within a few seconds the door opened and he was confronted by a cheery-looking dark haired lady with a pinafore wrapped around her waist and a small blob of flour on the end of her nose.

"Good morning!" she said, "You must be Ewan. Alan and I have been expecting you; would you and your buddies care to come in for some pancakes?"

Ewan still felt full from the breakfast he'd eaten but didn't have the heart to say no.

"And a very good morning to you too," he said cheerily, "I'd love a pancake, but if you'll excuse me first, I'll just go and check that my companions are ready."

"Sure," said the lady, "and tell them to come on in, the coffee's already made."

Ewan walked over to the Hummer and for the first time noticed how ominous it looked with the blackened out windows.

As he approached the rear window lowered down about an inch.

"She seems nice and we've been invited in for pancakes..." said Ewan into the void.

"Ask her her Christian name, middle name and her husband's middle name." said Rosie.

Ewan knew better than to argue; he walked back to the house and tapped on the screen door. The lady returned minus the flour on her nose.

"I'm sorry to be a nuisance," he said, "but my colleague wants to know your Christian name, your middle name and your husband's middle name."

The lady looked a little puzzled at first, then with the slightest shake of her head said, "My name's Deborah Elsie Farlington and Alan doesn't have a middle name."

Ewan thanked her and turned to walk away.

"And hey..." called Deborah.

Ewan turned back to face her.

"…I love your accent!"

Ewan smiled and walked back to the Hummer, the window lowered again and he reported the results to Rosie.

"Good!" said Rosie, "Anybody want more pancakes?"

Two doors opened and Rosie and Kitty disembarked whilst Lola stayed at his position behind the wheel.

"We'll bring hers out," said Rosie as they made their way indoors.

Formal introductions were followed by a very sociable second breakfast of delicious pancakes and fresh coffee after which Alan disappeared for a few moments.

Whilst he was gone, Deborah took some pancakes and coffee out to Lola.

Several minutes later Alan returned holding a very old looking wooden chest. It looked like the type of strongbox that every schoolboy dreamed about finding; a long lost chest stuffed with pirate gold and gleaming jewellery. It was approximately eighteen inches long by eight inches wide, had a flat lid and was about twelve inches deep. The metal bindings were old and pitted but looked in remarkably good condition and the lid was secured by a large mortise lock.

"May I?" said Ewan holding out his arms.

"Sure thing buddy," said Alan handing the chest to Ewan, "being a Chance, I guess you'll get as big a kick out of handling it as I do, especially as we believe it to have originally come from the Whitewall Estate in England."

Ewan's mouth fell open and he said, "What? What do you mean it came from the Whitewall Estate?"

"Didn't Naomi tell you about it?"

"No, she just told me to contact, Auntie… er, Rob here," he looked briefly at Rosie who nodded, "…and collect a chest from you. She didn't say anything about it being a family heirloom!"

Alan briefly explained the known history of the Matthew Chance legacy and about how the chest hadn't been opened in anybody's living memory. He said that Naomi's forthcoming visit was to supervise its opening for what the Farlingtons believed, would be the first time since it had left England.

Ewan was stunned. He sat down, placed the chest carefully on his lap and stared at it.

He'd grown up with the tales of Maria's quest and was fully aware of the history of that side of the Chance family, but he'd never heard of Matthew Chance before.

He slowly stroked the lid and tried to imagine what the old chest had been through. What journeys it had been on over the last two hundred odd years, and all the time carrying within its dark interior secrets about that side of the family.

"Do you know how or when the chest was brought to America?" he asked.

"According to my recently departed gran'ma," said Alan, "the chest was brought over by one of the Chances some time at the end of the 1700's."

"And has anybody *ever* attempted to open it?"

"Not to our knowledge, nor to the knowledge of gran'ma."

"Why?" said Ewan, "Weren't you curious?"

"Sure I was," said Alan, "I can't remember how many times as a kid I pleaded with her to let me look inside, but she kept on telling me that one day it would be mine and that if I wanted to bring the family curse down on me then that would be my business, but until that day it would stay locked."

"A family curse?" said Ewan.

"Yeah, she told us that she'd been told by her grandparents that the chest had to remain sealed until it was returned to the Whitewall Estate in England, otherwise whoever opened it would be cursed."

Ewan sat in awe. It was such a small box but with such a huge history. All he could say was, "Wow…"

He looked up at Alan and said, "And aren't you just a tad worried by the curse?"

Alan cocked his head to one side, thought for a few seconds and said, "I haven't really given it much thought to tell the truth, but I guess we'll soon find out if gran'ma was right…

Highly animated conversation followed until it was time to leave; all sorts of suggestions had been mooted about what could be contained within the chest and about how Naomi could gain access to the interior, but that was going to be for her to decide. One thing was for sure though, everybody who had seen the chest that day wanted to be there when she opened it.

A little after 10:00am, having enjoyed their second breakfast and the hospitality of the Farlingtons the four companions said their 'au revoir's' and set off on what was to be an uneventful return journey to Miami.

Only once en route did Ewan catch Rosie surreptitiously peering through a specially angled wing mirror at another vehicle, but Rosie didn't speak about it and he didn't see it.

He was dropped back at South Beach Marina at 5:00pm and promised his travelling companions to be in touch once Naomi had arrived. He bid them farewell and left the chest in the more than capable hands of Auntie Rosie.

"*Bye-bye sweet cheeks!*" called Lola noisily as Ewan walked towards Monty's Bar.

Ewan, who was much more relaxed with the guys than just twenty-four hours earlier turned and cheekily called, "*Toodle pip sweetie!*"

"*Ooh!*" came back the response, "*Get her…*"

Ewan waved and walked quickly away from the Hummer hoping that the regulars at Monty's hadn't heard him.

"*Yoo hoo! Yolanda!*" called Rosie.

Ewan cringed at the sound of his adoptive name and stopped. He turned around and placed a finger up to his lips in a vain attempt to quieten his new friend.

"*Give my love to Carol when you speak to her next.*"

Ewan nodded and waved as the Hummer departed, but he just knew that the guys at Monty's had heard them and that he would be in for another rough ride…

Amidst endless ribbing, he sauntered over to Paul and Jo-Anne who were seated at the round bar for an early evening livener.

Paul was the first to speak as he approached.

"Oi, Chancey!" he said heatedly, "I've got a bone to pick with you; did you give anybody at Camp Stanley my mobile number?"

"I had to," said Ewan, "in case we had to get a message to you, why?"

"Because dumb ass," said Paul angrily, "that bloody Lil's plaguing me with texts and calls. She, he, whatever, keeps calling me Eric the Red and wants me to let her know when I'm going on a fucking rampage!

Christ - you've got a lot of rounds to get in before I forgive you…"

Chapter 37

Thursday 22nd August 2002. Orlando, Florida

Thanks to the generosity of Walmsfield Borough Council and Giles Eaton, Naomi and Carlton had arrived in Orlando just after 05:00am in reasonable comfort. The long flight from London's Gatwick airport had seemed interminable but Giles had been 'thoughtful' enough to arrange car hire and a one night stay at a nearby Quality Inn.

The couple had picked up their transport, a full-sized green Ford saloon from the fast track section of the airport car hire facility and had made their way to the Inn by 06:20am in order to take a shower and a quick nap before meeting for breakfast at 10:00am.

Giles had specified adjoining rooms when making the bookings and despite both Carlton and Naomi secretly wishing it otherwise, they parted company and promised to meet at the arranged time.

Carlton was aware that he could hear Naomi moving about next door and though most of the sounds were pretty muffled, he realised that he could hear her shower running at the same time as his.

As the hot water soothed his muscled body he couldn't help thinking that she was standing naked just inches away from him through the thin hotel wall. He tried to imagine what she looked like as she moved about under the hot water, warm and covered in soft luxurious soap suds; how she would feel if he caressed her soft skin as the water washed away the soap to leave her glistening in the warmth of a steamy bathroom.

He turned to face the wall and wished that he could just beat it right down and get to her.

Outside their hotel a black Cadillac pulled into the parking space next to their green Ford; a smartly dressed man in a dark suit stepped out of the passenger side, walked to the rear of their car and positioned something just below the trunk.

Silently and without attracting any attention he walked back to the Cadillac, got in, and it departed.

On the opposite side of the car park two sets of eyes were watching the proceedings through the blackened glass of a large black powerful Jeep.

The driver, Corporal Pete 'Randy' Kincaid noted the registration number of the Cadillac whilst his companion Private Henry 'Hilda' Boxer passed it on to Rosie via his mobile phone.

"It also looks as though somebody has placed a tracking device below their car," said Hilda, "do you want me to place it on another vehicle?"

"Check it out first," said Rosie, "then if you're sure it is a tracking device leave it, we don't want to stop these guys from following them."

"O.K., and one more thing boss," said Randy, "the girl Naomi's a tall one. We're going to need Lanky Ada."

There was an exasperated sigh from the other end of the phone.

"And does she in anyway match up…?"

"Not a chance."

"Oh bollocks!" said Rosie.

Following her shower and a short fitful sleep, Naomi walked outside into the warm Florida sunshine and looked around her.

This was her first trip to America and she was thrilled by the whole experience. The delight of seeing new and exciting places, the prospect of opening the sealed chest and being alone with Carlton was very exhilarating and she relished every moment of it.

She took a deep breath and marvelled at how wonderful and unpredictable life could be.

Following the break-up of her marriage to Andy she had been terribly depressed; self-doubt had crept in about her attractiveness and sex appeal and she had begun to question if her big chance at happiness had eluded her.

Now it could hardly be more different, she bubbled with delight at the very sight of Carlton and daydreamed endlessly about him. She'd heard him in the shower next to her earlier in the day and she too had wanted to smash the wall down between them and have him where he stood. The very thought of his masculine body wet and naked had made her tremble with desire.

The door behind her opened and the man of her dreams stepped into the sunshine and walked over to her.

She instantly leaned forward and kissed him.

"Good morning handsome, I'm starving." she turned her head slightly away from him and muttered, "And not just for food…"

Carlton seemed oblivious to her comment as they walked arm in arm over to the diner. They went inside, were shown to a table and ordered a full fried breakfast complete with pancakes and maple syrup.

As the waitress thanked them for their order and walked away, Carlton looked at Naomi opposite him and said, "I'm starving too." He looked fully into her face, leaned over the table and said in a lowered voice, "And not just for food either!"

Naomi blushed.

Carlton winked and smiled as he saw her cheeks turn pink; he reached across the table, took hold of her hands and looked deeply into her eyes.

"And when I get a raging starve on," he said quietly, "I'm insatiable!"

Naomi was shocked and said "Carlton Wilkes!" She quickly looked around and saw that their intimacy was being watched surreptitiously by more than one set of eyes; she leaned forwards and whispered, "We're English, don't be naughty!"

Carlton whispered back, "I haven't even started yet!"

Naomi smiled and then in order to stop attracting attention she retrieved her hands and quickly changed the subject.

"I've spoken to Alan Farlington already and he and his wife are going to put us up for the night tonight if that's O.K. with you?"

Carlton nodded and said, "Does he think we're, you know, *together*?"

"Oh! I don't know!"

"Maybe they've only got one guest room. And maybe its only got a really big double bed in it!" whispered Carlton devilishly.

"Well if they have, I hope you'll be comfortable on the garage floor!"

Carlton smiled, leaned forwards and quietly said, "No harm in fantasising!"

Naomi reached over and lightly slapped his arm. She could have turned inside out with delight...

Half an hour later the two companions had checked out of the hotel and Carlton had set the car's satnav for the address in Dunnellon.

As they followed the same route that Ewan and co. had taken a week earlier, they were blissfully unaware of the two vehicles that were following them.

"It's the same black Caddy that planted the tracker." said Hilda to Rosie on his mobile as they followed in the rearmost vehicle.

"O.K.," said Rosie, "liaise directly with Lola and Kitty from now on, they're just north of where Route 44 crosses the I-75. Once you get past them, let them pick up the tail, you make yourselves scarce and proceed directly to the Days Inn in Marion Oaks. I'll pick up Lanky Ada and we'll fly up to Dunnellon tonight."

As instructed, Randy and Hilda discontinued following the Cadillac once Lola and Kitty had picked up the tail in the Hummer.

Just after 2:30pm Carlton swung the Ford into SW 136th Court Road and stopped outside the Farlington house; he asked Naomi to stay in the car until he had established that all was well.

Naomi had only ever been asked to do this once before and that had been thousands of miles away at Whitewall when Chief Inspector Crowthorne had been investigating the awful sounds from the finds room. She thought about that for a second and didn't argue.

The front door opened and a bright and happy looking man appeared.

"You must be Carlton," he said cheerily, "I'm Al!"

Carlton took the offered hand but to the surprise of Alan, increased his grip slightly and didn't let go.

"Sorry," he said, "but may I have yours and your wife's middle name?"

"Oh yes, Debs told me about this before, I have no middle name and Debs is Elsie."

Carlton smiled and released Alan's hand.

"Forgive me," he said, "I was just taking precautions..."

Alan nodded his approval and went across to the car.

"You've got to be Naomi," he said, "come on in cousin, you're most welcome!"

Carlton and Naomi grabbed their bags and were shown into the house; they deposited their belongings into their respective bedrooms, (much to Carlton's disappointment), freshened up and were shown out to the swimming pool.

"I hope you've brought your swimming costumes." said Alan, "'cos we've been asked to wait until another couple arrive this evening."

The afternoon seemed to rush by as Naomi and Carlton regaled Alan and Deborah with the events leading up to their visit.

The Farlingtons sat in almost total silence and were astonished that so much had happened. Their various sojourns into the Chance family history had been leisurely, internet researched affairs where they had read about the apparent skulduggery and alleged murders committed years ago in old Blighty; and on many occasions they'd kept their fascinated (and mildly jealous) all-American neighbours enthralled with the bleak and dastardly tales of evil goings on dating back to Queen Victoria's reign.

But to hear about modern day murders and conspiracies, especially on American soil, was an altogether different thing.

The evils of the past had unexpectedly and violently rushed into the present and Alan and Deborah suddenly had a stark insight into what it truly meant to be a member of the Chance family. A creeping feeling of unease and vulnerability slowly swept over them.

"God damn it Naomi," said Alan after listening to the various tales and caveats, "you're not doing an awful lot to boost my confidence in our safety here. You don't think that Debs and I could be in danger do you?"

"You two are perfectly safe," said Carlton reassuringly, "You know that the real chest is in Miami and it's highly unlikely that anybody would even consider stealing it from here.

For a start, nobody has any idea where the real chest is so it would be pointless attempting to snatch it until its location could be verified.

Hence, of course, our plan to take the replica to Miami

tomorrow."

"Why did you feel the need to concoct such an elaborate plan?" asked Deborah.

"Because we had to set a trap to catch a man we believe is complicit in two suspected murders in Orlando and another murder back in England.

Before he's arrested, the Brit police want to know if he's working in conjunction with anybody here so we informed him and him alone, about our planned itinerary to transport the chest to a specialist laboratory in Miami.

He booked our flights and accommodation and will know daily where we plan to be, so if any attempt to stop us occurs, we will know that it was he who passed on the information."

"Isn't that going to be dangerous for Naomi?" said Alan.

"Not in the slightest. Just as long as everybody does as we have planned."

A quarter of a mile further down the Ned Folks Highway from its junction with SW 136th Court Road, the black Cadillac was parked on the side of the road and Tel and Flynn the occupants, were enjoying the late evening sunshine. They had reported their position to their boss and had settled down to take turns keeping watch in case the green Ford made an unscheduled start for Miami, but as boredom had set in and the warm sunshine had made them drowsy, neither of them paid any attention to two people who ambled by and turned at the very junction that they were supposed to be watching.

The doorbell of the Farlington home rang; Alan noted that it was 8:35pm and got up to answer it.

Carlton held up his hand and said, "Let me go."

"All right," said Alan, "but you can check who's there through the viewing portal."

Carlton nodded and made his way to the front door, peered through the viewer then opened it wide.

"Carol!" said Rosie beaming from ear to ear; he stepped through the door and threw his arms around Carlton with genuine affection.

"Whoa! Steady on Rosie, you're squeezing the life out of me!"

"It's so good to see you!" said Rosie; he paused for a second and then added, "What's this I hear about you two-timing me?"

Carlton smiled and said, "Rosie, come on, would I?"

Rosie burst into laughter and the two friends hugged again. Suddenly they heard a distinct *'Ahem!'* behind them and they turned to look at the source.

Rosie stepped to one side and said, "Carol, this is Lanky Ada."

Carlton's eyes nearly popped out of his head.

Lanky Ada was every inch of six feet three inches tall, was slim, tanned, shapely and had a huge pair of boobs! He was truly stunning to look at; he wore a turquoise blue, low cut designer top, an over-the-top but obviously expensive necklace and his spectacular legs disappeared up into a white micro-mini skirt with a low slung silver belt.

"I was beginning to think that you'd forgotten me Rosie!" he said sulkily.

"Wow! My God in Heaven!" said Carlton, "How could anybody forget you!"

Ada shot a sideways glance at Rosie then turned and scrutinised Carlton from head to foot.

"Hmm – needs work, but has promise," he paused briefly then turned to Rosie.

"You said he was a charmer but who picks his clothes for crying out loud - his mother?"

Carlton opened his mouth to speak but was cut off.

"Still," said Ada pursing his lips, "it's obvious that he has a slick tongue in his mouth…" he turned and stared right back at Carlton and said, "Let's hope he knows how to use it properly."

Carlton was dumbfounded; he turned to Rosie and raised his eyebrows with a mild look of desperation, but Rosie just smiled and left them to it.

"Well Carol love," said Ada, "it seems I've rendered you speechless, so come on, take me by the gland and introduce me to your friends."

At 5:00am the following morning, Flynn had positioned himself in the trees near the Farlington house and was watching through a small pair of binoculars. Their car had been moved off the highway but was close enough to respond to any eventuality.

A second car, a dark blue Chevrolet saloon, had been positioned further down the Highway on the opposite side of the junction from which they expected the green Ford to appear thereby covering the possibility of Carlton and Naomi turning in either direction.

The man controlling their operations from his office in Miami was a retired gun-runner and drug smuggler named Grant Fitkern, now the CEO of GFK Logistics, one of Adrian Darke's preferred contractors.

He prided himself on being able to figure out what other people were planning and for the most part he was usually right. He was particularly good at logistics too; the movement of people fascinated him but unfortunately it was something of a paradoxical fascination, for once Fitkern had brought his logistical talent to fruition, they invariably never moved again.

The Cadilac driver Terence Anthony was a 'gelignite artiste' nicknamed Tel the Gel. He, too, was good at logistics; mostly because he had the unique ability to be able to site gelignite in places that assisted the more difficult GFK clients to be moved efficiently and very loudly in multiple directions all at once.

This made them invaluable assets to Darke Dealings, though Adrian had gone to incredible lengths to make sure that nobody could ever make a connection between them.

"You two and the guys in the Chevvy follow if they turn east," said Fitkern to Tel, "and make sure you hit them between Montverde Junction and Reavills Corner near Lake Apopka like we arranged. Jake's waiting in the truck stop on the turnpike and will do his part.

"Don't forget, once you've got the chest you veer off onto the old Highway 50 and leave Wes and Hux to disappear up County Road. O.K.?"

"Right boss, consider it done," said Tel, then as an afterthought he added "Once we've got the box, would you like me to plant a little going away present?"

"No. We ain't being paid for removal, just collection."

Just after 7:10am Flynn watched Naomi carefully place the chest in the trunk of the green Ford; he then quickly made his way back to the Cadillac and awaited their departure.

At 7:20am the Ford appeared at the end of SW 136th Court Road and turned east.

Tel turned on the engine and was about to engage drive when suddenly a large Hummer with blackened out windows pulled up directly in front of them and reversed to within inches of their hood.

Neither man was sure how to react and for a couple of seconds they just looked at each other in bewilderment.

Suddenly a loud hissing sound emanated from the Hummer followed by a bang and a thud as something hit their vehicle.

Both men reached for their handguns, but before they could draw them the Hummer pulled away and left them wondering what the hell had happened.

Once again they swapped puzzled expressions until Tel realised that their engine had stopped, he tried the ignition key a couple of times but nothing happened.

Flynn jumped out and looked at the front of the car.

"Goddam it Tel, take a look at this!" he said.

Tel got out and made his way to the front.

Protruding through the front of the vehicle's radiator vent was a one inch diameter stainless steel rod that had literally been blasted like a crossbow bolt into the car's engine.

"Shit!" he said, "What the hell is that?"

"Beats me," said Flynn, "I ain't *never* seen anything like that before!"

Several miles away Lola and Kitty were still laughing in the Hummer as they followed Carlton at a discreet distance.

"You should have seen their faces when Kitty shot her bolt!" said Lola to Rosie via the vhf radio.

"All right girls, keep it professional," said Rosie who was commanding ops from high above them in a Cessna light aircraft, *"this is an open frequency remember?"*

"Sorry boss," said Lola.

"O.K. Well done for now, but keep a weather eye out for that Chevvy and watch Carol's back."

As Carlton approached the outskirts of Orlando he noticed that he was being tailed by a dark blue saloon; he slowed down, speeded up, overtook and undertook but the car behind mirrored his every move. He became so obsessed by it that it was several more miles before he realised that another large black car had taken up a similar position in front. They continued playing cat and mouse on the Turnpike until they reached Lake Apopka then suddenly the vehicle in front dramatically slowed down.

He immediately tried to overtake but was blocked by a tractor/trailer unit that was obviously working in conjunction with them. A quick glance in the mirror confirmed that the dark blue saloon had now positioned itself directly behind him and that he was being boxed in and stopped.

As the vehicles slowed down to a halt the truck veered away. He was completely blocked in and considered ramming his way out, but remembered who he was with and decided that it would be safer to keep calm and comply.

Within seconds the driver of the rearmost car was out and sporting a handgun.

"Get out of the car and open the trunk!" he yelled pointing the gun directly at Carlton's head.

Carlton hesitated.

"Get out of the car and open the trunk!" shouted the man, this time much more menacingly.

Before Carlton could respond an even louder voice boomed through a handheld megaphone, *"Drop your weapon and lay face down on the ground."*

The driver of the rear vehicle whipped round and saw an armed Highway Patrol officer cautiously making his way towards him with a drawn weapon. Behind him was a patrol car concealed behind a large roadside billboard.

"I said drop your weapon and get down on the ground!" shouted the cop.

The black saloon that had forced Carlton to stop screeched away leaving the remaining driver to face the music.

Unsure of whether the officer was being covered by another, the driver dropped his gun, laid down and was 'cuffed and stuffed' into the back of the patrol car.

It had been a long time since Carlton's adrenalin had been pumping like that and he needed to collect his wits. He thought about Naomi for a second and then saw the Highway Patrol officer walking towards him.

The cop cautiously made his way to Carlton's vehicle then tapped lightly on the driver's window.

Carlton wound it down half expecting the usual dry and humourless request to see his driving licence.

"Not bad Carol," said an unmistakably English accent, "you kept really cool when those monkeys forced you off the road."

Carlton spun round and stuck his head out of the window.

"Randy!" he shouted as he got out and hugged his old buddy, "I don't believe it! How on earth…?"

"It's a long story Carol, but for now we've got to get out of here."

"But how on earth did you know where to stop?"

"Thanks to the info you passed on to Rosie we've been one step ahead of those goons all along. We've been watching them since you arrived and we saw a guy place a tracking device under your car. We followed him and found out where he lived.

Hilda and Kitty paid him a visit last night dressed in full night combat gear with face paint and scared the absolute shit out of him. They promised him a return visit with mortal consequences if he didn't reveal his boss's plans to deal with you guys and luckily for us, he spilled the beans."

Carlton shook his head and said, "Damn it Randy, you girls never fail to amaze me!"

Randy laughed as the Hummer with Lola and Kitty pulled in behind them.

They jumped out, greeted Carlton warmly and asked how Naomi was.

Carlton turned, opened the rear door and out stepped Lanky Ada.

"Just wait 'til I see that bitch Rosie," he said sullenly, "she could have warned me not to put my Dolce and Gabbana's on. That quick stop made me break a heel!"

"You shouldn't let things get on top of you Ada," said Kitty.

"I'll be the judge of what gets on top of me thank you very much Kitty Langdon, and it certainly isn't going to be you!"

Following a few seconds of light banter Randy looked around to make sure that the coast was clear then instructed Ada to travel with Lola and Kitty in the Hummer.

He then made his way to the rear of Carlton's car, removed the tracking device and attached it to the underside of the patrol car.

Content that everything was satisfactorily concluded, he made his way to Carlton's car and got in.

"Aren't you forgetting something?" said Carlton nodding towards the patrol car.

"No not really," said Randy as he fastened his seat belt, "the real Highway Patrol should be missing it anytime now…"

Carlton let out a gasp of amazement, jammed the car into gear and pulled away as quickly as he could, expecting at any second to hear the sound of a siren behind him!

"And where did you get the uniforms?" he asked as he accelerated away.

"From one of the reviews we put on at Camp Stanley…"

Carlton just shook his head and burst out laughing.

Back on the turnpike Hilda swept passed them in the Jeep and took up a position in front whilst Lola followed behind in the Hummer.

"The point has been proven," said Rosie from the Cessna, *"It's now obvious that your Town Clerk had a hand in this so it shouldn't be too difficult to tie up the loose ends. And if I was you Carol, I'd see if your policeman buddy in England can find out how he knew about GFK Logistics in Miami."*

Carlton agreed and said, "How's Naomi enjoying the view up there?"

"She's loving it," there was a brief pause and he heard Naomi say something to Rosie.

"She says to tell you she's starving again, so take care."

Carlton smiled and turned his head away so that Randy couldn't see.

"I doubt if those goons will try anything with Lola and Hilda in the back and front of you," said Rosie, *"so all being well, we'll see you back at Camp Stanley for dinner and a catch-up."*

Chapter 38

Cold salty spray splashed over the port bow of the Benetau 331 Clipper yacht as it breasted a short choppy sea on its way around Egypt Point on the last leg of its short journey from Lymington to Cowes on the Isle of Wight.

Giles could hardly believe he was there, the very centre of the sailing world. The skipper and brokerage salesman Steve Clark had wound in the mainsail and genoa prior to entering the River Medina.

Cowes was split into two distinct halves; East Cowes the least popular and West Cowes. This was the side that housed the main shopping centre, the most popular pubs, bars and restaurants and it was the one that most visiting yachtsmen craved to be berthed at.

As Giles motored the Benetau slowly up the Medina, Cowes Yacht Haven came into view on the starboard side.

"This is it Mr. Eaton," called Steve from the bow as he busied himself attaching fenders all round, *"The one and only Cowes."*

Giles could not have been happier. He looked down at his newly acquired red Gill sailing coat and Chatham Marine sailing shoes and felt wonderful.

"Any chance we could park the boat and grab some lunch?" he shouted back.

Steve looked at his watch and called, *"I'm afraid I can't stay for a full-blown lunch, but we could pop into 'The Anchor' for a swift half and quick bite before going back to Lymington."*

"Excellent!" called back Giles beaming from ear to ear. This was just as he had imagined it would be, a million miles from Walmsfield.

He'd been ultra careful with his bank accounts, ensuring that no trace of the fifty thousand that he'd received from Adrian Darke could ever be located and associated with him and though he was considering buying the yacht, it wasn't too over the top.

It was second-hand, albeit only twenty months old and worth

approximately £70,000 in total, but it was not a sum that a reasonably well paid and astute Town Clerk couldn't afford if he only had himself to consider.

He'd never married, and had never really wanted to; his looks, position and comfortable wealth had ensured that there was always a partner on hand when he needed one, even if he did have to pay for it the odd time.

He looked around soaking up the sights and sounds and felt part of a sailing fraternity; one of thousands of sailing brothers who like him, had thrilled at the very thought of being in Cowes *and* arriving by yacht!

Steve took the wheel as he gently rounded the boat into Cowes Yacht Haven's South basin and found an empty berth.

Having secured the vessel they made their way ashore, paid for their lunchtime stay at the marina office and walked to 'The Anchor' public house as arranged. They ordered their drinks and sandwiches and found a table next to the window allowing Giles to watch the meanderings of the numerous and varied folk outside.

He was in seventh heaven.

As they ate and chatted over the pros and cons of the Benetau, one of the bar staff who obviously knew Steve appeared at the table and courteously waited for a break in their conversation.

Giles was the first to see him and nodded his head in the barman's direction.

Steve turned around to face him.

"Excuse me Steve," he said, "I'm sorry to interrupt your conversation, but your boss has been on the phone and he wants you to ring him urgently."

"Why didn't he ring my mobile?"

"He says he thinks it's turned off..."

Steve immediately retrieved his mobile from his coat pocket and saw that it was off. He gave an exasperated shrug and thanked the barman who returned to the bar.

"I shan't be a tick," he said, "but I'd better get this, he'll give me enough gyp for having it switched off as it is!" He shuffled out from behind the table and made his way out onto the street as he was dialling.

Giles sat quietly taking in the ambience; he could hardly credit his luck and quietly reflected that the whole delightful situation had been initiated by the discovery of a bunch of dusty old papers.

His mind wandered on to Carlton and Naomi in America. He involuntarily shook his head at their feeble plan to catch him out. He'd realized that by passing on the information of Carlton and Naomi's whereabouts in Florida he could be implicated in anything that may occur in the States so he and Adrian had come up with a plan.

Naturally the chest had to be taken or destroyed at all costs there was no way of avoiding that; but it was how to do it without being directly implicated that was the tricky bit. He had as instructed by Adrian, secured funding for their flights, car hire and two nights' stay at the Quality Inn in Orlando. One had been for when they'd arrived, and the other was for the night before they returned.

He'd had to ask Naomi to provide him with an itinerary of planned events in order to arrange things, Naomi had obliged and in her usual highly efficient way had emailed him a detailed programme. He'd known better than to forward the email directly to Adrian, so he'd printed a copy and posted it instead. Next he forwarded a copy of Naomi's email to the Treasurer's Department with a copy to the Department Head and a further copy to the Mayor's Office.

He'd been perfectly aware that Tom Ramsbottom had not yet been replaced but that hadn't stopped him sending the email. He'd figured that the more places that had it the better. Finally, he'd called a small press conference on the day of Carlton and Naomi's departure to show how Walmsfield Borough Council cared about its history by funding their trip to America in order to try to resolve a local mystery that would be revealed upon their return.

The journo's from the local papers had bought into it; they'd avidly written about an unfolding historical mystery and had promised to return within a week to see the results. It had made interesting reading for the locals and it had had the added advantage of being able to fill columns for two weeks running.

He was then confident with any number of people being aware of Naomi and Carlton's itinerary, that he could never have been accused of being the only person to have known where they were and what they were doing at any one time in Florida.

He smiled to himself as he finished his sandwich and was just about to order another half pint of Guinness, when he saw Steve walk back into the bar with a perplexed look upon his face.

Steve walked over to Giles and said, "You haven't got any unpaid parking fines have you?"

"Not that I'm aware of, why?"

"My boss has just informed me that the police want to see you when you get back to Lymington…"

"What? Why?" said Giles.

"I've no idea," said Steve, "either my boss wouldn't tell me or they didn't tell him; regardless, he's asked me to ring him when we get back to Lymington so that he can arrange for the police to meet us at Town Quay."

Giles mind went into overdrive; he thought about Naomi and Carlton in Florida, his bank account in The Caymans…

Steve broke his train of thought.

"You look worried;" he said, "you've not stolen the family jewels to buy the Benetau have you?"

Giles tried to look nonchalant.

"No, definitely not," he said smiling back at his companion.

"You'll probably get back and find that they got an unpaid parking ticket or something," said Steve jokily.

Giles knew that Steve was trying to make light of the situation, but some subtle thing about his demeanour had changed.

"Anyway," said Steve light-heartedly, "I suppose that we'd better make a move, we don't want to keep the boys in blue waiting." He bent down picked up his glass and drained the contents, picked up his sandwich and gestured towards the door with his head.

Giles cased himself out from behind the table, departed 'The Anchor' and walked in silence back to the yacht.

"Short but sweet," said Steve as the boat slowly made its way out of the marina, "but maybe you'll come back if you buy this baby."

"You can bet your life on it," said Giles, but small talk was the last thing he wanted.

The thought of the waiting police was driving him crazy. His ordered mind chronologically went through all of the events of the last few months and he believed that he'd left nothing to chance. If anything had gone dramatically wrong in Florida the connection could be made of course, but nothing definitive.

'*And therein*', he thought, '*lay the problem*'. The police hardly ever acted on impulse; they invariably possessed some concrete piece of evidence before alerting a suspect.

"We could be in for a bit of a bumpy ride on the way back," said Steve as the western Solent came into view, "the wind's picked up and it's reacting against the opposing tide."

It was all double Dutch to Giles; he politely nodded an acknowledgement and didn't give Steve's comment any further thought.

As the vessel slowly made its way back to Lymington the sea colour changed to a slate grey; the wind picked up and white horses tinged the wave crests. The yacht handled the conditions very well but the closer it got towards the middle of The Solent, the more it had to breast battering waves. Several times the bow reared up alarmingly then plunged down the wave troughs causing huge sprays of water to cascade back into the cockpit.

Giles positioned himself behind the dark blue cockpit canopy and cast a nervous glance over his shoulder towards Steve at the wheel who whilst taking the full force of the spray, appeared to be completely at ease.

Steve saw Giles' concerned look and reassured him by being nonchalant.

"*I love it when it's like this!*" he said calling over the sound of the turbulence, "*To me, it's what being on the water is all about; one minute calm and peaceful, then in the blink of an eye you're on a fairground ride.*"

Giles smiled but took no comfort from the reassurance.

A look of consternation spread over Steve's face; he'd noticed a distinct change in his sailing companion and couldn't help harbouring a feeling that he was planning something.

Being a boat skipper often called for him to make snap decisions involving plenty of awkward possibilities coupled to very few options and over the years he'd developed a strong faith in his own judgement; now tiny alarm bells were ringing.

He couldn't rationalise it, but for whatever reason he now

wanted Giles off the boat.

He casually glanced at his watch and made a mental estimate of his ETE and ETA; he saw Giles watching him intently and called, "*At least it's summer and won't get dark too soon.*"

The very mention of the word 'dark' did it for Giles.

"*Dark, yes!*" he called back, "*Adrian bloody Darke!*"

Steve looked at Giles in a puzzled way, leaned forwards and called, "*Adrian bloody Dark? I don't follow…*"

'I'll bet that bastard has something to do with this!" said Giles quietly.

"*I'm sorry,*" called Steve, "*I didn't quite get that.*"

Giles suddenly realised that he wasn't making sense and called back, "*It's nothing, I was just thinking out loud.*"

Steve called, "*Is it anything I can help with?*"

Giles looked at Steve and called, "*How could you possibly help?*"

"*I don't know, but if it's something technical about the boat or some other nautical thing…*"

The penny dropped and Giles called, "*No, forget it. I wasn't even thinking about the boat, I was speculating about what the police might want.*"

"*And do you think this 'Adrian bloody Dark' has something to do with the police wanting to see you?*"

"*I really don't know,*" called Giles, "*but as you said, it's probably nothing important.*"

Steve nodded and resumed concentrating on helming.

Giles looked forwards and focused his thoughts on Adrian Darke.

He'd always been scathing; belittling him whenever he could and constantly telling him that thinking wasn't his strong point, and now he surmised that Adrian was trying to sever all ties with him and come out of the Whitewall affair unscathed.

And another thing played on his mind. Following the highly unsettling experience with FA Cup he'd carefully wiped out any trace of a paper trail that could connect the Darke family to him too.

Over and over he considered the possibilities, until one thing finally dominated his thoughts. That was, if he was to be implicated in any way, he wouldn't be the only one…

He was suddenly aware that the vessel's movement had calmed and quickly looked around. He could see that they'd entered the Lymington River entrance and knew that within thirty minutes they'd be back at Town Quay.

It was too quick; he needed time to think, to plan. He looked down at the controls, considered his options for a second and then dismissed the idea of taking the yacht.

He shook his head whilst still in thought and in doing so noticed how many small boats were tied up along the river bank.

"Another twenty minutes and we'll be there," said Steve interrupting his thoughts, "I'll call my boss and let him know that we've arrived and then he can call the police. You take the helm, stick to the right hand side of the river and keep the green posts to starboard."

Happy that Giles was fully au fait with the situation, Steve disappeared below and retrieved his mobile; he came back up on deck and stood with his back to Giles as he dialled.

Giles waited for his moment; he watched carefully as Steve lifted the phone to his ear and then moved quietly alongside the wheel. In one quick movement he raised his right foot in the air, stamped it hard down on the deck, made a loud yelling noise and then slammed his bodyweight into Steve's back.

Steve shot forwards and hit the bulkhead in front of him with such force that he lost his grip on his phone and it cascaded over the side and into the water.

"Jesus Christ!" he said regaining his footing, "What the hell happened there?"

"I'm sorry," said Giles, "I was coming forwards to ask you a question and I tripped."

Steve looked down at the deck and saw the uncoiled mainsheet lying in the cockpit sole.

"Oh I'm sorry," he said, "that's my fault, I should have stowed the line before I went down below."

"No harm done with me," said Giles smugly, "but what about your mobile?"

"Don't worry about it, it was a company one and they're covered by insurance. I'll get another when we get back."

"But what about your call to your boss?"

"No problem there either, this is a boat. We always have back-up plans; I'll contact the Harbour Master via vhf and ask him to pass on the message."

Giles hadn't seen that coming; he was no better off than before. Once again the grey matter went into overdrive.

As they made the penultimate turn prior to reaching Town Quay, Steve went forwards and started attaching fenders to the guardrails. He looked back at Giles and called, "*When we get up near the quay, slip the gear into neutral until I get back to you, O.K.?*"

Giles acknowledged Steve's instruction and slowly inched the boat towards their destination. Behind him he became aware of the deep guttural growl of a powerful engine.

"*Ahoy there!*" called a voice from astern.

Giles turned to look in his direction.

"*Are you tying up at the quay?*" It was the skipper of a powerboat behind him.

Giles nodded.

"*Then do you mind if I raft up alongside of you while I get some lunch?*"

Giles looked forward towards Steve who nodded and seemed happy enough to let him conduct the negotiations.

"*It's O.K. with me,*" he called back.

"Excellent!" said the powerboat skipper as he came alongside the yacht, "I'll attach some fenders then skull about until you're ready for me."

Giles watched the powerboat skipper as he put the boat's gear into neutral and noted that it was controlled pretty much the same as the Benetau. The skipper then made his way carefully forwards along the narrow sloping bow and started to attach fenders.

Slowly, the two vessels began to drift towards one another when Giles had an idea. The powerboat engine was still running and he thought that if he could get across to the cockpit before anybody knew what was happening he could be away. He could race the boat back down the river, disappear into The Solent and from there he could speed into any number of destinations to effect his getaway before anybody realised where he was going.

The powerboat drifted closer to the yacht; the skipper saw it and said, "It's O.K. mate, if we touch our fenders will cushion the impact."

With a tiny jolt the cockpit of the powerboat came to rest directly next to the cockpit of the yacht.

Giles took in the situation; the Town Quay was in view, the odd person was casually walking along the water's edge but it wasn't overly crowded and their preparations for mooring appeared to be of little interest to any of the passers-by.

"It looks like your ride has arrived!" said Steve jokily as a police car slowly pulled into the car park opposite them.

In a blur of action, Giles suddenly leapt over the rails of the yacht and dropped down into the cockpit of the powerboat. He snatched the gear lever backwards causing the boat to surge astern and plunge the unsuspecting powerboat skipper into the water.

The speed at which the boat reversed panicked him and without thinking he jammed the gear lever forwards to stop the movement. The gears engaged and the boat jumped forwards; it accelerated at an alarming speed and glanced off the side of the yacht knocking Steve into the water too. It then raced directly towards the powerboat skipper in the river and narrowly missed him as it surged forwards. He heard a scream from the quayside and saw people running towards the life-buoys in an effort to assist the men in the water.

The sudden sounds and uncharacteristic movement attracted the policeman who had just emerged from the car and he too ran down the jetty and started shouting.

With more self-control, Giles calmed his nerves, engaged the reverse gear and slowly backed away from the scene of mayhem in front. As the river widened he turned the boat, re-engaged the forward gear and powered back down the river from whence he had come.

At the Town Quay, the people who'd leapt into the river to help the stunned powerboat skipper were being pulled out by helpful passers-by.

The policeman who'd witnessed the proceedings from the beginning had made sure that everything was under control and had radioed the events through to his control room.

Back in the river Giles gained speed and confidence as he piloted the powerboat towards the open waters of The Solent. The vessel was very powerful, and though he had seen several notices requiring him to stick to six knots he had kept the power on, creating a rooster tail of water at his stern *and* a torrent of abuse from other outraged boaters. Port and starboard he swept as the river coursed one way and then the other on its way to the open sea.

As he roared around the narrowest and tightest bend he was suddenly confronted by the huge Yarmouth to Lymington car ferry. This was the biggest vessel to use the river and it all but filled the channel directly in front of him.

In a knee-jerk reaction he yanked the wheel left in an attempt to keep the ferry on his right-hand side as he passed.

This erroneous marine decision didn't go unnoticed by the ferry skipper who gave five loud warning blasts on his horn.

Oblivious of the meaning of the signal, Giles sped into the narrow stretch of water on the wrong side of the river and kept the power on.

He thought he'd got away with it until to his horror, the towering black hull of a large commercial fishing boat appeared from behind the ferry directly in his path.

In blind terror Giles swung the wheel over to the right causing the powerboat to crash into the side of the ferry.

Above him a collective gasp went out from the watching passengers as he yanked the wheel in the opposite direction causing the boat to turn once again into the path of the oncoming fishing boat.

The alarmed skipper of the fishing boat now sounded *his* horn as the powerboat came straight at him.

Giles reacted instinctively by swerving once again to the right and thudding for a second time into the side of the ferry.

Another gasp went out from above as the powerboat scraped and scratched along at high speed making all sorts of unhealthy sounds until it veered off to port and hammered into the side of the fishing boat. The unexpected impact caused Giles to lose his grip on the steering wheel and he fell heavily backwards into the bottom of the cockpit.

Now completely out of control but still under full power, the speedboat careered out of the river mouth and into the rough waters of The Solent.

In the short time since they'd arrived at Lymington the weather had further deteriorated and the local Coastguard had been forced to issue an unscheduled gale warning to all vessels via the vhf radio.

The rough state of the sea now caused the driverless boat to leapfrog across the waves with alarming speed and brutality. Giles desperately attempted to regain control, but the wild bucking as it crashed into the oncoming waves made it impossible for him to regain his feet without being knocked over each time he tried. Cold seawater blasted into his face, the wind seemed to be howling like a banshee and each time the propeller left the water the engine screamed in protest until it made contact again. Then just as he pulled himself up and peered over the bow, he saw it.

Directly in front of him was an enormous wave and behind it was a huge, solid wooden construction looming up out of the water.

The powerboat roared up the wave and launched itself into thin air as the foaming wave crest passed below him. For a brief second in time everything stood still; he became momentarily weightless and the howling of the wind ceased. He clearly saw the wooden structure as the boat arced through the air towards it then slowly, ever so slowly, descended.

He watched in slow motion as the glass reinforced plastic disintegrated before his very eyes; shattered pieces of hull danced in the turbulent air as the bow was pile-driven with colossal force into the woodwork.

And then with one last movement of his head, he looked up and saw the eighteen inch thick, solid oak cross member directly in front of his face.

With horrendous speed and ferocity the powerboat smashed itself into tiny smithereens, and took the headless body of Giles with it as it sank below the cold crashing waters of The Solent.

Back at the Town Quay, the policeman who was completely unaware of what had just transpired was trying to explain things over the radio to his controller.

"But if you were only there to inform him that somebody had hit his parked car," said the puzzled controller, "why did he hijack a boat and speed away?"

"That my friend," said the police driver, "is the one million pound question isn't it?"

Chapter 39

This was a day unlike any other at Camp Stanley; Rosie was in charge of everybody's well-being and he'd put on a good spread.

Carlton and Naomi had arrived a little after 10:15am followed soon afterwards by Deborah and Alan Farlington. The entire sewing circle had turned out, Randy, Kitty, Lola and Hilda and even Lil had turned up hoping for another shot at Paul, who much to his chagrin wasn't there. Last but by no means least, sitting preening in the far corner of the main bar was the spectacular and impressive Lanky Ada.

Naomi had contacted Doctor Eleanor Jayne Drascoe from the Antiquities Department of Florida State Museum who had in turn recommended her own father, a thick-set guy known to all as 'Solid' and a top quality locksmith to boot, for the job of getting into the chest and both were present, awaiting instructions to start.

Naomi had often encountered the problem of old locks with no key but they had generally been on pieces of furniture, not old sea chests. The principal however, remained the same.

Most mortise locks dating from between one hundred and fifty to two hundred and fifty years old could be impressive and imposing looking especially when they were large, such as those employed on chests and strongboxes, but by modern day standards they were pretty simple in design and certainly not beyond the skills of an experienced locksmith.

Sitting on the bar was the object of everybody's attention - the sealed chest.

Even in such a modest gathering it looked small and insignificant; the construction was simple and functional and it appeared to have only four distinguishing features.

Carved into the woodwork of the lid were the initials 'V' and 'C' generally accepted to be the initials of Valentine Chance,

Matthew's grandson, and whom it was believed first brought the chest to America; a simple engraving of a cow's head with pollarded horns situated between the letters, and a large circular indentation to the right-hand side of the letter 'C', that looked as though the lid had been struck heavily by a hammer or something similar.

None of the people present had any idea how much that old wooden box had affected so many lives in the past; how nobody had dared to open it because of the curse and how it had been revered and passed from generation to generation without ever revealing its contents. But all of that was about to change.

The time was getting on for 11 o' clock and most people were now impatient to see the contents, but one person was missing - Ewan Chance. Not surprisingly he was late, an annoying trait that had been the bane of Naomi's life.

"Come on Naomi," said Randy, "can't we at least let Solid start with his box of tricks?"

"I'll try Ewan's mobile and see where he is; if he's close we'll wait, but if he hasn't left the marina Solid can start."

Everybody was placated.

Then almost as though he had been awaiting the moment, the door to the club opened and Ewan walked in with Paul and Jo-Anne.

Lil's eyes lit up at the appearance of Paul and then immediately dulled when he caught sight of Jo-Anne.

"Hi sis!"

"Ewan!" Naomi ran across the room and flung herself into her big brother's arms.

"It's so good to see you!" she said hugging him in genuine affection, and then she noticed Paul and Jo-Anne too.

"Paul, Jo-Anne; how wonderful to see you!" She let go of Ewan and hugged Jo-Anne first, and then a delighted Paul.

Once again Lil pouted. He turned to Lanky Ada and said, "Just look at them, it's disgusting! Men and women; personally I can't stand mixed marriages..."

Paul overheard Lil, looked at Ewan and mouthed, "Oh shit, spare me...!"

Ewan grinned and mouthed back, "You're on your own Eric!"

Naomi made her way back to her brother.

"Ewan," she said, "there's somebody I'd like you to meet; the man I've been telling you about." She took her brother by the arm and walked him over to Carlton.

Carlton smiled and extended his hand.

Ewan smiled, shook the offered hand and then said, "I'm not sure about him sis, the last one you married turned out to be dodgy and now I'm meeting this one for the first time in a gay bar…!"

Carlton couldn't help himself, he stuck his hand on his hip and in as feminine a voice as he could muster said, "Well get you, cheeky!"

Brother and sister burst out laughing, then even more so when Rosie's voice cut through their merriment and said, "Carol love, you're a natural! There's hope for you yet!"

"That's more than can be said for my Eric with *her* in tow, isn't it!" said Lil, giving the bad eye to Jo-Anne.

"All right girls and boys," said Rosie, "the big moment has arrived. Shall we put Solid to work?"

"I'm game if he is!" said Lanky Ada from across the room.

Solid looked uncomfortably across to where Ada was sitting, did an obvious double take, made a 'harrumphing' sound and looked at Naomi.

"Very well," she said to no-one in particular, "but please remember to give him plenty of space. The contents of the chest are supposedly about two hundred and fifty years old so we don't want anything to happen to them now."

Solid nodded and reached for his canvas bag. He extracted several large key rings each holding numerous old-looking keys of various sizes and shapes and placed them on the bar next to the chest. There appeared to be an infinite number of variations with differing shank lengths, diameters, bit and ward sizes and he explained that in most cases the first steps were not highly technical, they were trial and error and that he had to estimate the size and shape of key required to undo the lock and keep on trying until he hopefully found one that fitted.

Everybody watched in fascination as Solid gently offered up different keys to the lock housing and cautiously checked to see if they would turn the mechanism.

A telephone rang on the end of the bar; Rosie made his way over to it and answered. Following an exchange of words he called over, "*Carol! It's for you!*"

Carlton looked at Naomi and said, "Who the hell knows I'm here right now?"

Naomi shrugged and said, "You'll soon find out…"

Carlton walked across to the phone and said, "Wilkes."

"Ah yes Mr. Wilkes, Bob Crowthorne here; I'm afraid I'm the bearer of rather bad tidings."

Carlton hated calls like this, he closed his eyes and said, "Go on."

"It concerns Mr. Giles Eaton."

There was a brief pause which sounded to Carlton as though the Chief Inspector was checking notes before committing himself.

"We have been informed by the Hampshire Constabulary that he has been killed in a boating incident in The Solent, near Lymington."

Carlton was flabbergasted; he could hardly believe his ears; first there was Sandra, then Tom and Peggy Ramsbottom and now Giles, all gone in such a short period of time.

"…Are you still there?" Crowthorne's voice brought him back to reality.

"Yes, forgive me, you said a boating incident in The Solent? That seems impossible! What was he doing there and what happened?"

"I'm sorry, I can't answer that; the Hampshire Police haven't finished their investigations yet, but they contacted the Lancashire Constabulary to ask us to inform his next of kin etcetera. When I received the news, I thought that you should know about it in case it had any bearing upon your activities in Florida."

"Yes thank you," said Carlton, "that was very thoughtful of you. Do you have any objection to me informing Naomi Draper?"

"No. The Hampshire Police have told me that as far as the death is concerned they don't suspect foul play, so withholding information about it is not an issue." Crowthorne paused for a second and then said, "Can I ask you, are you still expecting to return to the UK tomorrow as planned?"

"We are," said Carlton.

"Then I should be able to fill you in with the details upon your return."

Carlton and Crowthorne said their goodbyes and promised to

meet following their return to Walmsfield.

Carlton looked across the room and saw Naomi staring at him intently; he gestured for her to come over to him.

Naomi knew that something had happened. They had become much closer on this trip, far closer than she had dared hope and now she had developed some kind of emotional radar and could read his feelings by just looking at him. She walked across and said, "What is it?"

Carlton told her about the death of Giles.

Naomi was stunned; for a while she stared at Carlton in complete silence trying to mentally collate all of the unusual occurrences that had happened since the file had been opened.

Finally she said, "I don't know what's going on Cal but I don't like it, it is like a curse or something. We're the only original ones left alive who know about the contents of that file…"

Carlton was also deep in thought and quietly said, "Maybe, maybe not…"

Naomi opened her mouth to speak but from across the room there was a sudden buzz of excitement. Everybody had gathered around Solid and as she and Carlton approached, they heard him triumphantly say "Gotcha!"

The group parted to make way for Naomi; all their faces were alive with anticipation and excitement.

Solid turned to Naomi and said, "I got it for you ma'am."

Naomi looked down and saw one of the keys sitting neatly in the housing.

"It opened real smooth when we got the right key, it must have been a good quality lock in both material and workmanship."

Naomi thanked him and turned to his daughter, Eleanor Jayne.

"Do you have any reservations before I proceed?"

"No ma'am, let's just see what's in there shall we?"

Naomi looked down at the chest and to her amazement, found that she was trembling.

The contents of the little wooden box had the ability to change people's lives forever and she hardly dared to open the lid. She briefly thought about the Arc of the Covenant and wondered whether like that, the contents were best unseen.

She looked at the eager faces around her and remembered that everybody had played a part in getting to this moment of truth; and that they all deserved to be there when the contents were revealed regardless of the consequences.

"Come on then sis, let's see..." Ewan's voice broke the silence.

Naomi looked at him briefly and then turned to face them all.

"Before I open the chest," she said gravely, "I'd just like to thank you all on behalf of the Chance family, and in particular my great, great, great Aunt Maria whom we believe may have died without ever having seen what we may potentially see in a few minutes' time; for the tremendous support, help and encouragement you have all shown in helping us to arrive at this incredibly auspicious moment.

Some of you present cannot possibly know just how important her courage and tenacity was, yet despite having to endure unbelievable danger and hardship she managed to pass down to the present day members of the Chance family a legacy, a cause, and a belief that did not die.

It naturally behoves me to fully acknowledge that the small box we are about to open is thanks only to Matthew Chance from Alan's branch of the family; and for the care that they have shown in preserving such an important piece of family history, but if you would all kindly indulge me, I would like to dedicate this moment, this very last possibility of success in regaining our inheritance, to the one and only Maria without whose papers none of this would be happening."

"Here here," said Alan graciously, "to Maria"

The rest of the people in the room remained silent, but all heads nodded in agreement.

Naomi turned to face the chest, reached into her conservator's bag, retrieved a hair net, a pair of soft white cotton gloves and a face mask. She carefully put them on and placed her hands on each side of the lid and lifted.

Once it was fully opened she leaned over and peered inside. At first she couldn't see anything and then as she looked closer her face fell; all that she could see was dust and the remnants of a parchment style material scattered about the base.

To all intents and purposes the chest was empty and whatever had been inside had disintegrated.

She let out a groan of disappointment and all heads leaned forward for a look.

Everybody else's reaction was the same; they simply stood in crestfallen silence.

Naomi reached into the chest and carefully picked up the largest fragment of material; one side was blank but on the reverse she could just make out the faded lettering, '...*eus immit*...' She stared at it for a few seconds and racked her brain to make a connection, but to no avail.

She looked up and noticed Eleanor Jayne scrutinizing the fragment also, but she, too, eventually shook her head and gave a shrug of her shoulders.

Bit by tiny bit, Naomi methodically examined all the other pieces of parchment, but not a single letter or number was present on anything else.

Whitewall was now lost to the Chance family forever.

All about her the atmosphere was heavy with disappointment, she felt the emotion welling up in her chest and turned to look at the crestfallen Alan.

"I'm so sorry..." she said quietly shaking her head.

Alan said nothing but Deborah said, "We weren't responsible for that were we?"

Naomi frowned and said, "For what?"

"I mean," said Deborah defensively, "I hope that you don't think that the contents were spoiled because we didn't look after the chest properly because we haven't had it long. We haven't dropped it or mistreated it or anything..."

"No, no," said Naomi, "It's nothing to do with any of us. The contents have probably been like that for years and years; and without the aid of forensic science it would be impossible to state how or when the damage occurred."

Deborah breathed a sigh of relief and said, "Well thank the Lord for that at least."

As Deborah's statement sank in Naomi started to question herself, she wondered whether or not she could have done anything more to ensure the stability of the contents, but within a few minutes of mulling things over she accepted that all of her 'what if's?' were pure conjecture.

From across the room Ewan saw the look of self-doubt on his

sister's face and walked over to her.

"It's not your fault sis; we all know how fastidious you are so don't start feeling guilty about anything."

Naomi looked at her brother and smiled.

"That was our last possibility of reclaiming our inheritance," she said quietly, "and everything that Maria struggled for has finally gone."

"Fate," said Ewan decisively, "Fate. It obviously has other plans for us."

The day's disappointment didn't stop Rosie and the staff putting on a party at Camp Stanley that night.

As a precursor to the event Paul had tentatively invited everybody back to the marina for drinks aboard 'Las Ventanas' whilst he, Jo-Anne and Ewan had changed into more suitable clothing. He had not expected the entire sewing circle, including Lil and Lanky Ada in full drag to tag along too, but tag along they had.

The ensuing mayhem both in the marina and at Monty's bar some time later had been such that Jo-Anne, Paul and Ewan had never been able to live it down and it had become the stuff of bar talk legend...

That night at Camp Stanley Rosie excelled himself; he was the perfect 'hostess'. A wonderful spread had been put on followed by an inimitable cabaret, and everybody thoroughly enjoyed themselves.

During the evening Carlton noticed Naomi looking at him from across the table and gave her a questioning look.

She gestured for him to follow her outside.

"What is it love?" he softly enquired, "You've been looking at me oddly all night."

Naomi turned to face him and took hold of both of his hands.

"I love you Carlton Wilkes, that's what it is; and that's why I've been staring at you all night."

Carlton stared deeply into her eyes and whispered, "And I love you too." He put his arms around her and kissed her.

At the end of a wonderful evening, Rosie ascended the stage and called for silence.

"Ladies, gentlemen," he called, *"and those who have yet to make up their minds, I wish to propose a toast.*

I would like to thank the various members of the Chance and Farlington families for bringing us all together like this.

Without their unremitting dedication to preserving their family history, which I believe stretches back over two hundred and fifty years, we would not all be here today.

Now, I am not a party to all of the ins and outs of the proceedings, but being a lady of considerable good looks, taste and dress sense ..."

Lanky Ada cast a glance across to Lil, raised an eyebrow and mouthed, "As if..."

"...I have to admit harbouring a secret admiration for... wait for it... a woman!"

Various comments were shouted back at Rosie who quelled them all with a wave of his hand.

"Yes," he continued, *"it's true. Like Naomi, my favourite historical character has been Maria. For me she represented everything good in the opposite sex... so much so in fact, that I shall be checking out her medical records later to see if she was not actually a gentleman of our particular persuasion!"*

Everybody burst out laughing.

"So now please raise your glasses and toast the indomitable Maria!"

The cry went up, *"The indomitable Maria!"*

Chapter 40

25th February 1870

Maria stepped out into the chill winter air and inhaled deeply. She could hardly believe where she was and how things had turned out in the last six months.

The latter part of 1869 had been filled with firsts and not all of them had been pleasant.

She'd had to completely abandon her lodgings and personal possessions; she'd had to break all contact with every member of her family knowing that they'd be desperate to find out where she was *and* in the knowledge that it could last up to a year before she could contact them again. She'd had to move out of Cheshire altogether to avoid arrest by the police, and she'd substituted the Christian name Mary for Maria.

However, the scales of life swung both ways and for every down she'd had to endure there were an equal number of ups.

The bond that had been forged between her and her new friends was one of the most important things in her life and her appreciation of them was unsurpassed.

They'd risked persecution, prosecution and even gaol to help her escape from the Asylum and she didn't think that she would ever be able to repay them for their unbelievable kindness and unselfishness.

Sister Florence Parks had returned to work and had met with a total blank about the escape; it was as though nothing had ever happened. For weeks she'd waited for the axe to fall but just as surely as she'd made no reference to the housing of private patients at Parkway, or to Maria individually, neither had anyone else ever mentioned that an escape had taken place, and she'd continued to work there without any hint of trouble.

Indeed if anything, Florence was of the opinion that she was being treated better now than she had ever been before that fateful night.

Simeon Twitch had opted to leave his employment at the Asylum and had taken up a new position with his wife.

And then there was Silas. In September 1869, two months after her escape he'd proposed to her; she'd joyfully accepted and they'd married just before Christmas on December the 20th.

She was now known to all but her immediate family as Mary Cartwright.

But without a doubt the most astonishing turn of events had occurred following an idea first mooted by Silas several weeks after her escape from Parkway.

He had read a newspaper article describing how the police were trying to establish the whereabouts of Caleb Johnson following the reporting of a murder by a young boy who had clearly seen him shoot another man in the Roch Valley.

At the scene of the crime the police had discovered numerous bodies including Johnson's own father and close friend Hugo Darke at the bottom of a nearby rogue pit and a Warrant had been issued for his arrest.

He'd subsequently deserted his home at the Whitewall Estate and had gone into hiding.

The weeks had passed by and in the absence of any further news about the missing Johnson, Silas had contacted the Local Land Registry office about the possibility of applying for the tenancy of Whitewall until the rightful owners could either be contacted or established.

At the end of October 1869 they'd informed him that he'd been successful in securing the tenancy for a twenty year period in the absence of any legal claims.

Now here she was, living at Whitewall not as the rightful owner, but as the wife of tenant Silas Cartwright.

And Simeon and Martha Twitch had taken up their offer of employment as live-in senior farm hand and cook!

She didn't think that life could have possibly sprung any more surprises on her until midway through November.

Late one evening she and Silas had heard a large bang from somewhere in the yard and had gone out to investigate. As they'd stepped out they'd seen Simeon with a petrified expression on his face pointing to the split level door next to the barn. They'd made their way over to him and enquired what the trouble was but he'd just pointed towards the door without making a sound.

Silas had slowly edged up to it, pulled it open and to their utmost horror they'd seen Sugg staring back out at them.

Their first instinct had been to run for a shotgun, but something about his demeanour had stopped them and despite desperate pleas not to from her and Simeon, Silas had slowly approached.

Upon seeing this Sugg had submissively laid down and hadn't made any kind of aggressive move. It was obvious from his appearance that he was malnourished and unkempt but Maria remembered all too well what a dangerous dog he had been.

Very cautiously at first Silas had put food out for him and although he wouldn't eat when anybody was nearby, over time he'd slowly started to accept it.

Confidence had grown and a mutual trust borne out of kindness and care had resulted, and within weeks Sugg had become a healthy looking regular fixture at Whitewall that accompanied Silas nearly everywhere he went.

Now it was the day of Silas's fiftieth birthday and she couldn't have been happier; her new friends Len and his wife Catherine, Simeon and Martha, and Florence and her husband Cornelius were sitting indoors with Silas waiting for her to return to cut the cake that Florence had made.

She took several steps into the yard, looked around, smiled and went back indoors. She didn't even mind the hated 'L:J:M 1748' carved into the lintel anymore.

The door closed behind her and a pair of watching eyes sank down behind the perimeter wall adjacent to the yard entrance.

Caleb Johnson was stunned by what he had just seen.

Things had been hard since he'd been on the run and the funds had completely run out but he knew that his father had secreted a cache of money below the floorboards of the master bedroom at Whitewall and now he wanted it.

He looked up into the darkening sky and quietly said, "You aren't going to believe this pa. Not only am I going to get the money, I'm going to be able to finish the bitch that started all this trouble."

Chapter 41

Upon their return from Florida Carlton and Naomi extended the Bank Holiday weekend and went with Jane and Sam to see her grandmother Jocelyn at her home in Bournemouth.

Following the introductions and the cups of tea and coffee all round, Naomi brought her up to date, from the exciting beginnings to the disappointing conclusion.

"It's all gone nanny," she said finally, "We had what appeared to be two shots at it; the papers that were passed down to poppa, allied to the Deeds and Tenancy Agreement that were found and then lost again at Walmsfield. Then there was the possibility of seeing Matthew Chance's copy of the Deeds and Tenancy Agreement in America, but they had disintegrated over the years except for a tiny fragment of material with the lettering 'eus immit' on it."

"What on earth is 'eus immit'? And does it mean anything?" said Jocelyn.

"Not that anybody is aware of - at least for the present." said Sam.

Jocelyn remained silent and thoughtful. She was in her mid-eighties but was as sharp as a pin.

"So, despite all of ours and Maria's efforts," said Sam, "it was ultimately to no avail."

"And what of the documents lost in Walmsfield? Do you think they will ever be re-discovered?" asked Jocelyn.

"The police think that they were purposely destroyed," said Naomi.

"Well, I'm terribly sorry darlings," said Jocelyn, "especially after all the effort everybody has put in." She looked at Sam and said consolingly, ""Dad would have been proud of you."

Sam smiled and said, "Not just me mum, you wouldn't believe how many people helped us in the end."

Everybody lapsed into silence for a few minutes until Jane

looked up and said, "My old mum used to say, "Nowt passes you by that was meant for you.""

Sam and Jocelyn looked thoughtfully at her and nodded in agreement.

The following day and two-hundred-and-fifty miles north, Carlton and Naomi were walking to Carlton's office when they heard a dreadful cacophony ahead of them.

Three male voices could clearly be heard *apparently* singing, but they were all off key and completely out of time with one another.

Naomi and Carlton followed their tortured ears to the source of the noise and found Postcard Percy with two other men, all singing at the tops of their voices to the gathered staff of the general office. The sheer sound of it had people standing with their hands on their ears and with screwed-up faces; some were staring with incredulity while others were simply laughing. The singing trio was utterly undaunted by their audience's reaction and carried steadfastly on to the end of their number. Everybody clapped and cheered after which Percy shook his collection jar, and picked up contributions from all around.

At first one member of staff, then another, suddenly noticed their returned Department Head standing in their midst and hurriedly retreated to their work stations.

"Naomi! Carlton!" said Percy beaming from ear to ear. "Before I leave, I have a bit of information for you."

He spoke briefly to his two colleagues who turned and waved to everybody, then walked quietly out of the main office to await Percy at the main reception.

"Can we go into your office?" he said.

Carlton nodded and pointed to his door.

Once inside, Naomi had to ask, "That was the worst sounding trio I've ever heard Percy. I know that you've got a nice voice but theirs are dreadful; who are they and why on earth are you with them?"

"Ah!" said Percy, "double reverse psychology my dear!"

Carlton and Naomi didn't even try to respond…

"Do you recall that people were paying me more money to keep quiet rather than to sing?"

Naomi nodded.

"Well, I figured that even more people would pay me if my singing was really bad. Mind numbingly, cringingly bad I mean, so I asked two of my friends to help me - deaf Mitch and der der Dave."

"Deaf Mitch and der der Dave?" repeated Carlton.

"Yes. Mitch's hearing is really bad so he can't tell which key we're singing in, and der der Dave as the name implies, has a terrible stutter and can't keep up!"

"But it sounded awful!" said Naomi.

"Yes I know!" said Percy beaming from ear to ear, "Great wasn't it? And that's what's earning us so much money for charity!"

Naomi and Carlton looked at one another and smiled; they both knew that if he was nothing else, Percy was enterprising…

Percy reached down into his bag and extracted one of his notebooks.

"Now," he said, "It's about *the* Maria Chance. In your absence I checked out her medical records and death certificate and found out a bit more than I'd bargained for."

A sudden realisation dawned upon him.

"Oh, forgive me! Here am I bending your ears on your first day back and I haven't even asked how your trip went!"

"It was a disaster as far as proving anything," said Naomi, "but we'll explain it all to you after you've finished."

Percy raised his eyebrows and said, "I'm sorry to hear about that, but whilst you've been away I've located a few more missing pieces from the Chance family jigsaw puzzle for you."

Naomi sat back in her chair and said, "Sounds interesting."

"When I located the death certificate for Maria, I noted where she had died, made enquiries and was eventually allowed to look at all sorts of documents relating to her life." He paused for a second looked directly at Naomi and said, "And it seems that your Great Aunt was committed to the Cheshire Pauper Lunatic Asylum in Macclesfield, on the 1st July, 1869."

Naomi gasped in horror and disbelief.

"That's awful, I've heard all sorts about her from the past, but I can't ever recall being told about what happened to her later on in life."

"Well," continued Percy, "I hope that this isn't going to be a horrid shock too, because she finally died in October 1890, still an inmate of the Asylum."

Naomi *was* horribly shocked.

"My God!" she said, "That was over twenty years!" She sat back in her chair and tried to comprehend the enormity of what she'd just heard. "No wonder we lost touch with her."

She remained silent as she mulled over Maria's dreadful fate until the Estate crossed her mind. She sat back up and said, "Did you manage to find out who took over Whitewall after the Johnsons?"

Percy flicked through his papers, extracted one of his notes and said, "Yes, the estate was taken over by tenant farmers Silas and Mary Cartwright until it was passed on to the Hawthorns; Alan and Annie's forebears."

Naomi sat in silence as Percy ordered the rest of his paperwork.

"This is a photocopy of your Aunt Maria's entire twenty year medical history…" Percy carefully spread two pages of A4 paper onto Carlton's desk.

"What! Twenty years on two pieces of paper?" said Carlton, now equally appalled.

"Precisely, just have a read."

The document stated that Maria Chance had been committed to the Asylum suffering from 'Delusions of Exaltation'.

It was about as wildly nonspecific as it possibly could be. It also showed that she had only been permitted one medical examination per year and that each examination had resulted in the same equally nonspecific entry. 'Condition unchanged.'

Naomi was outraged.

"Twenty long years in a Lunatic Asylum!" she said angrily, "One annual examination, no chance of release and summed up in just two words; 'Condition unchanged!' That is absolutely appalling."

Both Naomi and Carlton were truly and profoundly horrified.

"There is no proof, nor will there ever be," said Percy, "but if you ask me, it looks as though somebody paid to have her locked up until the day that she died."

Naomi felt drained, she tilted her head back and was about to say something when the thumb pressed violently down on her shoulder.

"Ow!" she said reaching up and rubbing it.

Carlton instantly knew that something was wrong and said, "Are you all right love?"

Percy immediately picked up on Carlton's use of the word 'love' and knew that they had grown closer whilst abroad.

"*Look at the daguerreotype...*" The voice in Naomi's head was a less refined, deeper female one again. For several seconds she sat silently staring into space listening.

Percy cast a quick glance at Carlton and silently mouthed, "Is she O.K.?"

Carlton put his finger to his lips and nodded.

"*The daguerreotype,*" said the voice again, "*look at it...*"

Naomi slowly looked across to Percy and said, "Have you got a photograph of Maria?"

Percy was stunned; he looked quickly at Carlton and then looked back at Naomi.

"Why yes," he said, "I was saving it as a surprise for you!"

"Do you mind if I see it?"

"No of course not," he reached down into his bag and extracted a C5 sized envelope.

"I should warn you that this was taken after her death," he said sombrely.

"That's fine." said Naomi extending her arm.

Percy handed Naomi the envelope and watched as she extracted the photo. He said, "The Victorians were very good at making deceased people look life-like in their photographs, especially given the limited make-up at their disposal."

Naomi removed the photograph and looked at it.

"This isn't Maria!" she said.

Percy looked shocked for a second and said, "I can assure you that it is Naomi. I have always taken the utmost care in my research and I would never present anything for viewing without being absolutely sure about its authenticity."

"*This is not Maria!*" said Naomi defiantly. She reached down to her desk drawer, extracted a folder and rummaged through the contents until she found what she was looking for. She carefully extracted a similar sized photo and placed it alongside the one Percy had shown her.

"You decide." She turned both photo's to face Percy and Carlton.

Both men leaned forwards and studied the two photographs.

"I know it's difficult with these old photo's," said Carlton, "and I appreciate that in one she's much older and dead, but these two women look entirely different to me. They both have a full head of hair, but the photo you say is Maria shows a woman whose hairline runs straight across her forehead and who has a very distinctive face. Whereas Percy's photo shows a woman whose hairline has two deep 'v's running back from her forehead and who has a very plain and uninteresting face.

To me," he said finally pointing to Percy's photo, "this face has either massively changed with age or it is definitely not the same woman."

Percy studied the photographs in silence for a little while longer and then said, "I have to agree. I too think that these are different women but look at this…" He turned the photograph over and pointed to some handwriting on the rear.

Naomi saw the inscription;

"*Maria Chance D.O.B. 6.10.1820 – Deceased 6.10.1890.*
Cheshire Lunatic Asylum, Parkway, Macclesfield"

"Oh my goodness!" said Naomi, "Maria was born and died on the same day as my birthday, the 6th of October!"

Percy smiled and said, "Yes very interesting, but the point is my dear, this photograph seems to indicate that either someone at the Asylum has mixed things up and put your Aunt Maria's details on somebody else's photo, or the woman who died on the 6th October, 1890 in Parkway, wasn't your Aunt at all."

Naomi looked at Carlton and Percy in turn and said, "Wow, intriguing; just when I thought that the dust was beginning to settle, Maria surprises me yet again!"

"It is only speculation," said Percy cautiously, "so we can't go jumping to conclusions…"

"Yes I appreciate that…" said Naomi leaning back in her chair, "but, if she did somehow manage to escape, I wonder what actually happened to her." She paused for reflection and then said, "And I wonder if we'll ever discover the truth about Whitewall…"

The thumb that had been pressing heavily down on her shoulder suddenly lifted and within seconds depressed again. A gentle male voice said, *"Dat Deus immiti cornua curta bovi"* and was gone.

She frowned and opened her mouth to speak but didn't know what to say. She had no idea what she'd just heard and doubted if she could even remember it verbatim. For several seconds she sat in puzzled silence until she decided that for the present she'd had enough.

She looked at the two men, smiled and said, "Anyone fancy a cuppa?"

Chapter 42

1:20am Monday 28th February 1870. The Whitewall Estate

As Caleb Johnson waited quietly in the drive to Whitewall he was filled with self-doubt; not about the task in hand, but about whom he'd seen two days earlier.

When he'd left the Estate that evening he'd been utterly convinced that it was Maria Chance that he'd seen, but now two days later he wasn't so sure.

He knew that he'd been in hiding for the last six months; he knew that Hugo and his father were dead, but he also knew that Hugo had paid Parkway Asylum twelve months in advance to keep the Chance woman locked up. And once private money had exchanged hands the one thing that Asylums were good for was keeping people well and truly locked up without any chance of counter-payment for release, or parole.

Every week he'd avidly read the local newspapers in case anything had been mentioned about the police force's search for him, and during all of that time he hadn't read about anybody escaping from an Asylum.

He got out his pocket watch and saw that it was just after quarter past one; he looked down and double checked that the hessian sacking he'd wound around his boots was still secure and then he got up and quietly walked down the last few yards of the drive, confident that he would know if it was her or not the moment he laid eyes upon her.

And of course, the bonus was the cash under the floorboards in the master bedroom.

He crept quietly into the courtyard and made his way across to the front door. He reached down and unravelled the hessian sacking from around his boots and tossed it to one side. He then slipped two number four cartridges into the breech of his double-barrelled shotgun and left it uncocked over his left arm.

He'd arrived just after midnight on a crystal clear night but the moon was past its last quarter and it gave him just enough light to see without particularly illuminating him.

There had been no obvious signs of activity from indoors and the only false light he'd seen in the last hour or so appeared to be coming from the master bedroom.

He stood quietly assessing the situation and decided against subtlety.

He had Hugo's fully loaded pistol in his coat pocket and guessed that he wouldn't need to loose off more than two rounds to finish off any other occupant than the Chance woman. On her he wanted to use his knife.

He knew that the sound of shots would carry a long way on such a night and could possibly arouse some of the nearby tenant crofters but he reckoned that if no more than two, possibly three were fired they would soon settle down again.

He looked at the door, remembered how well it was made and knew that a single blast from a shotgun wouldn't open it; he looked to the right and opted to go through the window. There was a hefty-looking stone on the ground in front of it and he decided that that would do nicely.

Almost instantly everything started to go wrong.

He took a couple of steps forward to pick up the stone, his leather soled boots scraped lightly on the ground and the split level door next to the barn burst open with an almighty crash.

He wheeled around and to his horror saw Sugg coming at him head on. He snapped the breech of the shotgun shut and immediately fired at the dog.

The shot screamed over Sugg's head but knocked *him* off balance; in blind panic he fired off the other round and then fell flat on his back. He scrambled backwards expecting to be attacked at any moment, but nothing happened. He peered over the top of the forearm protecting his face and saw no sign of Sugg. Within seconds he guessed that the sound, if not an injury had sent the dog running for cover and he now needed to act quickly.

He jumped to his feet, picked up the stone, smashed the glass out of the window and clambered into the hall.

Upstairs Maria and Silas were wide awake and wondering what had happened. Silas had immediately ordered Maria to get under their bed and was ready facing the door with his service revolver in his hand.

He heard heavy footsteps come lumbering up the stairs, along the landing and then stop just outside their bedroom door. He cocked the pistol and lifted it to shoulder height.

The door burst open, he fired and missed, and a split second later a bullet thudded into his left shoulder and spun him partially around. He saw a bulky figure launch himself across the room and turned to meet him face on.

The pain in his shoulder was agonizing but as he saw the intruder lift his weapon to fire again he lashed out with his right foot and sent the gun flying. It slithered across the floor and came to a stop by the window.

Both men went for it but Caleb got there first. His fingers touched the handle but before he get a grip on it Silas grabbed him around the torso and wrenched him to one side.

Caleb stood up and rammed him into the wall next to the window frame causing him to lose his grip. He quickly turned around and landed a swingeing blow with his fist to the right side of Silas' face sending him reeling back towards the window.

Momentarily Silas was framed in the moonlight and Caleb saw his chance.

He lunged forwards with outstretched arms, hit Silas full in the chest and sent him crashing through the glass pane.

He looked down and saw that his adversary was lying motionless fifteen feet below on the stone floor of the courtyard.

During the scuffle, Caleb's heavy knife had fallen from his jacket pocket next to the bed and Maria had quickly grabbed it. She clutched it to her breast and laid quietly, hardly daring to breathe. For what seemed like an eternity nothing happened and then all hell erupted. In one violent movement the bed was suddenly thrust up above her head and then pushed over into the wall at the back of her.

Caleb shouted, *"Got you!"* grabbed hold of one of Maria's ankles and yanked her towards him.

As quick as a flash Maria sat up and slashed the knife around and under Caleb's left arm with all of her might, it plunged into the left side of his rib cage and sank at least three inches in. She knew that she had done some damage.

Caleb yelled in alarm as he felt a searing pain in his left side and knew that something bad had happened. He looked down, saw the knife and snatched it out but could feel that his breathing felt different in his left lung.

As soon as Caleb let go of her ankle, Maria leapt to her feet, pushed him to one side and ran out of the bedroom door and onto the landing. She cascaded down the stairs and across to the front door.

The key was hanging in its usual place, but in her panic to get it she knocked it off the hook and under a nearby sideboard. She dropped to her knees and started wildly scrabbling around for it.

Behind her she heard Caleb coming down the stairs.

"You didn't really think that you could get away from me did you, you ugly bitch? I knew it was you when I saw your sour face under the bed..."

Maria spun around and saw Caleb standing at the foot of the stairs with his pistol in his hand. She had to think quickly.

"Who are you and what do you want?" she said.

"What do you mean who am I? Have you forgotten our last encounter?"

"I don't know what you're talking about; I haven't ever seen you before..."

"*Don't talk shit!* You know who I am and you're going to pay for all the trouble you've caused..."

Caleb put the pistol down onto the stairs and pulled the already bloodied knife from his jacket pocket. He suddenly coughed and blood sprayed out of his mouth.

"And you've done this!" he yelled, coughing and spitting more blood onto the floor.

"Are you the man who attacked my twin sister Maria?"

Caleb frowned and said "What?"

"I said, are you the man who attacked my twin sister Maria here a couple of years ago?"

Caleb said, "What are you talking about you stupid bitch?"

"You are aren't you? You're the pig she told me about; the coward who set that dog onto her?"

Caleb faltered and wasn't sure what to say.

"And now she's disappeared completely! What did you do, kill her?"

Caleb stared in silence.

"Well answer me - that's the least you can do if you're going to kill me too!"

Caleb said, "She's in an asylum, and that's where she's going to stay."

He thought for a second and then started to become suspicious; he said, "Wait, how do I know you aren't lying? You're a cunning cow…"

Maria remembered what she was wearing and said, "Because of my necklace."

"What about your necklace?"

"Maria and I were both given one by my father. Hers has her name on it, mine has mine." She reached up to the top of her cotton nightdress ripped it open and kept on tearing until her right nipple popped momentarily into view in the moonlight.

"Come and see," she said.

Caleb saw the bare expanse of flesh and started to walk across to where she was standing.

Maria purposely pulled the nightdress aside with her left hand and fully exposed her left breast. "Look," she said, "I'll turn to the light so that you can see."

Caleb approached with his eyes fixed intently upon her breast; her pert nipple stood out in the moonlight as she turned towards the window. He swallowed hard and walked right up to her with his head down.

In an instant Maria grabbed a heavy brass candlestick from atop the sideboard and brought it crashing into Caleb's left temple. She saw him stumble back and fall over; she turned and yanked herself through the broken window into the courtyard.

She saw Silas lying on the floor and was tempted to stop and tend to him, but she saw that he was alive and conscious and beckoning for her to go. She nodded and set off.

As she got to the courtyard gatepost she turned and saw Caleb climbing out of the window.

Caleb saw her and yelled, *"I'm going to kill you…"* he then raised the pistol and fired.

The bullet ricocheted off the stone gatepost and whined away into the distance.

Maria was petrified; she'd run up the drive before and knew

how slow and arduous it was; and that it could afford her pursuer a shot or two at her. She decided that she would be safer in the trees of the copse behind the main buildings.

As quickly as she could with bare feet, she climbed over the dry stone wall, dropped down into the field and set off running. She could see that she had at least two hundred yards to go before she got to cover and ran for all her worth.

Caleb reached the wall and realised where Maria had gone, he climbed over and lowered himself gently into the field. He saw Maria running in the distance, aimed the pistol and fired.

The shot whistled past Maria's right ear and thudded into the ascending ground in front of her. A second shot rang out and another bullet whistled past her left side, this time much closer.

She turned around to look and tripped over the hem of her nightdress and fell heavily down onto the ground.

Caleb saw this and started to half run, half walk towards her as quickly as his wound would allow him.

Maria was panic-stricken; she jumped up, attempted to run away and tripped a second time over the hem of her nightdress, this time twisting her ankle. She scrambled to her feet and then almost fell over again; the pain was excruciating. She saw Caleb gaining precious ground and started to hobble frantically towards the trees.

A shot rang out and a searing pain ripped across the flesh of her left inner calf. She fell over onto her side and lay gripping her leg; she knew that she couldn't get away from Caleb anymore but was determined to show no sign of weakness when he got to her.

Caleb hobbled up the incline and grinned evilly as he saw the blood coursing from Maria's leg. He slowly made his way towards her; got level with her ankles and raised the gun. Slowly and deliberately he aimed at her lower stomach and pulled back the hammer.

"No more talking whore. This is for pa and..."

In a blur of movement Caleb had gone. Maria sat bolt upright and looked at what had happened.

Fifty yards in front of her Sugg had her attacker by the head and was dragging him towards the trees. Caleb appeared to lash out and flail around for a few seconds but Sugg suddenly stopped and shook his head ferociously from side to side. Almost instantly

Caleb went still and she presumed from the unnatural angle of his head that his neck was broken.

She continued watching in silence until Sugg disappeared from view, and then looked down at the wound to her leg. She could see that it wasn't really serious, so she tore a strip off her cotton nightdress and bound it around her calf.

A few minutes later she saw Simeon running towards her; he helped her to her feet and told her that Martha was looking after Silas.

Two months later Maria and Silas were well on the way to full recovery. Silas had sustained a flesh wound to the shoulder, some very nasty bruising and a sprained ankle when he'd been pushed out of the window but he was in good spirits; the damage to the buildings had been repaired and the cache of money had been found in their bedroom - but nobody ever spoke about what had happened. They had decided that it would be far too risky involving the police in case any investigations resulted in exposing Maria's escape from Parkway.

Sugg had returned to his room the morning after the attack and had appeared to be entirely unaffected by what had happened, but although Maria had been convinced that she'd seen him kill Caleb, she'd needed to be sure.

Simeon had volunteered to go. He'd made his way into the copse and had seen all the evidence that he'd needed to convince him that Caleb had been dead. During his dubious past and his brief military conscription, he'd seen animal attacks on bodies and carcasses and what he'd found had been wholly reminiscent of that.

Two hours later he'd buried everything that he could find; clothing, bone, body parts and other bits of human detritus in a shallow grave in the copse and had returned to the house.

He'd simply confirmed to Maria and Silas that he'd found and disposed of Caleb's body and had never said another word about it.

Now a Chance was back at Whitewall. Maria had succeeded in her quest and knew that her father would have approved.

She knew that history would record Mary and Silas Cartwright as the tenants and not the owners of the Estate, but she accepted that that was the price she would have to pay to hide her true identity.

She looked up and smiled at Silas and decided that as soon as she was able, she would give her sister Charlotte all of the paperwork that she'd amassed in her attempt to return Whitewall to Chance family ownership, so that one day perhaps, her story would inspire one of her descendants to take up the gauntlet that she had so reluctantly had to put down.

Chapter 43

In March 2006 the Newton Regeneration Scheme in Hyde was well under way and most of the old Victorian houses had been demolished to make way for the new Vical Centre.

The name 'Vical' had been chosen because it contained elements of Victoria and Albert in whose reign the houses had originally been built.

As per the norm, a team of archaeologists had been called in to record and catalogue the development site for posterity but it had been decided due to its size, and the repetitive nature of the brick built terraced houses that not all had to be recorded.

On the site, Neale Brent the driver of one of the JCB hydraulic diggers was responsible for clearing the footings and cellars of the houses from the old Newton High Street and each day had seemed much the same to him until the morning of Tuesday, the 21st March.

The JCB lurched from side to side as Neale slowly drove it into the next cellar whilst his co-driver and workmate Pete Milton, stood on the sidelines watching and directing. He halted the huge machine and waited for Pete to select the next area to be demolished.

Both men wore hard hats and ear defenders but had become used to one another's sign language.

Pete made his choice, indicated to Neale and backed away to a safe zone.

Neale raised the bucket, positioned it in such a way that the prongs would descend behind the brickwork and then engaged the levers to bring it down.

The top third of the wall collapsed as expected and Pete signalled to Neale to pull down the adjacent section.

Once again the bucket rose, Neale positioned it and operated the levers. The arm descended, but instead of the brickwork simply collapsing the prongs struck something that caused so much resistance, the front wheels of the JCB momentarily lifted off the floor.

"Whoa! Whoa!" shouted Pete.

Neale quickly reversed the controls and raised the arm.

As it lifted a whole shower of brickwork and mortar cascaded onto the cellar floor.

Neale immediately halted the upward swing suspending the arm and bucket in mid-air. He jumped down from the cab and shouted, *"Bloody hell!"*

Both he and Pete stood open mouthed looking at the sight before them, for skewered to the prongs of the bucket was a small wall safe.

"Where the hell did that come from?" said Pete.

"I don't know mate," said Neale, "I didn't see any signs of it before we hit it, did you?"

Pete shook his head and said, "No, not a thing."

They stared at it for a few seconds longer until Pete finally said, "I suppose we'd better get the foreman…"

Two days later, the safe and its contents were being recorded and catalogued by four members of an archaeological preservation team led by a Professor Craig Brompton.

Amongst the finds was a small wooden cash box containing a considerable sum of old style pound notes of differing denominations; various odd files and one or two sealed letters. From the numerous references on the paperwork the team had established that the wall safe must have at one time belonged to an old firm of local solicitors generically named Messrs. Josiah Hubert & Sons of Hyde.

Nina Clements, one of the conservators looked across to her associates Helen and Charlotte and said, "Anybody good with French?"

"Mine's O.K. why?" said Helen.

Nina held up an old sealed envelope and said, "There's something written on the reverse of this envelope, and I don't understand it…"

Helen got up from her position and walked across to her colleague.

"What's inside it?" she asked.

"I don't know," said Nina, "it's sealed with wax and I've been instructed to leave opening things like this to Craig."

Helen took the envelope and examined it. It was in remarkably good condition given its age, and the writing was perfectly legible.

"Ah, yes, I see," she said, "John and Matthew Chance - Cestui que Vie."

She paused for a moment and then quietly repeated, "Cestui que Vie... Hmm, that's a new one to me..." She turned the envelope around and looked at the opposite side.

"That's odd," she said to nobody in particular, "there's a name but no address; it just says 'Matthew Chance'..."

The next day, the telephone rang on Naomi's desk.

"Good morning," she said cheerily, "Walmsfield Historic Research Department, Naomi *Wilkes* speaking..."

If you enjoyed this novel look out for the sequel:

The Matthew Chance Legacy